MÖ

"Reintegration complete," ZORAC advised. "We're back in the universe again . . ." An unusually long pause followed, ". . . but I don't know which part. We seem to have changed our position in space." A spherical display in the middle of the floor illuminated to show the starfield surrounding the ship.

"Several large, artificial constructions are approaching us," ZORAC announced after a short pause. "The designs are not familiar, but they are obviously the products of intelligence. Implications: we have been intercepted deliberately by a means unknown, for a purpose unknown, and transferred to a place unknown by a form of intelligence unknown. Apart from the unknowns, everything is obvious."

**Also by James P. Hogan
Published by Ballantine Books:**

THE GENESIS MACHINE

THE GENTLE GIANTS OF GANYMEDE

INHERIT THE STARS

THRICE UPON A TIME

THE TWO FACES OF TOMORROW

Giants' Star

James P. Hogan

A Del Rey Book

BALLANTINE BOOKS • NEW YORK

TO JACKIE

A Del Rey Book
Published by Ballantine Books

Copyright © 1981 by James Patrick Hogan

Library of Congress Catalog Card Number: 80-66570

ISBN 0-345-28771-1

Printed in Canada

First Edition: July 1981

Cover art by Darrell K. Sweet

prologue

By the beginning of the fourth decade of the twenty-first century, it seemed that the human race was finally beginning to learn to live together and that it was on its way to the stars. Having abandoned the crippling arms race and disbanded the bulk of their strategic forces, the superpowers were instead pouring their billions into a massive transfer of Western technology and know-how to the nations of the Third World. With the increased wealth and living standards that came universally with global industrialization, and the security and variety that accompanied more affluent life-styles, population became self-limiting, and hunger, poverty, along with most of mankind's other traditional age-old scourges, at last looked as if they were on the brink of being eradicated permanently. While the U.S.-U.S.S.R. rivalry transformed itself into a war of wits and diplomacy for economic and political influence among the stabilizing nation-states, Man's adventure lust found its expression in a revitalized, multinational space program, which burst outward across the solar system in a new wave of exploration and expansion coordinated under a specially formed UN Space Arm. Lunar development and exploitation proceeded rapidly, permanent bases appeared on Mars and in orbit above Venus, and a series of large-scale manned missions reached the outer planets.

But probably the greatest revolution of the times was the upheaval in science that had followed some of the discoveries made on the Moon and out at Jupiter in the course of these explorations. In the space of just a few years, a series of astonishing discoveries had toppled beliefs unquestioned since the beginnings of science, forced a complete rewriting of the history of the solar system itself, and culminated in Man's first encounter with an advanced alien species.

A hitherto unknown planet, christened Minerva by the

investigators who unraveled its story, had once occupied the position between Mars and Jupiter in the solar system as originally formed, and had been inhabited by an advanced race of eight-foot-tall aliens who came to be known as the "Ganymeans" after the first evidence of their existence came to light on Ganymede, largest of the Jovian moons. The Ganymean civilization, which flourished up until twenty-five million years before the present, vanished abruptly. Some of Earth's scientists believed that deteriorating environmental conditions on Minerva might have forced the "Giants" to migrate to some other star system, but the matter had not been settled conclusively. Much later—some fifty thousand years prior to the current period in Earth's history—Minerva was destroyed. The bulk of its mass, thrown outward into an eccentric orbit on the edge of the solar system, became Pluto. The remainder of the debris was dispersed by Jupiter's tidal effect and formed the Asteroid Belt.

While the pieces of this puzzle were still being fitted together, a starship from the ancient Ganymean civilization returned. Having undergone a relativistic time dilation that was compounded by a technical problem in the vessel's spacetime-distorting drive system, the net result was that an elapsed time of twenty-odd years for the ship corresponded to the passing of something on the order of a million times that number on Earth. The *Shapieron* had departed from Minerva before the onset of whatever had befallen the rest of the Ganymean race, and its occupants were therefore unable to either confirm or refute the theories of the terrestrial researchers involved with the subject. The Giants stayed for six months, combining their efforts with those of Earth's scientists in a search for more clues and mingling harmoniously into Earth's society. Mankind had found a friend, and the remnants of the Ganymean race had, it was assumed, found a home.

But it was not to be. Investigations uncovered a hint that the Ganymean civilization had migrated to a star located near the constellation of Taurus—a star that came to be called the "Giants' Star"; there was no guarantee, but there was hope. Shortly afterward the *Shapieron* departed, leaving behind a sad, but in many ways wiser, world.

Radio observatories on lunar Farside beamed a signal toward the Giants' Star to forewarn of the *Shapieron*'s coming. Though the signal would take years to cover the distance, it would still arrive well ahead of the ship. To the astonishment of the scientists who composed the transmission, a reply purporting to have come from the Giants' Star and confirming that it was indeed the new home of the Ganymeans was received only hours after they first began sending. But by that time the *Shapieron* had already left, and news of the message could not be relayed to it because of the spacetime distortion induced around the craft by its drive, which prevented electromagnetic signals from being received coherently. There was nothing more that the scientists on Earth could do; the *Shapieron* had vanished back into the void from whence it had come, and many more years of uncertainty would pass before the Ganymeans aboard it would know whether or not their quest was in vain.

The transmitters on lunar Farside continued sending intermittently during the three months that followed, but no further reply was evoked.

chapter one

Dr. Victor Hunt finished combing his hair, buttoned on a clean shirt, and paused to contemplate the somewhat sleepy-eyed but otherwise presentable image staring back at him from the bathroom mirror. He detected a couple of gray strands here and there among his full head of dark brown waves, but somebody would have had to be looking for them to notice them. His skin had an acceptably healthy tone to it; the lines of his cheeks and jaw were solid and firm, and his belt still rested loosely on his hips to serve its intended purpose of keeping his pants up and not to keep his waistline in. All in all, he decided, he wasn't doing too badly for thirty-nine. The face in the mirror frowned suddenly as the ritual reminded him of a typical specimen of middle-age male wreckage in a TV commercial; all it wanted now was for the mentally defective, bottle-brandishing wife to appear in the doorway behind to deliver the message on baldness cures, body deodorants, remedies for bad breath, or whatever. Shuddering at the thought, he tossed the comb into the medicine cabinet above the sink, closed the door, and ambled through into the apartment's kitchen.

"Are you through in the bathroom, Vic?" Lyn's voice called from the open door of the bedroom. It sounded bright and cheerful, and should have been illegal at that time in the morning.

"Go ahead." Hunt tapped a code into the kitchen terminal to summon a breakfast menu onto its screen, studied the display for a few seconds, then entered an order to the robochef for scrambled eggs, bacon (crisp), toast with marmalade, and coffee, twice. Lyn appeared in the hallway outside, Hunt's bathrobe hanging loosely on her shoulders and doing little to hide her long, slim legs and golden-tanned body. She flashed him a smile, then vanished into

5

the bathroom in a swirl of the red hair that hung halfway down her back.

"It's coming up," Hunt called after her.

"The usual," her voice threw back from the doorway.

"You guessed?"

"The English are creatures of habit."

"Why make life complicated?"

The screen presented a list of grocery items that were getting low, and Hunt okayed the computer to transmit an order to Albertson's for delivery later that day. The sound of the shower being turned on greeted him as he emerged from the kitchen and walked through into the living room, wondering how a world that accepted as normal the nightly spectacle of people discussing their constipation, hemorrhoids, dandruff, and indigestion in front of an audience of a million strangers could possibly find something obscene in the sight of pretty girls taking their clothes off. "There's now't so strange as folk," his grandmother from Yorkshire would have said, he thought to himself.

It wouldn't have needed a Sherlock Holmes to read the story of the night before from the scene that confronted him in the living room. The half-filled coffee cup, empty cigarette pack, and the remains of a pepperoni pizza surrounded by scientific papers and notes strewn untidily in front of the desk terminal told of an evening that had begun with the best and purest of intentions to explore another approach to the Pluto problem. Lyn's shoulder bag on the table by the door, her coat draped across one end of the couch, the empty Chablis bottle, and the white cardboard box containing traces of a beef-curry dinner-to-go all added up to an interruption in the form of an unexpected but not exactly unwelcome arrival. The crumpled cushions and the two pairs of shoes lying where they had fallen between the couch and the coffee table said the rest. Oh well, Hunt told himself, it wouldn't make much difference to the rest of the world if the solution to how Pluto had wound up where it was had to wait an extra twenty-four hours.

He walked over to the desk and interrogated the terminal for any mail that might have come in overnight. There was a draft of a paper being put together by Mike Barrow's team at Lawrence Livermore Labs, suggesting that an aspect of Ganymean physics that they had been studying implied the possibility of achieving fusion at low temperatures. Hunt scanned it briefly and rerouted it to his office for closer reading there. A couple of bills and statements of account . . . file away and present again at the end of the month. Videorecording from Uncle William in Nigeria; Hunt entered a command for a replay and stood back to watch. Beyond the closed door the shower noises stopped, then Lyn sauntered back into the bedroom.

William and the family had enjoyed having Vic over on vacation recently and had especially liked hearing his personal account of his experiences at Jupiter and later back on Earth with the Ganymeans. . . . Cousin Jenny had gotten an admin job at the nuclear steelmaking complex that was just going into operation outside Lagos. . . . News from the family in London was that all were well, except for Vic's older brother, George, who had been charged with threatening behavior after an argument about politics at his local pub. . . . The postgraduate students at Lagos University had been enthralled by Hunt's lecture about the *Shapieron* and were sending on a list of questions that they hoped he'd find time to reply to.

Just as the recording was finishing, Lyn came out of the bedroom wearing her chocolate blouse and ivory crêpe skirt from the night before, then disappeared again into the kitchen. "Who's that?" she called, to the accompaniment of cupboard doors being opened and closed and plates being set down on a working surface.

"Uncle Billy."

"The one in Africa that you visited a few weeks ago?"

"Uh huh."

"So how are they doing?"

"He looks fine. Jenny's got herself fixed up at the new nuplex I told you about, and brother George is in trouble again."

"Uh-oh. What now?"

"Doing his pub lawyer act by the sound of it. Somebody didn't agree that the government ought to guarantee paychecks to anybody on strike."

"What is he—some kind of nut?"

"Runs in the family."

"You said it, not me."

Hunt grinned. "So never say you weren't warned."

"I'll remember that. -. . . . Food's ready."

Hunt flipped off the terminal and walked into the kitchen. Lyn, perched on a stool at the breakfast bar that divided the room in two, had already started eating. Hunt sat down opposite her, drank some coffee, then picked up his fork. "Why the rush?" he asked. "It's still early. We're not pushed for time."

"I'm not coming straight in. I ought to go home first and change."

"You look okay to me—in fact, not a bad piece of womanry at all."

"Flattery will get you anywhere you like. No . . . Gregg's got some special visitors coming down from Washington today. I don't want to look 'groped' and spoil the Navcomms image." She smiled and mimicked an English accent. "One must maintain standards, you know."

Hunt snorted derisively. "It needs more practice. Who are the visitors?"

"All I know is they're from the State Department. Some hush-hush stuff that Gregg's been mixed up with lately . . . lots of calls coming in on secure channels, and couriers showing up with for-your-eyes-only things in sealed bags. Don't ask me what it's about."

"He hasn't let you in on it?" Hunt sounded surprised.

She shook her head and shrugged. "Maybe it's because I associate with crazy, unreliable foreigners."

"But you're his personal assistant," Hunt said. "I thought you knew about everything that happens around Navcomms."

Lyn shrugged again. "Not this time . . . at least, not so far. I've got a feeling I might find out today, though. Gregg's been dropping hints."

"Mmm . . . odd . . ." Hunt returned his attention to his plate and thought about the situation. Gregg Caldwell, Executive Director of the Navigation and Communications Division of the UN Space Arm, was Hunt's immediate chief. Through a combination of circumstances, under Caldwell's direction Navcomms had played a leading role in piecing together the story of Minerva and the Ganymeans, and Hunt had been intimately involved in the saga both before and during the Ganymeans' stay on Earth.

Since their departure, Hunt's main task at Navcomms had been to head up a group that was coordinating the researches being conducted in various places into the volume of scientific information bequeathed by the aliens to Earth. Although not all the findings and speculations had been made public, the working atmosphere inside Navcomms was generally pretty frank and open, so security precautions taken to the extreme that Lyn had described were virtually unheard of. Something odd was going on, all right.

He leaned against the backrest of the bar chair to light a cigarette, and watched Lyn as she poured two more coffees. There was something about the way her gray-green eyes never quite lost their mischievous twinkle and about the hint of a pout that was always dancing elusively around her mouth that he found both amusing and exciting—"cute," he supposed an American would have said. He thought back over the three months that had elapsed since the *Shapieron* left, and tried to pinpoint what had happened to turn somebody who had been just a smart-headed, good-looking girl at the office into somebody he had breakfast with fairly regularly at one apartment or the other. But there didn't seem to be any particular where or when; it was just something that had happened somehow, somewhere along the line. He wasn't complaining.

She glanced up as she set the pot down and saw him looking at her. "See, I'm quite nice to have around, really. Wouldn't the morning be dull with only the viscreen to stare at." She was at it again . . . playfully, but only if he didn't want to take it seriously. One rent made more sense than two, one set of utility bills was cheaper, et cetera, et cetera, et cetera.

"I'll pay the bills," Hunt said. He opened his hands appealingly. "You said it yourself earlier—Englishmen are creatures of habit. Anyhow, I'm maintaining standards."

"You sound like an endangered species," she told him.

"I am—chauvinists. Somebody's got to make a last stand somewhere."

"You don't need me?"

"Of course not. Good Lord, what a thought!" He scowled across the bar while Lyn returned an impish smile.

Maybe the world could wait another forty-eight hours to find out about Pluto. "What are you up to tonight—anything special?" he asked.

"I got invited to a dinner party over in Hanwell . . . that marketing guy I told you about and his wife. They're having a big crowd of people in, and it sounded as if it could be fun. They told me to bring a friend, but I didn't think you'd be all that interested."

Hunt wrinkled his nose and frowned. "Isn't that the ESP-and-pyramid bunch?"

"Right. They're all excited because they've got a super-psychic going there tonight. He predicted everything about Minerva and the Ganymeans years ago. It has to be true—*Amazing Supernature* magazine said so."

Hunt knew she was teasing but couldn't suppress his irritation. "Oh for Christ's sake . . . I thought there was supposed to be an educational system in this bloody country! Don't they have any critical faculties at all?" He drained the last of his coffee and banged the mug down on the bar. "If he predicted it years ago, why didn't anybody hear about it years ago? Why do we only hear about it after science has told him what he was supposed to predict? Ask him what the *Shapieron* will find when it gets to the Giants' Star and make him write it down. I bet that never gets into *Amazing Supernature* magazine."

"That would be taking it too seriously," Lyn said lightly. "I only go there for the laughs. There's no point in trying to explain Occam's Razor to people who believe that UFOs are timeships from another century. Besides, apart from all that, they're nice people."

Hunt wondered how this kind of thing could still go on after the Ganymeans, who flew starships, created life in laboratories, and built self-aware computers, had affirmed repeatedly that they saw no reason to postulate the existence of any powers existing in the universe beyond those revealed by science and rational thinking. But people still wasted their lives away with daydreams.

He was becoming too serious, he decided, and dismissed the matter with a wave of his hand and a grin. "Come on. We'd better do something about sending you on your way."

Lyn headed for the living room to collect her shoes, bag, and coat, then met him again at the front door of the apartment. They kissed and squeezed each other. "I'll see you later, then," she whispered.

"See you later. Watch out for those crazies."

He waited until she had disappeared into the elevator, then closed the door and spent five minutes clearing the kitchen and restoring some semblance of decency to the rest of the place. Finally he put on a jacket, stuffed some items from the desk into his briefcase, and left in an elevator heading for the roof. Minutes later his airmobile was at two thousand feet and climbing to merge into an eastbound traffic corridor with the rainbow towers of Houston gleaming in the sunlight on the skyline ahead.

chapter two

Ginny, Hunt's slightly plump, middle-aged, meticulous secretary, was already busy when he sauntered into the reception area of his office, high in the skyscraper of Navcomms Headquarters in the center of Houston. She had three sons, all in their late teens, and she hurled herself into her work with a dedication that Hunt sometimes thought might represent a gesture of atonement for having inflicted them on society. Women like Ginny always did a good job, he had found. Long-legged blondes were all very nice, but when it came to getting things done properly and on time, he'd settle for the older mommas any day.

"Good morning, Dr. Hunt," she greeted him. One thing he had never been able to persuade her to accept fully was that Englishmen didn't expect, or really want, to be addressed formally all the time.

"Hi, Ginny. How are you today?"

"Oh, just fine, I guess."

"Any news about the dog?"

"Good news. The vet called last night and said its pelvis isn't fractured after all. A few weeks of rest and it should be fine."

"That's good. So what's new this morning? Anything panicky?"

"Not really. Professor Speehan from MIT called a few minutes ago and would like you to call back before lunch. I'm just finishing going through the mail now. There are a couple of things I think you'll be interested in. The draft paper from Livermore, I guess you've already seen."

They spent the next half-hour checking the mail and organizing the day's schedule. By that time the offices that formed Hunt's section of Navcomms were filling up, and he left to update himself on a couple of the projects in progress.

Duncan Watt, Hunt's deputy, a theoretical physicist who had transferred from UNSA's Materials and Structures Division a year and a half earlier, was collecting results on the Pluto problem from a number of research groups around the country. Comparisons of the current solar system with records from the *Shapieron* of how it had looked twenty-five million years before established beyond doubt that most of what had been Minerva had ended up as Pluto. Earth had been formed originally without a satellite, and Luna had orbited as the single moon of Minerva. When Minerva broke up, its moon fell inward, toward the Sun, and by a freak chance was captured by Earth, about which it had orbited stably ever since. The problem was that so far no mathematical model of the dynamics involved had been able to explain how Pluto could have acquired enough energy to be lifted against solar gravitation to the position it now occupied. Astronomers and specialists in celestial mechanics from all over the world had tried all manner of approaches to the problem but without success, which was not all that surprising since the Ganymeans themselves had been unable to produce a satisfactory solution.

"The only way you can get it to work is by postulating a three-body reaction," Duncan said, tossing up his hands in exasperation. "Maybe the war had nothing to do with it. Maybe what broke Minerva up was something else passing through the solar system."

Thirty minutes later and a few doors farther along the corridor, Hunt found Marie, Jeff, and two of the students on loan from Princeton, excitedly discussing the set of partial-differential tensor functions being displayed on a large mural graphics screen.

"It's the latest from Mike Barrow's team at Livermore," Marie told him.

"I've already seen it," Hunt said. "Haven't had a chance to go through it yet, though. Something about cold fusion, isn't it?"

"What it seems to be saying is that the Ganymeans didn't have to generate high thermal energies to overcome proton–proton repulsion," Jeff chipped in.

"How'd they do it then?" Hunt asked.

"Sneakily. They started off with the particles being neutrons so there wasn't any repulsion. Then, when the particles were inside the range of the strong force, they increased the energy gradient at the particle surfaces sufficiently to initiate pair production. The neutrons absorbed the positrons to become protons, and the electrons were drawn off. So there you've got it—two protons strongly coupled. Pow! Fusion."

Hunt was impressed, although he had seen too much of Ganymean physics by that time to be astounded. "And they could control events like that down at that level?" he asked.

"That's what Mike's people reckon."

Shortly afterward, an argument developed over one of the details, and Hunt left the group as they were in the process of placing a call to Livermore for clarification.

It seemed as if the information left by the Ganymeans was all starting to bear fruit at once, causing something new to break out every day. Caldwell's idea of using Hunt's section as an international clearinghouse for the research into Ganymean sciences was starting to produce results. When the first clues concerning Minerva and the Ganymeans were coming to light, Caldwell had set up Hunt's original pilot group to do exactly this kind of thing. The organization had proved well suited to the task, and now it formed a ready-made group for tackling the latest studies.

Hunt's last call was on Paul Shelling, whose people occupied a group of offices and a computer room on the floor below. One of the most challenging aspects of Ganymean technology was their "gravitics," which enabled them to deform spacetime artificially without requiring large concentrations of mass. The *Shapieron*'s drive system had utilized this capability by creating a "hole" ahead of the ship into which it "fell" continuously to propel itself through space; the "gravity" inside the vessel was also manufactured, not simulated. Shelling, a gravitational physicist on a sabbatical from Rockwell International, headed up a mathematical group which had been delving into Ganymean field equations and energy-metric transforms for six months. Hunt found him staring at a display of isochrons and distorted spacetime geodesics, and looking very thoughtful.

"It's all there," Shelling said, keeping his eyes fixed on the softly glowing colored curves and speaking in a faraway voice. "Artificial black holes . . . just switch 'em on and off to order."

The information did not come as a big surprise to Hunt. The Ganymeans had confirmed that the *Shapieron*'s drive had in fact achieved this, and Hunt and Shelling had talked about its theoretical basis on many occasions. "You've figured it out?" Hunt asked, slipping into a vacant chair and studying the display.

"We're on our way, anyhow."

"Does it get us any nearer instant point-to-point transfers?" That was something the Ganymeans had not achieved, although the possibility was implicit in their theoretical constructs. Black holes distantly separated in normal space seemed to link up via a hyperrealm within which unfamiliar physical principles operated, and the ordinary concepts and restrictions of the relativistic universe simply didn't apply. As the Ganymeans had agreed, the promises implied by this were staggering, but nobody knew how to turn them into realities yet.

"It's in there," Shelling answered. "The possibility is in there, but there's another side to it that bothers me, and it's impossible to separate out."

"What's that?" Hunt asked.

"Time transfers," Shelling told him. Hunt frowned. Had he been talking to anybody else, he would have allowed his skepticism to show openly. Shelling spread his hands and gestured toward the screen. "You can't get away from it. If the solutions admit point-to-point transfers through normal space, they admit transfers through time too. If you could find a way of exploiting one, you'd automatically have a way of exploiting the other as well. Those matrix integrals are symmetric."

Hunt waited for a moment to avoid appearing derisive. "That's too much, Paul," he said. "What happens to causality? You'd never be able to unscramble the mess."

"I know . . . I know the theory sounds screwy, but there it is. Either we're up a dead end and none of it works, or we're stuck with both solutions."

They spent the next hour working through Shelling's equations again but ended up none the wiser. Groups at Cal Tech, Cambridge, the Ministry of Space Sciences in Moscow, and the University of Sydney, Australia, had found the same thing. Obviously Hunt and Shelling were not about to crack the problem there and then, and Hunt eventually left in a very curious and thoughtful mood.

Back in his own office, he called Speehan at MIT, who turned out to have some interesting results from a simulation model of the climatic upheavals caused fifty thousand years earlier by the process of lunar capture. Hunt then took care of a couple of other urgent items that had come in that morning, and was just settling down to study the Livermore paper when Lyn called from Caldwell's suite at the top of the building. Her face was unusually serious.

"Gregg wants you in on the meeting up here," she told him without preamble. "Can you get up right away?"

Hunt sensed that she was pushed for time. "Give me two minutes." He cut the connection without further ado, consigned Livermore to the uncharted depths of the Navcomms databank, told Ginny to consult Duncan if anything desperate developed during the rest of the day, and left the office at a brisk pace.

chapter three

From the web of communications links interconnecting UNSA's manned and unmanned space vehicles with orbiting and surface bases all over the solar system, to the engineering and research establishments at places such as Houston, responsibility for the whole gamut of Navcomms activities ultimately resided in Caldwell's office at the top of the Headquarters Building. It was a spacious and opulently furnished room with one wall completely of glass, looking down over the lesser skyscrapers of the city and the ant colony of the pedestrian precincts far below. The wall opposite Caldwell's huge curved desk, which faced inward from a corner by the window, was composed almost totally of a battery of display screens that gave the place more the appearance of a control room than of an office. The remaining walls carried a display of color pictures showing some of the more spectacular UNSA projects of recent years, including a seven-mile-long photon-drive star probe being designed in California and an electromagnetic catapult being constructed across twenty miles of Tranquillitatis to hurl lunar-manufactured structural components into orbit for spacecraft assembly.

Caldwell was behind his desk and two other people were sitting with Lyn at the table set at a T to the desk's front edge when a secretary ushered Hunt in from the outer office. One of them was a woman in her mid- to late forties, wearing a high-necked navy dress that hinted of a firm and well-preserved figure, and over it a wide-collared jacket of white-and-navy check. Her hair was a carefully styled frozen sea of auburn that stopped short of her shoulders, and the lines of her face, which was not unattractive in a natural kind of way beneath her sparse makeup, were clear and assertive. She was sitting erect and seemed composed and fully in command of herself. Hunt had the feeling that he had seen her somewhere before.

Her companion, a man, was smartly attired in a charcoal three-piece suit with a white shirt and two-tone gray tie. He had a fresh, clean-shaven look about him and jet-black hair cut short and brushed flat in college-boy fashion, although Hunt put him at not far off his own age. His eyes, dark and constantly mobile, gave the impression of serving an alert and quick-thinking mind.

Lyn flashed Hunt a quick smile from the side of the table opposite the two visitors. She had changed into a crisp two-piece edged with pale orange and was wearing her hair high. She looked distinctly un-"groped."

"Vic," Caldwell announced in his gravelly bass-baritone voice, "I'd like you to meet Karen Heller from the State Department in Washington, and Norman Pacey, who's a presidential advisor on foreign relations." He made a resigned gesture in Hunt's direction. "This is Dr. Vic Hunt. We send him to Jupiter to look into a few relics of some extinct aliens, and he comes back with a shipful of live ones."

They exchanged formalities. Both visitors knew about Hunt's exploits, which had been well publicized. In fact Vic had met Karen Heller once very briefly at a reception given for some Ganymeans in Zurich about six months earlier. Of course! Hadn't she been the U.S. Ambassador to —France, wasn't it, at the time? Yes. She was representing the U.S. at the UN now, though. Norman Pacey had met some Ganymeans too, it turned out—in Washington—but Hunt hadn't been present on that occasion.

Hunt took the empty chair at the end of the table, facing along the length of it toward Caldwell's desk, and watched the head of wiry, gray, close-cropped hair while Caldwell frowned down at his hands for a few seconds and drummed the top of his desk with his fingers. Then he raised his craggy, heavily browed face to look directly at Hunt, who knew better than to expect much in the way of preliminaries. "Something's happened that I wanted to tell you about earlier but couldn't," Caldwell said. "Signals from the Giants' Star started coming in again about three weeks ago."

Even though he should have known about such a development if anyone did, Hunt was too taken aback for the moment to wonder about it. As months passed after the sole reply to the first message transmitted from Giordano Bruno at the time of the *Shapieron*'s departure, he had grown increasingly suspicious that the whole thing had been a hoax—that somebody with access to the UNSA communications net had somehow arranged a message to be relayed back from some piece of UNSA hardware located out in space in the right direction. He was open-minded enough to admit that with an advanced alien civilization anything could be possible, but a hoax had seemed the most likely explanation for the fourteen-hour turnaround time. If Caldwell were right, it made so much nonsense of that conviction.

"You're certain they're genuine?" he asked dubiously when he had recovered from the initial shock. "It couldn't all be a sick joke by a freak somewhere?"

Caldwell shook his head. "We have enough data now to pinpoint the source interferometrically. It's way out past Pluto, and UNSA does not have anything anywhere near it. Besides, we've checked every bit of traffic through all our hardware, and it's clean. The signals are genuine."

Hunt raised his eyebrows and exhaled a long breath. Okay, so he'd been wrong on that one. He shifted his gaze from Caldwell to the notes and papers lying along the middle of the table in front of him, and frowned as another thought occurred to him. Like the original message from Farside, the reply from the Giants' Star had been composed in the ancient Ganymean language and communications codes from the time of the *Shapieron*. After the ship's departure, the reply had been translated by Don Maddson, head of the Linguistics section lower down in the building, who had made a study of Ganymean during the aliens' stay. That had required considerable effort, short though the reply had been, and Hunt knew of no one else anywhere who could have handled the more recent signals that Caldwell was talking about. As a rule Hunt didn't have much time for protocol and formality, but if Maddson was in on this, he sure-as-hell should have known about it too. "So who did the translating?" he asked suspiciously. "Linguistics?"

"There wasn't any need," Lyn said simply. "The signals

are coming through in standard datacomm codes. They're in English."

Hunt slumped back in his chair and just stared. Ironically that said definitely that it was no hoax; who in their right mind would forge messages from aliens in English? And then it came to him. "Of course!" he exclaimed. "They must have intercepted the *Shapieron* somehow. Well, that's good to—" He broke off in surprise as he saw Caldwell shaking his head.

"From the content of the dialogue over the last few weeks, we're pretty certain that's not the case," Caldwell said. He looked at Hunt gravely. "So if they haven't talked to the Ganymeans who were here, and they know our communications codes and our language, what does that say to you?"

Hunt looked around and saw that the others were watching him expectantly. So he thought about it. And after a few seconds his eyes widened slowly, and his mouth fell opened in undisguised disbelief. "*Je-sus!*" he breathed softly.

"That's right," Norman Pacey said. "This whole planet must be under some kind of surveillance . . . and has been for a long time." For the moment Hunt was too flabbergasted to offer any reply. Little wonder the whole business had been hushed up.

"That supposition was backed up by the first of the new signals that came in at Bruno," Caldwell resumed. "It said in no uncertain terms that nothing whatsoever relating to the contact was to be communicated via lasers, comsats, datalinks, or any kind of electronic media. The scientists up at Bruno who received the message went along with that directive, and told me about it by sending a courier down from Luna. I passed the word up through Navcomms to UNSA Corporate in the same way and told the Bruno guys to carry on handling things locally until somebody got back to them."

"What it means is that at least part of the surveillance is in the form of tapping into our communications network," Pacey said. "And whoever is sending the signals, and whoever is running the surveillance, are not the same . . . 'people,' or whatever. And the ones who are talking to us don't want the other ones knowing about it." Hunt nodded, having figured that much out already.

"I'll let Karen take it from there," Caldwell said and nodded in her direction.

Karen Heller leaned forward to rest her arms lightly along the edge of the table. "The scientists at Bruno established fairly early on that they were indeed in contact with a Ganymean civilization descended from migrants from Minerva," she said, speaking in carefully modulated tones that rose and fell naturally and made listening easy. "They inhabit a planet called Thurien, in the planetary system of the Giants' Star, or 'Gistar,' to use the contraction that seems to have been adopted. While this was going on, UNSA in Washington referred the matter to the UN." She paused to look over at Hunt, but he had no questions at that point. She went on, "A special working party reporting to the Secretary General was formed to debate the issue, and the ruling finally came out that a contact of this nature was first and foremost a political and diplomatic affair. A decision was made that further exchanges would be handled secretly by a small delegation of selected representatives of the permanent-member nations of the Security Council. To preserve secrecy, no outsiders would be informed or involved for the time being."

"I had to hold things right there when that ruling came down the line," Caldwell interjected, looking at Hunt. "That was why I couldn't tell you about any of this before." Hunt nodded. Now that it had been explained, at least he felt a little better on that score.

He was still far from completely happy, however. It sounded as if there had been a typical bureaucratic overreaction to the whole thing. Playing safe was all very well up to a point, but surely this supersecrecy was taking things too far. The thought of the UN keeping everybody out of it apart from a handful of select individuals who had probably had few, if any, dealings with Ganymeans was infuriating.

"They didn't want *anybody* else included?" he asked dubiously. "Not even a scientist or two—somebody who knows Ganymeans?"

"*Especially* not scientists," Caldwell said, but volunteered nothing further. The whole thing was beginning to sound nonsensical.

"As a permanent member of the Council, the U.S.A. was

informed from high up in the UN and applied sufficient pressure to be represented on the delegation," Heller continued. "Norman and myself were assigned that duty, and for most of the time since then we've been at Giordano Bruno, participating in the exchange of signals that has been continuing with the Thuriens."

"You mean everything is being handled locally from there?" Hunt asked.

"Yes. The ban on communicating anything to do with it electronically is being strictly adhered to. The people up there who know what's going on are all security-cleared and reliable."

"I see." Hunt sat back and braced his arms along the table in front of him. So far there was a mystery and some reason for being uncomfortable, but nothing that had been said so far explained what Heller and Pacey were doing in Houston. "So what's been going on?" he asked. "What have you been talking to Thurien about?"

Heller motioned with her head to indicate a lockable document folder lying by her elbow. "Complete transcripts of everything received and sent are in there," she told him. "Gregg has a full set of copies, and since you'll no doubt be involved from now on, you'll be able to read them for yourself shortly. To sum up, the first messages from Thurien asked for information about the *Shapieron*—its condition, the well-being of its occupants, their experiences on Earth, and that kind of thing. Whoever was sending the messages seemed concerned . . . as if they considered us a threat to it for some reason." Heller paused, seeing the look of noncomprehension that was spreading across Hunt's face.

"Are you saying they didn't know about the ship before we beamed that first signal out from Farside?" he asked.

"So it would appear," Heller replied.

Hunt thought for a moment. "So again, whoever is handling the surveillance isn't talking to whoever is sending these messages," he said.

"Exactly," Pacey agreed, nodding. "The ones handling the surveillance could hardly have not known about the *Shapieron* while it was here if they have any access to our communications network. There were enough headlines about it."

"And that's not the only strange thing," Heller went on. "The Thuriens that we have been in contact with seem to have formed a completely distorted picture of Earth's recent history. They think we're all set for World War III only this time interplanetary, with orbiting bombs everywhere, radiation and particle-beam weapons commanding the surface from the Moon . . . you name it."

Hunt had been growing even more bemused as he listened. He could see now why it looked as if the *Shapieron* couldn't have been intercepted—at least not by the Thuriens who were talking to Earth; the Ganymeans from the ship would have cleared up any misunderstandings like that straight away. But even if the Thuriens who were doing the talking hadn't intercepted the *Shapieron*, they had an impression of Earth nonetheless, which meant that they could only have obtained it from the Thuriens who were handling the surveillance. The impression they had obtained was wrong. Therefore, either the surveillance wasn't very effective, or the story being passed on was being distorted. But if the messages had been coming in composed in English, the surveillance methods had to be pretty effective, which therefore implied that the Thuriens passing on the story weren't passing it on straight.

But that didn't make a lot of sense, either. Ganymeans didn't play Machiavellian games of intrigue or deceive one another knowingly. Their minds didn't work that way; they were far too rational . . . unless the Ganymeans who now existed on Thurien had changed significantly in the course of the twenty-five million years that separated them from their ancestors aboard the *Shapieron*. That was a thought. A lot of changes could have taken place in that time. He couldn't arrive at any definite conclusions now, he decided, so the information was simply filed away for retrieval and analysis later.

"It sounds strange, all right," Hunt agreed after he had sorted that much out in his head. "They must be pretty confused by now."

"They were already," Caldwell said. "The reason they reopened the dialogue is that they want to come to Earth physically—I guess to straighten out the whole mess. That's what they've been trying to get the UN people to arrange."

"Secretly," Pacey explained in answer to Hunt's questioning look. "No public spectacles or anything like that. What it seems to add up to is that they're hoping to do some quiet checking up without the outfit that's running the surveillance knowing about it."

Hunt nodded. The plan made sense. But there was a note in Pacey's voice that hinted of things not having gone so smoothly. "So what's the problem?" he asked, shifting his eyes to glance at both Pacey and Heller.

"The problem is the policy that's been handed down from the top levels inside the UN," Heller replied. "To put it in a nutshell, they're scared of what it might mean if this planet simply opens up to a civilization that's millions of years ahead of us . . . our whole culture could be torn up by the roots; our civilization would come apart at the seams; we'd be avalanched with technology that we're not ready to absorb . . . that kind of thing."

"But that's ridiculous!" Hunt protested. "They haven't said they want to take this place over. They just want to come here and talk." He made an impatient throwing-away motion in the air. "Okay, I'll accept that we'd have to play it softly and exercise some caution and common sense, but what you're describing sounds more like a neurosis."

"It is," Heller said. "The UN's being irrational—there's no other word for it. And the Farside delegation is following that policy to the letter and operating in go-slow, stall-stall-stall mode." She waved toward the folder she had indicated earlier. "You'll see for yourself. Their responses are evasive and ambiguous, and do nothing to correct the wrong impressions that the Thuriens have got. Norman and I have tried to fight it, but we get outvoted."

Hunt caught Lyn's eye as he sent a despairing look around the room. She sent back a faint half-smile and a barely perceptible shrug that said she knew how he felt. A faction inside the UN had fought hard and for the same reasons to prevent the Farside transmissions being continued after the first, unexpected reply had come in, he remembered, but had been overruled after a deafening outcry from the world's scientific community. That same faction seemed to be active again.

"The worst part is what we suspect might be behind it," Heller continued. "Our brief from the State Department was to help move things smoothly toward broadening

Earth's communications with Thurien as fast as developments allowed, at the same time protecting this country's interests where appropriate. The Department didn't really agree with the policy of excluding outsiders, but had to go along with it because of UN protocols. In other words, the U.S. has been trying to play it straight so far, but under protest."

"I can see the picture," Hunt said as she paused. "But that just says that you're becoming frustrated by the slow progress. You sounded as if there's more to it than that."

"There is," Heller confirmed. "The Soviets also have a representative on the delegation—a man called Sobroskin. Given the world situation—with us and the Soviets competing everywhere for things like the South Atlantic fusion deal, industrial-training franchises in Africa, scientific-aid programs, and so on—the advantage that either side could get from access to Ganymean know-how would be enormous. So you'd expect the Soviets to be just as impatient to kick some life into this damn delegation as we are. But they aren't. Sobroskin goes along with the official UN line and doesn't bitch about it. In fact he spends half his time throwing in complications that slow things down even further. Now when those facts are laid down side by side, what do they seem to say?"

Hunt thought over the question for a while, then tossed out his hands with a shrug. "I don't know," he said candidly. "I'm not a political animal. You tell me."

"It could mean that the Soviets are planning to set up their own private channel to fix a landing in Siberia or somewhere so that they get exclusive rights," Pacey answered. "If that's so, then the UN line would suit them fine. If the official channel stays clogged up, and the U.S. plays straight and sticks with the official channel, then guess who walks off with the bonanza. Think of the difference it would make to the power balance if a few heads of select governments around the world were quietly tipped off that the Soviets had access to lots of know-how that we didn't. You see—it all fits with the way Sobroskin is acting."

"And an even more sobering thought is the way in which the UN's policy fits in with that so conveniently," Heller added. "It could mean that the Soviets have ways that we don't even know about of pulling all kinds of strings and levers right inside the top levels of the UN itself. If that's true, the global implications for the U.S. are serious indeed."

The facts were certainly beginning to add up, Hunt admitted to himself. The Soviets could easily set up another long-range communications facility in Siberia, up in orbit, out near Luna maybe, and operate their own link to whatever was intercepting Farside's signals out beyond the edge of the solar system. Any reply coming back would probably be in the form of a fairly wide beam by the time it got to Earth, which meant that anybody could receive it and know that somebody somewhere other than the UN was cheating. But if the replies were in a prearranged code, nobody would be able to interpret them or know for whom they were intended. The Soviets might be accused, in which case they would deny the charge vehemently . . . and that would be about as much as anybody would be able to do about it.

He thought he could see now why he had been brought in on all this. Heller had given herself away earlier when she said that the U.S. had been trying to play it straight, *"so far."* As insurance the State Department had decided that it needed its own private line too, but nothing crude enough to be detected anywhere within a few hundred thousand miles of Earth. So who would they have sent Heller and Pacey to talk to? Who else but someone who knew a lot about Ganymeans and Ganymean technology, somebody who had also been among the first people to receive them on Ganymede?

And that was another point—Hunt had spent a lot of time on Ganymede, and he still had many close friends among the UNSA personnel there with the *Jupiter Four* and *Jupiter Five* missions. Jupiter was a long, long way from the vicinity of Earth, which meant that no receivers anywhere near Earth would ever know anything about a beam aimed toward Jupiter from the fringe of the solar system, whether the beam diverged appreciably or not. And, of course, the J4 and J5 command ships were linked permanently to Earth by laser channels . . . which Caldwell and Navcomms just happened to control. It couldn't possibly be all just a coincidence, he decided.

Hunt looked up at Caldwell, held his eye for a second, then turned his head to gaze at the two people from Washington. "You want to set up a private wire to Gistar via Jupiter to arrange a landing here, without any more messing around, before the Soviets get around to doing something," he told them. "And you want to know if I can come up with an idea for telling the people at Jupiter what we want them to do, without the risk of any Thuriens who might be bugging the laser link finding out about it. Is that right?" He turned his eyes back toward Caldwell and inclined his head. "What do I get, Gregg?"

Heller and Pacey exchanged glances that said they were impressed.

"Ten out of ten," Caldwell told him.

"Nine," Heller said. Hunt looked at her curiously. There was a hint of laughter in her expression. "If you can come up with something, we'll need all the help we can get handling whatever comes afterward," she explained. "The UN might have decided to try going it alone without their Ganymean experts, but the U.S. hasn't."

"In other words, welcome to the team," Norman Pacey completed.

chapter four

Joseph B. Shannon, Mission Director of *Jupiter Five*, orbiting two thousand miles above the surface of Ganymede, stood in an instrumentation bay near one end of the mile-and-a-quarter-long ship's command center. He was watching a large mural display screen from behind a knot of spellbound ship's officers and UNSA scientists. The screen showed an undulating landscape of oranges, yellows, and browns as it lay cringing beneath a black sky made hazy by a steady incandescent drizzle falling from somewhere above, while in the far distance half the skyline was erupting in a boiling column of colors that exploded upward off the top of the picture.

It had been fifty-two years before—the year that Shannon was born—when other scientists at the Jet Propulsion Laboratory in Pasadena had marveled at the first close-ups of Io to be sent back by the *Voyager I* and *II* probes, and dubbed the extraordinary disk of mottled orange "the great pizza in the sky." But Shannon had never heard of any pizza being cooked in the way this one had.

Orbiting through a plasma flux of mean particle energies corresponding to 100,000° Kelvin sustained by Jupiter's magnetic field, the satellite acted as an enormous Faraday generator and supported internal circulating currents of five million amperes with a power dissipation of a thousand billion watts. And as much energy again was released inside it as heat from tidal friction, resulting from orbital perturbations induced as Europa and Ganymede lifted Io resonantly up and down through Jupiter's gravity. This amount of electrically and gravitationally produced heat maintained large reservoirs of molten sulfur and sulfur compounds below the moon's surface, which eventually penetrated upward through faults to explode into the virtually zero-pressure of the outside. The result was a regular succession of spectacular volcanoes of solidifying sulfur and sulfur-dioxide frost that ejected at velocities of up to a thousand meters per second, and sometimes reached heights of 300 kilometers or more.

Shannon was looking at a view of one of those volcanoes now, sent back from a probe on Io's surface. It had taken the mission's engineers and scientists more than a year of back-to-the-drawing-board experiences to devise an instrumentation package and shielding method that would function reliably under Jupiter's incessant bombardment of radiation, electrons, and ions, and Shannon had felt an obligation to be present in person to observe the results of their eventual success. Far from being the chore he had expected, the occasion had turned out an exhilaration and served as a reminder of how easy it was for supreme commanders of anything to allow themselves to become remote and lose touch with what was happening in the trenches. In future, he thought to himself, he would make a point of keeping more up to date on the progress of the mission's scientific projects.

He remained in the command center discussing details of the probe for a full hour after he was officially off duty, and then at last excused himself and retired to his private quarters. After a shower and a change of clothes he sat down at the desk in his stateroom and interrogated the terminal for a listing of the day's mail. One item that had come in was qualified as a text message from Vic Hunt at Navcomms Headquarters. Shannon was both pleasantly surprised and intrigued. He had had many interesting talks with Hunt during the latter's stay on Ganymede, and didn't perceive him as being somebody with much time for idle socializing, which suggested that something interesting was afoot. Curious, he keyed in a command for Hunt's message to be displayed. Five minutes later he was still sitting there staring at the message, his brows knitted in a mystified frown. It read:

Joe,

To avoid any further cross words on this subject, I looked for some clues in the book you mentioned and came across some references on pages 5, 24, and 10. When you get down to sections 11 and 20, it all makes more sense.

How they got 786 is still a puzzle.

Regards

Vic

Not a word of it meant anything to him. He knew Hunt well enough to be reasonably sure that something serious was behind the message, and all he could think of was that Hunt was trying to tell him something highly confidential. But why would Hunt go to this kind of trouble when UNSA possessed a perfectly adequate system of security codes? Surely it wasn't possible that somebody could be eavesdropping on the UNSA net, somebody equipped with enough computer power to render its protective measures unreliable. On the other hand, Shannon reflected soberly, the Germans had thought exactly that in World War II, and the British, with their "Turing Engine" at Bletchley, had been able to read the complete radio traffic between

Hitler and his generals, frequently even before the intended recipients. Certainly this message would mean nothing to any third party even though it had come through in plain English, which made it appear all the more innocuous. The problem was that it didn't mean anything to Shannon, either.

Shannon was still brooding about the message early the next morning when he sat down for breakfast in the senior officers' dining quarters. He liked to eat early, before the captain, the first navigation officer, and the others who were usually on early shift appeared. It gave him time to collect his thoughts for the day and keep up with events elsewhere by browsing through the *Interplanetary Journal*—a daily newspaper beamed out from Earth by UNSA to its various ships and installations all over the solar system. The other reason he liked to be early was that it gave him an opportunity to tackle the *Journal*'s crossword puzzle. He'd been an incurable addict for as long as he could remember, and rationalized his addiction by claiming that an early-morning puzzle sharpened the mental faculties in preparation for the demands of the day ahead. He wasn't really sure if that were true, and didn't care all that much either, but it was as good an excuse as any. There was nothing sensational in the news that morning, but he skimmed dutifully through the various items and arrived gratefully at the crossword page just as the steward was refilling his coffee cup. He folded the paper once, then again, and rested it against the edge of the table to scan through the clues casually while he felt inside his jacket for a pen. The heading at the top read: JOURNAL CROSSWORD PUZZLE NUMBER 786.

Shannon stiffened, his hand still inside his jacket, as the number caught his eye. *"How they got 786 is still a puzzle"* replayed itself instantly in his mind. Every word of Hunt's mysterious message had become firmly engraved by that time. *"786"* and *"puzzle"* . . . both appearing in the same sentence. It couldn't be a coincidence, surely. And then he remembered that Hunt had been a keen crossword solver too in his rare moments of free time; he had introduced Shannon to the particularly cryptic puzzles contained in the London *Times*, and the two of them had spent many a good hour solving them over drinks at the bar. Suppressing the urge to leap from his chair with a shout of *Eureka!*, he pushed the pen back into his pocket and felt behind it for the copy of the message tucked inside his wallet. He drew out the sheet of paper, unfolded it, and smoothed it flat on the table between the *Journal* and his coffee cup. He read it once again, and the words took on a whole new light of meaning.

Right there in the first line it said *"cross words,"* and a little further on, *"clues."* Their significance was obvious now. What about the rest of it? He had never mentioned any book to Hunt, so that part had to be just padding. Presumably the numbers that followed meant something, though. Shannon frowned and stared hard at them: 5, 24, 10, 11, and 20. . . . The sequence didn't immediately jump out and hit him for any reason. He had already tried combining them in various ways and gotten nowhere, but when he read through the message again in its new context, two of the phrases that he had barely noticed before did jump out and hit him: ". . . came *across* . . . ," associated with 5, 24, and 10, and immediately after: ". . . get *down* to . . . ," associated with 11 and 20, had obvious connotations to do with crosswords: they referred to the across and down sets of clues. So presumably whatever Hunt was trying to say would be found in the answers to clues 5, 24, and 10 across, and 11 and 20 down. That had to be it.

With rising excitement he transferred his attention to the *Journal.* At that moment the captain and the first navigation officer appeared in the doorway across the room, talking jovially and laughing about something. Shannon rose from his seat and picked up the *Journal* in one movement. Before they were three paces into the room he had passed them, walking briskly in the opposite direction and tossing back just a curt "Good morning, gentlemen," over his shoulder. They exchanged puzzled looks, turned to survey the doorway through which the Mission Director had already vanished, looked at each other again and shrugged, and sat down at an empty table.

Back in the privacy of his stateroom, Shannon sat down at his desk and unfolded the paper once more. The clue to 5 across read, "Find the meaning of a poem to Digital

Equipment Corporation (6)." The company name was well known among UNSA and scientific people; DEC computers were used for everything from preprocessing the datastreams that poured incessantly through the laser link between Jupiter and Earth to controlling the instruments contained in the robot landed on Io. *"DEC"*! Those letters had to be part of the solution. What about the rest of the clue? "Poem." A list of synonyms paraded through Shannon's head: "verse" . . . "lyric" . . . "epic" . . . "elegy." They were no good. He wanted something of three letters to complete the single-word answer of six letters indicated in the parentheses. *"Ode"*! Added *to* "DEC" it gave "DECODE," which meant, "Find the meaning of." Not too difficult. Shannon penned in the answer and shifted his attention to 24 across.

"Dianna's lock causes heartache (8)." "Dianna's" was an immediate giveaway, and after some reflection Shannon had succeeded in obtaining Di's tress (lock of hair), which gave heartache in the form of "DISTRESS."

10 across read, "A guiding light in what could be a confused voyage (6)." The phrase "could be a confused voyage" suggested an anagram of "voyage," which comprised six letters. Shannon played with the letters for a while but could form them into nothing sensible, so moved on to 11 down. "Let's fit a date to reorganize the experimental results (4,4,4)." Three words of four letters each made up the solution. "Reorganize" looked like a hint for an anagram again. Shannon searched the clue for a combination of words containing twelve letters and soon picked out "Let's fit a date." He scribbled them down randomly in the margin of the page and juggled with them for a few minutes, eventually producing "TEST DATA FILE," which his instinct told him was the correct answer.

The clue for 20 down was, "Argon beam matrix (5)." That didn't mean very much, so Shannon began working out some of the other clues to obtain some cross-letters in the words he had missed. The "guiding light" in 10 across turned out to be "BEACON," which was *in* the remainder of the clue and staring him in the face all the time as it had said: ". . . could *be a con*fused . . ." The suggestion of an anagram had been made deliberately to mislead. He wondered what kind of warped mentality was needed to

JOURNAL CROSSWORD PUZZLE, NUMBER 786
(Compiler: D. Maddson, Navcomms HQ, Houston)

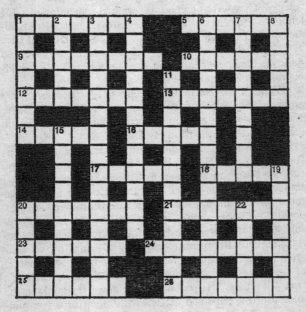

ACROSS

1 Watery Irish flower (6)
5 Find the meaning of a poem to Digital Equipment Corporation (6)
9 Guilty of having no money after the pub? Quite the opposite! (8)
10 A guiding light in what could be a confused voyage (6)
12 Writer, jumping into action, arrives at a profound conclusion (4, 3)
13 The ultimate in text remedies (7)
14 Oriental rule changed by Swiss mathematician (5)
16 Wild riot about the point of a short preamble, colloquially speaking (5)
17 Expert loses two-thirds but takes back art for something more (5)
18 A separated piece (5)
20 Continental one-fan car, maybe (7)
21 Ringing around to abolish a right (7)
23 Keep the elephant's head and tail in the rain (6)
24 Dianna's lock causes heartache (8)
25 After six months, men and I find a type of Arab (6)
26 Surrounds North Carolina with ease, to a point (7)

DOWN

1 Win in a sled, perhaps? It's not fair! (7)
2 But the arms this noted lady was advised to get wouldn't have been much good to Venus! (5)
3 Powerful response, right from the heart? (7, 8)
4 Possibly did on gin? Can't—it's not habit-forming (3-9)
6 A wave from a charge of the Light Brigade (15)
7 Hydrogen makes harmony in turbulent star-core (9)
8 Norman's head in the lake? No—some other guy (5)
11 Let's fit a date to reorganize the experimental results (4, 4, 4)
15 It sounds like a lumberjack's musical number (9)
19 Hoover, initially in trust over the South, urges progress (7)
20 Argon beam matrix (5)
22 Deposit nothing in the smaller amount (5)

qualify as a crossword compiler. Finally the "argon beam" was revealed as "Ar" (chemical symbol) plus "ray" (beam), to give "ARRAY," i.e., a matrix. Interestingly the answer to the first clue of all, 1 across, was "SHANNON," a river in Ireland, presumably slipped in as a confirmation to him personally.

The complete message with the words placed in the same order as the numbers that Hunt had given now read:

DECODE DISTRESS BEACON
TEST-DATA-FILE ARRAY.

Shannon sat back in his chair and studied the final result with some satisfaction, although it so far still told him far from everything. It was evident, however, that it had something to do with the Ganymeans, which tied in with Hunt's being involved.

Some time before the *Shapieron* appeared out of the depths of space at Ganymede, the UNSA missions exploring the Jovian moon system had discovered the wreck of an ancient Ganymean spaceship from twenty-five million years back entombed beneath Ganymede's ice crust. In the process of experimenting with some of the devices recovered from the vessel, Hunt and a group of engineers at Pithead—one of the surface bases on Ganymede—had managed to activate a type of Ganymean emergency transmitter that utilized gravity waves since the propulsive method used by Ganymean ships precluded their receiving electromagnetic signals while under main drive; that was what had attracted the *Shapieron* to Ganymede after reentering the solar system. Shannon remembered that there had been a suggestion to use that same device to relay the news of the surprise reply from the Giants' Star on to the *Shapieron* after its departure, but Hunt had grown suspicious that the reply was a hoax and had vetoed the idea.

That had to be the "Distress Beacon" in Hunt's message. So what was the "Test-Data-File Array" that Shannon was supposed to decode? The Ganymean beacon had been shipped to Earth along with many other items that various institutions had wanted to experiment with firsthand, and the researchers conducting those experiments usually made a point of sending their results back to Jupiter via the laser link to keep interested parties there informed. The only thing that Shannon could think of was that Hunt had somehow arranged for some information to be sent over the link disguised as a file of ordinary-looking experimental test data purportedly relating to the beacon and probably consisting of just a long list of numbers. Now that Shannon's attention had been drawn to the file, the way the numbers were supposed to be read would hopefully, with close enough scrutiny, make itself clear.

If that was it, the only people likely to know anything about unusual files of test data coming in from Earth would be the engineers down at Pithead who had worked on the beacon after it was brought up from beneath the ice. Shannon activated the terminal on his desk and entered a command to access the *Jupiter Five* personnel records. A few minutes later he had identified the engineering project leader in charge of that work as a Californian called Vincent Carizan, who had joined *J5* from UNSA's Propulsion Systems and Propellants Division, where he had worked for ten years after obtaining a master's degree in electrical and electronic engineering at Berkeley.

Shannon's first impulse was to put a call through to Pithead, but after a minute or two of further reflection he decided against it. If Hunt had taken such pains to avoid any hint of the subject being interpretable from what went over the communications network, anything could be happening. He was still pondering on what to do when the call-tone sounded from the terminal. Shannon cleared the screen and touched a key to accept. It was his adjutant officer calling from the command center.

"Excuse me, sir, but you are scheduled to attend the Operations Controller's briefing in G-327 in five minutes. Since nobody's seen you this morning, I thought maybe a reminder might be called for."

"Oh . . . thanks, Bob," Shannon replied. "Look, something's come up, and I don't think I'm going to be able to make it. Make excuses for me, would you."

"Will do, sir."

"Oh, and Bob . . ." Shannon's voice rose suddenly as a thought struck him.

The adjutant looked up just as he had been about to cut the call. "Sir?"

"Get here as soon as you've done that. I've got a message that I want couriered down to the surface."

"Couriered?" The adjutant appeared surprised and puzzled.

"Yes. It's to go to one of the engineers at Pithead. I can't explain now, but the matter is urgent. If you don't waste any time, you should be able to make the nine o'clock shuttle down to Main. I'll have it sealed and waiting by the time you get here. Treat this as grade *X-ray*."

The adjutant's face at once became serious. "I'll be there right away," he said, and the screen went blank.

Shannon received a brief call from Pithead shortly before lunch, advising that Carizan was on his way up to *Jupiter Five* via Ganymede Main Base. When Carizan arrived, he brought with him a printout of a file of data, supposedly relating to tests performed on the Ganymean beacon, that had materialized in the computers at Pithead that very morning after coming in from Earth over the link and being relayed down to the surface. The engineers at Pithead had been puzzled because the file header was out of sequence and contained references that didn't match the database indexing system. And nobody had known anything about any tests being scheduled of the kind that the header mentioned.

As Shannon had anticipated, the file contained just numbers—many groups of numbers, each group consisting of a long list of pairs; it was typical of the layout of an experimental report giving readings of interrelated variables and would have meant nothing more to anybody who had no reason not to accept it at face value. Shannon called together a small team of specialists whose discretion could be trusted, and it didn't take them long to deduce that each group of pairs formed a set of datapoints defined by x–y coordinates in a 256-by-256 matrix array; the hint had been there in the crossword. When the sets of points were plotted on a computer display screen, each set formed a pattern of dots that looked just like a statistical scattering of test data about a straight-line function. But when the patterns of dots were superposed they formed lines of words written diagonally across the screen, and the words formed a message in English. The message contained pointers to other files of numbers that had also been beamed through from Earth and gave explicit instructions for decoding them, and when this was done the amount of information that they yielded turned out to be prodigious.

The result was a set of detailed directions for *Jupiter Five* to transmit a long sequence of Ganymean communications coding groups not into the UNSA net but outward, toward coordinates that lay beyond the edge of the solar system. The contents of any replies received from that direction were, the directions said, to be disguised as experimental data in the way that had thus been established and communicated to Navcomms via the laser link.

Shannon was weary and red-eyed due to lack of sleep by the time he sat down at the terminal in his stateroom and composed a message for transmission to Earth, addressed to Dr. Victor Hunt at Navcomms Headquarters, Houston. It read:

Vic,

  I've talked to Vince Carizan, and it's all a lot clearer now. We're running some tests on it as you asked, and if anything positive shows up I'll have the results sent straight through.

  Best wishes,
  Joe

chapter five

Hunt lounged back in the pilot's seat and stared absently down at the toytown suburbs of Houston while the airmobile purred along contentedly, guided by intermittent streams of binary being directed up at it from somewhere below. It was interesting, he thought, how the patterns of movement of the groundcars, flowing, merging, slowing, and accelerating in unison on the roadways below seemed to reveal some grand, centrally orchestrated design—as if

they were all parts of an unimaginably complex score composed by a cosmic Bach. But it was all an illusion. Each
vehicle was programmed with only the details of its own
destination plus a few relatively simple instructions for
handling conditions along the way; the complexity emerged
as a consequence of large numbers of them interacting
freely in their synthetic environment. It was the same with
life, he reflected. All the magical, mystical, and supernatural forces invoked through the ages to explain it were
inventions that existed in the minds of misled observers,
not in the universe they observed. He wondered how much
untapped human talent had been wasted in futile pursuit of
the creations of wishful thinking. The Ganymeans had entertained no such illusions, but had applied themselves dili-
gently to understanding and mastering the universe as it
was, instead of how it seemed to be or how they might
have wanted it to be. Maybe that was why the Ganymeans
had reached the stars.

In the seat next to him, Lyn looked up from the half-
completed crossword in the *Interplanetary Journal* of a few
days earlier. "Got any ideas for this—'It sounds like a lumberjack's musical number.' What do you make of that?"

"How many letters?" Hunt asked after a few moments
of thought.

"Nine."

Hunt frowned at the flight-systems status summaries
being routinely updated on the console display in front of
him. "Logarithm," he said after another pause.

Lyn thought about it, then smiled faintly. "Oh, I see
. . . sneaky. It sounds like 'logger rhythm.' "

"Right."

"It fits okay." She wrote the word in on the paper resting on her lap. "I'm glad that Joe Shannon had fewer problems with it than this."

"You and me both."

Shannon's confirmation that the message was understood
had arrived two days earlier. The idea had occurred to
Hunt and Lyn one evening while they were at Lyn's apartment, solving a puzzle in one of Hunt's books of London
Times crosswords. Don Maddson, the linguistics expert at
Navcomms who had studied the Ganymean language, was
one of the regular compilers of the *Journal* puzzles and also

a close friend of Hunt's. So with Caldwell's blessing, Hunt had told Maddson as much as was necessary about the Gistar situation, and together they had constructed the message transmitted to Jupiter. Now there was nothing to do but wait and hope that it produced results.

"Let's hope Murphy takes a day off," Lyn said.

"Never hope that. Let's hope somebody remembers Hunt's extension to the Law."

"What's Hunt's extension?"

" 'Everything that can go wrong, will . . . unless somebody makes it his business to do something about it.' "

The stub wing outside the window dipped as the airmobile banked out of the traffic corridor and turned to commence a shallow descent. A cluster of large white buildings standing to attention on a river bank about a mile away moved slowly around until they were centered in the windshield and lying dead ahead.

"He must have been an insurance salesman," Hunt murmured after a short silence.

"Who?"

"Murphy. 'Everything's going to screw up—sign the application now.' Who else but an insurance salesman would have thought of saying something like that?"

The buildings ahead grew to take on the smooth, clean lines of the Westwood Biological Institute of UNSA's Life Sciences Division. The vehicle slowed to a halt and hovered fifty feet above the roof of the Biochemistry building, which with Neurosciences and Physiology formed a trio facing the elongated bulk of Administration and Central Facilities across a plaza of colorful mosaic paving broken up by lawns and a bevy of fountains playing in the sun. Hunt checked the landing area visually, then cleared the computer to complete the descent sequence. Minutes later he and Lyn were checking in at the reception desk in the building's top-floor lobby.

"Professor Danchekker isn't in his office," the receptionist informed them as she consulted her screen. "The route-through code entered against his number is for one of the basement labs. I'll try there." She keyed in another code, and after a short delay the characters on the screen vanished in a blur of colors which immediately assembled themselves into the features of a lean, balding man wearing a pair of anachronistic gold-rimmed spectacles perched at the top of a thin, somewhat aquiline nose. His skin gave the impression of having been stretched over his bones as an afterthought, with barely enough left over to cover his defiant, outthrust chin. He didn't seem too pleased at the interruption.

"Yes?"

"Professor Danchekker, top lobby here. I have two visitors for you."

"I am extremely busy," he replied curtly. "Who are they and what do they want?"

Hunt sighed and pivoted the flatscreen display around to face him. "It's us, Chris—Vic and Lyn. You're expecting us."

Danchekker's expression softened, and his mouth compressed itself into a thin line that twitched briefly upward at the ends. "Oh, of course. I do apologize. Come on down. I'm in the dissecting lab on Level E."

"Are you working alone?" Hunt asked.

"Yes. We can talk here."

"We'll see you in a couple of minutes."

They walked on through to the elevator bank at the rear of the lobby. "Chris must be working with his animals again," Lyn remarked as they waited.

"I don't think he's come up for air since we got back from Ganymede," Hunt said. "I'm surprised he hasn't started looking like some of them."

Danchekker had been with Hunt on Ganymede when the *Shapieron* reappeared in the solar system. In fact Danchekker had made the major contribution to piecing together what was probably the most astounding part of the whole story, the more sensitive details of which still had not been cleared for publication to an unsuspecting and psychologically unprepared world.

Not surprisingly, the Ganymeans had made visits to Earth during the period that their civilization had flourished on Minerva—twenty-five million years before. Their scientists had predicted an epoch of deteriorating environmental conditions on Minerva in the form of an increasing concentration of atmospheric carbon dioxide, for which they had only a low inherent tolerance, so one of the reasons for their interest in Earth had been to assess it as a possible candidate for migration. But they soon abandoned the idea. The Ganymeans had evolved from ancestors whose biochemistry had precluded the emergence of carnivores, thus inhibiting the development of aggressiveness and ruthlessness together with most of the related traits that had characterized the survival struggle on Earth. The savagery that abounded in the environment of late-Oligocene, early-Miocene Earth made it altogether too inhospitable for the placid Ganymean temperament, and the notion of settling there unthinkable.

These visits to Earth did, however, have one practical outcome in addition to satisfying the Ganymeans' scientific curiosity. In the course of their studies of the forms of animal life they discovered, they identified a totally new, gene-based mechanism for absorbing CO_2, which gave terrestrial fauna a far higher and more adaptable inherent tolerance. It suggested an alternative approach to solving the problem on Minerva. The Ganymeans imported large numbers of terrestrial animal species back to their own planet to conduct genetic experiments aimed at transplanting the functional terrestrial coding groups into their own species, thereafter to be inbred automatically into their descendants. Some well-preserved specimens of these early terrestrial animals had been recovered from the wrecked ship on Ganymede, and Danchekker had brought many of them back to Westwood for detailed studies.

The experiments were not successful, and soon afterward the Ganymeans disappeared. The terrestrial species left on Minerva rapidly wiped out the virtually defenseless native forms, adapted and radiated to flourish across the planet, and continued to evolve. . . .

Almost twenty-five million years later—around fifty thousand years before the current period on Earth—an intelligent, fully human form had established itself on Minerva. This race was named the "Lunarians" after the first traces of their existence came to light in the course of lunar explorations being conducted in 2028, which was when Hunt had first gotten involved and moved from England to join UNSA. The Lunarians were a violent and warlike race who developed advanced technology rapidly and eventually polarized into two superpowers, Cerios and Lambia, which clashed in a final, cataclysmic war fought across the entire

surface of Minerva and beyond. In the violence of this conflict Minerva had been destroyed, Pluto and the Asteroids
born, and Luna orphaned.

A few survivors were left stranded on the lunar surface
at the end of these events. Somehow, when at last the
Moon stabilized in orbit around Earth after being captured,
some of these survivors succeeded in reaching the only haven left for them in the entire solar system—the surface of
Earth itself. For millennia they clung precariously to the
edge of extinction, reverting to barbarism for a period and
in the process losing the thread that traced their origins.
But in time they grew strong and spread far and wide.
They supplanted the Neanderthals, who were descended
from the primates that had continued to evolve undisturbed
on Earth, and eventually came to dominate the entire
planet in the form of Modern Man. Only much later, when
at last they rediscovered the sciences and ventured back
into space, did they find the evidence to reconstruct the
story of their origins.

They found Danchekker attired in a stained white lab
smock, measuring and examining parts taken from a large,
brown, furry carcass lying on the dissection table. It was
powerfully muscled, and its fearsome, well-developed car-
nivore's teeth were exposed where the lower jaw of the
snout had been removed. Danchekker informed them that
it was an intriguing example of a relative to *Daphoenodon*
of the Lower Miocene. Despite its evidently distinct digiti-
grade mode of locomotion, moderately long legs, and heavy
tail, its three upper molars distinguished it as an ancestor
of *Amphicyon* and through it of all modern bears—unlike
Cynodesmus, of which Danchekker also had a specimen,
whose upper dentition of two molars put it between *Cynod-
ictis* and contemporary Canidae. Hunt took his word for it.

Hunt had practically insisted to Caldwell that if they
succeeded in arranging a landing for a ship from Thurien,
Danchekker would have to be included in the reception
party; he probably knew more about Ganymean biology
and psychology than anybody else in the world's scientific
community. Caldwell had broached the subject confiden-
tially with the Director of the Westwood Institute, who had
agreed and advised Danchekker accordingly. Danchekker

had not needed very much persuading. He was far from happy at the manner in which the eminent personages responsible for managing Earth's affairs had been handling things, however.

"The whole situation is preposterous," Danchekker declared irritably while he was loading the instruments he had been using into a sterilizer on one side of the room. "Politics, cloak-and-dagger theatrics—this is an unprecedented opportunity for the advancement of knowledge and probably for a quantum leap in the progress of the whole human race, yet here we are having to plot and scheme as if we were dealing in illicit narcotics or something. I mean, good God, we can't even talk about it over the phone! The situation's intolerable."

Lyn straightened up from the dissecting table, where she had been curiously studying the exposed innards of *Daphoenodon*. "I guess the UN feels it has an obligation to humanity to play safe," she said. "It's a contact with a whole new civilization, and they figure that up front it ought to be handled by the professionals."

Danchekker closed the sterilizer lid with a bang and walked over to a sink to rinse his hands. "When the *Shapieron* arrived at Ganymede, the only repesentatives of *Homo sapiens* there to meet it were, as I recall, the scientific and engineering personnel of the UNSA Jupiter missions," he pointed out coolly. "They conducted themselves in exemplary fashion and had established a perfectly civilized relationship with the Ganymeans long before the ship came to Earth. That was without any 'professionals' being involved at all, apart from sending inane advice from Earth on how the situation should be managed, and which those on the spot simply laughed at and ignored."

Hunt looked across from a chair by a desk that stood in one corner of the lab, almost surrounded by computer terminal equipment and display screens. "Actually there is something to be said for the UN line," he said. "I don't think you've thought yet just how big a risk we might be taking."

Danchekker sniffed as he came back around the table. "What are you talking about?"

"If the State Department wasn't convinced that if we

don't go it alone and fix a landing the Soviets will, we'd be a lot more cautious too," Hunt told him.

"I don't follow you," Danchekker said. "What is there to be cautious about? The Ganymean mind is incapable of conceiving anything that could constitute a threat to our, or anybody else's, well-being, as you well know. They simply have not been shaped by the factors that have conditioned *Homo sapiens* to be what he is." He waved a hand in front of his face before Hunt could reply. "And as for your fears that the Thuriens may have changed in some fundamental way, you may forget that. The fundamental traits that determine human behavior were established, not tens but hundreds of millions of years ago, and I have studied Minervan evolution sufficiently to be satisfied that the same may safely be said of Ganymeans also. On such timescales, twenty-five million years is scarcely significant, and quite incapable of giving rise to changes of the magnitude that your suggestion implies."

"I know that," Hunt said when he could get a word in. "But you're going off at a wrong tangent. That's not the problem. The problem is that we might not be talking to Ganymeans at all."

Danchekker seemed taken aback for a moment, then frowned as if Hunt should have known better. "That's absurd," he declared. "Who else could we be talking to? The original transmission from Farside was encoded in Ganymean communications format and understood, was it not? What reason is there to suppose its recipients were anything else?"

"They're talking in English now, but it's not coming from London," Hunt replied.

"But they are talking from Gistar," Danchekker retorted. "And isn't that where, from independently derived evidence, we deduced that the Ganymeans went?"

"We don't *know* that those signals are coming from Gistar," Hunt pointed out. "They say they are, but they've been saying all kinds of other strange things as well. Our beams are being aimed *in the direction of* Gistar, but we've no idea what's out there past the edge of the solar system picking them up. It could be some kind of Ganymean relay that transforms signals that our physics knows nothing about into electromagnetic waves, but then again it might not."

"Surely it's obvious," Danchekker said, sounding a trifle disdainful. "The Ganymeans left some kind of monitoring device behind when they migrated to Gistar, probably to detect and alert them to any signs of intelligent activity."

Hunt shook his head. "If that were the case, it would have been triggered by early radio over a hundred years ago. We'd have known about it long before now."

Danchekker thought about it for a moment, then showed his teeth. "Which proves my point. It responded only to Ganymean codes. We've never sent anything out encoded in Ganymean before, have we? Therefore it must be of Ganymean origin."

"And now it's talking English. Does that mean it was made by Boeing?"

"Obviously the language was acquired via their surveillance operation."

"And maybe they learned Ganymean the same way."

"You're being absurd."

Hunt threw out his arms in appeal. "For Christ's sake, Chris, all I'm saying is let's be open-minded for now and accept that we might be letting ourselves in for something we didn't expect. You're saying they have to be Ganymeans, and you're probably right; I'm saying there's a chance they might not be. That's all I'm saying."

"You said yourself that Ganymeans don't play cloak-and-dagger games and twist facts around, Professor," Lyn injected in a tone that she hoped would calm things a little. "But whoever it is seems to have some funny ideas about how to open up interplanetary relations. . . . And they've got some pretty weird ideas on how Earth is coming along these days, so somebody hasn't been talking straight to somebody somewhere. That hardly sounds like Ganymeans, does it?"

Danchekker snorted but seemed hard-pressed for a reply. The terminal on a side table by the desk saved him by emitting a call-tone. "Excuse me," he muttered, leaning past Hunt to accept. "Yes?" Danchekker inquired.

It was Ginny, calling from Navcomms HQ. "Hello, Professor Danchekker. I believe Dr. Hunt is with you. I have an urgent message for him. Gregg Caldwell said to find him and let him know right away."

Danchekker moved back a pace, and Hunt rolled his chair forward in front of the screen. "Hi, Ginny," he acknowledged. "What's new?"

"A message has come in for you from *Jupiter Five.*" She looked down to read something below the edge of the screen. "It's from the Mission Director—Joseph B. Shannon. It reads, 'The lab tests worked out just as you hoped. Complete file of results being assembled for transmission now. Good luck.'" Ginny looked up again. "Is that what you wanted to know?"

Hunt's face was radiating jubilation. "It sure is, Ginny!" he said. "Thanks . . . a lot." Ginny nodded and tossed him a quick smile; the screen blanked out.

Hunt swiveled his chair around to find two awed faces confronting him. "I guess we can stop arguing about it," he told them. "It looks as if we'll know for sure before very much longer."

chapter six

The main receiver dish at Giordano Bruno was like a gigantic Cyclopean eye—a four-hundred-foot-diameter paraboloid of steel latticework towering into the starry blackness above the lifeless desolation of lunar Farside. It was supported by twin lattice towers moving in diametric opposition around the circular track that formed the most salient surface feature of the observatory and base. As it stood motionless, listening to whispers from distant galaxies, the lines of its lengthening shadow lay draped as a distorted mesh across the domes and lesser constructions huddled around it, spilling over on one side to become indistinct and lost among the boulders and craters scattered beyond.

Karen Heller stood gazing up at it through the transparent wall of an observation tower protruding from the roof of the two-story Main Block. She had gone there to be alone and recompose herself after yet another acrimonious meeting of the eleven-person UN Farside delegation, which had gotten nowhere. Their latest scare was that the signals might not be coming from Ganymeans at all, which was her own fault for ill-advisedly introducing the thought that Hunt had voiced when she was in Houston a week earlier. She wasn't sure even now why she had brought that possibility up at all, since with hindsight it provided an opportunity for procrastination that they were bound to latch onto. As she had commented to a surprised Norman Pacey afterward, it had been a badly calculated attempt at a shock tactic to spur any positive reaction, and had misfired. Perhaps in her frustration she hadn't been thinking too clearly at the time. Anyway it was done now, and the latest transmission sent out toward Gistar had discounted the possibility of any landing in the immediate future and instead talked reams of insignificant detail to do with rank and protocol. Ironically this in itself should have said clearly enough that the aliens, Ganymean or not, harbored no hostile intentions; if they did, they would surely have just arrived, if that was what they wanted to do, without waiting for a cordial invitation. It all made the UN policy more enigmatic and reinforced her suspicions, and the State Department's, that the Soviets were setting themselves up to go it alone and were manipulating the UN somehow. Nevertheless the U.S. would continue to follow the rules until Houston succeeded in establishing a channel via Jupiter—assuming Houston succeeded. If they did, and if none of the efforts to speed things up at Bruno had borne fruit by that time, the U.S. would feel justified in concluding that its hand had been forced.

As she gazed up at the lines of metal etched against the blackness by the rays of the setting sun, she marveled at the knowledge and ingenuity that had created an oasis of life in a sterile desert a quarter of a million miles from Earth, and built instruments such as this, which even as she watched might be silently probing the very edges of the universe. One of the scientific advisors from NSF had told her once that all of the energy collected by all the world's radiotelescopes since the beginnings of that branch of astronomy almost a century earlier was equivalent to no more than that represented by the ash from a cigarette falling through a distance of several feet. And somehow the whole fantastic picture painted by modern cosmology—of collapsed stars, black holes, X-ray-emitting binaries, and a universe consisting of a "gas" of galaxy "molecules"—had all been reconstructed from the information contained in it.

She had ambivalent views about scientists. On the one hand, their intellectual accomplishments were baffling, and at times like this awesome; on the other, she often felt that at a deeper level their retreat into the realm of the inanimate represented an abdication—an escape from the burdens of the world of human affairs within which the expression of knowledge acquired meaning. Even biologists seemed to reduce life to terms of molecules and statistics. Science had created the tools to solve humanity's problems a century ago, but had stood by helplessly while others took the tools and forged them into means of attaining other ends. It was not until the 2010s, when the UN emerged as a truly coherent global influence to be reckoned with, that strategic disarmament had become fact and the resources of the superpowers were at last mobilized toward building a safer and better world.

It was all the more tragic and inexplicable that the UN—until so recently the epitome of the world's commitment to meaningful progress and the realization of the full potential of the human race—should be the obstacle in the road along which the arrow of that progress surely pointed. It seemed a law of history for successful movements and empires to resist further change after the needs that had motivated them into promoting change had been satisfied. Perhaps, she reflected, the UN was already, in keeping with the universally accelerating pace of the times, beginning to show the eventual senility symptom of all empires—stagnation.

But the planets continued to move in their predicted orbits, and the patterns being revealed by the computers connected to the instruments at Giordano Bruno didn't change. So was her "reality" an illusion built on shifting sands, and had scientists shunned the illusion for some vaster, unchanging reality that was the only one of permanence that mattered? Somehow she couldn't picture the Englishman Hunt or the American she had met in Houston as fugitives who would idle their lives away tinkering in ivory towers.

A moving point of light detached itself from the canopy of stars and enlarged gradually into the shape of the UNSA surface transporter ship due in from Tycho. It came to a halt above the far side of the base, and after pausing for a few seconds sank slowly out of sight between Optical Dome 3 and a clutter of storage tanks and laser transceivers. Aboard it would be the courier with the latest information from Houston via Washington. The experts had decreed that if Ganymean technology was behind the surveillance of Earth's communications anything was possible, and the ban on using even supposedly secure channels was still being rigidly enforced. Heller turned away and walked across the floor of the dome to call an elevator at the rear wall. A minute or two later she stepped out into a brightly lit, white-walled corridor three levels below the surface and began walking in the direction of the central hub of Bruno's underground labyrinth.

Mikolai Sobroskin, the Soviet representative on Farside, came out of one of the doors as she passed and turned to walk with her in the same direction. He was short but broad, completely bald, and pink-skinned, and he walked with a hurried, jerking gait, even in lunar gravity, that made her feel for a moment like Snow White. From a dossier that Norman Pacey had procured, however, she knew that the Russian has been a lieutenant-general in the Red Army, where he had specialized in electronic warfare and countermeasures, and a counterintelligence expert for many years after that. He came from a world about as far removed from Walt Disney's as it was possible to get.

"I spent three months in the Pacific conducting equipment trials aboard a nuclear carrier many years ago," Sobroskin remarked. "It seemed that it was impossible to get from anywhere to anywhere without interminable corridors. I never did find out what lay in between half those places. This base reminds me of it."

"I'd say the New York subway," Heller replied.

"Ah, but the difference is that these walls get washed more regularly. One of the problems with capitalism is that only the things that pay get done. So it wears a clean suit which conceals dirty undershorts."

Heller smiled faintly. At least it was good that the differences that erupted across the table in the conference room could be left there. Anything else would have made life intolerable in the cramped, communal atmosphere of the base. "The shuttle from Tycho has just landed," she said. "I wonder what's new."

"Yes, I know. No doubt some mail from Moscow and Washington for us to argue about tomorrow." The original UN charter had ruled against representatives receiving instructions from their national governments, but nobody at Farside kept up any pretenses about that.

"I hope not too much," she sighed. "We should be thinking of the future of the whole planet. National politics shouldn't come into this." She glanced sideways as she spoke, searching his face for a hint of a reaction. Nobody at Washington had yet been able to decide for sure if the UN stance was being dictated from the Kremlin, or if the Soviets were simply playing along with something they found expedient to their own ends. But the Russian remained inscrutable.

They came out of the corridor and entered the "common room"—normally the UNSA Officers' Mess, but assigned temporarily for off-duty use by the visiting UN delegation. The air was warm and stuffy. A mixed group of about a dozen UN delegates and permanent residents of the base was present, some reading, two engrossed in a chess game, and the others talking in small groups around the room or at the small bar at the far end. Sobroskin continued walking and disappeared through the far door, which led to the rooms allocated for office space for the delegation. Heller had intended going the same way, but she was intercepted by Niels Sverenssen, the delegation's Swedish chairman, who detached himself from a small group standing near where they had entered.

"Oh, Karen," he said, catching her elbow lightly and steering her to one side. "I've been looking for you. There are a few points from today's meeting that we ought to resolve before finalizing tomorrow's agenda. I was hoping to discuss them before it's typed up." He was very tall and lean, and he carried his elegant crown of silver hair with a haughty uprightness that always made Heller think of him as the last of the true blue-blooded European aristocrats. His dress was always impeccable and formal, even at Bruno where practically everyone else had soon taken to more casual wear, and he gave the impression somehow of looking on the rest of the human race with something approaching disdain, as if condescending to mix with them only as an imposition of duty. Heller was never able to feel quite at ease in his presence, and she had spent too much time in Paris and on other European assignments to attribute it simply to cultural differences.

"Well, I was on my way to check the mail," she said. "If the discussion can wait for an hour or so, I could see you back here. We'll go through it over a drink maybe, or use one of the offices. Was it anything important?"

"A few questions of procedure and some definitions that need clarifying under one or two headings." Sverenssen's voice had fallen from its public-address mode of a moment earlier, and as he spoke he moved around as if to shield their conversation from the rest of the room. He was looking at her with a curious expression—an intrigued detachment that was strangely intimate and distant at the same time. It made her feel like a kitchen wench being looked over by a medieval lord-of-the-manor. "I was thinking of something perhaps a little more comfortable later," he said, his tone now ominously confidential. "Possibly over dinner, if I might have the honor."

"I'm not sure when I'll be having dinner tonight," she replied, telling herself that she was getting it all wrong. "It might be late."

"A more companionable hour, wouldn't you agree," Sverenssen murmured pointedly.

It was getting to her again. His words implied that the honor would be his, but his manner left no doubt that she should consider it hers. "I thought you said that you needed to talk before the agenda gets typed," she said.

"We could clear that matter up in an hour as you suggest. That would make dinner a far more relaxing and enjoyable occasion . . . later."

Heller had to swallow hard to maintain her composure. He *was* propositioning her. Such things happened and that was life, but the way this was happening wasn't real. "I

think you must have misjudged something," she told him
curtly. "If you have business to discuss, I'll talk to you in
an hour. Now would you excuse me please?" If he left it at
that, it would all soon be forgotten.

He didn't. Instead he moved a pace closer, causing her
to back away a step instinctively. "You are an extremely
intelligent and ambitious, as well as an attractive, woman,
Karen," he said quietly, dropping his former pose. "The
world has so many opportunities to offer these days—
especially to those who succeed in making friends among
its more influential circles. I could do a lot for you that
you would find extremely helpful, you know."

His presumption was too much. "You're making a mistake," Heller breathed harshly, striving to keep her voice at
a level that would not attract attention. "Please don't com-
pound it any further."

Sverenssen was unperturbed, as if the routine were familiar and mildly boring. "Think it over," he urged, and
with that turned casually and rejoined the group he had
left. He'd paid his dollar and bought a ticket. It was no
more than that. The fury that Heller had been suppressing
boiled up inside as she walked out of the room, managing
with some effort to keep her pace normal.

Norman Pacey was waiting for her when she reached
the U.S. delegate's offices a few minutes later. He seemed
to be having trouble in containing his excitement over
something. "News!" he exclaimed without preamble as she
entered. Then his expression changed abruptly. "Hey,
you're looking pretty mad about something. Anything up?"

"It's nothing. What's happened."

"Malliusk was here a little while ago." Gregor Malliusk
was the Russian Director of Astronomy at Bruno and one
of the privileged few among the regular staff there who
knew about the dialogue with Gistar. "A signal came in
about an hour ago that isn't intended for us. It's in some
kind of binary numeric code. He can't make anything out
of it."

Heller looked at him numbly. It could only mean that
somebody else, either somewhere on Earth or in its vicinity,
had begun transmitting to Gistar and wanted the reply kept
private. "The Soviets?" she asked hoarsely.

Pacey shrugged. "Who knows? Sverenssen will probably call a special session, and Sobroskin will deny it, but I'd stake a month's pay."

His voice didn't carry the defeat that it should have, and what he had said didn't account for the jubilant look that Heller had caught on his face as she entered. "Anything else?" she asked, praying inwardly that the reason was what she thought it might be.

Pacey's face split into a wide grin that he could contain no longer. He scooped up some papers from a wad lying in front of the opened courier's bag on a table beside him and waved them triumphantly in the air. "Hunt got through!" he exclaimed. "They've done it via Jupiter! The landing is already fixed for a week from now, and the Thuriens have confirmed it. It's all arranged for a disused airbase in Alaska. It's all fixed up!"

Heller took the papers from him and smiled with relief and elation as she scanned rapidly down the first sheet. "We'll do it, Norman," she whispered. "We'll beat those bastards yet!"

"You've got a recall to Earth from the Department so you can be there as planned. You'll be getting space-happy with all these lunar flights." Pacey sighed. "I'll be thinking about you while I'm holding the fort up here. I only wish I was coming too."

"You'll get your chance soon enough," Heller said. Everything looked bright again. She lifted her face suddenly from the papers in her hand. "I'll tell you what— tonight we'll both have a special dinner to celebrate . . . a kind of farewell party until whenever. Champagne, a good wine, and the best poultry the cook here's got in his refrigerator. How does that sound?"

"Sounds great," Pacey replied, then frowned and rubbed his chin dubiously. "Although . . . would it really be a good idea? I mean, with this unidentified signal coming in only an hour ago, people might wonder what the hell we're celebrating. Sverenssen might think it's us, not the Soviets, who are being underhanded."

"Well we are, aren't we?"

"Yeah, I guess so—but for a good reason. That's different."

"So let them. If the Soviets think the heat's on us, they might get a false sense of security and not move too fast." A look of grim satisfaction came into Heller's eyes as she thought of something else. "And let Sverenssen think anything he damn well likes," she said.

chapter seven

Clad in a standard-issue UNSA arctic jacket, quilted over-trousers, and snowboots, Hunt stood in the center of a small group of muffled figures stamping their feet and breathing frosty clouds of condensation into the air on the concrete apron of McClusky Air Force Base, situated in the foothills of the Baird Mountains one hundred miles inside the Arctic Circle. The ground fog of the previous day had thinned somewhat to become a layer of overcast through which the washy blob of the sun was just able to impart a drab mix of off-white and grays to the texture of the surrounding landscape. Most of the signs of life among the huddle of semiderelict buildings behind them were concentrated around the former mess hall, which had been hastily patched up and windproofed to provide makeshift accommodation and a command post for the operation. A gaggle of UNSA aircraft and other vehicles parked among a litter of supplies and equipment along the near edge of the apron, and a team of handpicked UNSA personnel positioned in the background with cameras and microphone booms set up ready to record the impending event, completed the scene. The command post had landline links into the area radar net, and a homing beacon had been set up for the Ganymean ship. A strangely tense silence predominated, broken only by the intermittent cries of kittiwakes wheeling and diving above the frozen marshes beyond the perimeter fence, and the humming of a motor generator supplying power from one of the parked trailers.

McClusky was about as far from population centers and

major air-traffic lanes as it was possible to get without going outside the U.S., but like every other point on the Earth's surface it was still subject to satellite scrutiny. In an attempt to mask the landing, UNSA had given notice that tests of a new type of reentry vehicle would be conducted in the area during that week, and had requested airlines and other organizations to reroute flights accordingly until further notice. To accustom the region's radar controllers to an abnormal pattern of activity, UNSA had also been staging irregular flights over Alaska for several days and altering their announced flight plans at short notice. Beyond that there was little they could do. How anything like the arrival of a starship could be kept secret from terrestrial observers, never mind an advanced alien surveillance system, was something nobody was quite sure of. Whoever was sending the messages through Jupiter had seemed satisfied with the arrangements, however, and had stated that they would take care of the rest.

The last message to go out via Jupiter had given the names of the persons who would make up the reception party, their positions, and a brief summary of what they did and why each was included. The aliens had reciprocated with a reply advising that three of their members would be prominent in conducting their dealings with Earth. The first was "Calazar," who was described as personifying the government of Thurien and its associated worlds—the figure nearest to a "president" that the planet seemed to possess. Accompanying him would be Frenua Showm, a female "ambassador" whose function had to do with affairs between the various sectors of Thurien society, and Porthik Eesyan, who was involved with policies of scientific, industrial, and economic importance. Whether or not more than just these three would be involved, the aliens hadn't said.

"This is all a striking contrast to the *Shapieron*'s arrival on this planet," Danchekker muttered, surveying the scene around them. That event on the shore of Lake Geneva had been witnessed by tens of thousands and shown live over the news grid.

"It reminds me of Ganymede Main," Hunt replied. "All we need is helmets on and a few Vegas around. What a way to start a new era!"

On Hunt's other side, Lyn, looking lost in the outsize, fur-trimmed hood pulled closely around her face, thrust her hands deeper into her jacket pockets and ground down a block of slush with her foot. "They're about due," she said. "I hope they've got good brakes." Assuming all was on schedule, the ship would have left Thurien, over twenty light-years away, just about twenty-four hours earlier.

"I don't think we need entertain any fears of ineptitude on the part of the Ganymeans," Danchekker said confidently.

"*If* they turn out to be Ganymeans," Hunt remarked, even though by this time he no longer had any real doubts about the matter.

"*Of course* they're Ganymeans," Danchekker snorted impatiently.

Behind them Karen Heller and Jerol Packard, the U.S. Secretary of State, stood motionless and silent. They had persuaded the President to go ahead with the operation on the strength of the implication that the aliens, Ganymean or not, were friendly, and if they were wrong they could well have committed their country to the worst blunder in its history. The President had hoped to be present in person, but in the end had accepted reluctantly the advice of his aides that the absence of too many important people at the same time without explanation would be inviting undesirable attention.

Suddenly the voice of the operations controller inside the mess hall barked over the loudspeaker mounted on a mast at the rear. "Radar contact!" The figures around Hunt stiffened visibly. Behind them the team of UNSA technicians hid their nervousness behind a frenzied outbreak of last-minute preparations and adjustments. The voice came again: "Approaching due west, range twenty-two miles, altitude twelve thousand feet, speed six hundred miles per hour, reducing." Hunt swung his head around instinctively to peer upward along with all the others, but it was impossible to make out anything through the overcast.

A minute went by in slow motion. "Five miles," the controller's voice announced. "It's down to five thousand feet. Visual contact any time now." Hunt could feel the blood pumping solidly in his chest. Despite the cold, his body suddenly felt clammy inside his heavy clothing. Lyn wriggled her arm through his and pulled herself closer.

And then the wind blowing down from the mountains to the west brought the first snatch of a low moaning sound. It lasted for a second or two, faded away, then came back again and this time persisted. It swelled slowly to a steady drone. A frown began forming on Hunt's face as he listened. He turned and glanced back, and saw that several of the UNSA people were exchanging puzzled looks too. There was something wrong. That sound was too familiar to be from any starship. Mutterings started breaking out, then ceased abruptly as a dark shape materialized out of the cloud base and continued descending on a direct line toward the base. It was a standard Boeing 1227 medium-haul, transonic VTOL—a model widely used by domestic carriers and UNSA's preferred type for general-purpose duties. The tension that had been building up around the apron released itself in a chorus of groans and curses.

Behind Heller and Packard, Caldwell, his face dark with fury, spun around to confront a bewildered UNSA officer. "I thought this area was supposed to have been cleared," he snapped.

The officer shook his head helplessly. "It was. I don't understand. . . . Somebo—"

"Get that idiot out of here!"

Looking flustered, the officer hurried away and disappeared through the open door of the mess hall. At the same time voices from the control room inside began pouring out over the loudspeaker, evidently left inadvertently live in the confusion.

"I can't get anything out of it. It's not responding."

"Use the emergency frequency."

"We've already tried. Nothing."

"For Christ's sake what's happening in here? Caldwell just chewed my balls off outside. Find out from Yellow Six who it is."

"I've got 'em on the line now. They don't know, either. They thought it was ours."

"Gimme that goddam phone!"

The plane leveled out above the edge of the marshes about a mile away and kept coming, heedless of the volley of brilliant red warning flares fired from the top of

McClusky's control tower. It slowed to a halt above the open area of concrete in front of the reception party, hung motionless for a moment, and then started sinking toward the ground. A handful of UNSA officers and technicians ran forward making frantic crossed-arms signals over their heads to wave it off, but fell back in disarray as it came on down regardless and settled. Caldwell strode ahead of the group, gesticulating angrily and shouting orders at the UNSA figures who were converging around the nose and making signs up at the cockpit.

"Imbeciles!" Danchekker muttered. "This kind of thing should never happen."

"It looks as if Murphy's back from vacation," Lyn said resignedly in Hunt's ear. But Hunt only half heard. He was staring hard at the Boeing with a strange look on his face. There was something very odd about that aircraft. It had landed in the middle of a sea of watery snow and slush churned up by the activity of the last few days, yet its landing jets hadn't thrown up the cloud of spray and vapor as they should have. So maybe it didn't have any landing jets. If that were so it might have looked like a 1227, but it certainly wasn't powered like one. And there didn't seem to be much response from the cockpit to the antics of the people below. In fact, unless Hunt's eyes were deceiving him, there wasn't anybody in the cockpit at all. Suddenly his face broke into a wide grin as the penny dropped.

"Vic, what is it?" Lyn asked. "What's funny?"

"What's the obvious way to hide something in the middle of an airfield from a surveillance system?" he asked. He gestured toward the plane, but before he could say any more a voice that could have belonged to a natural-born American boomed out across the apron from its direction.

"Greetings from Thurien to Earth, et cetera. Well, we made it. Too bad about the lousy weather."

All movement around the craft ceased instantly. A total silence fell. One by one the heads on every side jerked around and gaped at each other speechlessly as the message percolated through.

This was a starship? The *Shapieron* had stood nearly half a mile high. It was like having a little old lady show up at Tycho on a bicycle.

The forward passenger door opened, and a flight of

steps unfolded itself to the ground. All eyes were riveted to
the open doorway. The UNSA people up front drew back
slowly while Hunt and his companions, with Heller and
Packard a pace behind, moved forward to close in behind
Caldwell and then slowed to a halt again uncertainly. Behind them the expectant cameras focused unwaveringly on
the top of the steps.

"You'd better come on in," the voice suggested. "No
sense in catching colds out there."

Heller and Packard exchanged bemused glances; none of
their talks and briefings in Washington had prepared them
for this. "I guess we just ad-lib as we go," Packard said in
a low voice. He tried to summon up a reassuring grin, but
it died somewhere on its way to his face.

"At least it's not happening in Siberia," Heller murmured.

Danchekker was fixing Hunt with a satisfied look. "If
those utterances are not indicative of Ganymean humor at
work, I'll accept creationism," he said triumphantly. The
aliens could have warned them about the ship's disguise,
Hunt agreed inwardly, but apparently they had been unable to resist making a mild joke out of it. And they obviously had little time for pomp and formality. It sounded
like Ganymeans, all right.

They began moving toward the steps with Caldwell in
the lead while the UNSA people opened up to let them
pass through. Hunt was a couple of paces behind Caldwell
as Caldwell was about to step onto the first stair. Caldwell
emitted a startled exclamation and seemed to be lifted off
the ground. As the others froze in their tracks, he was
whisked upward over the stairway without any part of his
body seeming to touch it, and deposited on his feet inside
the doorway apparently none the worse for wear. He
seemed a trifle shaken when he turned to look back down
at them, but composed himself rapidly. "Well, what are
you waiting for?" he growled. Hunt was obviously next in
line. He drew a long, unsteady breath, shrugged, and
stepped forward.

A strangely pleasant and warm sensation enveloped him,
and a force of some kind drew him onward, carrying his
weight off his legs. There was a blurred impression of the
steps flowing by beneath his feet, and then he was standing

beside Caldwell, who was watching him closely and not without a hint of amusement. Hunt was finally convinced—this was not a 1227.

They were in a fairly small, bare compartment whose walls were of a translucent amber material and glowed softly. It seemed to be an antechamber to whatever lay beyond another door leading aft, from which a stronger light was emanating. Before Hunt could take in any more of the details, Lyn sailed in through the doorway and landed lightly on the spot he had just vacated. "Smoking or non-smoking?" he asked.

"Where's the stewardess? I need a brandy."

Then Danchekker's voice shouted in sudden alarm from outside. "What in God's name is happening? Do something with this infernal contraption!" They looked back down. He was hanging a foot or two above the stairway, flailing his arms in exasperation after having apparently come to a halt halfway through the process of joining them. "This is ridiculous! Get me down from here!"

"You're crowding the doorway," the voice that had spoken before advised from somewhere around them. "How about moving on through and making more room?" They moved toward the inner doorway, and Danchekker appeared behind somewhat huffily a few seconds later. While Heller and Packard were following, Hunt and Lyn followed Caldwell into the body of the craft.

They found themselves in a short corridor that ran twenty feet or so toward the tail before stopping at another door, which was closed. A series of partitions extending from floor to ceiling divided the space on either side into a half-dozen or so narrow cubicles facing inward from left and right. As they moved along the corridor, they found that all the cubicles were identical, each containing some kind of recliner, luxuriously upholstered in red, facing inward toward the corridor and surrounded by a metal framework supporting panel inlays of a multicolored crystalline material and a bewildering layout of delicately constructed equipment whose purpose could have been anything. There was still no sign of life.

"Welcome aboard," the voice said. "If you'd each take a seat, we can begin."

"Who's doing the talking?" Caldwell demanded, looking

around and overhead. "We'd appreciate the courtesy of your identifying yourself."

"My name is VISAR," the voice replied. "But I'm only the pilot and cabin crew. The people you're expecting will be here in a few minutes."

They were probably through the door at the far end, Hunt decided. It seemed odd. The voice reminded him of his first meeting with the Ganymeans, inside the *Shapieron* shortly after it had arrived in orbit over Ganymede. On that occasion, too, contact with the aliens had been through a voice functioning as interpreter, which turned out subsequently to belong to an entity called ZORAC—a supercomputer complex distributed through the ship and responsible for the operation of most of its systems and functions. "VISAR," he called out. "Are you a computer system built into this vehicle?"

"You could say that," VISAR answered. "It's about as near as we're likely to get. A small extension is there. The rest is scattered all over Thurien plus a whole list of other planets and places. You've got a link into the net."

"Are you saying this ship isn't operating autonomously?" Hunt asked. "You're interacting between here and Thurien in realtime?"

"Sure. How else could we have turned around the messages from Jupiter?"

Hunt was astounded. VISAR's statement implied a communications network distributed across star systems and operating with negligible delays. It meant that the point-to-point transfers, at least of energy, that he had often talked about with Paul Shelling at Navcomms were not only proved in principle, but up and running. No wonder Caldwell was looking stunned; it put Navcomms back in the Stone Age.

Hunt realized that Danchekker was now immediately behind him, peering curiously around, with Heller and Packard just inside the door. Where was Lyn? As if to answer his unvoiced question, her voice spoke from inside one of the cubicles. "Say, it feels great. I could stand this for a week or two, maybe." He turned and saw that she was already lying back in one of the recliners and apparently enjoying it. He looked at Caldwell, hesitated for a moment, then moved into the adjacent cubicle, turned, and sat down, allowing his body to sink back into the recliner's yielding contours. It felt right for human rather than Ganymean proportions, he noted with interest. Had they built the whole craft in a week specifically for the occasion? That would have been typical of Ganymeans too.

A warm, pleasant feeling swept over him again and made him feel drowsy, causing his head to drop back automatically into the concave rest provided. He felt more relaxed than he could ever remember and suddenly didn't care if he never had to get up again. There was a vague impression of the woman—he couldn't recall her name—and the Secretary of something-or-other from Washington floating in front of him as if in a dream and gazing down at him curiously. "Try it. You'll like it," he heard himself murmuring distantly.

Some part of his mind was aware that he had been thinking clearly only moments before, but he was unable to remember what or really to care why. His mind had stopped functioning as a coherent entity and seemed to have disassembled into separate functions that he could observe in a detached kind of way as they continued to operate as isolated units instead of in concert. It should be troubling him, part of himself told the rest casually, and the rest agreed . . . but it wasn't.

Something was happening to his vision. The view of the upper part of the cubicle collapsed suddenly into meaningless blurs and smears, and then almost as quickly reassembled itself into an image that swelled, shrank, then faded and finally brightened once again. When it stabilized all the colors were wrong, like those of a false-color, computer-generated display. The colors reversed into complementary tones for a few insane seconds, overcorrected, and then suddenly were normal.

"Excuse these preliminaries," VISAR's voice said from somewhere. At least Hunt thought it was VISAR's; it was barely comprehensible, with the pitch sliding from a shrill whine through several octaves to finish in an almost inaudible rumble. "This process . . ." something completely unintelligible followed, ". . . one time, and after that there will be no . . ." a confusion of telescoped syllables, ". . . will be explained shortly." The last part was free from distortion.

And then Hunt became acutely conscious of the pressure of the recliner against his body, of the touch of his clothes against his skin, and even of the sensation of air flowing through his nostrils as he breathed. His body started to convulse, and he felt a sudden spasm of alarm. Then he realized that he was not moving at all; the impression was due to rapid variations in sensitivity taking place all over his skin. He felt hot all over, then cold, itchy for a moment, prickly for a moment, and then completely numb—and then suddenly normal once more.

Everything was normal. His mind had reintegrated itself, and all his faculties were in order. He wriggled his fingers and found that the invisible gel that had been immersing him was gone. He tried moving an arm, then the other arm; everything was fine.

"Feel free to get up," VISAR said. Hunt climbed slowly to his feet and stepped back into the corridor to find the others emerging and looking as bewildered as he felt. He looked past them at the door blocking the far end, but it was still closed.

"What do you suppose may have been the object of that exercise?" Danchekker asked, for once looking at a loss. Hunt could only shake his head.

And then Lyn's voice sounded from behind him. "Vic." It was just one word, but its ominous tone of warning spun him around instantly. She was staring wide-eyed along the corridor toward the door through which they had entered. He turned his head farther to follow her gaze.

Filling the doorway was the huge frame of a Ganymean, clad in a silvery garment that was halfway between a short cape and a loose jacket, worn over a trousered tunic of dark green. The deep, liquid violet, alien eyes surveyed them for a few seconds from the elongated, protruding face while they watched silently, waiting for a first move. Then the Ganymean announced, "I am Bryom Calazar. You are the people we have been expecting, I see. Please step this way. It's a little too crowded in here for introductions." With that he moved out of sight toward the outer door. Danchekker thrust out his jaw, drew himself up to his full height, and went back into the antechamber after him. After a moment's hesitation Lyn followed.

"This is absurd." Danchekker's voice reached Hunt just

as he was stepping through behind Lyn. The statement was uttered in the tone of somebody clinging obstinately to reason and flatly denying that what his senses were reporting could be real. A split second later Lyn gasped, and an instant after that Hunt could see why. He had assumed that Calazar had come from another compartment leading forward from the antechamber, but there was no such compartment. There didn't need to be. The other Ganymeans were outside.

For McClusky Air Force Base, Alaska, and the Arctic had all gone. Instead he was looking out at a completely different world.

chapter eight

The plane, starship, or whatever the vessel was no longer stood in the open at all. Hunt found himself staring out at the interior of an enormous enclosed concourse formed by a mind-defying interpenetration of angled planes and flowing surfaces of glowing amber and shades of green. It seemed to be the hub of an intricate, three-dimensional dovetailing of thoroughfares, galleries, and shafts extending away up, down, and at all angles through a conjunction of variously oriented spaces that baffled the senses. He felt as if he had stepped into an Escher drawing as he fought to extract some shred of sense from the contradictions of the same surfaces serving as floors here, walls there, and transforming into roofs overhead elsewhere, while all over the scene dozens of Ganymean figures went unconcernedly about their business, some in inverted subsets of the whole, others perpendicular, with one merging somehow into the other until it was impossible to tell which direction was what. His brain balked and gave up. He couldn't take in any more of it.

A group of about a dozen Ganymeans was standing a short distance back from the doorway with the one who had introduced himself as Calazar positioned a few feet ahead. They seemed to be waiting. After a few seconds Calazar beckoned. In a complete daze and with his mind only barely able to register what was happening, Hunt felt himself being pulled almost hypnotically through the door and was aware only vaguely that he was stepping out at floor level.

Everything exploded around him. The whole scene burst into a spinning vortex of color that whirled around him on every side to destroy even the sense of orientation of his immediate surroundings that he had retained. The noise of a thousand banshees was crushing him. He was trapped inside a shrieking avalanche of light.

The vortex became a spinning tunnel into which he was hurtling helplessly at increasing speed. Shapes of light hurled themselves out of the formlessness ahead and exploded away into fragments only inches from his face. Never in his life had he known true panic, but it was there, clawing and tearing, paralyzing any ability to think. He was in a nightmare that he could neither control nor wake up from.

A black void opened up at the tunnel end and rushed at him. Suddenly it was calm. The blackness was . . . space. Black, infinite, star-studded space. He was out in space, looking at stars.

No. He was inside somewhere, looking at stars on a large screen. His surroundings were shadowy and indistinct—some kind of control room with vague suggestions of figures around him . . . human figures. He could feel himself shaking and perspiration drenching his clothes, but part of the panic had let go and was allowing his mind to function.

On the screen a bright object was enlarging steadily as it appeared to be approaching from the background of stars. There was something familiar about it. He felt as if he were reliving something he had experienced a long time ago. Part of a large metallic structure loomed in the foreground to one side of the view, highlighted by an eerie reddish glow coming from offscreen. It suggested part of whatever place the view was being captured from—a spacecraft of some kind. He was aboard a spacecraft watching something approaching on a screen, and he had been there before.

The object continued to enlarge, but even before it became recognizable he knew what it was: It was the *Shapieron*. He had gone back almost a year in time and was back inside the command center of *Jupiter Five* watching the arrival of the *Shapieron* as he had been when it first reappeared over Ganymede. He had watched this sequence replayed from UNSA's archives many times since then and knew every detail of what was coming next. The ship slowed gradually and maneuvered to come to relative rest standing five miles off in parallel orbit, swinging around to present a side view of the graceful curves of its half-mile length of astronautic engineering.

And then something happened that he was completely unprepared for. Another object, moving fast and blazing white at the tail, curved into the scene from one side, passed close by the *Shapieron*'s nose, and exploded in a huge flash a short distance beyond. Hunt stared at it, stunned. That wasn't the way it had happened.

And then a voice sounded from the screen—an American voice, speaking in the clipped tones of the military. "Warning missile launched. Attack salvo primed and locked on target. T-beams being directed in near-miss pattern, and destroyers moving in to take up close-escort formation. Orders are to fire for effect if alien attempts evasion."

Hunt shook his head and looked wildly from side to side, but the shadow figures around him paid no heed to his presence. "No!" he shouted. "It wasn't like that! This is all wrong!" The shadows remained heedless.

On the screen a flotilla of black, sinister-looking vessels moved into view from all directions to take up position around the Ganymean starship. "Alien is responding," the voice announced neutrally. "Commencing descent into parking orbit."

Hunt shouted out again in protest and leaped forward, at the same time wheeling around to appeal for a response from the shadow figures. But they had gone. The command center had gone. All of *Jupiter Five* had gone.

He was looking down on a huddle of metal domes and buildings standing beside a line of Vega ferries amid an icy wilderness that lay naked beneath the stars. It was Main Base on the surface of Ganymede. And on an open area to one side of the complex, dwarfing the Vegas behind, stood the awesome tower of the *Shapieron*. He had advanced by several days and was witnessing again the moment when the ship had just landed.

But instead of the simple but touching welcoming scene that he remembered, he saw a column of forlorn Ganymeans being herded across the ice from their ship between lines of impassive, heavily armed combat troops, under the muzzles of heavy weapons being trained from armored vehicles positioned farther back. And the base itself had acquired defense works, weapons emplacements, missile batteries, and all kinds of things that had never existed. It was insane.

He couldn't tell whether he was inside one of the domes and looking out over the scene as he had been at the time, or whether he was somehow floating disembodied at some other viewpoint. Again his immediate surroundings were indistinct. He swung around, moving in a dreamlike way in which his body had lost its substance, and found that he was alone. Even surrounded by ice and endless empty space he felt clammy and claustrophobic. The terror that had gripped him when he first stepped out of the alien vessel was still there, gnawing insistently and stripping away his powers of reason. "What is this?" he demanded in a voice that choked somewhere at the back of his throat. "I don't understand. What does this mean?"

"You don't remember?" the voice boomed deafeningly from nowhere and everywhere.

Hunt looked wildly in every direction, but there was nobody. "Remember what?" he whispered. "I remember none of this."

"You do not remember these events?" the voice challenged. "You were there."

An anger surged up inside him suddenly—a delayed-action reflex to protect him from the merciless assault on his mind and senses. *"No!"* he shouted. "Not like *that!* They never happened like that. What kind of lunacy is this?"

"How, then, did they happen?"

"They were our friends. They were welcomed. We gave

gifts." His anger boiled over into a quivering rage. "Who are you? Are you mad? Show yourself."

Ganymede vanished, and a series of confused impressions poured by in front of his eyes, which inexplicably his mind assembled together into coherent meaning. There was a vision of the Ganymeans being taken into captivity by a stern and uncompromising American military . . . being allowed to repair their ship only after agreeing to divulge details of their technology . . . being taken to Earth to keep their side of the bargain . . . being dispatched ignominiously back into the depths of space.

"Was it not so?" the voice demanded.

"For Christ's sake, NO! Whoever you are, you're insane!"

"What parts are untrue?"

"All of it. What is the—"

A Soviet newscaster was talking hysterically. Although it was in Russian, Hunt somehow understood. The war had to start now, before the West could turn its advantage into something tangible . . . speeches from a balcony; crowds chanting and cheering . . . launchings of U.S. MIRV satellites . . . propaganda from Washington . . . tanks, missile transporters, marching lines of Chinese infantry . . . high-power radiation weapons hidden in deep space across the solar system. A race that had gone insane was marching off to doomsday with bands playing and flags waving.

"NO-O-O-O!" He heard his own voice rise to a shriek that seemed to come from all sides to engulf him, and then die somewhere far off in the distance. His strength evaporated abruptly, and he felt himself collapsing.

"He speaks the truth," a voice said from somewhere. It was calm and decisive, and sounded like a lone rock of sanity amid the maelstrom of chaos that had swept him out of the universe.

Collapsing . . . falling . . . blackness . . . nothing.

chapter nine

Hunt was dozing in what felt like a soft and very comfortable armchair. He was relaxed and refreshed, as if he had been there for some time. The memory of his experience was still vivid, but it lingered only as something that he regarded in a detached, almost academically curious, kind of way. The terror had gone. The air around him smelt fresh and slightly scented, and subdued music was playing in the background. After a few seconds it registered as a Mozart string quartet. What kind of insanity was he part of now?

He opened his eyes, straightened up, and looked around. He was in an armchair, and the chair was part of an ordinary-looking room, furnished in contemporary style with another, similar chair, reading desk, a large wooden table in the center, a side-table near the door set with an ornate vase of roses, and a thick carpet of dark brown pile that blended fairly well with the predominantly orange and brown decor. There was a single window behind him, covered by heavy drapes that were closed and billowing gently in the breeze coming through from the outside. He looked down at himself and found that he was wearing a dark blue, open-necked shirt and light gray slacks. There was nobody else in the room.

After a few seconds he got up, found that he felt fine, and strolled across the room to part the drapes curiously. Outside was a pleasant, summery scene that could have been part of any major city on Earth. Tall buildings gleamed clean and white in the sun, familiar trees and open green spaces beckoned, and Hunt could see the curve of a wide river immediately below, an older-style bridge with a railed parapet and rounded arches, familiar models of groundcars moving along the roadways, and processions of airmobiles in the sky. He let the drapes fall back as they had been and glanced at his watch, which seemed to be working normally. Less than twenty minutes had passed since the "Boeing" touched down at McClusky. Nothing made sense.

He turned his back to the window and thrust his hands into his pockets while he thought back and tried to remember something that had been puzzling him even before he stepped out of the spacecraft. It had been something trivial, something that had barely registered in the few moments that had elapsed between Calazar's brief appearance inside the craft and Hunt's first glimpse of the stupefying scene that had greeted him outside just before everything went crazy. It had been something to do with Calazar.

And then it came to him. In the *Shapieron*, ZORAC had interpreted between Ganymeans and humans by means of earpiece and throat-mike devices that provided normal-sounding synthesized voices, but which did not synchronize with the facial movements of the original speakers. But Calazar had spoken without any such aids, and apparently quite effortlessly. What made it all the more peculiar was that the Ganymean larynx produced a low, guttural articulation and was utterly incapable of reproducing a human pitch even approximately. So how had Calazar done it, and without looking like a badly dubbed movie at that?

Well, he wasn't going to get nearer any answers by standing here, he decided. The door looked normal enough, and there was only one way to find out whether it was locked or not. He was halfway toward it when it opened and Lyn walked in, looking cool and comfortable in a short-sleeved pullover top and slacks. He stopped dead and stared at her while part of him braced itself instinctively for her to hurl herself across the room and throw her arms around his neck while sobbing in true heroine tradition. Instead she stopped just inside the door and stood casually inspecting the room.

"Not bad," she commented. "The carpet's too dark, though. It should be a more red rust." The carpet promptly changed to a more red rust.

Hunt stared at it for a few seconds, blinked, and then looked up numbly. "How the hell did you do that?" he asked, looking down again to make sure that he hadn't imagined it. He hadn't.

She looked surprised. "It's VISAR. It can do anything. Haven't you been talking to it?" Hunt shook his head. Lyn's face became puzzled. "If you didn't know, how come you're wearing different clothes? What happened to your Nanook outfit?"

Hunt could only shake his head. "I don't know. I don't know how I got here, either." He stared down at the red rust carpet again. "Amazing . . . I think I could use a drink."

"VISAR," Lyn said in a slightly raised voice. "How about a Scotch, straight, no ice?" A glass half filled with an amber liquid materialized from nowhere on the table beside Hunt. Lyn picked it up and offered it to him nonchalantly. He reached out hesitantly to touch it with a fingertip, at the same time half hoping that it wouldn't be there. It was. He took the glass unsteadily from her hand and tested it with a sip, then downed a third of the remainder in one gulp. The warmth percolated smoothly down through his chest and after a few moments had worked a small miracle of its own. Hunt drew a long breath, held it for a few seconds, then exhaled it slowly but still shakily.

"Cigarette?" Lyn inquired. Hunt nodded without thinking. A cigarette, already lit, appeared between his fingers. Don't even ask about it, he told himself.

It all had to be some kind of an elaborate hallucination. How, when, why, or where he didn't know, but it seemed that he had little choice for the moment but to go along with it. Perhaps this whole preliminary interlude had been staged by the Thuriens to provide a period of adjustment and familiarization or something like that. If so, he could see their point. This was like dumping an alchemist from the Middle Ages into the middle of a computerized chemical plant. Thurien, or wherever this was, was going to take some getting used to, he realized. Having decided that much, he felt that probably he was over the biggest hurdle already. But how had Lyn managed to adapt so quickly? Maybe there were disadvantages to being a scientist that he hadn't thought about before.

When he looked up and studied her face, he could see now that her superficial calm was being forced in order to control an underlying bemusement not far short of his own. Her mind was temporarily blocking itself off from the full impact of what it all meant, probably in a way similar to the delayed shock that was a common reaction to exceptionally painful news such as the death of a close relative. He could detect no sign of her having been through anything as traumatic as he had. At least that was something to be thankful for.

He moved over to one of the chairs and turned to perch himself on an arm. "So . . . how did you get here?" he asked.

"Well, I was right behind you on the gravity conveyor, or whatever you'd call it, from that crazy place that we all walked out into from the plane, and then . . ." She broke off as she caught the perplexed expression creeping across Hunt's face. "You don't know what I'm talking about, do you?"

He shook his head. "What gravity conveyor?"

Lyn frowned at him uncertainly. "We all walked out of the plane? . . . There was this big bright place with everything upside down and sideways? . . . Something like whatever lifted us up the stairs picked us all up and took us off along one of the tubes—a big yellow-and-white one? . . ." She was listing the items slowly and intoning them as questions, all the while watching his face intently as if trying to help him identify the point at which he had lost the thread, but it was obvious already that she had experienced something quite different right from the beginning.

He waved a hand in front of his face. "Okay, skip the details. How did you get separated from the others?"

Lyn started to reply and then stopped suddenly and frowned, as if realizing for the first time that her own recollections were by no means as complete as she had thought. "I'm not sure . . ." She hesitated. "Somehow I ended up . . . I don't know where it was. . . . There was this big organization chart—colored boxes with names in them, and lines of who reports to who—that had to do with some crazy kind of United *States* Space *Force*." Her face grew more confused as she replayed the memory in her mind. "There were lots of UNSA names on it that I knew, but with ranks and things that didn't make any sense. Gregg's name was there as a general, and mine was right underneath as a major." She shook her head in a way that told Hunt not to bother asking her to explain it.

Hunt remembered the transcripts he had read of the Thurien messages received at Farside, which had been baffling in their suggestion of a militarized Earth divided in an East-West lineup that was strangely reminiscent of the reconstructions of how Minerva had been just before the final, cataclysmic Cerian-Lambian war. And the grilling that he had just gone through, if that was the right word for it, had echoed the same theme. There had to be a connection. "What happened then?" he asked.

"VISAR started talking and asked me if that was an accurate representation of the outfit I worked for," Lyn replied. "I told it that most of the names were right, but the rest was garbage. It asked some questions about a couple of weapons programs that Gregg was supposed to be mixed up with. Then it showed me some pictures of a surface-bombardment satellite that this U.S.S.F. was supposed to have put in orbit, and of a big radiation projector on the Moon that never existed. I told VISAR it was out of its mind. We talked about it for a bit, and in the end we got quite friendly."

All that hadn't happened in ten minutes, Hunt thought. There must have been some kind of time-compression process involved. "There wasn't anything . . . 'high-pressure' about all this?" he inquired.

Lyn looked at him surprised. "No way. It was all very civilized and nice. That was when I mentioned that I felt strange wearing those clothes indoors, and suddenly—zap!" She gestured down at herself. "Instant outfit. Then I found out more about VISAR's tricks. How long do you think it'll be before IBM gets one on the market?"

Hunt stood up and began pacing across the room, noting absently as he moved that his cigarette didn't seem to be accumulating any ash to be disposed of. It was some kind of interrogation procedure, he decided. The Thuriens had obviously gotten confused over the situation on today's Earth, and for some reason it was important to them to have the correct story. If that was the case, they certainly hadn't wasted any time over it. Perhaps Hunt's experience had been a shock tactic designed to guarantee straight answers at the optimum moment when he had been totally unprepared and too disoriented to have fabricated anything. If so, it had certainly worked, he reflected grimly.

"After that I asked where you were. VISAR directed me out through a door and along a corridor, and here I am," Lyn completed.

Hunt was about to say something more when the phone rang. He looked around and noticed it for the first time. It was a standard domestic datagrid terminal and went so naturally with the surroundings that it hadn't registered previously. The call-tone sounded again.

"Better answer it," Lyn suggested.

Hunt walked over to the corner, pulled up a chair, sat down, and touched a key on the terminal to accept. His jaw dropped open in disbelief as he found himself staring at the features of the operations controller at McClusky.

"Dr. Hunt," the controller said, sounding relieved. "Just a routine check to see if everything's okay. You people have been in there for a while now. Any problems?"

For what seemed a long time, Hunt could only stare back blankly. He'd never heard of phone calls from the real world intruding into hallucinations before. It had to be part of the hallucination too. What was somebody supposed to say to hallucinatory operations controllers? "How are you talking to us?" he managed at last, succeeding with some effort in making his voice almost normal.

"We got a transmission from the plane a while ago saying it would be okay for us to use a low-power, narrow beam aimed straight at it," the controller replied. "We set it up and waited, but when nothing came through we thought we'd better try calling you."

Hunt closed his eyes for a moment, then opened them again and glanced sideways at Lyn. She didn't understand it, either. "Are you saying that plane is still out there?" he asked, looking back at the screen.

The controller looked puzzled. "Why . . . sure . . . I'm looking right at it out the window." Pause. "Are you sure everything's okay in there?"

Hunt sat back woodenly, and his mind jammed up. Lyn stepped past him and stooped in front of the screen. "Everything's okay," she said. "Look, we're a bit busy right now. Call you back in a few minutes, okay?"

"Just as long as we know. Okay, talk to you later." The controller vanished from the screen.

Lyn's composure evaporated with the picture. She looked down at Hunt, visibly worried and frightened for the first time since entering the room. "It's still out there. . . ." Her voice was coming unevenly as she struggled to keep it under control. "Vic—what's happening?"

Hunt scowled around the room as the indignation that he had been suppressing at last came surging up inside. "VI-SAR," he called on impulse. "Can you hear me?"

"I'm here," the familiar voice answered.

"That plane that landed at McClusky—it's still there. We just talked to them on the phone."

"I know," VISAR agreed. "I put the call through."

"Isn't it about time you told us what the hell's going on?"

"The Thuriens were intending to explain it when you meet them very shortly," VISAR replied. "You are due an apology, and they want to make it personally, not second-hand through me."

"Then would you mind telling us where the hell we are?" Hunt said, not feeling very mollified by the statement.

"Sure. You're in the *perceptron,* which as you've just told me is still on the apron at McClusky." Hunt caught Lyn's eye in a mute exchange of baffled looks. She shook her head weakly and sank down into one of the chairs. "You don't look very convinced," VISAR commented. "A small demonstration, perhaps?"

Hunt felt his mouth opening and closing, and heard sounds coming out. But he wasn't making it happen. He was moving like a puppet to the pulls of invisible strings. "Excuse me," his mouth said as his head turned itself toward Lyn. "Don't worry about this—VISAR will explain. I'll be back in a few minutes."

And then he was lying back on something yielding and soft.

"Voilà!" VISAR's voice pronounced from somewhere overhead.

He opened his eyes and looked around, but a few seconds went by before he realized where he was.

He was back in the recliner inside one of the cubicles in the ship that had landed at McClusky.

Everything seemed very quiet and still. He rose to his feet and moved out into the corridor to peer into the adjacent cubicle. Lyn was still there, lying back in the recliner looking relaxed, her eyes closed and her face serene. He looked down and noticed for the first time that, like her, he was wearing UNSA arctic clothing again. He moved along to inspect the other cubicles and found all the others were there too, looking much the same.

"Take a walk outside and check it out," VISAR's voice suggested. "We'll still be here when you get back."

Hunt made his way dazedly to the door at the forward end of the corridor, stopped for a moment and braced himself for anything, and stepped through into the antechamber. McClusky and Alaska were back again. Through the open outer door he could see figures stirring and starting to move forward as they saw him. He moved toward the door, and seconds later was on his feet at the bottom of the access stairway. The figures converged around him, and excited questions assailed him from all sides as he began walking across the apron toward the mess hall.

"What's happening in there?"

"Are there Ganymeans inside?"

"Are they coming out?"

"How many of them are there?"

"Just . . . talking so far. What? Yes . . . well, sort of. I'm not sure. Look, give me a few minutes. I need to check something."

Inside the mess hall he made straight for the control room, set up in one of the front rooms. The controller and his two operators had watched Hunt through the window that looked out across the apron and were waiting expectantly. "Vic, how's it going?" the controller greeted as he came in the door.

"Fine," Hunt murmured absently. He stared hard at the consoles and screens set up around the room and forced his mind to go back over what had happened since they entered the craft. What he was seeing right now was real. Everything around him was real. The phone call had been part of something that hadn't been real. Obviously it couldn't have worked the other way around; reality couldn't communicate into the realm of the hallucinatory via radio. Obviously?

"Have you had any contact from that plane since we went inside?" he asked, turning to glance at the control-room crew.

"Why . . . yes." The controller looked suddenly worried. "You talked to us yourself a few minutes ago. You're sure everything's . . . all right?"

Hunt brought a hand up to massage his brow and give the confusion boiling inside his head time to die down a little. "How did you get through?" he asked.

"We got a signal from it earlier telling us we could couple in via a low-power beam, like I told you. I just asked for you by name."

"Do it again," Hunt said.

The controller moved in front of the supervisory console, tapped a command into its touchboard array, and spoke toward the two-way audio grille above the main screen. "McClusky Control to alien. Alien vessel, come in please."

"Acknowledged," a voice answered.

"VISAR?" Hunt said, recognizing it.

"Hi again. Convinced now?"

Hunt's eyes narrowed thoughtfully as he stared at the blank screen. At last the wheels of his brain felt as if they were sorting themselves out and lining themselves up on the right axles again. There was one obvious thing for him to try. "Put me through to Lyn Garland," he said.

"One moment."

The screen came to life, and a second later Lyn was looking out at him, framed by the background of the room he had recently been in. It must have been equally clear that Hunt was calling from McClusky, but her face did not register undue surprise. VISAR must have been doing some explaining.

"You sure get around," she commented drily.

A shadow of a smile formed on Hunt's face as the first glimmer of light began showing through it all. "Hi," he said. "Question: What happened after I last talked to you?"

"You vanished into thin air—just like that. It gave me a bit of a fright, but VISAR's been straightening me out about a lot of things." She held up a hand and wriggled her fingers in front of her face, at the same time shaking her head wonderingly. "I can't believe I'm not really doing this. It's all happening inside my head? It's incredible!"

Right at that moment she probably knew more about what was going on than he did, Hunt reflected. But he thought he had the general idea now. An instant communications link to Thurien . . . miracles worked to order . . . Ganymeans talking in English. . . . And what had VISAR called that vessel—the *perceptron*? The pieces started dropping into place.

"Just keep talking to VISAR," he said. "I'll be back in a few minutes." Lyn smiled the kind of smile that said she knew everything would work out okay; Hunt winked, then cut off the screen.

"Would you mind telling us what's going on?" the controller asked. "I mean . . . we're only supposed to be running this operation."

"Just give me a second," Hunt said, entering the code to reactivate the channel. He turned his face toward the grille. "VISAR?"

"You rang?"

"That place we walked out of the perceptron into—does it exist, or did you invent it?"

"It exists. It's part of a place called Vranix, which is an old city on Thurien."

"Did we see it the way it is right now?"

"Yes, you did."

"So you have to be relaying instantly between here and Thurien."

"You're getting the idea."

Hunt thought for a second. "What about the room with the carpet?"

"I invented that. A special effect—faked. We thought that maybe some familiar-looking surroundings would help you get used to how we do things. Figured the rest out yet?"

"I'll try a long shot," Hunt said. "How about total sensory stimulation and monitoring, plus an instant communications link. We never went to Thurien; you brought Thurien here. And Lyn never answered any phone call. You pumped it straight into her nervous system along with everything else she thinks she's doing, and you manufactured all the appropriate AV data to send through the local beam. How's that?"

"Pretty good," VISAR replied, managing to inject a strong

note of approval into its voice. "So are you ready to rejoin the party? You're due to meet the Thuriens in a few minutes."

"I'll talk to you later," Hunt said, and cut the connection.

"Now would you mind telling us what the hell this is all about?" the controller invited.

Hunt's expression was distant, his voice slow and thoughtful. "That's just a flying phone booth out there on the apron. It's got equipment inside that somehow couples directly into the perceptual parts of the nervous system and transfers a total impression from a remote place. What you saw on the screen a minute ago was extracted straight out of Lyn's mind. A computer translated it into audiovisual modulations on a signal beam and directed it into your antenna. It processed the transmission from here in the opposite direction."

Ten minutes later Hunt reentered the perceptron and sat down in the same recliner that he had occupied before. "What do I say—'Home, James'?" he asked aloud.

This time there were no preliminary sensory disturbances. He was instantly back in the room with Lyn, who seemed to have been expecting him to reappear; VISAR had evidently forewarned her. He looked around the room curiously to see if he could detect any hint of its being a creation manufactured by a computer, but there was nothing. Every detail was authentic. It was uncanny. As with VISAR's command of English and the data needed to disguise the perceptron as a Boeing, all the information must have been extracted from Earth's communications links; practically everything necessary had been communicated electronically from somewhere to somewhere at some time or another. No wonder the Thuriens had been particular about keeping everything connected with this business out of the network!

He reached out and ran a finger experimentally down Lyn's arm. It felt warm and solid. The whole thing was exactly what he had said to VISAR—a *total* sensory stimulation process, probably acting on the brain centers directly and bypassing the neural imputs. It was astounding.

Lyn glanced down at his hand, then looked up and eyed him suspiciously. "I don't know if it's that authentic, either," she told him. "And right now I'm not that curious. Forget it."

Before Hunt could reply, the phone rang again. He answered it. It was Danchekker, looking ready to commit mayhem.

"This is monstrous! Outrageous!" The veins at his temples were throbbing visibly. "Have you any idea of the provocation to which I have been subjected? Where are you in this computerized lunatic asylum? What kind of—"

"Hold it, Chris. Calm down." Hunt held up a hand. "It's not as bad as you think. All that's—"

"*Not as bad?* Where in God's name are we? How do we get out of it? Have you talked to the others? By what right do these alien creatures presume to—"

"You're not anywhere, Chris. You're still on the ground at McClusky. So am I. We all are. What's happened is—"

"Don't be preposterous! It's quite evident that—"

"Have you talked to VISAR? It'll explain it all far better than I can. Lyn's with me and—"

"No I have not, and what's more I have no intention of doing anything of the kind. If these Thuriens do not possess the common courtesy to—"

Hunt sighed. "VISAR, take the professor home and straighten him out, could you. I don't think I'm up to dealing with him right now."

"I'll handle it," VISAR replied, and Danchekker promptly vanished from the screen leaving an empty room in the frame.

"Amazing," Hunt murmured. There were times, he thought, when he would have liked to be able to pull that stunt with Danchekker himself.

A knock sounded lightly on the door. Hunt and Lyn's heads jerked around to look at it, turned back to meet each other's questioning looks, then stared at the door again. Lyn shrugged and moved across the room toward it. Hunt switched off the terminal and looked up to find the eight-foot-tall figure of a Ganymean straightening up after ducking through the doorway. Lyn stood speechless with surprise as she held the door open.

"Dr. Hunt and Miss Garland," the Ganymean said. "First, on behalf of all of us, I apologize for the somewhat bizarre welcome. It was necessary for some very important reasons, which will be explained when we all get together very shortly. I hope that our leaving you on your own like this hasn't seemed too bad-mannered, but we thought that perhaps a short period of adjustment might be beneficial. I am Porthik Eesyan—one of those you were expecting to meet."

chapter ten

Eesyan was subtly different in form from the Ganymeans of the *Shapieron*, Hunt noticed as they walked. He had the same massive torso lines beneath his loose-fitting yellow jerkin and elaborately woven shirt of red and amber metallic threads, and the same six-fingered hands, each with two thumbs, but his skin was darker than the grays that Hunt remembered—almost black—and seemed smoother in texture; his build was lighter and more slender, his height slightly less than would have been normal, and his lower face and skull, though still elongated significantly, had receded and broadened into a more rounded head that was closer to the human profile.

"We can move objects from place to place instantaneously by means of artificially generated spinning black holes," Eesyan told them. "As your own theories predict, a rapidly spinning black hole flattens out into a disk, and eventually becomes a toroid with the mass concentrated at the rim. In that situation the singularity exists across the central aperture and can be approached axially without catastrophic tidal effects. The aperture affords an 'entry port' into a hyperrealm described by laws not subject to the conventional restrictions of ordinary spacetime. Creating such an entry port also gives rise to a hypersymmetric effect that appears as a projection elsewhere in normal space, and which functions as a coupled exit port. By controlling the dimensions, spin, orientation, and certain other parameters of the initial hole, we can select with considerable accuracy the location of the exit up to distances in the order of several tens of light-years."

Eesyan between Vic and Lyn, they were walking along a broad, enclosed, brightly illuminated arcade of soaring lines, gleaming sculptures, and vast openings, which led into other spaces. There were more Escher-like distortions and inversions here and there in the scene, but nothing as overwhelming as the sight they had first seen from the perceptron. Apparently Ganymean gravitic engineering tricks came with the architecture on Thurien. For this was Thurien. They had emerged from the room and walked through a series of galleries and a huge domed space bustling with Ganymeans, eventually to this place, the illusory blending so smoothly into reality that Hunt had missed the point along the way at which the switch from one to the other had taken place. The meeting between the two worlds was about to take place, Eesyan had informed them, and he had been assigned to escort them there personally. No doubt VISAR could have transferred them there instantly, Hunt thought, but this seemed a more natural way while they were still "acclimatizing." And having an opportunity to get to know at least one of the aliens informally in advance helped the process further. Probably that was the idea.

"That must be how you got the perceptron to Earth," Hunt said.

"Almost to Earth," Eesyan told him. "A black hole large enough to take a sizable object creates a significant gravitational disturbance over a large distance. Therefore we don't project things like that into the middle of planetary systems; it would disrupt clocks and calendars and so on. We exited the perceptron outside the solar system, and it had to make the last lap in a more conventional way."

"So a round trip needs four conventional stages," Lyn commented. "Two one way, and two the other."

"Correct."

"Which explains why it took something like a day to make it from Thurien to Earth," Hunt said.

"Yes. Instant planet-to-planet hopping is out. But *communications* is another matter entirely. We can send messages by beaming a gamma frequency microlaser into a microscopic black-hole toroid that can be generated in equipment capable of operating on planetary surfaces without undesirable side effects. So instant planet-to-planet datalinks are practicable. What's more, generating the microscopic black holes needed for them doesn't require the enormous amount of energy that holes big enough to send ships through do. So we don't do a lot of instantaneous people-moving unless we have to; we prefer moving *information* instead."

It fitted in with what Hunt already knew: he and Lyn were really at McClusky, and all the information they were perceiving was being transmitted there through VISAR. "That explains how the information gets sent," he said. "But what's the input to the system? How is it originated in the first place?"

"Thurien is a fully 'wired' planet," Eesyan explained. "So are most of the other planets in the portions of the Galaxy where we have spread. VISAR exists all over those worlds, and in other places between, as a dense network of sensors located inside the structures of buildings and cities, distributed invisibly across mountains, forests, and plains, and in orbit above planetary surfaces. By combining and interpolating between its data inputs, it is able to compute and synthesize the complete sensory input that would be experienced by a person located at any particular place.

"VISAR bypasses the normal input channels to the brain and stimulates symbolic neural patterns directly with focused arrays of high-resolution spatial stress-waves. Thus it can inject straight into the mind all the information that would be received by somebody physically present at whatever place is specified. Also it monitors the neural activity of the voluntary motor system and reproduces faithfully all the feedback sensations that would accompany muscular movements and so forth. The net result is to create an illusion of actually being at a remote location which is indistinguishable from the real thing. Physically transporting the body would add nothing."

"Star travel the easy way," Lyn murmured. She gazed around as they came to the end of the arcade and turned off to begin walking across a curved, sweeping surface that had looked like a wall a minute ago, but now seemed to be pivoting slowly as they moved onto it and lifting the whole of the arcade and the structures connected to it up at an increasing angle behind them. "This is all real and twenty light-years away?" she said, still sounding disbelieving. "I really haven't come here?"

"Can you tell the difference?" Eesyan asked her.

"How about you, Porthik?" Hunt asked as a new thought struck him. "Are you actually here . . . there . . . whatever, in Vranix, or what?"

"I'm on an artificial world twenty million miles from Thurien," Eesyan replied. "Calazar is on Thurien, but six thousand miles from Vranix at a place called Thurios—the principal city of Thurien. Vranix is an old city that we keep preserved for sentimental and traditional reasons. Frenua Showm, whom you were also expecting to meet and will very shortly, is on a planet called *Crayses,* which is in a star system about nine light-years from Gistar."

Lyn was looking puzzled. "I'm not quite sure I get this," she said. "How do we all manage to get consistent impressions when we're in different places? How do I see you there, Vic next to you, and all this around us when it's scattered all over the Galaxy?" Hunt was still too boggled by what Eesyan had said a moment earlier to be able to ask anything.

"VISAR manufactures composite impressions from data originated in different places and delivers them as a total package," Eesyan replied. "It can combine visual, tactile, audile, and other details of an environment with data synthesized from monitoring the neural activity of other persons linked into the system, and provide each individual with a complete, personalized impression of being in that environment and interacting physically and verbally with the others. Hence we can visit other worlds, travel among other cultures, convene for meetings in other star systems, and make visits to artificial worlds out in space . . . and be home in an instant. We do move around physically to some degree, of course, for example in recreation or for activities that require physical presence, but for the most part our long-range business and travel is conducted via electronics and gravitics."

The surface continued curving over and brought them out into a wide circular gallery that looked down over a railed parapet on a fairly busy plaza of some kind a level below. Between the flowing curves and surfaces enclosing the space from above, they could see part of the floor of the arcade that they had been walking along a few minutes earlier. At least, it had seemed like a floor at the time. But by now they were beginning to get used to that kind of thing.

"When we first sat down inside that plane at McClusky, all my senses went haywire for a while," Lyn said as she thought back. "What was that all about?"

"VISAR tuning in to your personal cerebral patterns and activity levels," Eesyan told her. "It was making adjustments until it obtained correct feedback responses. They vary somewhat from individual to individual. The process is a one-time thing. You could think of it as somewhat like fingerprinting."

"Porthik," Hunt said after they had continued for some distance in silence. "That stunt you pulled on me right at the beginning—you've been getting some mixed-up stories about Earth, and you needed to check them out. Right?"

"It was extremely important, as Calazar will explain," Eesyan answered.

"But was it necessary?" Hunt queried. "If VISAR can access symbolic neural patterns directly, why couldn't it have simply pulled whatever it wanted to know straight out of my memory? That way there wouldn't have been any risk of wrong answers."

"Technically that would be possible," Eesyan agreed. "However, for reasons of privacy such things are not permitted under our laws, and VISAR is programmed in a way that restricts it to supplying primary sensory inputs to the brain and monitoring motor and certain other terminal outputs only. It communicates only what would be seen, heard, felt, and so on; it does not read minds."

"How about the others?" Hunt inquired. "Do you have any idea how they're getting along? I wouldn't exactly recommend your welcoming ceremonies as the best way of making friends."

Eesyan's mouth puckered in the way that Hunt had long ago recognized as the Ganymean equivalent of a smile. "You needn't worry. They haven't all been getting to the bottom of VISAR as quickly as you did, so some of them are still a little confused, but apart from that they're fine."

The confusion had been intentional, Hunt realized suddenly. It was a deliberate measure calculated to defuse any animosity left lingering as a result of the initial shock tactics. Eesyan's showing up to escort them to wherever they were going was no doubt part of the plan too. "It didn't seem quite like that when I talked to Chris Danchekker on the phone a few minutes before you arrived," he said, grinning to himself as he caught the expression on Lyn's face.

"As a matter of fact, you and Professor Danchekker did have comparatively hard rides," Eesyan admitted. "We're sorry about that, but the two of you were unique in that you both possessed firsthand knowledge of certain events connected with the *Shapieron* that we were particularly anxious to obtain. The experiences of your companions were more in the nature of discussions concerning their various specialized fields. Their accounts corroborated one another's perfectly. It was very illuminating."

"What happened with you and Chris?" Lyn asked, looking across at Hunt.

"I'll tell you about it later," he replied. What they did might have been unconventional, but it had certainly worked, he told himself with grudging admiration. In those first few minutes the Ganymeans had obtained and verified more information than they could have in days of talking. If it was that important, he could hardly blame them after the way they had been messed around by the UN at Farside. He wondered if Caldwell and the others saw things the same way. It wouldn't be long before he found out, he saw as he looked ahead of them. They seemed to have arrived at their destination.

They were walking down a shallow, fan-shaped ramp that was taking them through a final arch out into the open. They emerged into a descending arrangement of interlocking geometric forms, terraces, and esplanades that formed one side of a large circular layout echoing the same theme. The lowermost, central part, directly ahead of them, consisted of a forum of seats set in tiers and facing one another from all four sides of a rectangular floor. The whole place was a vast composition of color and form set among pools of liquid fluorescence fed by slow-motion rivers and fountains of shimmering light. A number of figures were assembled on three sides of the floor, all Ganymean. They were standing and seemed to be waiting. At the front and in the center of a raised section of seats on one side was Calazar, recognizable by his dark green tunic and silvery cape.

And then Hunt saw Caldwell's stocky frame emerge from another entrance on the far side of an open area to his right, accompanied by a Ganymean . . . and beyond Caldwell, Heller and Packard appeared with another Ganymean, Heller walking calmly and with assurance, Packard staring from side to side and looking bewildered. Hunt turned his head the other way in time to see Danchekker walking through an archway, waving his arms and remonstrating to a Ganymean on either side; evidently it was taking two of them to handle him. The arrivals had been synchronized perfectly. It couldn't have been accidental.

Suddenly Lyn gasped and stopped, her face raised to stare at something overhead. Hunt followed her gaze . . . and stopped . . . then gasped.

From three sides beyond the raised rim of the place they were in, three slim spires of pink ivory converged upward above their heads for an inestimable distance before blending into an inverted cascade of terraces and ramparts that broadened and unfolded upward and away for what must have been miles. Above it—it didn't make sense, but above it, where the sky should have been, the scene mushroomed out into a mind-defying fusion of structures of staggering dimensions that marched away as far as the eye could see in one direction, and fringed a distant ocean in the other. It had to be the city of Vranix. But it was all hanging miles over their heads, and upside down.

And then the realization hit him. They had walked out into the sky. The three pink spires "rising" from around them in fact surmounted an enormous tower that projected upward from the city, supporting a circular platform that held the place they were in. But they had come out on the *underside* of it! Their senses had become sufficiently disoriented in the Ganymean labyrinth for them to have inverted without realizing it, and they had walked outside in some locally generated gravity effect to find themselves gazing down over the surface of Thurien stretching away over their heads.

Caldwell and the others had seen it too, and were just standing, staring. Even Danchekker had stopped talking and was looking upward, his mouth hanging half open. It was the Ganymeans' final trump card and master stroke, Hunt realized. Even if any of his companions had been harboring any lingering resentments, they would be too overwhelmed by this—timed precisely to hit them minutes before the meeting was due to begin—to protest very strongly. He liked these aliens, he decided, strange though the thought seemed in some ways at that particular moment. He always enjoyed seeing professionals in action.

One by one the dazed figures of the Terrans came slowly back to life and began moving again, down toward the central forum where the Ganymeans were waiting.

chapter eleven

"We owe you an apology," Calazar said bluntly as soon as the introductions had been completed. "I know that's not supposed to be the best way of starting a meeting by Earth's customs, but I've never really understood why. If it needs saying, let's say it and get it out of the way. As you no doubt appreciate by now, we needed to check some facts that are important to us, and to you too I would imagine. It seems just as well that we did."

It was going to be a far less formal affair than he had been half prepared for, Hunt noted with relief. He wondered if what he was hearing was an accurate translation of Calazar's words or a liberal interpretation concocted by VISAR. He had assumed that an opening on this note would be unavoidable, and was ready for some fireworks there and then. But as he looked around he could see that the Ganymean defusing tactics appeared to be having their desired effect. Caldwell and Heller seemed in command of themselves and were looking purposeful as if by no means ready to let the matter just go at that, but at the same time they were subdued sufficiently to wait and see what developed before making an issue out of anything. Danchekker had obviously come in spoiling for a fight, but the psychological left hook that the Ganymeans had delivered out of the blue—literally—at the last moment had temporarily knocked it out of him. Packard appeared to be in some kind of trance; in his case the tranquilizer had, perhaps, worked too well.

After pausing, Calazar continued, "On behalf of our entire race, we welcome you to our world and to our society. The threads that have traced the evolution of our two kinds, and which have remained separated until now, have at last crossed. We hope that from this point on they will continue to remain entwined for the benefit and greater learning of all of us." With that he sat down. It was simple, Hunt thought, and seemed a good way of getting things moving.

The Terran faces turned toward Packard, who was officially the most senior in rank and therefore the designated spokesman. It took him a few seconds to realize that the others were looking at him. Then he looked uncertainly from side to side, gripped the sides of his chair, moistened his lips, and rose slowly and somewhat unsteadily to his feet. "On behalf of the . . . government of . . ." The words dried up. He stood swaying slightly and staring dumbstruck at the rows of alien countenances arrayed before him, and then raised his head and shook it disbelievingly at the spectacle of the tower falling away into the metropolis of Vranix and the panorama of Thurien stretching off on every side beyond. For an instant Hunt thought he was going to collapse. And then he vanished.

"I regret that the Secretary of State appears to be temporarily indisposed," VISAR informed the assembly.

That was enough to break the spell. At once Caldwell was on his feet, his eyes steely and his mouth clamped in a downturned line. Heller had also started to rise, but she checked herself and sank back into her seat as Caldwell beat her to it by a split second. "This has gone too far," Caldwell grated, fixing his eyes on Calazar. "Save the niceties. We came here in good faith. You owe us an explanation."

Instantly everything changed. The forum, the tower, Vranix, and the overhead canopy of Thurien were gone. Instead they were all indoors in a fairly large but not huge room with a domed ceiling, which contained a wide, circular table of iridescent crystal as a centerpiece. The principal participants were placed around it in the same relative positions as before with Caldwell still standing; the other Ganymeans who had been present earlier were looking on from raised seats behind. Compared to the previous setting this one felt protective and secure.

"We underestimated the impact," Calazar said hastily. "Perhaps this will be closer to what you are used to."

"Never mind the Alice-in-Wonderland effects," Caldwell said. "Okay, you've made your point—we're impressed. But we came here at your request and somebody just flipped out as a consequence. We don't find it amusing."

"That was not intentional," Calazar replied. "We have already expressed our regrets. Your colleague will be back to normal very soon."

The exchange did not have the connotations that it would have if this confrontation were taking place on Earth, Hunt knew as he listened. Because of their origins Ganymeans simply didn't seek to intimidate nor did they respond to intimidation. They didn't think that way. Calazar was simply stating the facts of the matter, no more and no less. The standards and conditioning of human culture did not apply to this situation. Caldwell knew it too, but somebody had to be seen to set the limits.

"So let's get down to some straight questions and answers," Caldwell said. "You said that our two races have evolved separately until now. That's not entirely true—the two lines come together a long way back in the past. Since the story you've been getting about us seems to have become confused somewhere, it might help clear up a lot of uncertainty and save us some time if I sum up what we already know." Without waiting for a response he went on, "We know that your civilization existed on Minerva until around twenty-five million years ago, that you shipped a lot of terrestrial life there, possibly to attempt a genetic-engineering solution to the environmental problems, and that the Lunarians evolved from ancestors included among them after you left. We also know about the Lunarian war of fifty thousand years ago, about the Moon being captured by Earth, and about ourselves having descended from Lunarian survivors that came with it. Are we talking the same language so far?"

A ripple of murmurings broke out among the Ganymeans. They seemed surprised. Evidently the Terrans knew a lot more than they had expected. That could put an interesting new perspective on things, Hunt thought.

Frenua Showm, the female ambassador of Thurien, who had been introduced at the commencement of the proceedings, replied. "If you already know about the Lunarians, you shouldn't have any difficulty in finding the answer to one of the questions that you have no doubt been asking," she said. "Earth has been under surveillance because of our concern that it might go the way of its Lunarian ancestors and become a technically advanced, belligerent planet. The Lunarians destroyed themselves before they spilled out of the solar system. Earth might not have. In other words we saw in Earth a potential threat to other parts of the Galaxy, and perhaps, one day, to all of it." Showm gave the impression that she was far from convinced, even now, that it wasn't so. Definitely not a Terranophile, Hunt decided. The reason did not come as a surprise. With the Ganymeans being the way they were and the Lunarians having been the way they had, it had to be something like that.

"So why all the secrecy?" Heller asked from beside Caldwell. Caldwell sat down to allow her to take it from there. "You claim to represent the Thurien race, yet it's obvious that you don't speak for everybody. You don't want this dialogue brought to the attention of whoever is responsible for the surveillance. So are you what you say you are? If so, why do you need to conceal your actions from your own people?"

"The surveillance is operated by an autonomous . . . shall we say, 'organization' within our system," Calazar replied. "We had reason to suspect the accuracy of some of the information being reported. It became necessary for us to verify it . . . but discreetly, in case we were wrong."

"Suspect the accuracy!" Hunt repeated, spreading his hands in an imploring gesture around the table. "You're making it sound like just a minor aberration here and there. Christ . . . they didn't even tell you that the *Shapieron* had returned and was on Earth at all—your own ship with your own people in it! And the picture you got of

Earth wasn't just inaccurate; it was systematically distorted. So what the hell's been going on?"

"That is an internal affair of Thurien that we will now be in a position to do something about," Calazar assured him. He seemed a little off balance, perhaps as a result of his having been unprepared for the Terrans knowing as much as Caldwell had revealed.

"It's not just an internal affair," Heller insisted. "It concerns our whole planet. We want to know who's been misrepresenting us, and why."

"We don't know why," Calazar told her simply. "That's what we're trying to find out. The first step was to get our facts straight. My apologies again, but I think we have now achieved that."

Caldwell was scowling. "Maybe you ought to let us talk to this 'organization' direct," he rumbled. "We'll find out why."

"That's not possible," Calazar said.

"Why?" Heller asked him. "Surely we've got a legitimate interest in all this. You've carried out your discreet checking of facts now, and you've got your answers. If you in fact represent this planet, what's to stop you acting accordingly?"

"Are you in a position to make such demands?" Showm challenged. "If our interpretation of the situation is correct, you do not constitute an officially representative group of the whole of Earth's society, either. That function surely belongs rightfully to the United Nations, does it not?"

"We've been communicating with them for weeks," Calazar said, taking Showm's point. "They have done nothing to dispel any wrong impressions of Earth that we may have, and they seem disinclined to meet us. But your transmissions were directed from another part of the solar system entirely, suggesting perhaps that you did not wish our replies to become general knowledge, and therefore that you are equally concerned with preserving secrecy."

"What is the reason for the UN's curious attitude?" Showm asked, looking from one to another of the Terrans and allowing her eyes to rest finally on Heller.

Heller sighed wearily. "I don't know," she admitted. "Perhaps they're wary of the possible consequences of colliding with an advanced alien culture."

"And so it might be with some of our own race," Calazar said. It seemed unlikely since Earth was hardly advanced by Thurien standards, but strange things were possible, Hunt supposed.

"So maybe we should insist on talking to that organization directly," Showm suggested pointedly. There was no response to that.

There was still something Hunt didn't understand when he sat back and tried to reconstruct in his mind the probable sequence of events as the Thuriens would have perceived them. For some time they had been building up a picture of a belligerent and militarized Earth from the accounts forwarded by the mysterious "organization," none of which had mentioned the *Shapieron*. Then a signal, coded in Ganymean, had suddenly come in direct to Calazar's side of the operation, advising that the ship was on its way home. After that, the further transmissions from Farside would have accumulated to hint of an Earth significantly different from that which the surveillance reports had described. But why had it been so important for the Thuriens to establish which version was correct? The measures that they had employed to find out said very clearly that the issue had been taken much more seriously than could be explained by mere academic curiosity or the need to straighten out some internal management problems.

"Let's start at the beginning with this relay device—or whatever you'd call it—that you've got outside the solar system," he suggested when he had that much clear in his head.

"It's not ours," Eesyan said at once from his position next to Calazar, opposite Showm. "We don't know what it is, either. You see, we didn't put it there."

"But you must have," Hunt protested. "It uses your instant communications technology. It responded to Ganymean protocols."

"Nevertheless it's a mystery," Eesyan replied. "Our guess is that it must be a piece of surveillance hardware, not operated by us but by the organization responsible for that activity, which malfunctioned in some way and routed the signal through to our equipment instead of to its intended destination."

"But you replied to it," Hunt pointed out.

"At the time we were under the impression it was from the *Shapieron* itself," Calazar answered. "Our immediate concern was to let its people know that their message had been received, that they had correctly identified Gistar, and that they were heading for the right place." Hunt nodded. He would have done the same thing.

Caldwell frowned in a way that said he still wasn't clear about something. "Okay, but getting back to this relay—why didn't you find out what it was? You can send stuff from Thurien to Earth in a day. Why couldn't you send something to check it out?"

"If it was a piece of surveillance hardware that had gone faulty and given us a direct line, we didn't want to draw attention to it," Eesyan replied. "We were getting some interesting information through it."

"You didn't want this—'organization' to know about it?" Heller queried, looking puzzled.

"Correct."

"But they already knew about it. The reply from Gistar was all over Earth's newsgrid. They must have known about it if they run the surveillance."

"But they weren't picking up *your* signals *to* the relay," Eesyan said. "We would have known if they were." Suddenly Hunt realized why Gistar hadn't responded to the Farside transmissions that had continued for months after the *Shapieron*'s departure: the Thuriens didn't want to reveal their direct line via Earth's news network. That fitted in with their insistence on nothing being communicated via the net when at last they had elected to reopen the dialogue.

Heller paused for a moment and brought her hand up to her brow while she collected her thoughts. "But they couldn't have left it at that," she said, looking up. "From what they picked up out of the newsgrid, they would have known that you knew about the *Shapieron*—something they hadn't been telling you about. They couldn't have just done nothing . . . not without arousing suspicion. They'd have to tell you about it at that point, because they knew if they didn't you'd be going to them and asking some awkward questions."

"Which is exactly what they did," Calazar confirmed.

"So didn't you ask them why they hadn't gotten around

to it earlier?" Caldwell asked. "I mean—hell, the ship had been there for six months."

"Yes, we did," Calazar replied. "The reason they gave was that they were concerned for the *Shapieron*'s safety, and feared that attempts to interfere with the situation might only jeopardize it further. Rightly or wrongly, they had come to the decision that it would be better for us to know only after it was out of the solar system."

Caldwell snorted, obviously not impressed by the mysterious "organization's" excuse. "Didn't you ask to see the records they had acquired through their surveillance?" ·

"We did," Calazar answered. "And they produced ones that had every appearance of justifying their fears for the *Shapieron* completely."

Now Hunt knew where the phony depictions that he had witnessed of the *Shapieron*'s arrival at Ganymede had come from: the "organization" had faked them just as they had been faking their reports of Earth all along. Those were the versions that Calazar's people had been shown. If those scenes with their frighteningly authentic blending of reality and fantasy were typical of what had been going on, it was no wonder that the deception had gone unsuspected for years.

"I've seen some of those records," Hunt said. He sounded incredulous. "How did you ever come to suspect that they might not be genuine? They're unbelievable."

"We didn't," Eesyan told him. "VISAR did. As you may be aware, the drive method of the *Shapieron* creates a spacetime deformation around the ship. It is most pronounced when main drive is operating, but exists to some extent even under auxiliary drive—sufficient to displace the apparent positions of background stars close to the vessel's outline by a measurable amount. VISAR noticed that the predicted displacements were present in some of the views we were shown, but completely missing from others. Hence the reports of the *Shapieron* were suspect."

"And not only those," Calazar said. "By implication, every other report that we had ever received of Earth was in doubt too, but we had no comparable way of testing them." He moved his eyes solemnly along the row of Terran faces. "Perhaps now you can see why we were concerned. We had two conflicting impressions of Earth, and no way of knowing how much of each might be true. But suppose that Earth was as aggressive and as irrational as we had been led to believe for years, and that the occupants of the *Shapieron* had indeed been received and treated in the ways described to us. . . ." He left the sentence unfinished. "Well, in our position what might you have thought?"

A silence descended around the table. The Thuriens wouldn't have known what to believe, Hunt conceded inwardly. Their only way to check the facts would have been to reopen the dialogue with Earth secretly and establish face-to-face contact, which was precisely what they had done. So why had it been so important?

Suddenly Lyn's mouth dropped open, and she stared wide-eyed at Calazar. "You were afraid that we might have bombed the *Shapieron* or something!" she gasped, horrified. "If we were the way those stories said, we'd never have let that ship get to Thurien to tell anybody about it." The shocked looks coming from around her said that it suddenly all made sense to the others too. Even Caldwell seemed deflated for the moment. It was a shame about Jerol Packard, but nobody could blame the Thuriens for acting as they had.

"But you didn't have to wait to find out," Hunt said after a few seconds. "You can project black-hole ports across light-years. Why didn't you simply intercept the ship and get it here fast? Surely they'd have been the obvious people to check your surveillance reports with; they had been on Earth for six months."

"Technical reasons," Eesyan replied. "A Thurien vessel can clear a planetary system in about a day, but only because it carries on-board equipment that interacts with the transfer port and keeps the gravitational disturbance relatively localized. Naturally the *Shapieron* does not have such equipment. We needed to give it months if we were to avoid perturbing your planetary orbits. That would have been embarrassing if our fears were groundless. But we've been taking a risk. We finally reached the point where we had to know whether or not that ship was safe—*now*, without any further delays and obstructions."

"We had decided to go ahead anyway when it became clear that we were not making progress with the UN," Calazar told them. "Only when your messages from Jupiter started coming in did we decide to leave it a little longer. We had the necessary ships and generators ready then, and they have been standing by ever since. All they needed was one signal from us to commence the operation."

Hunt sank back in his chair and released a long breath. It had been a close thing. If Joe Shannon on *Jupiter Five* had not been thinking too clearly for a day or two, all of Earth's astronomical tables would have needed to be worked out all over again from square one.

"You'd better send the signal."

The voice sounded suddenly from one end of the Terran group. Everyone looked round, surprised, and found Danchekker directing a challenging look from one part of the table to another as if inviting them to make some obvious deduction. A score of Terran and Ganymean faces stared back at him blankly.

Danchekker removed his spectacles, polished them with a handkerchief, and then returned them to his nose in the manner of a professor allowing a class of slow students time to reflect upon some proposition he had put to them. There was no reason why VISAR would make lenses that existed only in somebody's head go cloudy, Hunt thought to himself; the ritual was just an unconscious mannerism.

At last Danchekker looked up. "It seems evident that this, er, 'organization' responsible for the surveillance activities, whatever its nature, would not see its interests served by the *Shapieron* reaching Thurien." He paused to let the full implication sink in.

"And now let me conjecture as to what might be my disposition now, were I in the position of the leaders of that organization," he resumed. "I assume that I know nothing about this meeting or that any dialogue between Thurien and Earth is taking place at all since my source of information would be the terrestrial communications network, and all references to such facts have been excluded from that system. Therefore I would have no reason to believe that my falsified accounts of Earth have been questioned. Now, that being so, if the *Shapieron* were to encounter an unfortunate, shall we say, accident, somewhere in the void between the stars, I would have every reason to feel confident that, if perchance the Thuriens should suspect foul play,

Earth would top their list as the most likely culprit." He nodded and showed his teeth briefly as the appalled expressions around the table registered the impact of what he was driving at.

"Precisely!" he exclaimed, and looked across at Calazar. "If you have at your disposal the means of extracting that vessel from its present predicament, I would strongly advise that you proceed with such action without a moment of further delay!"

chapter twelve

Niels Sverenssen lay propped against the pillows in his executive-grade quarters at Giordano Bruno, watching the girl dress by the vanity on the far side of the room. She was young and quite pretty, with the clear complexion and open features typical of many Americans, and her loose black hair cut an intriguing contrast against her white skin. She should use the sunray facilities provided in the gymnasium more often, he thought to himself. As with most of her sex, her superficial layer of college-applied pseudointellectualism went no deeper than the pigment in her skin; beneath it she was as facile as the rest of them—a regrettably necessary but not unpleasant diversion from the more serious side of life. "You only want my body," they had cried indignantly down through the ages. "What else can you offer?" was his reply.

She finished buttoning her shirt and turned toward the mirror to run a comb hurriedly through her hair. "I know it's a strange time to be leaving," she said. "Trust me to be on early shift this morning. I'm going to be late again as it is."

"Don't worry about it," Sverenssen told her, putting more concern into his voice than he felt. "First things must come first."

She picked her jacket up off the back of a chair next to

the vanity and slung it over her shoulder. "Have you got the cartridge?" she asked, turning back to face him.

Sverenssen opened the drawer of the bedside unit, reached inside, and took out a matchbook-size, computer micromemory cartridge. "Here. Remember to be careful."

The girl walked over to him, took the cartridge and folded it inside a tissue, then slipped it into one of the pockets of her jacket. "I will. When will I see you again?"

"Today will be very busy. I'll have to let you know."

"Don't make it too long." She smiled, stooped to kiss him on the forehead, and left, closing the door softly behind her.

Professor Gregor Malliusk, the Director of Astronomy at the Giordano Bruno observatory, was not looking pleased when she arrived in the main-dish control room ten minutes later. "You're late again, Janet," he grumbled as she hung her jacket in one of the closets by the door and put on her white working coat. "John had to leave in haste because he's going to Ptolemy today, and I've had to cover. I've got a meeting in less than an hour and things to do beforehand. This situation is becoming intolerable."

"I'm sorry, Professor," she said. "I overslept. It won't happen again." She walked quickly across to the supervisory console and began going through the routine of calling up the night's status logs with deft, practiced movements of her fingers.

Malliusk watched balefully from beside the equipment racks outside his office, trying not to notice the firm, slim lines of her body outlined by the white material of her coat and the raven black curls tumbling carelessly over her collar. "It's that Swede again, isn't it," he growled before he could stop himself.

"That's my business," Janet said without looking up, making her voice as firm as she dared. "I've already said— it won't happen again." She compressed her mouth into a tight line and stabbed savagely at the keyboard to bring another screen of data up in front of her.

"The check correlation on 557B was not completed yesterday," Malliusk said icily. "It was scheduled for completion by fifteen hundred."

Janet hesitated from what she was doing, closed her eyes

momentarily, and bit her lip. "Damn!" she muttered beneath her breath, then louder, "I'll skip break and get it done then. There's not a lot of it left."

"John has already completed it."

"I'm . . . sorry. I'll do an extra hour off his next shift to make up."

Malliusk scowled at her for a few seconds longer, then turned on his heel abruptly and left the control room without saying anything more.

When she had finished checking the status logs, she switched off the screen and walked over to the transmission subsystem communications auxiliary processor cabinet, opened a cover panel, and inserted the cartridge that Sverenssen had given her into an empty slot. Then she moved around to the front of the system console and ran through the routine of integrating the contents of the cartridge into the message buffer already assembled for transmission later that day. Where the transmission was intended for she didn't know, but it was part of whatever had brought the UN delegation to Bruno. Malliusk always took care of the technical side of that personally, and he never talked about it with the rest of the staff.

Sverenssen had told her that the cartridge contained some mundane data that had come in late from Earth for appending to the transmission that had been already composed; everything that went out was supposed to be approved formally by all of the delegates, but it would have been silly to call them all together merely to rubber-stamp something as petty as this. But a couple of them could be touchy, he had said, and he cautioned her to be discreet. She liked the feeling of being confided in over a matter of UN importance, even if it had only to do with some minor point, especially by somebody so sophisticated and worldly. It was so deliciously romantic! And, who knew? From some of the things that Sverenssen had said, she could be doing herself a really big favor in the long run.

"He is a guest here, like the rest of you, and we have done our best to be accommodating," Malliusk told Sobroskin later that morning in the Soviet delegate's offices. "But this is interfering with the observatory's work. I do not expect to have to be accommodating to the point of having my own work disrupted. And besides that, I object to such conduct in my own establishment, particularly from a man in his position. It is not becoming."

"I can hardly intervene in personal matters that are not part of the delegation's business," Sobroskin pointed out, doing his best to be diplomatic as he detected more than merely outraged propriety beneath the scientist's indignation. "It would be more appropriate for you to try talking to Sverenssen directly. She is your assistant, after all, and it *is* the department's work that is being affected."

"I have already done that, and the response was not satisfactory," Malliusk replied stiffly. "As a Russian, I wish my complaint to be conveyed to whichever office of the Soviet Government is concerned with the business of this delegation, with the request that they apply some appropriate influence through the UN. Therefore I am talking to you as the representative here of that office."

Sobroskin was not really interested in Malliusk's jealousies, and he didn't particularly want to stir up things in Moscow over something like this; too many people would want to know what the delegation was doing on Farside in the first place, and that would invite all kinds of questions and poking around. On the other hand, Malliusk obviously wanted something done, and if Sobroskin declined there was no telling whom the professor might be on the phone to next. There really wasn't a lot of choice. "Very well," he agreed with a sigh. "Leave it with me. I'll see if I can talk to Sverenssen today, or maybe tomorrow."

"Thank you," Malliusk acknowledged formally, then marched out of the office.

Sobroskin sat there thinking for a while, then reached behind himself to unlock a safe, from which he took a file that an old friend in Soviet military intelligence had sent up to Bruno unofficially at his request. He spent some time thumbing through its contents to refresh his memory, and as he thought further, he changed his mind about what he was going to do.

There were a number of strange things recorded in the file on Niels Sverenssen—the Swede, supposedly born in Malmo in 1981, who had vanished while serving as a mercenary in Africa in his late teens and then reappeared ten years later in Europe with inconsistent accounts of where he had been and what he had been doing. How had he suddenly reemerged from obscurity as a man of considerable wealth and social standing with no record of his movements during that time that could be traced? How had he established his international connections without it being common knowledge?

The pattern of womanizing was long and clear. The affair with the German financier's wife was interesting . . . with the rival lover who had publicly sworn vengeance and then met with a skiing accident less than a month later in dubious circumstances. A lot of evidence implied people had been bought off to close the investigation. Yes, Sverenssen was a man with connections he would not like to see aired publicly and the ruthlessness to use them without hesitation if need be, Sobroskin thought to himself.

And more recently—within the last month, in fact—why had Sverenssen been communicating regularly and secretly with Verikoff, the space-communications specialist at the Academy of Sciences in Moscow who was intimately involved with the top-secret Soviet channel to Gistar? The Soviet Government did not comprehend the UN's apparent policy but it suited them, and that meant that the existence of the independent channel had to be concealed from the UN more than from anybody else; the Americans had doubtless deduced what was happening, but they were unable to prove it. That was their loss. If they insisted on tying themselves down with their notions of fair play, that was up to them. But why was Verikoff talking to Sverenssen?

And finally, in years gone by Sverenssen had always been a prominent figure in leading the UN drive for strategic disarmament, and a champion of world-wide cooperation and increased productivity. Why was he now vigorously supporting a UN policy that seemed opposed to seizing the greatest opportunity the human race had ever had to achieve those very things? It seemed strange. Everything to do with Sverenssen seemed strange.

Anyhow, what was he going to do about Malliusk's assistant? She was an American girl, Malliusk had said. Perhaps there was a way in which he could clear this irritating business up without inviting Sverenssen's close attention at a time when he was particularly anxious to avoid it. Their national loyalties aside, he admired the way in which Pacey had continued battling to promote his country's views after Heller left, and he had got to know the American quite well socially. In fact it was a shame in some ways that over this particular issue the U.S.S.R. and the U.S.A. were not together on the same side of the table; at heart they seemed to have more in common with each other than with the rest of the delegation. Very probably it wouldn't make much difference for a lot longer anyway, he admitted to himself. As Karen Heller had said on one occasion, it was the future of the whole race they should be thinking about. As a man he tended to agree with her; if the contact with Gistar meant what he thought it meant, there would be no national differences to worry about in fifty years' time, nor maybe even any nations. But that was as a man. In the meantime, as a Russian, he had a job to do.

He nodded to himself as he closed the file and returned it to the safe. He would talk to Norman Pacey and see if Pacey would talk to the American girl quietly. Then, with luck, the whole thing would resolve itself with no more than a few ripples that would soon die away.

chapter thirteen

Framed in the screen that took up most of one wall of the room was the image of a planet, captured from several thousand miles out in space. Most of its surface was ocean blue or stirred into spirals of curdled clouds through which its continents varied from yellowy browns and greens at its equator to frosty white at the poles. It was a warm, sunny, and cheerful world, but the image failed to recreate the sense of wonder at the energy of the life teeming across its surface that Garuth had felt at the time the image was captured months earlier.

As Garuth, commander of the long-range scientific mission ship *Shapieron*, sat in his private stateroom staring at the last view to be obtained of Earth, he pondered on the incredible race of beings that had greeted the return of his ship from its long exile in the mysterious realm of compoundly dilated time. Twenty-five million years before, although only a little over twenty by the *Shapieron*'s clocks, Garuth and his companions had left a flourishing civilization on Minerva to conduct a scientific experiment at a star called Iscaris; if the experiment had gone as planned, they would have been gone for twenty-three years of elapsed time back home, having lost less than five years from their own lifetimes. But the experiment had not gone as planned, and before the *Shapieron* was able to return, the Ganymeans had vanished from Minerva; the Lunarians had emerged, built their civilization, split into opposing factions, and finally destroyed themselves and the planet; and *Homo sapiens* had returned to Earth and written several tens of thousands of years of history.

And so the *Shapieron* had found them. What had been a pathetically deformed mutant left by the Ganymeans to fend for itself against hopeless odds in a harsh and uncompromising environment had transformed itself into a creature of pride and defiance that had not only survived, but laughed its contempt at every obstacle that the universe had tried to throw in its path. The solar system, once the exclusive domain of the Ganymean civilization, had become rightfully the property of the human race. And so the *Shapieron* had departed once more into the void on a forlorn quest to reach the Giants' Star, the supposed new home of the Ganymeans.

Garuth sighed. Supposed for what reasons? Speculations based upon nothing that even the most elementary student of logic would accept as evidence; a frail straw of possibility clutched at to rationalize a decision taken in reality for reasons that only Garuth and a few of his officers knew about; a fabrication in the minds of Earthmen, whose optimism and enthusiasm knew no bounds.

The incredible Earthmen . . .

They had persuaded themselves that the myth of the Giants' Star was true and gathered to wish the Ganymeans well when the ship departed, believing, as most of Garuth's own people still believed, the reason he had stated—that Earth's fragile civilization was still too young to withstand the pressures of coexistence with an alien population that would have grown in numbers and influence. But there must have been a few, like the American biologist Danchekker, and the Englishman Hunt, who had guessed the real reason—that long ago the Ganymeans had created the ancestors of *Homo sapiens*. The human race had survived and flourished in spite of all the handicaps that the Ganymeans had inflicted upon them. Earth had earned its right to freedom from Ganymean interference; the Ganymeans had already interfered enough.

And so Garuth had allowed his people to believe the myth and follow him into oblivion. The decision had been hard, but they deserved the comfort of hope, at least for a while, he told himself. Hope had sustained them through the long voyage from Iscaris; they trusted him again now as they had then. Surely it was not wrong to allow them that until the time came when they would have to know what only Garuth and a select few knew at present, and probably what Earthmen like Danchekker and Hunt already knew. But he would never be certain how much those two friends from that astounding race of impetuous and at times aggressively inclined dwarves had really known. He would never see them again.

Garuth had stared silent and alone at this image many times since the ship's departure from Earth, and at the star maps showing its distant destination, still many years away and gleaming as just another insignificant pinpoint among millions. There was a chance, of course, that the scientists of Earth had been right. There was always a shred of hope that— He checked himself abruptly. He was allowing himself to slip into wishful thinking. It was all nothing but wishful thinking.

He straightened up in his chair and returned from his reverie. There was work to do. "ZORAC," he said aloud. "Delete the image. Inform Shilohin and Monchar that I would like to see them later today, immediately after this evening's concert if possible." The image of Earth disappeared. "Also I'd like to have another look at the proposal for revising the Third Level Educational curriculum." The screen came to life at once to present a table of statistics and some text. Garuth studied it for a while, voiced some comments for ZORAC to record and append, then called up the next screen in the sequence. Why was he worried at all about an educational curriculum that was nothing more than part of a pattern of normality that had to be preserved? Condemned by his decision along with the rest of his people, the children were destined to perish ignominiously and unmourned in the emptiness between the stars, knowing no home other than the *Shapieron*. Why did he concern himself with details of an educational curriculum that would serve no purpose?

He pushed the thought firmly from his mind and returned his attention fully to the task.

chapter fourteen

"Look, I know I don't have any right to interfere in your private life, and I'm not trying to," Norman Pacey said from an armchair in his private room at Bruno some hours after Sobroskin had talked to him about Janet. He tried to make his voice reasonable and gentle, but at the same time firm. "But when it gets to the point where I get dragged in and it affects the delegation's business, I have to say something."

From the chair opposite, Janet listened without changing expression. There was just a trace of moisture in her eyes, but whether that was due to remorse, anger, or to a sinus condition that had nothing to do with either, Pacey couldn't tell. "I suppose it was a bit silly," she said at last in a small voice.

Pacey sighed inwardly and did his best not to show it. "Sverenssen should have known better anyway," he said, hoping that it might be a consolation. "Hell—look, I can't tell you what to do, but at least be smart. If you want my advice for what it's worth, I'd say forget the whole thing and concentrate on your job here. But it's up to you. If you decide not to, then keep things so that they don't give Malliusk anything to come bitching about to us. There—that's as frank as I can be."

Janet stroked her lip with a knuckle and smiled faintly. "I'm not sure if that would be possible," she confided. "If you want the real reason why it's bugging him, it's because he's had this thing about me ever since I came up here."

Pacey groaned under his breath. He had felt himself slipping into a father role, and her responding to it. Now her whole life story was about to come pouring out. He didn't have the time. "Oh Jesus . . ." He spread his hands appealingly. "I really don't want to get too involved in your personal life. I just felt there was an aspect that I ought to say something about purely as the U.S. member of the delegation. Suppose we simply leave it at that and stay friends, huh?" He pushed his mouth into a grin and looked at her expectantly.

But she had to explain everything. "I guess it was just that everything here was so strange and different . . . you know . . . out here on the back of the Moon." She looked a little sheepish. "I don't know . . . I suppose it was nice to meet someone friendly."

"I understand." Pacey half-raised a hand. "Don't imagine you're the first—"

"And he was such a different kind of man to talk to. . . . He understood things too, like you." Her expression changed suddenly, and she looked at Pacey in a strange way, as if unsure about voicing something that was on her mind. Pacey was about to stand up and bring the matter to a close before she turned the room into a private confessional, but she spoke before he could move. "There's something else I've been wondering about . . . whether I ought to mention it to somebody or not. It seemed okay at the time, but . . . oh, I don't know—it's been kind of bothering me." She looked at him as if waiting for a signal to go on. Pacey stared back without the slightest indication of interest. She went on anyway. "He gave me some micromemories with some additional data in for appending to the transmissions that Malliusk has been handling. He said it was just some extra trivial stuff, but . . . I don't know . . . there was something strange about the way he said it." She released her breath sharply and seemed relieved. "Anyhow, there—now you know about it."

Pacey's posture and manner had changed abruptly. He was leaning forward and staring at her, a shocked look on his face. Her eyes widened in alarm as she realized that what she had said was more serious than she thought.. "How many?" he demanded crisply.

"Three . . . The last was early this morning."

"When was the first?"

"A few days ago . . . more maybe. It was before Karen Heller left."

"What did they say?"

"I don't know." Janet shrugged helplessly. "How would I know that?"

"Aw, come on." Pacey waved a hand impatiently. "Don't tell me you weren't curious. You've got the equipment to read a memory onto a screen."

"I tried to," she admitted after a few seconds. "But they had a lockout code that wouldn't permit a read from the console routine. They must have had a built-in, one-time activating sequence from the transmission call. They'd self-erased afterward."

"And that didn't make you suspicious?"

"At first I thought it was just some kind of routine UN security procedure. . . . Then I wasn't so sure. That was when it started bothering me." She looked across at Pacey nervously for a few seconds, then added timidly, "He did say it was only some trivial additions." Her tone said she didn't believe that now, either. Then she lapsed into silence while Pacey sat back with a distant expression on his face, gnawing unconsciously at the knuckle of his thumb while his mind raced through the possible meaning of what she had said.

"What else has he said to you?" he asked at last.

"What else?"

"Anything. Try and remember anything strange or unusual that he might have done or talked to you about—even things that sound stupid. This is important."

"Well . . ." Janet frowned and stared at the wall behind him. "He told me about all the work he did for disarmament and how he was mixed up in turning the UN into an efficient global power since then . . . all the people in high places that he knows all over."

"Uh huh. We know about that. Anything else?"

A smile flickered on Janet's mouth for a second. "He gets mad because you seem to give him a hard time at the delegation meetings. I get the impression he thinks you're a mean bastard. I can't think why, though."

"Yes."

Her expression changed suddenly. "There was something else, not long ago. . . . Yesterday, it was." Pacey waited and said nothing. She thought for a moment. "I was in his quarters—in the bathroom. Somebody else from the delegation came in the front door suddenly, all excited. I'm not sure which one it was. It wasn't you or that little bald Russian guy, but somebody foreign. Anyhow, he couldn't have known I was in there and started talking straight away. Niels shut him up and sounded really mad, but not before this other guy had said something about some news coming in that something out in space a long way off would be destroyed very soon now." She wrinkled her brow for a moment, then shook her head. "There wasn't anything else . . . not that I could make out, anyway."

Pacey was staring at her incredulously. "You're sure he said that?"

Janet shook her head. "It sounded like that . . . I can't be sure. The faucet was running and . . ." She let it go at that.

"You can't remember hearing anything else?"

"No . . . sorry."

Pacey stood up and walked slowly over to the door. After pausing for a while he turned and came back, halting to stand staring down in front of her. "Look, I don't think you realize what you've got yourself into," he said, injecting an ominous note into his voice. She looked up at him fearfully. "Listen hard to this. It is absolutely imperative that you tell nobody else about this. Understand? *Nobody!* If you're going to start being sensible, the time is right now. You must *not* let one word of what you've told me go a step further." She shook her head mutely. "I want your word on that," he told her.

She nodded, then after a second or two asked, "Does that mean I can't see Niels?"

Pacey bit his lip. The chance to learn more was tempting, but could he trust her? He thought for a few seconds, then replied, "If you can keep your mouth shut about what you heard and what you've said. And if anything else unusual happens, let me know. *Don't* go playing at spies and looking for trouble. Just keep your eyes and ears open, and if you see or hear anything strange, let me know and nobody else. And don't write anything down. Okay?"

She nodded again and tried to grin, but it didn't work. "Okay," she said.

Pacey looked at her for a moment longer, then spread his arms to indicate that he was through. "I guess that's it for now. Excuse me, but I've got things waiting to get done."

Janet got up and walked quickly to the door. She was just about to close it behind her when Pacey called, "And Janet . . ." She stopped and looked back. "For Christ's sake try to get to work on time and stay out of the hair of that Russian professor of yours."

"I will." She managed a quick smile, and left.

Pacey had noted for some time that, like himself, Sobroskin seemed excluded from the clique that revolved around Sverenssen, and he had come to believe increasingly that the Russian was playing a lone game on behalf of Moscow and merely finding the UN policy expedient. If so, Sobroskin would not be a party to whatever information Janet had caught a snippet of. Unwilling to break radio silence on Thurien-related matters with Earth, he decided to risk playing his hunch and arranged to meet the Russian later that evening in a storage room that formed part of a rarely frequented section of the base.

"Obviously I can't be sure, but it could be the *Shapieron*," Pacey said. "There seem to be two groups of Thuriens who aren't exactly on open terms with each other. We've been talking to one group, who appear to have the best interests of the ship at heart, but how do we know that other people back here haven't been talking to the other group? And how do we know that the other group feels the same way?"

Sobroskin had been listening attentively. "You're referring to the coded signals," he said. As expected, everybody had denied having anything to do with them.

"Yes," Pacey answered. "We assumed it was you because we know damn well it isn't us. But I'm willing to concede that we might have been wrong about them. Suppose the

UN has set up this whole thing at Bruno for appearance's sake while it plays some other game behind the scenes. They could be stalling both of us while all the time they're talking behind our backs to . . . I don't know, maybe one Thurien side, maybe the other, or maybe even both."

"What kind of game?" Sobroskin asked. He was obviously fishing for ideas, probably through having few of his own to offer just then.

"Who knows? But what I'm worried about is that ship. If I'm wrong about it I'm wrong, but we can't just do nothing and hope so. If there's reason to suppose that it might be in danger, we have to let the Thuriens know. They might be able to do something." He had thought for a long time about risking a call to Alaska, but in the end decided against it.

Sobroskin thought deeply for a while. He knew that the coded signals were coming in in response to the Soviet transmissions, but there was no reason to say so. Yet another oddity had come to light concerning the Swede, and Sobroskin was anxious to follow it through. Moscow wished for nothing other than good relations with the Thuriens, and there was nothing to be lost by cooperating in warning them by whatever means Pacey had in mind. If the American's fears proved groundless, no permanent harm would result that Sobroskin could see. Either way, there was no time to consult with the Kremlin. "I respect your confidence," he said at last, and meant it, as Pacey could see he did. "What do you want me to do?"

"I want to use the Bruno transmitter to send a signal," Pacey replied. "Obviously it can't go through the delegation, so we'd have to go to Malliusk directly to take care of the technical side. He's a pain, but I think we could trust him. He wouldn't respond to an approach from me alone, but he might from you."

Sobroskin's eyebrows raised a fraction in surprise. "Why did you not go to the American girl?"

"I thought of it, but I'm not convinced she's reliable enough. She's too close to Sverenssen."

Sobroskin thought for a moment longer, then nodded. "Give me an hour. I'll call you in your room then, whatever the news." He sucked his teeth pensively as if weighing up something in his mind and then added, "I would suggest taking things easy with the girl. I have reports on Sverenssen. He can be dangerous."

They met Malliusk in the main-dish control room after the evening shift was over and while the astronomers booked for the night were away having coffee. Malliusk agreed to their request only after Sobroskin had consented to sign a disclaimer stating that the action was requested by him, acting in his official capacity as a representative of the Soviet Government. Malliusk locked the statement among his private papers. He then closed the control-room doors and used the main screen of the supervisory console to compose and transmit the message that Pacey dictated. Neither of the Russians could understand why Pacey insisted on appending his own name to the transmission. There were some things that he was not prepared to divulge.

chapter fifteen

Monchar, Garuth's second-in-command, was visibly tense when Garuth arrived in response to the emergency call to the *Shapieron*'s Command Deck. "There's something we've never seen before affecting the stress field around the ship," he said in answer to Garuth's unvoiced question. "Some kind of external bias is interfering with the longitudinal node pattern and degrading the geodesic manifolds. The gribase is going out of balance, and ZORAC can't make sense of it. It's trying to recompute the transforms now."

Garuth turned to Shilohin, the mission's chief scientist, who was in the center of a small group of her staff, taking in the information appearing on a battery of screens arrayed around them. "What's happening?" he asked.

She shook her head helplessly. "I've never heard of anything like this. We're entering some kind of spacetime asymmetry with coordinates transforming inversely into an exponential frame. The whole structure of the region of space that we're in is breaking down."

"Can we maneuver?"

"Nothing seems to work. The divertors are ineffective, and the longitudinal equalizers can't compensate even at full gain."

"ZORAC, what's your report?" Garuth called in a louder voice.

"Impossible to construct a gridbase that couples consistently into normal space," the computer replied. "In other words I'm lost, don't know where we are, where we're going, or even if we're going anywhere, and don't have control anyway. Otherwise everything's fine."

"System status?" Garuth inquired.

"All sensors, channels, and subsystems checked and working normally. No—I'm not sick, and I'm not imagining it."

Garuth stood nonplussed. Every face on the Command Deck was watching and waiting for his orders, but what order could he give when he had no idea what was happening and what, if anything, could be done about it. "Call all stations to emergency readiness and alert them to stand by for further instructions," he said, more to satisfy expectations than for any definite reason. A crewman to one side acknowledged and turned toward a panel to relay the order.

"Total stress-field dislocation," Shilohin murmured, taking in the latest updates on the screens. "We're dissociated from any identifiable reference." The scientists around her were looking grim. Monchar nervously gripped the edge of a nearby console.

Then ZORAC's voice sounded again. "The trends reported have begun reversing rapidly. Coupling and translation functions are reintegrating to a new gridbase. References are rotating back into balance."

"We might be coming out of it," Shilohin said quietly. Hopeful mutterings broke out all around. She studied the displays again and appeared to relax somewhat.

"Stress field not returning to normal," ZORAC advised. "The field is being externally suppressed, forcing reversion to subgravitic velocity. Full spatial reintegration unavoidable and imminent." Something was slowing the ship down and forcing it to resume contact with the rest of the universe. "Reintegration complete. We're in touch with the universe again . . ." An unusually long pause followed. "But I don't know which part. We seem to have changed our position in space." A spherical display in the middle of the floor illuminated to show the starfield surrounding the ship. It was nothing like that visible from the vicinity of the solar system, which should not have altered beyond recognition since the *Shapieron*'s departure from Earth.

"Several large, artificial constructions are approaching us," ZORAC announced after a short pause. "The designs are not familiar, but they are obviously the products of intelligence. Implications: we have been intercepted deliberately by a means unknown, for a purpose unknown, and transferred to a place unknown by a form of intelligence unknown. Apart from the unknowns, everything is obvious."

"Show us the constructions," Garuth commanded.

Three screens around the Command Deck displayed views obtained in different directions of a number of immense craft, the like of which Garuth had never seen, moving slowly inward from the background of stars. Garuth and his officers could only stand and stare in silent awe. Before anybody could find words, ZORAC informed them, "We have communications from the unidentified craft. They are using our standard high-spectrum format. I'm putting it on the main monitor." Seconds later, the large screen overlooking the floor presented a picture. Every Ganymean in the Command Deck froze, stupefied by what they saw.

"My name is Calazar," the face said. "Greetings to you who went to Iscaris long ago. Soon you will arrive at our new home. Be patient, and all will be explained."

It was a Ganymean—a slightly modified Ganymean, but a Ganymean sure enough. Elation and joy mixed with disbelief surged in the confused emotions exploding in Garuth's head. It could only mean that . . . the signal that the Earthmen had beamed outward from their Moon had been received. Suddenly his heart went out to the impetuous, irrepressible, unquenchable Earthmen. They had been right after all. He loved them, every one.

Gasps of wonder were erupting on every side as one by one the others realized what was happening. Monchar was turning circles and waving his arms in the air in an uncontrollable release of emotion, while Shilohin had sunk into an empty seat and was just gaping wide-eyed and speechless up at the screen.

Then ZORAC confirmed what they already knew. "I've matched the starfield with extrapolations from records and fixed our location. Don't ask me how, but it seems that the voyage is over. We're at the Giants' Star."

Less than an hour later, Garuth led the first party of Ganymeans out of the lock of one of the *Shapieron*'s daughter vessels and into a brilliantly lit reception bay in one of the craft from Thurien. They approached the line of figures that were waiting silently, and went through a short welcoming ritual in which the dam finally broke and all the pent-up anguish and hope that the wanderers had carried with them burst forth in a flood of laughter and not a few tears. It was over. The long exile was over, and the exiles were finally home.

Afterward the new arrivals were conducted to a side chamber and required to recline on couches for a few minutes. The purpose of this was not explained. The Ganymeans experienced a strange sequence of sensory disturbances, after which all was normal again. They were then told that the process was complete. Minutes later, Garuth left the side chamber with his party to reenter the area where the Thuriens were assembled . . . and suddenly stopped dead in his tracks, his eyes popping in disbelief.

Slightly ahead of the Thuriens, grinning unashamedly at the Ganymeans' total bemusement, stood a small group of familiar pink dwarves. Garuth's mouth fell open, hung limply for a moment, and then closed again without making any sound. For the two figures moving toward him, ahead of the other humans, were none other than—

"What kept you, Garuth?" Hunt asked cheerfully. "Did you miss a sign somewhere along the way?"

"Do forgive my amusement at your expense," Danchekker said, unable to suppress a chuckle. "But I'm afraid the expression on your face is irresistibly provocative."

Behind them Garuth could see another familiar figure—stocky and broad, with wiry hair streaked with gray and deeply etched features; it was Hunt's superior from Houston, and next to him was the red-haired girl who also worked there. Beside them were another man and woman, neither of whom he recognized. Garuth forced his feet to move again, and through his daze saw that Hunt was extending a hand in the customary manner of greeting of Earth. Garuth shook hands with him warmly, then with the others. They were not optical images of some kind; they were real. The Thuriens must have brought them from Earth for this occasion by methods unknown at the time of Minerva.

As he stood back to allow his companions to surge forward toward the Terrans, Garuth spoke quietly into the throat microphone that still connected him with the *Shapieron*, riding not far away from the Thurien vessel. "ZORAC, I am not dreaming? This is really happening?" ZORAC could monitor visual scenes via the miniaturized TV-camera headbands that Ganymeans from the ship wore most of the time.

"I don't know what you mean," ZORAC's voice replied in the earpiece that Garuth was also wearing. "All I can see is a ceiling. You're all lying in chairs of some kind in there, and you haven't moved for almost ten minutes."

Garuth was at a loss. He looked around and saw Hunt and Calazar making their way toward him through the throng of Ganymeans and Terrans. "Can't you see them?" he asked, mystified.

"See who?"

Before Garuth could answer, another voice said, "Actually that wasn't ZORAC. It was me, repeating and imitating ZORAC. Allow me to introduce myself—my name is VISAR. Perhaps it's time we explained a few things."

"But not in the lobby," Hunt said. "Let's go on through into the ship. There's quite a lot that needs explaining." Garuth was even more perplexed. Hunt had heard and understood the exchange even though he was not wearing communications accessories and the exchange had been in Ganymean.

Calazar stood waiting until the rest of the welcomes and

introductions had been completed. Then he beckoned and led the mixed group of Ganymeans and Terrans into the body of the huge spacecraft from Thurien, now only a matter of hours away.

chapter sixteen

Hunt and Danchekker were somewhere out in the vastness of space. Around them was a large, darkened area made up of walled enclosures that looked like booths and interconnecting stretches of open floor, extending away beneath pools of subdued local lighting into the shadows on all sides. The dominant light was a soft, ghostly whiteness coming from the stars overhead, every one bright and unblinking.

After the reception of the *Shapieron* some distance outside the system of Gistar, Jerol Packard, by then his normal self once more, had decided to leave the two groups of Ganymeans alone for some time without Terran intrusion. The others had agreed. They seized the opportunity thus presented to make some instant "visits," courtesy of VISAR, to experience other parts of the Thurien civilization. Packard and Heller went to Thurios to learn more of the system of social organization while Caldwell and Lyn were taken on a tour of light-years between stops to observe more of Thurien space engineering in action. Hunt and Danchekker, intrigued after following the operation that had been mounted to intercept the *Shapieron*, were curious about how the energy had been generated to form the enormous black-hole toroid thrown in the ship's path, and how it was hurled across such an immense distance. VISAR had offered to show them a Thurien power plant, and an instant later they had found themselves here.

They were beneath a huge, transparent blister that formed part of some form of construction hanging in space. But what scale of construction was this? To left and right outside the blister, and in front and behind, the external parts of the structure swept away and upward in four gently curving arms of intricately engineered metal architecture that shrank into the distance to give an impression of immensity that was almost frightening. They seemed to be standing at the crossover point of two shallow crescents that met at right angles like sections of the equator and a longitude line drawn on a globe. The tips of the four crescent arms carried four long, narrow, cylindrical forms whose axes seemed to converge on some distant point like those of four gigantic gun barrels trained to concentrate fire on a remote target. How far away they were was impossible to guess since there was nothing familiar to give any visual cue of size.

Farther away and to one side, positioned almost edge-on to their vantage point, was another structure identical to the one they were in, comprising a similar cruciform of two crescents and carrying its own quadruplet of cylinders, details of its far side losing themselves in foreshortening and distance. And on the other side of the view was another, also edge-on, and another above, and yet another below. The whole set of them, Hunt realized as he looked, was positioned symmetrically in space around a common center to form sections of an imaginary spherical surface like parts of an engineer's exploded drawing, and the gun barrels were pointing inward radially. And far away at the focus of this configuration, an eerie halo of blurred, scrambled starlight was hanging in the void, tinted with a dash of violet.

After giving them some time to take in the scene VISAR informed them, "You are now something like five hundred million miles outside the system of Gistar. You're standing in something called a *stressor*. There are six of them, and together they define a boundary around a spherical volume of space. Each of the arms outside is of the order of five thousand miles long. That's how far away those cylinders are, which should give you some idea of their size."

Danchekker looked at Hunt dumbfounded, raised his head again to take in the scene above, then looked at Hunt once more. Hunt just stared back glassy-eyed.

VISAR continued, "The stressors induce a zone of enhanced spacetime curvature that increases in intensity to-

ward the center until, right at the focus, it collapses into a
black hole." A bright red circle, obviously superposed on
their visual inputs by VISAR, appeared from nowhere to surround the hazy region. "The hole is in the center of the
circle," VISAR told them. "The halo effect is distorted light
from background stars—the region acts like a gravitic lens.
The hole itself is about ten thousand miles from you, and
the space you're in is actually highly distorted. But I can
censor confusing data, so you feel and act normal.

"Behind the shell defined by the stressors are batteries
of projectors that create intense beams of energy by matter
annihilation and direct them between the stressors and into
the hole. From there the energy is redirected and distributed through a higher-order dimension grid and extracted
back into ordinary space wherever it's needed. In other
words this whole arrangement forms the input into an h-
space distribution grid that delivers to anywhere you like,
instantaneously, and over interstellar distances. Like it?"

A while went by before Hunt found his voice. "What
kinds of things hook on the other end?" he asked. "I mean,
would this feed a whole planet . . . or what?"

"The distribution pattern is very complex," VISAR replied. "Several planets are being fed from Garfalang,
which is what the place you're at is called. So are a number
of high-energy projects that the Thuriens are engaged in at
various places. But you can hook smaller units into the grid
wherever they happen to be, such as spacecraft, other vehicles, machines, dwellings—anything that uses power. The
local equipment needed to tap into the grid is not large in
size. For instance the perceptron that we landed in Alaska
was powered from the grid on the conventional stage from
its exit port to Earth. It would have had to be much larger
if it carried its own on-board propulsion source. Hardly any
of our machines have local, self-contained power sources.
They don't need them. The grid feeds everything from
large centralized generators and redirectors, like the one
you're in, located far out in space."

"This is unbelievable," Danchekker breathed. "And to
imagine, fifty years ago people were frightened of their energy sources being exhausted. This is stupefying . . . quite
stupefying."

"What's the prime source?" Hunt asked. "You said the

input beams were produced by matter annihilation. What gets annihilated?"

"Mainly the cores of burned-out stars," VISAR answered. "Part of the energy generated is tapped off to drive a network of transfer ports for conveying material from the remote sites, where the cores are dismantled, to the annihilator batteries. The net production of useful energy fed into the grid from Garfalang is equivalent to about one lunar mass per day. But there's plenty of fuel around. We're a long way from any crisis. Don't worry about it."

"And you can concentrate the energy from here across light-years of space through some kind of . . . hyperdimension and create a transfer toroid remotely," Hunt said. "Is it always as elaborate as the operation we watched?"

"No. That was a special case that required exceptionally precise control and timing. An ordinary transfer is pretty simple by comparison, and just routine."

Hunt fell silent while he took in more of the spectacle overhead, and went back in his mind over the details of the operation he had witnessed.

Calazar had decided to go ahead with the interception of the *Shapieron* without further delay when a baffling message, signed personally by Norman Pacey, came in from Bruno to warn of a possibility that the ship could be in some kind of danger. How Pacey could have known about a risk that had been recognized on Thurien only with the benefit of information that Pacey couldn't possibly have possessed was a mystery.

Apparently the "organization" possessed equipment capable of tracking the *Shapieron* just as Calazar's people did, and Calazar had been unwilling to reveal his actions by simply allowing the ship to vanish from the course it had been following. Therefore he had called upon Eesyan's engineers to modify the operation to cover not only the fishing of a vessel out of the void twenty light-years away, but also the substitution of a dummy object constructed to give identical readings on the "organization's" tracking instruments. There was a risk that the gravitational disturbance produced in the process might itself be detected, but since continuous monitoring was not practicable for technical reasons, there was a good chance that the substitution could be made invisible provided the operation was pulled off in minimum time. As planned, the switch had gone quickly and smoothly, and if all had gone well the "organization" would by now be receiving tracking-data updates originating from the decoy while the *Shapieron* was in fact light-years away and almost at Thurien. Time would no doubt tell if the switch had gone quickly and smoothly enough.

Hunt didn't know what to make of this game of deception and counterdeception between two, possibly rival, groups of Ganymeans. As Danchekker had maintained from the beginning, the response simply did not fit with the way Ganymean minds worked. Hunt had tried several times to squeeze a hint of what was behind it all out of VISAR, but the machine, evidently acting under a firm directive not to discuss the matter, merely reaffirmed that Calazar would broach the subject himself at the appropriate time.

But whatever the reasons, the *Shapieron* had not been attacked or interfered with in whatever way Pacey had feared, and it was now in safe hands. The only conclusion Hunt could draw was that Pacey had totally misinterpreted something and overreacted, which seemed strange for the kind of person Hunt had judged Pacey to be. To be fair, Hunt conceded as he thought about it again, Pacey hadn't actually said for certain that it was the *Shapieron* that was threatened; what he had said was that he had reason to believe that *something* well out in space was in danger of destruction, and he had expressed concern that it might be the *Shapieron*. Calazar had decided not to take any chances, and Hunt couldn't blame him for that. What the warning did seem to indicate was that Pacey had been hopelessly wrong about something. Or had he? Hunt wondered.

Suddenly Hunt realized he was feeling physically uncomfortable. Surely not, he thought. Surely the package of sensations that made up his computer-simulated body couldn't be that complete. What would be the point?

He looked around him instinctively and discovered he was back in his own body in the recliner inside the perceptron. "Facing you at the back end of the corridor," VISAR's voice informed him. Hunt sat up, shaking his head in wonder. As always, the Ganymeans had thought of everything. So *that* was what the mysterious door was for.

He was back at Gistar a few minutes later, and found Danchekker waiting for him wearing a grave expression. "Some alarming news has come through while you were absent," the professor informed him. "It appears that our friend at Giordano Bruno was not quite as mistaken as we had supposed."

"What's happened?" Hunt asked.

"The device that has been relaying the communications between Farside and Thurien has ceased operating. According to VISAR, indications are that something destroyed it."

chapter seventeen

How could Norman Pacey, isolated and incommunicado on lunar Farside, have known that the relay was about to be destroyed? His only source of information from outside the solar system was the signals coming in from the Thuriens at Gistar, and the Thuriens themselves hadn't known about it. And why had Pacey apparently acted independently of the official UN delegation on Farside in sending the warning? Furthermore, how had he gained access to the equipment there, and how had he been able to operate it? In short, just what was going on at Farside?

Jerol Packard requested from the Thuriens a complete set of their versions of all the messages that had been exchanged with Earth since the whole business began. Calazar agreed to supply them, and VISAR hard-copied them through to McClusky by means of equipment contained in the perceptron. When the team there compared the Thuriens' transcripts with their own, some peculiar discrepancies emerged.

The first set comprised one-way traffic from Earth and were from the period immediately following the *Shapieron*'s departure, when scientists at Bruno had resisted UN pressure and continued transmitting in the hope of renewing the dialogue that the first brief, unexpected signal from the Giants' Star had initiated. These messages contained information regarding Earth's civilization and state of scientific progress that over the months had begun adding up to form a picture which was not at all consistent with that reported to the Thuriens for years by the still mysterious and undefined "organization." Perhaps these inconsistencies had been the cause of the Thuriens becoming suspicious about the reports in the first place. In any event, the two sets of transcripts of these messages matched perfectly.

The next group of exchanges dated from the time that Thurien began talking again, and the UN stepped in to handle Earth's end. At this point the tone of the transmissions from Farside took on a distinctly different flavor. As Karen Heller had told Hunt at his first meeting with her in Houston, and as he had verified for himself since, the messages became negative and ambivalent, doing little to dispel the Thuriens' notions of a militarized Earth and rejecting their overtures for a landing and direct talks. Among these transmissions the first discrepancies appeared.

Every one of the communications sent during the period in which Heller was on Farside was reproduced faithfully in the Thuriens' records. But there were two additional ones—identifiable by their format and header conventions as having undoubtedly originated from Bruno—that she had never seen before. What made these even more mysterious was that their contents were overtly belligerent and hostile to a degree that the UN delegation would never have condoned even with its negative attitude. Some of the things they said were simply untrue, the gist of them being that Earth was capable of managing its own affairs, didn't want and wouldn't tolerate alien interference, and would respond with force if any landing was attempted. More inexplicable still was the fact that some of the details correlated with and reinforced the falsified picture of Earth that Hunt and the others had learned of only after meeting the Thuriens. How could anyone at Bruno have known anything about that?

Then Hunt's signals had started coming in from Jupiter—coded in Ganymean, welcoming the suggestion for a landing, suggesting a suitable location, and projecting a different image completely. No wonder the Thuriens had been confused!

After that came the Soviet signals, complete with details of the security code to be used for replies. Packard had persuaded Calazar to include them by playing up the grilling that the Terrans had been put through and especially its effect on him personally. The Soviets, too, had expressed interest in a landing, though in a manner distinctly more cautious than Hunt's messages from Jupiter. This theme traced consistently through most of the Soviet signals, but again there were some, in this case three, that stood out as exceptions and conveyed similar sentiments to those of the "unofficial" transmissions from Bruno. And even more amazingly, they tallied in some significant details with the Bruno exceptions in ways that couldn't have been coincidental.

How could the Soviets have known about unofficial signals from Bruno that even Karen Heller hadn't known about when she was there? The only way, surely, was if the Soviets were responsible for them. Did that mean that the Kremlin was so dominating the UN that the whole Bruno operation had been simply a sham to distract the U.S. and other prominent nations that knew about Gistar, and that the delegation's ostensibly mild but nevertheless counterproductive actions had been secretly derailed, presumably by somebody put there for the purpose—perhaps in the form of Sobroskin? That the Director of Astronomy at Bruno was also a Russian gave further credibility to the thought, but against it was the unavoidable fact that the Soviets' own effort had been sabotaged in exactly the same manner. Again nothing made sense.

Later a third unofficial message from Bruno, sent after Karen Heller had left, reached a new peak of aggressiveness, announcing that Earth was severing relations and had taken steps to insure that the dialogue would be discontinued permanently. Finally there was Norman Pacey's warning of something about to be destroyed out in space, and shortly afterward the relay had ceased operating.

The answers to these riddles would not be found in Alaska. Packard waited until a State Department courier arrived at McClusky with the official news that communications with Gistar had ceased and the UN delegation was returning to Earth, and then left for Washington with Caldwell. Lyn went with them for the purpose of returning to McClusky with an update as soon as they had talked to Pacey.

Hunt and Danchekker stood on the apron at McClusky, watching the UNSA jet that had just lifted off to take Packard, Caldwell, and Lyn to Washington turn and begin climbing away steeply toward the south. Not far from them, a ground crew was busy shoveling snow over the holes in the concrete left by the landing gear of the perceptron, which had moved itself into line with the other UNSA aircraft parked along one side of the apron in order to provide a more natural scene for the "organization's" surveillance instruments. Although the black hole contained in the vessel's communications system was microscopic, it still had the equivalent mass of a small mountain; McClusky's apron hadn't been designed for that.

"It's funny when you think about it," Hunt remarked as the plane shrank to a dot above the distant ridgeline. "It's twenty light-years from Vranix to Washington, but the last four thousand miles take all the time. Maybe when we get this business cleared up, we could think about wiring a few parts of this planet into VISAR."

"Maybe." Danchekker's voice was noncommittal. He had been noticeably quiet since breakfast.

"It would save Gregg a lot of charges from Transportation Services."

"I suppose so."

"How about wiring up Navcomms HQ and Westwood? Then we'd be able to go straight to Thurien from the office and be back for lunch."

"Mmm . . ."

They turned and began walking back toward the mess hall. Hunt glanced sideways to give the professor a curious look, but Danchekker appeared not to notice and kept walking.

Inside they found Karen Heller hunched over a pile of communications transcripts and notes she had made while at Bruno. She pushed the papers away and sat back in her chair as they entered. Danchekker moved over to a window and stared silently out at the perceptron; Hunt turned a chair around and straddled it to face the room from a corner. "I just don't know what to make of this," Heller said with a sigh. "There just isn't any way that some of this information could have been known to anybody here or on the Moon except us—unless they've been in contact with Calazar's 'organization.' Could that be possible?"

"I wondered the same thing," Hunt replied. "How about the coded signals? Maybe Moscow wasn't transmitting to Calazar's bunch at all."

"No, I've checked." Heller gestured toward the papers around her. "Every one that we picked up was sent by Calazar's aide. They're all accounted for."

Hunt shook his head and folded his arms on the backrest of the chair. "It's got me beat too. Let's wait and see what they find out from Norman when he gets back." A silence descended. Lost in thoughts of his own, Danchekker continued staring out through the window. After a while Hunt said, "You know, it's funny—sometimes when things become so confusing that you think you'll never make any kind of sense out of them, it just needs one simple, obvious thing that everybody's overlooked to make everything come together. Remember a couple of years back when we were trying to figure out where the Lunarians came from. Nothing added up until we realized that the Moon must have moved. Yet looking back, that should have been obvious all along."

"I hope you're right," Heller said as she collected papers and returned them to their folders. "Something else I don't understand is all this secrecy. I thought Ganymeans weren't supposed to be like that. Yet here we are with one group doing one thing, another doing something else, and neither wanting to let the other know anything about it. You know them better than most people. What do you make of it?"

"I don't know," Hunt confessed. "And who bombed the relay? Calazar's bunch didn't, so it must have been the other bunch. If so, they must have found out about it despite all the precautions, but why would they want to bomb it, anyway? It's definitely a strange way for Ganymeans to be carrying on, all right . . . or at least, it is for the kind of Ganymeans that existed twenty-five million years ago." He turned his head unconsciously and directed his last words at Danchekker, who still had his back to them. Hunt had not yet been convinced that such a span of time couldn't have been sufficient to bring about some fundamental change in Ganymean nature, but Danchekker had remained intractable. He thought that Danchekker hadn't heard, but after a few seconds the professor replied without moving his head.

"Perhaps your original hypothesis deserved more consideration than I was prepared to give it at the time."

Hunt waited for a few seconds, but nothing further happened. "What hypothesis?" he asked at last.

"That perhaps we are not dealing with Ganymeans at all." Danchekker's voice was distant. A short silence fell. Hunt and Heller looked at each other. Heller frowned; Hunt shrugged. Of course they were dealing with Ganymeans. They looked back at Danchekker expectantly. He wheeled around to face them suddenly and brought his hands up to clasp his lapels. "Consider the facts," he invited. "We are confronted by a pattern of behavior that is totally inconsistent with what we know to be true of the Ganymean nature. That pattern concerns the relationship between two groups of beings. One of these groups we have met and know to be Ganymean. The other group we have not been permitted to meet, and the reasons that have been offered, I have no hesitation in dismissing as pretexts. A logical conclusion to draw, therefore, would be that the second group is *not* Ganymean—would it not?"

Hunt just stared back at him blankly. The conclusion was so obvious that there was nothing to be said. They had all been assuming that the "organization" was Ganymean, and the Thuriens had said nothing to change their minds. But the Thuriens had never said anything to confirm it either.

"And consider this," Danchekker went on. "The structural organizations and patterns of neural activity at the symbolic level in human and Ganymean brains are quite dissimilar. I find it impossible to accept that an equipment designed to interact in a close-coupled mode with one form would be capable of functioning at all with the other. In other words, the devices inside that vessel standing out on the apron cannot be standard models designed for use by Ganymeans, which, purely by good fortune, happen to operate effectively with human brains too. Such a situation is impossible. The only way in which those devices could operate as they do is by virtue of having been *specifically constructed to couple with the human central nervous system in the first place!* Therefore the designers must have been intimately familiar with the most detailed inner workings of that system—far more so than they could have been by any amount of study of contemporary terrestrial medical science through their surveillance activities. Therefore that knowledge could only have been acquired on Thurien itself."

Hunt looked across at him incredulously. "What are you saying, Chris?" he asked in a strained voice, although it was already plain enough. "That there are *humans* on Thurien as well as Ganymeans?"

Danchekker nodded emphatically. "Exactly. When we first entered the perceptron, VISAR was able, in a matter of mere seconds, to adjust its parameters to produce normal levels of sensory stimulation and to decode the feedback commands from the motor areas of our nervous systems. But how did it know what stimulation levels were normal for humans? How did it know what patterns of feedback were correct? The only possible explanation is that VISAR already possessed extensive prior experience in operating with human organisms." He looked from one to the other to invite comment.

"It could be," Karen Heller breathed, nodding her head slowly as she digested what he had said. "And maybe that explains why the Ganymeans haven't exactly been rushing themselves to tell us about it until they've got a better feel for how we might react—especially with the accounts they've been getting of what we're like. And it could make sense that if they *are* human, they got the job of running a surveillance program to keep an eye on Earth." She thought over what she had said and nodded again to herself, then frowned as something else occurred to her. She looked up at Danchekker. "But how could they have gotten there? Could they be from some independent family of evolution that already existed on Thurien before the Ganymeans got there . . . something like that maybe?"

"Oh, that's quite impossible," Danchekker said impatiently. Heller looked mildly taken aback and opened her mouth to object, but Hunt shot her a warning glance and gave a barely perceptible shake of his head. If she got Danchekker into a lecture on evolution, they'd be listening all day. She signaled her acceptance with a slight raising of an eyebrow and let it go at that.

"I don't think we have to search very far for the answer to that question," Danchekker informed them airily, drawing himself upright and tightening his hold on his lapels. "We know that the Ganymeans migrated to Thurien from Minerva approximately twenty-five million years ago. We also know that by then they had acquired numerous species of terrestrial life, including primates as advanced as any of the period. Indeed we discovered some of them ourselves in the craft on Ganymede, which we have every reason to believe was involved in that very migration." He paused for a moment as if doubting that the rest needed spelling out, then continued. "Evidently they took with them some representatives of early prehuman hominids, the descendants of which have since evolved and increased to become a human population enjoying full cocitizenship within the society of Thurien, as is evidenced by the fact that VISAR accommodates both them and Ganymeans equally." Danchekker dropped his hands to clasp them behind his back and thrust his chin out with evident satisfaction. "And that, Dr. Hunt, unless I am very much mistaken, would appear to be the simple and obvious missing factor that you were looking for," he concluded.

chapter eighteen

Norman Pacey held up his hand in a warning gesture and closed the door to cut off the room from the secretary giving directions to two UNSA privates who were loading boxes onto a cart in the outer office. Janet watched from a chair that she had cleared of a stack of papers and document holders waiting to be packed in preparation for the delegation's departure from Bruno. "Now start again," he told her, turning away from the door.

"It was last night, maybe early this morning . . . I'm not sure what time." Janet fiddled awkwardly with a button on her lab coat. "Niels got a call from somebody—I think it was the U.S. European, Daldanier—about something they needed to discuss right away. He started saying something about somebody called Verikoff, it sounded like, but Niels stopped him and said he'd go and talk to him at his place. I pretended I was still asleep. He got dressed and slipped out . . . kind of creepily, as if he were being careful not to wake me up."

"Okay," Pacey said with a nod. "Then what?"

"Well . . . I remembered he'd been looking at some papers earlier when I came in. He put them away in a holder, but I was sure he hadn't locked it. So I decided to take a chance and see what they were about."

Pacey clenched his teeth in the effort not to let his feelings show. That was exactly the kind of thing he had told her *not* to do. But the outcome sounded interesting. "And," he prompted.

Janet's face took on a mystified look. "There was a folder among the things inside. It was bright red around the edges and pink inside. What made me notice it was that it had your name on the front."

Pacey's brow creased as he listened. What Janet had described sounded like a standard UN-format document wallet that was used for highly confidential memoranda. "Did you look inside it?"

Janet nodded. "It was weird . . . the report criticized the way you'd been obstructing the meeting here and stated in a *Conclusions* section that the delegation would have made more progress if the U.S. had shown a more cooperative attitude. It didn't sound like you at all, which was why I thought it was weird." Pacey was staring at her speechlessly. Before he could find words to reply, she shook her head as if feeling a need to disclaim responsibility for what she was going to say next. "And there was this part about you and—Karen Heller. It said that you two were . . ." Janet hesitated, then raised a hand with her index and second fingers intertwined, " . . . like that, and that such—how was it put?—such 'blatant and indiscreet conduct was not becoming to a mission of this nature, and possibly had some connection with the counterproductive contribution of the United States to the proceedings.' " Janet sat back and shook her head again. "I knew the report simply wasn't true. . . . And coming from him, well . . ." She let the sentence trail away and left it at that.

Pacey sat down on the edge of a half-filled packing case and stared at her incredulously. A few seconds went by before he found his voice. "You actually saw all this?" he asked at last.

"Yes . . . I can't give you all of it word for word, but that was what it said." She hesitated. "I know it's crazy, if that helps. . . ."

"Does Sverenssen know you saw this report?"

"I don't see how he could. I put everything back exactly the way it was. I guess I could have got you more of it, but I didn't know how long he'd be away. As it turned out, he was gone quite a while."

"That's okay. You did the right thing not risking it." Pacey stared down at the floor for a while, feeling totally bewildered. Then he looked up again and asked, "How about you? Has he been acting strange now that we're leaving? Anything . . . ominous, maybe?"

"You mean sinister warnings to keep my mouth shut about the computer?"

"Mmm . . . yes, maybe." Pacey looked at her curiously.

She shook her head and smiled faintly. "Quite the opposite as a matter of fact. He's been very gentlemanly and said what a shame it is. He even hinted that we could get together again sometime back on Earth—he could fix me up with a job that pays real money, all kinds of interesting people to meet . . . stuff like that."

A smarter move, Pacey thought to himself. High hopes and treachery had never gone together. "Do you believe him?" he asked, cocking an eyebrow.

"No."

Pacey nodded in approval. "You *are* growing up fast." He looked around the office and massaged his forehead wearily. "I'm going to have to do some thinking now. I'm glad you told me about it. But you've got your coat on, which says you probably have to get back to work. Let's not start upsetting Malliusk again."

"He's off today," Janet said. "But you're right—I do have to get back." She stood up and moved toward the door, then turned back as she was about to open it. "I hope it was okay. I know you said to keep this away from the delegation offices, but it seemed important. And with everybody leaving . . ."

"Don't worry about it. It's okay. I'll see you again later."

Janet departed, leaving the door open in response to Pacey's wave request. Pacey sat for a while and began turning what she had told him over again in his mind, but was interrupted by the UNSA privates coming in to sort out the boxes ready for moving. He decided to go and think about it over a coffee in the common room.

The only people in the common room when Pacey entered a few minutes later were Sverenssen, Daldanier, and two of the other delegates, who were all together at the bar. They acknowledged his arrival with a few not overfriendly nods of their heads and continued talking among themselves. Pacey collected a coffee from the dispenser on one side of the room and sat down at a table in the far corner, wishing inwardly that he had picked somewhere else. As he studied them surreptitiously over his cup, he listed in his mind the unanswered questions that he had collected concerning the tall, immaculately groomed Swede who was standing in the center of the vassals gathered around him at the bar.

Perhaps Pacey's fears about the *Shapieron* had been misplaced. Could what Janet had overheard have been connected with the communications from Gistar ceasing so abruptly? It had happened suspiciously soon afterward. If so, how could Sverenssen and at least one other member of the delegation have known about it? And how were Sverenssen and Daldanier connected with Verikoff, whom Pacey knew from CIA reports to be a Soviet expert in space communications? If there were some conspiracy between Moscow and an inner clique of the UN, why had Sobroskin cooperated with Pacey? Perhaps that had been part of some even more elaborate ruse. He had been wrong to trust the Russian, he admitted to himself bitterly. He should have used Janet and kept Sobroskin and Malliusk out of it.

And last of all, what was the motive behind the attempt to character-assassinate him personally, compromise Karen Heller, and misrepresent the role they had played at Bruno? It seemed strange that Sverenssen had expected the plan to work, because the document Janet had described would not be substantiated by the official minutes of all the delegation's meetings, a copy of which would also be forwarded to UN Headquarters in New York. Furthermore, Sverenssen knew that as well as anybody; and whatever his other faults, he was not naive. Then a sick feeling formed slowly in his stomach as the truth dawned on him—he had no way of being certain that the minutes which *he* had read and approved, which had recorded the debates verbatim, would be the versions that would go to New York at all. From what Pacey had glimpsed of whatever strange machinations were in progress behind the scenes, anything was possible.

"In my opinion it would be a good thing if the South Atlantic deal did go to the Americans," Sverenssen was saying at the bar. "After the way the United States almost allowed its nuclear industry to be wrecked just before the turn of the century, it's hardly surprising that the Soviets gained a virtual monopoly across most of Central Africa. An equalizing of influence in the general area and the stiffening of competition it would produce could only be in the better long-term interests of all concerned." The three heads around him nodded obediently. Sverenssen made a casual throwing-away motion. "After all, in my position I can hardly allow myself to be swayed by mere national politics. The longer-term advancement of the race as a whole is what is important. That is what I have always stood for and shall continue to stand for."

After everything else this was too much. Pacey choked down his mouthful of coffee and slammed his cup down hard on the table. The heads at the bar turned toward him in surprise. "Hogwash!" he grated across the room at them. "I've never heard such garbage."

Sverenssen frowned his distaste for the outburst. "What do you mean?" he asked coldly. "Kindly explain yourself."

"You had the biggest opportunity ever for the advancement of the race right in your hand, and you threw it away. That's what I mean. I've never listened to such hypocrisy."

"I'm afraid I don't follow you."

Pacey couldn't believe it. "Goddammit, I mean this whole farce we've been having here!" He heard his voice rising to a shout, knew it was bad, but couldn't stop himself in his exasperation. "We were talking to Gistar for weeks. We said nothing, and we achieved nothing. What kind of 'standing for advancement' is that?"

"I agree," Sverenssen said, maintaining his calm. "But I find it strangely inappropriate that *you* should protest in this extraordinary fashion. I would advise you instead to take the matter up with your own government."

That didn't make any sense. Pacey shook his head, momentarily confused. "What are you talking about? The U.S. policy was always to get this moving. We wanted a landing from the beginning."

"Then I can only suggest that your efforts to project that policy have been singularly inept," Sverenssen replied.

Pacey blinked as if unable to believe that he had really heard it. He looked at the others, but found no sympathy for his predicament on any of their faces. The first cold fingers of realization as to what was going on touched at his spine. He shifted his eyes rapidly across their faces in a silent demand for a response, and caught Daldanier's gaze in a way that the Frenchman couldn't evade.

"Let us say it has been apparent to me that the probability of a more productive dialogue would have been improved considerably were it not for the negative views persistently advanced by the representative of the United States," Daldanier said, avoiding the reference to Pacey by name. He spoke in the reluctant voice of somebody who had been forced to offer a reply he would have preferred left unsaid.

"Most disappointing," Saraquez, the Brazilian, commented. "I had hoped for better things from the nation that placed the first man on the Moon. Hopefully the dialogue might be resumed one day, and the lost time made good."

The whole situation was insane. Pacey stared at them dumbfounded. They were all part of the plot. If that were the version that was going to be talked about back on Earth, backed by documentary records, nobody would believe his account of what had happened. Already he wasn't sure if he believed it himself, and he hadn't left Bruno yet. His body began shaking uncontrollably as a rising anger took hold. He got up and moved forward around the table to confront Sverenssen directly. "What is this?" he demanded menacingly. "Look, I don't know who you think you are with the high-and-mighty act and the airs and graces, but you've been making me pretty sick ever since I arrived here. Now let's just forget all that. I want to know what's going on."

"I would strongly advise you to refrain from bringing personal issues into this," Sverenssen said, then added pointedly, "*especially* somebody of your inclination toward the . . . indiscreet."

Pacey felt his color rising. "What do you mean by that?" he demanded.

"Oh, come . . ." Sverenssen frowned and looked away for an instant like somebody seeking to avoid a delicate subject. "Surely you can't expect your affair with your American colleague to have escaped notice completely. Really . . . this kind of thing is embarrassing and uncalled for. I would rather we dropped the matter."

Pacey stared at him for a moment in frank disbelief, then turned his gaze toward Daldanier. The Frenchman turned to pick up his drink. He looked at Saraquez, who avoided his eyes and said nothing. Finally he turned to Van Geelink, the South African, who had only been listening so far. "It was very unwise," Van Geelink said, almost managing to sound apologetic.

"*Him!*" Pacey gestured in Sverenssen's direction and swept his eyes over the others again, this time offering a challenge. "You let *him* stand there and spew something like that? Him of all people? You can't be serious."

"I'm not sure that I like your tone, Pacey," Sverenssen said. "What are you trying to insinuate?"

The situation was real. Sverenssen was actually brazening it out. Pacey felt his fist bunch itself against his side but resisted the urge to lash out. "Are you going to try and tell me I dreamed that too?" he whispered. "Malliusk's assistant—it never happened? Are these puppets of yours going to back you up on that too?"

Sverenssen made a good job of appearing shocked. "If you are suggesting what I think you are suggesting, I would advise you to retract the remark at once and apologize. I find it not only insulting, but also demeaning to somebody in your position. Pathetic fabrications will not impress anybody here, and are hardly likely to do anything to restore the doubtlessly somewhat tarnished image that you will have made for yourself on Earth. I would have credited you with more intelligence."

"Bad, very bad." Daldanier shook his head and sipped his drink.

"Unheard of," Saraquez muttered.

Van Geelink stared uncomfortably at the floor, but said nothing.

At that moment a call from the speaker concealed in the ceiling interrupted. "Calling Mr. Sverenssen of the UN Delegation. Urgent call holding. Would Mr. Sverenssen come to a phone, please."

"You must excuse me, gentlemen," Sverenssen sighed. He looked sternly at Pacey. "I am prepared to attribute this sad exhibition to an aberration occasioned by your having to acclimatize to an extraterrestrial environment, and will say no more about it." His voice took on a more ominous note. "But I must warn you that should you persist in repeating such slanderous accusations when we leave the confines of this establishment, I will be obliged to take a far more serious view. If so, you would not find the consequences beneficial either to your personal situation or to your future prospects professionally. I trust I make myself clear." With that he turned and conveyed himself regally from the room. The other three drank up quickly and left in rapid succession.

That night, his last at Bruno, Pacey was too bewildered, frustrated, and angry to sleep. He stayed up in his room and paced about the floor going over every detail of all that had happened and examining the whole situation first from one angle and then from another, but he could find no pattern that fitted everything. Once again he was tempted to call Alaska, but resisted.

It was approaching 2 A.M. local time when a light tap sounded on the door. Puzzled, Pacey rose from the chair in which he had been brooding and went over to answer it. It was Sobroskin. The Russian slipped in quickly, waited until Pacey closed the door, then reached inside his jacket and produced a large envelope that he passed over without speaking. Pacey opened it. Inside was a pink wallet with a bright red border. The title label on the front read: CONFIDENTIAL. REPORT 238/2G/NTS/FM. NORMAN H. PACEY—PERSONAL PROFILE AND NOTES.

Pacey looked at it incredulously, opened it to ruffle quickly through the contents, then looked up. "How did you get this?" he asked in a hoarse voice.

"There are ways," Sobroskin said vaguely. "Did you know of it?"

"I . . . had reason to believe that something like it might exist," Pacey told him guardedly.

Sobroskin nodded. "I thought you might wish to put it somewhere safe, or perhaps burn it. There was only one other copy, which I have already destroyed, so you may rest with knowledge that it will not get to where it was supposed to go." Pacey looked down at the wallet again, too stunned to reply. "Also, I came across a very strange volume of minutes of the delegation's sessions—nothing at all like what I remembered. I substituted a set of the copies that you and I both saw and approved. Take my word for it that those are the ones that will reach New York. I resealed them myself in the courier's bag just before it was taken to Tycho."

"But . . . how?" was all Pacey could say.

"I have not the slightest intention of telling you." The Russian's voice was curt, but his eyes were twinkling.

Suddenly Pacey grinned as the message at last got through that not everybody in the world was his enemy. "Perhaps it's about time we sat down and compared notes," he said. "I guess I don't have any vodka in the place. How about gin?"

"Precisely the conclusion that I have come to also," Sobroskin said, extracting a sheaf of notes from an inside pocket. "Gin would be fine—I'm very partial to it." He hung his jacket by the door and sat down to make himself comfortable in one of the armchairs while Pacey went into the next room for some glasses. While he was there he checked to make sure the ice maker was well stocked. He had a feeling it was going to be a long night.

chapter nineteen

Garuth had spent twenty-eight years of his life with the *Shapieron*.

A group of scientists on ancient Minerva had advocated a program of extensive climatic and geological engineering to control the predicted buildup of carbon dioxide. The project would have been extremely complicated, however, and simulation models revealed a high risk of rendering the planet uninhabitable sooner rather than later by disrupting the greenhouse effect that enabled Minerva to support life at its considerable distance from the Sun. As an insurance against this risk, another group proposed a method for increasing the Sun's radiation output by modifying its self-gravitation, the idea being that the climatic-engineering program could go ahead, and if instabilities did set in to the point of destroying the greenhouse effect, the Sun could be warmed up to compensate. Thus, overall, Minerva would be no worse off.

As a precaution, the Minervan government decided to test the later idea first by dispatching a scientific mission aboard the *Shapieron* to conduct a full-scale trial on a sun-like star called Iscaris, whose planets supported no life of any kind. It was as well that they did. Something went wrong that caused Iscaris to go nova, and the expedition had been forced to flee without waiting for completion of the repairs to the ship's main-drive system, which were in progress at the time. Hurled to maximum speed and with its braking system inoperative, the *Shapieron* returned to the vicinity of the solar system and circled for over twenty years by its own clocks under conditions of compounded time dilation while a million times that amount sped by in the rest of the Universe. And so, eventually, the ship had come to Earth.

As Garuth stood in the doorway of one of the lecture theaters of the ship's school and gazed across the rows of empty seats and scratched worktops to the raised dais and array of screens at the far end, his mind recalled those years. Many who had left Minerva with him had not survived to see this day. At times he had believed that none of them would ever see it. But, as was the pattern of life, a new generation had replaced those who were gone—a generation born and raised in the emptiness of space, who, apart from the brief stay on Earth, had known no other home than the inside of the ship. In many ways Garuth felt like a father to all of them. Although his own faith had wavered at times, theirs had not, and as they had never thought to doubt, he had brought them home. What would happen to them now? he wondered.

Now that the day had arrived, he found he had mixed feelings. The rational part of him was joyful, naturally, that the long exile of his people was over, and they were at last reunited with their kind; but at a deeper level, another part of him would miss this miniature, self-contained world, which for so long now had been the only one he had known. The ship, its way of life, and its tiny, close-knit community were as much part of him as he was part of them. Now all that was over. Would he ever be able to belong in the same way in the mind-defying, overwhelming civilization of Thurien with technologies that bordered on magic and a population of hundreds of billions flung across light-years of stars and space? Could any of them? And if not, could they ever belong anywhere again?

After a while he turned away and began walking slowly through the deserted corridors and communications decks toward an access point into a transfer tube that would take him back to the ship's command section. The floors were worn by years of treading feet, the corners of the walls abraded and smoothed by the passings of innumerable bodies. Every mark and score had its own tale to tell of some event that had occurred somewhere in the course of all those years. Would all that now be forgotten?

In some ways he felt that it already had been. The *Shap-*

ieron was in high orbit over Thurien, and most of its occupants had been taken down to accommodations prepared for them on the surface. There had been no public celebrations or welcoming ceremonies; the fact that the ship had been intercepted still had to be concealed. Only a handful of Thuriens were aware that Garuth and his people existed at all.

Shilohin was waiting on the Command Deck when he arrived, studying information on one of the displays. She looked around as he approached. "I had no idea just how complex the operation to intercept the ship was," she said. "Some of the physics is quite remarkable."

"How so?" Garuth inquired.

"Eesyan's engineers created a composite hyperport—a dual-purpose toroid that functioned as an entry port in one direction and an exit in the other at the same time. That was how they made the substitution so quickly: the dummy came out of one side as we went into the other. But to control it, they had to get their timing down to picoseconds." She paused and gave him a searching look. "You seem sad. Is something wrong?"

He gestured vaguely in the direction he had just come from. "Oh, it's just . . . walking through the ship . . . empty, with nobody around. It takes some getting used to after so long."

"Yes, I know." Her voice fell to an understanding note. "But you shouldn't feel sad. You did what you promised. They will all have their own lives to live again soon. It will be for the better."

"I hope so," Garuth said.

At that moment ZORAC spoke. "I've just received another message through VISAR: Calazar is free now and says he'll see you as soon as you're ready. He suggests meeting at a planet called Queeth, approximately twelve light-years from here."

"We're on our way," Garuth said. He shook his head wonderingly at Shilohin as they left the Command Deck. "I'm not sure I'll ever get used to this."

"The Earthpeople seem to be adapting well," she replied. "The last time I talked to Vic Hunt, he was trying to find a way of getting a coupler installed in his office."

"Earthpeople can adapt to anything," Garuth said with a sigh.

They entered the room in which the Thuriens had installed a row of four portable percepto-coupling cubicles, which represented the only means of using the Thurien system since the *Shapieron* was not wired for VISAR; hence Calazar could not "visit" the ship. Had the ship not been in orbit and therefore in free-fall, the weight of the microtoroid contained in the communications module of the equipment would have buckled the deck at best. Garuth entered one of the cubicles as Shilohin selected another, and he settled back in the recliner to couple his mind into VISAR. An instant later he was standing alongside Calazar in a large room that was part of an artificial island floating fifty miles above the surface of Queeth. Shilohin appeared next to him a few seconds later.

"Terrans are shrewder than you give them credit for," Garuth stated after the three of them had been talking for some time. "We lived among them for six months, and we know. What is difficult for the Ganymean mind to grasp is that deception and the recognition of deception are parts of their way of life. They have a natural feel for it and will soon get to the truth. Trying to conceal it any longer will only make the situation more embarrassing for all of us when they do. You should be frank with them now."

"And besides, this is not the Ganymean way," Shilohin said. "We have told you the true situation on Earth and how we were made welcome and helped there in every way possible. Your earlier doubts were justified because of the lies reported to you by the Jevlenese, but that no longer holds. You owe it to the Terrans, and to us, to tell them the whole truth now."

Calazar moved away a short distance and turned to stand with his hands clasped behind his back while he considered what they had said. The room they were in formed an oval projection hanging from the underside of the island. Its interior comprised a sunken floor surrounded by a continuous, sloping transparent wall that looked down over the purple, cloud-flecked surface of Queeth in every direction. Outside the wall and above, the mass of the island loomed in a series of metallic contours, blisters, and prominences converging together as they curved away out of sight overhead. "So . . . we won't be able to keep the truth from them," Calazar said at last without turning his head.

"Remember it was the Terrans who first recognized the risk that the Jevlenese could have planned to destroy the *Shapieron* with Earth set up to take the blame," Garuth reminded him. "The Thuriens would never have thought of it. Let's be honest—Terran and Jevlenese minds think very much alike, and Ganymean minds think very differently. We are not predators, and we have not evolved the art of sensing predators."

"And for the same reason you might well find you *need* the Terrans to help get to the bottom of exactly what the Jevlenese are up to," Shilohin added. "Are you any nearer to finding out why they have been systematically falsifying their reports of Earth for years?"

Calazar turned from the viewing wall and faced them again. "No," he admitted.

"Years," Garuth repeated pointedly. "And you suspected nothing until you began receiving the communications from Farside."

Calazar thought for a while, then sighed and nodded in resignation. "You are right—we suspected nothing. Until recently we believed the Jevlenese had integrated well into our society as enthusiatic students of our science and culture. We saw them as cocitizens who would spread outward with us to other worlds. . . ." He gestured behind him and downward. "This one, for example. We even helped them to establish their own autonomously administered and completely self-governed planet as the cradle of a new civilization that would cross the Galaxy in partnership with our own."

"Well, something has obviously gone badly wrong somewhere," Shilohin commented. "Maybe it needs a Terran mind to fathom out what and why."

Calazar looked at them for a moment longer, then nodded again. "Officially Frenua Showm is responsible for our dealings with Earth," he said. "We should talk to her about this. I'll see if I can get her here now." He turned his face away and called in a slightly raised voice, "VISAR, find out if Frenua Showm is available. If she is, show her a replay of our conversation here and ask if she'd join us when she has seen it."

"I'll see to it," VISAR acknowledged.

After a short silence Shilohin remarked, "She didn't strike me as being overfond of Earthpeople in the replay of the Vranix meeting."

"She has never trusted the Jevlenese," Calazar answered. "Her sentiments apparently extend to include Terrans also. Maybe it's not surprising." After another silence he commented, "Queeth is an interesting world, with an emergent intelligent race spread across much of its surface. The Jevlenese have cooperated in bringing many similar planets into our system in the past. They seem to possess a natural aptitude for dealing with primitive races in a way that would not come easily to Ganymeans. I'll show you an example of what I mean. VISAR, let's have another view of the place I was looking at earlier."

A solid image appeared above the open area in the center of the floor. It was of a view looking down on a township in which blocks of hewn rock or baked clay had been built into crude buildings of strangely curved designs. They were huddled around the base of a larger and more imposing edifice of ramps and columns set at the top of an arrangement of broad flat steps ascending on all of its six sides. As Garuth looked at the structure, it reminded him in a vague way of the depictions of ancient temples that he had seen while he was on Earth. The space at the foot of the steps on one side was densely packed with figures.

"Queeth is not integrated into VISAR yet," Calazar informed them as they watched. "Therefore we can't go down there. The view is being captured under high resolution from orbit and injected into your visual cortexes."

The view narrowed, and the magnification increased. The crowd consisted of beings who were bipeds with two arms and a head, but the parts not covered by their roughly cut clothes seemed to be formed from what looked like a pink, glinting crystal rather than skin. Their heads were elongated vertically and covered with reddish mats on top and behind, their limbs were long and slender, and they moved with a flowing grace that Garuth found strangely captivating.

What made his eyes open wider in surprise was the

group of five figures posing above the crowd at the top of the steps, standing motionless and erect in flowing garments and high, elaborate headdresses. They seemed aloof and disdainful. And then Garuth realized suddenly what the movements of the slender, pink aliens meant. The movements were signaling supplication and reverence—worship, almost. The starship commander turned his head sharply to direct a questioning look at Calazar.

"The Queeths think that the Jevlenese are gods," Calazar explained. "They come down from the sky in magic vessels and work miracles. The Jevlenese have been experimenting with the technique for some time as a means of pacifying primitive races and instilling respect and trust in them before moving them from barbarism toward civilization. Apparently they got the idea from Earth—from their surveillance observations of long ago."

Shilohin seemed concerned. "Is it wise?" she asked. "How could a race hope to advance toward rational methods and effective control of its environment if its foundations are built on such unreason? We know what happened on Earth."

"I was wondering if you'd say something like that," Calazar said. "I myself have been wondering the same thing. Perhaps, before these recent developments, we have been altogether too trusting of the Jevlenese." He nodded soberly. "I think we will see some big changes in the not-too-distant future."

Before either of the others could reply, VISAR informed them, "Frenua Showm will join you now."

"We don't need the view anymore," Calazar said. The image of Queeth vanished, and a second or two later Showm was standing by Calazar.

"I don't like it," she said frankly. "The Terrans will want a confrontation with the Jevlenese, and that would mean all kinds of problems. The whole situation is complicated enough as it is."

"But we did set the Jevlenese up to handle the surveillance of Earth," Calazar pointed out. "Why shouldn't we expect to accept the consequences?"

"We didn't set them up," Showm said. "They argued and pressed demands until the Thurien administration of the time conceded. They practically took it over." She shook her head apprehensively. "And the idea of the Terrans getting involved in our investigations makes me nervous. I don't like the thought of them gaining access to Thurien-level technology. Remember what happened to the Lunarians. And look at what the Jevlenese have been doing since they acquired their own version of VISAR. It's simply a fact with all their kind—if they get their hands on advanced technology, they abuse it." She glanced at Garuth and Shilohin and then looked back at Calazar. "Our concern was for the *Shapieron*. It is now safely at Thurien. If the rest were up to me alone, I'd break off contact with Earth now and leave them out of it completely while we straighten out the situation with the Jevlenese. We don't need Terrans. They've served their purpose."

"I must protest!" Garuth exclaimed. "We regard them as close friends. If it hadn't been for their help, we would never have reached Thurien at all. We cannot simply disregard them. It would be an insult to every Ganymean on the *Shapieron*."

Before Calazar could reply, VISAR interrupted with another announcement. "Excuse me again, but Porthik Eesyan is asking to join you. He says it's urgent."

"Well, we're not going to resolve this in minutes," Calazar said. "Very well, VISAR. We will receive him."

Eesyan materialized at once. "I've just left Hunt and Danchekker at Thurien," he said. The Thuriens took VISAR so much for granted that they never bothered with preliminaries. "I was half expecting it—they've found out about the Jevlenese. They're demanding to talk to us all about them."

Calazar stared at him in astonishment. The others looked equally taken aback. "How?" Calazar asked. "How could they? VISAR has been censoring all references to them from the datastream beamed to Earth. They couldn't have witnessed one scene with a single Jevlenese in it."

"They've deduced that humans are here," Eesyan replied, modifying his previous statement. "They've worked out that the surveillance has to have been run by humans. We'll have to do something. I don't think I can stall them much longer—especially Danchekker."

Garuth turned toward Calazar and Showm, at the same time spreading his hands wide. "I hate to say I told you so, but it is as I said—you *can't* keep secrets from Terrans. Now you've got to talk to them." Calazar looked inquiringly at Showm.

Showm searched her mind for an alternative but couldn't find one. "Very well," she agreed wearily. "If it must be. Let's bring them here while we're together and tell them the facts."

"What about Karen Heller, VISAR?" Calazar asked. "Is she coupled into the system at this moment too?"

"She's at Thurien examining surveillance reports from earlier years," VISAR replied.

"In that case invite her to join us," Calazar instructed. "Then bring them all here as soon as they're ready."

"One second." A short pause followed. Then, "She's just finishing hard-copying some notes through to McClusky. She'll be here in half a minute." Simultaneously Hunt and Danchekker materialized in the middle of the floor.

"I still say I'll never get used to this," Garuth muttered to Shilohin.

chapter twenty

"We have conducted surveillance of Earth since the beginning of human civilization," Calazar declared. "For most of that time the operation has been entrusted to a race within our society known as the Jevlenese, which until now we have not brought to your attention. As you appear to have deduced for yourselves already, the Jevlenese are fully human in form."

"*Homo sapiens* are somewhat . . . volatile," Frenua Showm added, as if feeling that some additional explanation was called for. "Humans possess an intense instinct for rivalry. We felt that the issue was potentially sensitive. It could always be revealed tomorrow, but never unsaid again once said today."

"You see," Danchekker pronounced, looking toward

Hunt with some evident satisfaction from where he was standing on the far side of Karen Heller. "As I maintained—an independent hominid line descended from ancestral primates taken to Thurien at the time of the migration from Minerva."

"Er . . . no," Calazar said apologetically.

Danchekker blinked and stared at the alien as if he had just uttered a blasphemy. "I beg your pardon."

"The Jevlenese are far more closely related to *Homo sapiens* than that. In fact they are descended from the same Lunarian ancestors as yourselves—of fifty thousand years ago." Calazar glanced anxiously at Showm, then looked back at the Terrans to await their reactions. Garuth and Shilohin waited in silence; they knew the whole story already.

Hunt and Danchekker looked at each other, equally confused, and then at the Ganymeans again. The Lunarian survivors had reached Earth from the Moon; how could any of them have got to Thurien? The only possible way was if the Thuriens had taken them there. But where could the Thuriens have taken them from? There couldn't have been any survivors on Minerva itself. All of a sudden so many questions began boiling inside Hunt's head that he didn't know where to begin. Danchekker seemed to be having the same problem.

Eventually Karen Heller said, "Let's go back to the start of it all and check some of the basics." She was still looking at Calazar and directing her words to him. "We've been assuming that the Lunarians evolved on Minerva from terrestrial ancestors that you left behind when you went to Thurien. Is that correct, or have you been leaving out something?"

"No, that is correct," Calazar replied. "And by fifty thousand years ago they had developed to the level of a fairly advanced technological civilization very much as you supposed. Up to that point all was as you reconstructed."

"That's good to know, anyhow." Heller nodded and sounded relieved. "So why don't you take the story from there and fill in what happened after that, in the order it happened," she suggested. "That'll save a lot of questions."

"A good idea," Calazar agreed. He paused to collect his thoughts, then looked from side to side to address all three of them, and went on, "When the Ganymeans migrated to Thurien, they left behind an observation system to monitor developments on Minerva. At that time they did not possess the sophisticated communications that we have today, so the information they received was somewhat sporadic and incomplete. But it was enough to give a reasonably complete account of what took place. Perhaps you would like to see Minerva as captured by the sensors operating at that time." He gave an instruction to VISAR, moved back a few paces, and looked expectantly at the center of the floor. A large image appeared, looking solid and real enough to touch. It was an image of a planet.

Hunt knew every coastal outline and surface feature of Minerva by heart. One of the most memorable discoveries of recent years—in fact the one that had started off the investigations which had culminated in proof of Minerva's and the Ganymeans' existence even before the *Shapieron* appeared—had been that of "Charlie," a spacesuit-clad Lunarian corpse uncovered in the course of excavations on the Moon. From maps found on Charlie, the researchers at Navcomms had been able to reconstruct a six-foot-diameter model of the planet. But the image that Hunt was examining now did not exhibit the enormous ice caps and narrow equatorial belt that Hunt remembered from the model. The two land masses were there, though changed appreciably in outline, but as parts of a more extensive system of continents that stretched north and south to ice caps much smaller—not much larger than those of contemporary Earth. For this was not the Minerva of the Lunarians of fifty thousand years back; it was the Minerva of twenty-five million years before the Lunarians existed. And it was captured live, as it had been; it was no mere model reconstructed from maps. Hunt looked around at Danchekker, but the professor was too spellbound to respond.

For the next ten minutes they watched and listened as Calazar replayed a series of close-ups captured from orbit that showed the imported terrestrial animal species evolving and spreading, extinguishing the native Minervan forms, adapting and radiating at the rate of over two million years per minute, until eventually the first social manapes emerged from a line that had begun with an artificially modified type of the originally imported primates.

The pattern was very much as had been conjectured for many years on Earth, except that until 2028 it had all been assumed to have taken place on the wrong planet, or at least the fossils discovered from the pre-fifty-thousand-less-a-bit years B.C. period had been attributed to the wrong hominid family. But there was a completely unexpected phase that had never appeared in the story put together by the anthropologists on Earth: early in the man-ape era, the species had returned for a period to a semiaquatic environment, mainly as a consequence of not being equipped physically to deal with predators on land. Thus they had commenced the path that whales and other aquatic mammals had taken, but they reversed it and came out of the water again when their increasing intelligence provided them with other means of protecting themselves, which happened before any significant physical adaptations had developed. This phase accounted for their upright posture, loss of body hair, rudimentary webbing between thumb and index finger, the salt-excreting function of their tear ducts, and several other peculiarities that experts on Earth had been arguing about for years. Danchekker would have spent the rest of the week talking about that alone, but Hunt persuaded him to take it up again with Eesyan at some other time.

After that came the discovery of tools and fire, tribalization, and the sequence of evolving social order that led from primitive hunter-gatherer economies through agriculture and city-building to the discovery of the sciences and the beginnings of industrialization. And there was something about this part of their history too that set them apart from terrestrial humans in Hunt's eyes: the practical and realistic approach that the Lunarians had adopted to everything they did. They had exploited their resources and talents efficiently, without drifting off into fruitless reliance on superstitions and magic to solve their problems as had so many millennia of Earth people. For the early hunters, better weapons and greater skill decided success, not the whims of imaginary gods who needed to be placated. For the crop growers, better knowledge of plants, the land, and the elements improved yields; rituals and incantations did not, and were soon abandoned. And not very long afterward it was measurement, observation, and the powers of reason that uncovered the laws governing the universe and opened up new horizons for the harnessing of energy and the creation of wealth. As a result the Lunarian sciences and industries had mushroomed almost overnight in comparison with the halting, faltering groping toward enlightenment that had come later when the same general pattern repeated itself on Earth.

The scientists on Earth who had recovered the information on the Lunarians had pictured them as an incurably aggressive and warlike breed whose discoveries of advanced technology had inevitably spelled their eventual self-destruction. Hunt and the others now learned that this picture was not really accurate. There had been some feuding and fighting in the earlier periods of Lunarian history, it was true, but by the time of the early industrial period such things had become rare. A greater common cause had united the Minervan nations. Their scientists recognized the deteriorating conditions that were descending with the coming Ice Age, and the whole race embarked on a feverish development of the sciences that would enable them to move to a warmer planet in the centuries ahead. The astronomers of the time singled out Mars and Earth as the most promising candidates. The stakes were survival, and there were no resources to be squandered on internal conflicts, until . . .

About two hundred years before the final, catastrophic war, something happened to change all that. Calazar explained, "It could have been a result of extreme genetic instabilities still inherent in the race. At about the time they had learned to harness steam and were just beginning to explore electricity, a superbreed of Lunarians appeared quite suddenly and advanced a quantum leap ahead of anything else in existence anywhere on the planet. Exactly where or when they appeared we don't know. Numerically they were few to begin with, but they spread and consolidated rapidly."

"Was that when the planet started to polarize?" Heller asked.

"Yes," Calazar replied. "The superbreed became the Lambians. They were totally ruthless. They militarized and formed a totalitarian regime that imposed itself by force on a large portion of the planet before the other nations could

muster the strength to resist. Their aim was to gain control
of Minerva's industrial and technical capabilities totally
and exclusively to guarantee their own move to Earth,
which meant taking over the nations that had been pursu-
ing that goal collectively. Submission would have meant extinction. The other nations had no choice but to unite, arm,
and defend their security. They became the Cerians. The
course was set irrevocably toward a struggle to the death
between the two factions."

Hunt watched more scenes showing the gradual transformation of Minerva into one enormous military and manufacturing machine dedicated to preparations for war. The
tragedy of what had happened appalled him. There had
been no need for it. More effort had gone into armaments
than would have been needed to move the whole Lunarian
race to Earth twice over. If the Lambians hadn't appeared
on the scene when they did, the people on Minerva would
have done it. After millennia they had gotten to within two
hundred years of achieving the goal that would have saved
them from extinction and preserved their civilization, and
then they had thrown it all away.

VISAR began showing scenes from the war itself. A world
quaked under the shocks of miles-high fireballs that vapor-
ized cities; oceans boiled, and forests flared into carpets of
sterile ash writhing and twisting in an atmosphere in turmoil. Then blankets of smoke and dust blotted out the surface and turned the planet into a murky ball of black and
brown. Spots of red and slowly pulsating yellow appeared,
isolated and glowing dimly at first, but becoming brighter
and spreading, then merging as continents ruptured and
the planet's interior exploded through and hurled fragments of crust into the void. The asteroids were being born,
and what would eventually become Pluto was being carved
into a tombstone for a whole race, destined to drift forever
far from the Sun. Although Garuth and Shilohin had
watched these scenes before, they became very quiet; they
alone among all those present had known Minerva as
home.

Calazar waited a while for the mood to lighten, then resumed, "The Ganymeans had long been troubled by their
consciences over their genetic interference with the early
Lunarian ancestors. Therefore their policy toward Minerva

had been one of nonintervention in its affairs. You've just seen the result of that. After the calamity a few survivors were left stranded on the Moon with no hope of survival. By that time Thurien had perfected the black-hole technology that made instant communications and transfers of objects possible, so the Ganymeans were aware of events in realtime, and they were in a position to intervene. After witnessing the results of their policy, they could not simply stand aside and allow the survivors to perish. Accordingly, they organized a rescue mission and sent several large vessels to the close vicinity of Luna and Minerva."

It took Hunt a few seconds to see the implications of what Calazar had just said. He stared at the Ganymean in sudden surprise. "Not outside the solar system?" he queried. "I thought you said you didn't establish large toroids inside planetary systems."

"It was an emergency," Calazar replied. "The Ganymeans decided to forget their rules for once. They didn't have any time to spare."

Hunt's eyes opened wider as the implication hit him: *that* was how Pluto had gotten to where it was! And *that* was what had broken the gravitational coupling between Minerva and its moon. One simple statement had put half his people at Navcomms out of business.

"So the Lunarian ancestors of the human race never came to Earth with the Moon at all," Karen Heller said. "They were *taken* there—by the Ganymeans. The Moon only showed up later."

"Yes," Calazar replied simply.

That answered another mystery. All the math models of the process had required a long transit time for the Moon to get from Minerva to the orbit of Earth. A lot of doubt had been expressed that a handful of Lunarian survivors could have lasted for any length of time at all, let alone with the resources necessary to reach Earth. But with Ganymean intervention added into the equation, all that changed. With some Ganymean help that handful would have established a secure settlement for themselves and been able to make a viable start at rebuilding their culture. So why had they plunged back into a barbarism that had taken tens of thousands of years to recover from? The only answer could be the upheavals caused by Luna being captured later. The truth was so ironic, Hunt thought: if they hadn't been stabbed in the back by their own Moon, they could have been back into space by 45,000 B.C., if not sooner.

"But not all were taken to Earth," Danchekker concluded. "Another group was taken back to Thurien, and have since become the Jevlenese."

"It was so," Calazar confirmed.

"Even after all that had happened,". Showm explained, "the Cerians and the Lambians were unmixable. Since the Lambians had been the cause of the trouble, the Ganymeans of that time considered that more good would come out of the Lambians being taken to Thurien and—it was hoped—being integrated into Ganymean ways and society. The Cerians were taken to Earth at their own request. They were offered ongoing aid to rebuild, but they declined. So a surveillance system was set up instead to keep an eye on them—as much for their own protection as anything." Hunt was surprised. If the surveillance system had been in place that long, the Ganymeans would have known about the collapse of the colony which they themselves had helped found. Why had they let it happen?

"So how did the others make out—the Lambians?" Heller asked. "They couldn't have been running the surveillance that far back. How did they get their hands on it?"

Calazar emitted a heavy sigh. "They caused a lot of problems for the Thuriens of that time, so much so that when Luna came to be captured by Earth and caused widespread catastrophes that demolished the fragile beginnings of the new Cerian society that had started to take root there, it was decided to leave things be. With troubles of their own at home, the Thuriens were not eager to see another human civilization rushing headlong toward advancement, perhaps to repeat the Minervan disaster." He shrugged as if to say that right or wrong, that was the way it had been, then resumed, "But as time went by and further generations of Lambians came and went, the situation seemed to improve. Signs appeared that they could be integrated fully into Ganymean society, so the Ganymean leaders adopted a policy of appeasement in an attempt to accelerate the process. As a result the Jevlenese, as the descendants of the Lambians were called by then, acquired control of the surveillance program."

"A mistake," Showm commented. "They should have been exiled."

"With hindsight, I think I agree," Calazar said. "But that was long before either my time or yours."

"How about telling us something about this system," Hunt suggested. "How does it work?"

Eesyan answered. "Mostly from space. Until about a century ago, it was comparatively simple. Since Earth entered its electronics and space era, the Jevlenese have had to be more careful. Their devices are very small and virtually undetectable. Most of their information comes from intercepting and retransmitting your communications, such as the laser links between Jupiter and Earth. At one time in the early years of your space program they manufactured instrument packages to resemble pieces of your own space debris, but they had to stop when you started clearing things up. That experiment had its uses though; that was where we got the idea of building a perceptron that looked like a Boeing."

"But how could they fake the reports as well as they did?" Hunt asked. "They must have something of their own like VISAR. No Mickey Mouse computer did that."

"They have," Eesyan told him. "Long ago, when there seemed reason to feel optimistic about the Jevlenese, the Thuriens helped them establish their own autonomous world. It's called Jevlen, on the fringe of our developed region of space, and it's equipped with a system known as JEVEX, which is VISAR-like but independent of VISAR. Like VISAR, JEVEX operates across its own system of many stars. The surveillance system from Earth is coupled into JEVEX, and the reports that we receive are transmitted indirectly from JEVEX through VISAR."

"So it isn't difficult to understand how the fabrications and distortions were engineered," Showm said. "So much for philanthropy. They should never have been allowed to operate such a system."

"But why did they do it?" Karen Heller asked. "We still don't have an answer. Their reports were pretty accurate up until about the time of World War II. The problems of the late twentieth century were somewhat exaggerated, but for the last thirty years it's turned into pure fiction. Why would they want you to think we were still heading for World War III?"

"Who can understand the contortions of human minds?" Showm asked, using the general term unconsciously.

Hunt just caught the look that she flashed involuntarily at Calazar as she spoke. There was something more behind it all, he realized—something that the Thuriens were not divulging even now. Whatever it was, he was just as certain in that same split second that Garuth and Shilohin didn't know about it, either. But he didn't feel this was the time to force a confrontation. Instead he steered the discussion back into technicalities as he remembered something else. "What kind of archives does JEVEX have?" he asked. "Do they go all the way back to the Ganymean civilization on Minerva, like VISAR's?"

"No," Eesyan replied. "JEVEX is of much more recent vintage. There was no need to load it with VISAR's complete archives, which concerned only Ganymeans." He studied Hunt curiously for a few seconds. "Are you thinking about the anomalies in the displacements of background stars that VISAR noticed in the shots of the *Shapieron*?"

Hunt nodded. "That explains it, doesn't it. JEVEX couldn't have known about the displacements. VISAR had access to the original design data for the ship; JEVEX didn't."

"Correct," Eesyan said. "There were a few other anomalies too, but all similar—all to do with an old Ganymean technology that JEVEX couldn't have known very much about. That was when we became suspicious." At which point everything that had ever come from JEVEX would be suspect, Hunt saw. But there would have been no way of checking any of the rest without bypassing the Jevlenese completely and going straight to the source of the information—Earth. And that was precisely what the Thuriens had done.

Calazar seemed anxious to move them away from the whole topic. When a lull presented itself, he said, "Garuth wanted me to show you another sequence that he thought you would find interesting. VISAR, show us the Ganymean landing at Gorda."

Hunt jerked his head up in surprise. The name was familiar. Danchekker was looking incredulous as well. Heller was looking from one to the other of the men with a puzzled frown; she was less conversant with Charlie's story than they were.

Don Maddson's linguistics team at Navcomms had eventually succeeded in deciphering a notebook of Charlie's that had remained a mystery for a long time. It gave a day-by-day account of Charlie's experiences as one member of a rapidly diminishing band of Cerian survivors making a desperate trek across the lunar surface to reach a base that offered their last hope of escape from the Moon, if any hope remained at all. The account had covered events up to the point of Charlie's arrival at the place at which he had been found, by which time attrition of various kinds had reduced his band to just two—him, and a companion whose name had been Koriel. Charlie had collapsed there from the effects of a malfunctioning life-support system, and Koriel had left on a lone bid to reach the base. Apparently he had never returned. The base was called Gorda.

A new image appeared above the center of the floor. It was of a wilderness of dust and boulders etched harshly beneath a black sky thick with stars. The landscape had been seared and churned by forces of unimaginable violence to leave just the twisted and mutilated wreckage of what could once have been a vast base. Amid the desolation stood a single structure that appeared to have survived almost intact—a squat, armored dome or turret of some kind, blown open on one side. Its interior was in darkness.

"That was all that was left of Gorda," Calazar commented. "The view you are seeing is from a Thurien ship that had landed a few minutes before."

A small vehicle, roughly rectangular but with pods and other protuberances cluttering its outside, moved slowly into view from behind the camera, flying twenty feet or so above the ground. It landed near the dome, and a group of Ganymeans wearing spacesuits emerged and began moving cautiously through the wreckage toward the opening. Then they stopped suddenly. There were movements in the shadows ahead of them.

A light came on from somewhere behind to light up the opening. It revealed more figures, also in suits, standing in front of what looked like an entrance leading down to an underground section of whatever the dome had been part of. Their suits were different, and they stood a full head and shoulders shorter than the Ganymeans facing them from a few yards away. They were carrying weapons, but they appeared unsure of themselves as they looked nervously at one another and at the Ganymeans. None of them seemed to know what to do or what to expect. None of them, except one . . .

He was standing in front of the others in a blue spacesuit that was plastered with dust and grotesquely discolored by scorch marks, his feet planted firmly astride, and a rifle-like weapon held unwaveringly in one hand to cover the leading Ganymean. With his free arm he made a gesture behind him to wave the others forward. The movement was decisive and commanding. They obeyed, some moving up to stand on either side of him, others moving out to cover the aliens from protected positions among the surrounding debris. He was taller than the others and heavy in build, and the lips of the face behind his visor were drawn back in a snarl to reveal white teeth that contrasted sharply with his dark, unshaven chin and cheeks. Something unintelligible came through on audio. Although the words meant nothing, the tone to challenge and defiance was unmistakable.

"Our surveillance methods were not as comprehensive then," Calazar commented. "The language was not known."

In the scene before them, the Ganymean leader was replying in his own tongue, evidently relying on intonation and gesture to dispel alarm. As the exchange continued, the tension seemed to ease. Eventually the human giant lowered his weapon, and the others who had taken cover began emerging again. He beckoned for the Ganymeans to follow, and as the ranks behind him opened to make way, he turned away to lead them down into the inner entrance.

"That was Koriel," Garuth said.

Hunt had already guessed that. For some reason he felt very relieved.

"He succeeded!" Danchekker breathed. Elation was showing on his face, and he swallowed visibly. "He *did* get to Gorda. I'm—I'm glad to know that."

"Yes," Garuth said, reading the further question written

across Hunt's face. "We have studied the ship's log. They did return, but Koriel's companion had already died. They left him as they found him. They did manage to rescue some of the others who had been left strung out along the way, however."

"And after that?" Danchekker queried. "Another thing we have often wondered is whether or not Koriel was among those who finally reached Earth. It seems now that he may well have been. Do you happen to know if he in fact was?"

In reply Calazar called up another image. It was a view of a settlement formed from a dozen or so portable buildings of unfamiliar design, situated on a river bank against a background of semitropical forest with the hazy outline of mountains rising in the distance beyond. On one side was what looked like a supply dump, with rows of stacked crates, drums, and other containers. A crowd of two or three hundred figures was assembled in the foreground— human figures, dressed mainly in simple but serviceable-looking shirts and pants, and many of them carrying weapons either holstered at the waist or slung across the shoulder.

Koriel was standing ahead of them, huge, broad-shouldered, with dense, black hair, unsmiling features, and his thumbs hooked loosely in his belt. Two lieutenants were standing one either side and a pace behind him. Some of the arms in the crowd began rising in a farewell salutation.

Then the view began to fall away and tilt. The settlement shrank quickly and lost itself among a carpet of tree-tops, which in turn faded to become just a hazy area of green on a patchwork of colors taking form as the scale reduced and more of the surrounding landscape flowed into view from the sides. "The last view from the ship as it departed from Earth to return to Thurien," Calazar said. A coastline that was recognizable as part of the Red Sea moved into the picture and shrank to become part of a familiar section of Middle East geography despite being distorted at the periphery by perspective. Finally the edge of the planet itself appeared, already looking distinctly curved.

They watched in silence for a long time. Eventually

Danchekker murmured, "Imagine . . . the whole human race began with that tiny handful. After all that they had endured, they conquered a whole world. What an extraordinary race they must have been."

This was one of the few occasions on which Hunt had seen Danchekker genuinely moved. And he felt it too. He thought back again to the scenes from the Lunarian war and the visions that the Jevlenese had created of Earth stampeding toward exactly the same catastrophe. And yet it had almost come true. It had been close—far too close. If Earth had not changed course when it did, just two or three decades more would have made that come true. And then Charlie, Koriel, Gorda, the efforts of the Thuriens, the struggles of the handful of survivors that he had just seen—and all that they endured after that—would have been for nothing.

It brought to mind Wellington's words after Waterloo: "It was a close-run thing, a damned close-run thing—the closest-run thing you ever saw in your life."

chapter twenty-one

After hearing Norman Pacey's account of the events at Bruno, Jerol Packard lodged a confidential request with an office of the CIA for a compendium of everything that had accumulated in its files over the years concerning Sverenssen and, for good measure, the other members of the UN Farside delegation as well. Clifford Benson, the CIA official who had dealt with the request, summarized the findings a day later at a closed-door session in Packard's State Department office.

"Sverenssen reappeared in Western Europe in 2009 with a circle of social and financial contacts already established. How that happened is not clear. We can't find any authenticated traces of him for about ten years before then—in fact from the time he was supposed to have been killed in

Ethiopia." Benson gestured at a section of the summary charts of names, photographs, organizations, and interconnecting arrows pinned to a wallboard. "His closest ties were with a French-British-Swiss investment-banking consortium, a big part of which is still run by the same families that set up a network of financial operations around Southeast Asia in the nineteenth century to launder the revenues from the Chinese opium trade. Now here's an interesting thing—one of the biggest names on the French side of that consortium is a blood relative of Daldanier. In fact the two names have been connected for three generations."

"Those people are pretty tightly knit," Caldwell commented. "I don't know if I'd attach a lot of significance to something like that."

"If it were an isolated case, I wouldn't, either," Benson agreed. "But look at the rest of the story." He indicated another part of the chart. "The British and Swiss sides control a sizable part of the world's bullion business and are connected through the London gold market and its mining affiliations to South Africa. And look what name we find prominent among the ones at the end of that line."

"Is that Van Geelink of the same family as Sverenssen's cohort?" Lyn asked dubiously.

"It's the same," Benson said. "There are a number of them, all connected with different parts of the same business. It's a complicated setup." He paused for a moment, then resumed, "Up until around the first few years of this century, a lot of Van Geelink–controlled money went into preserving white dominance in the area by undermining the stability of black Africa politically and economically, which is one reason why nobody seemed interested in backing resistance to the Cuban and Communist subversions that were going on from the '70s through '90s. To maintain their own position militarily in the face of trade embargoes, the family organized arms deals through intermediaries, frequently South American regimes."

"Is this where the Brazilian guy fits in?" Caldwell asked, raising an eyebrow.

Benson nodded. "Among others. Saraquez's father and grandfather were both big in commodity financing, especially to do with oil. There are links from them as well as from the Van Geelinks to the prime movers behind the destabilization of the Middle East in the late twentieth century. The main reason for that was to maximize short-term oil profits before the world went nuclear, which also accounts for the orchestrated sabotage of public opinion against nuclear power at around the same time. A side effect that worked in the Saraquezes' interests was that it boosted the demand for Central American oil." Benson shrugged and tossed out his hands. "There's more, but you can see the gist of it. The same kind of thing shows up with a few more who were on that delegation. It's one happy family, in a lot of cases literally."

Caldwell studied the charts with a new interest once Benson had finished. After a while he sat back and asked, "So what does it tell us? What's the connection with what went on at Farside? Figured that out yet?"

"I just collect facts," Benson replied. "I leave the rest to you people."

Packard moved to the center of the room. "There is another interesting side to the pattern," he said. "The whole network represents a common ideology—feudalism." The others looked at him curiously. He explained, "Cliff's already mentioned their involvement in the antinuclear hysteria of thirty or forty years ago, but there's more to it than that." He waved a hand at the charts that Benson had been using. "Take the banking consortium that gave Sverenssen his start as an example. Throughout the last quarter of the 1900s they provided a lot of behind-the-scenes backing for moves to fob the Third World off with 'appropriate technologies,' for various antiprogress, antiscience lobbies, and that kind of thing. In South Africa we had another branch of the same net pushing racism and preventing progressive government, industrialization, and comprehensive education for blacks. And across the ocean we had a series of right-wing fascist regimes protecting minority interests by military takeovers and at the same time obstructing general advancement. You see, it all adds up to the same basic ideology—preserving the feudal privileges and interests of the power structure of the time. What it says, I guess, is that nothing's changed all that much."

Lyn appeared puzzled. "But it has, hasn't it?" she said. "That's not the way the world is these days. I thought this guy Sverenssen and the rest were committed to just the opposite—advancing the whole world all over."

"What I meant was that the same people are still there," Packard replied. "But you're right—their underlying policy seems to have shifted in the last thirty years or so. Sverenssen's bankers provided easy credit for Nigerian fusion and steel under a gold-backed standard that couldn't have worked without the cooperation of people like the Van Geelinks. South American oil helped defuse the Middle East by leading the changeover to hydrogen-based substitutes, which was one of the things that made disarmament possible." He shrugged. "Suddenly everything changed. The backing was there for things that could have been done fifty years earlier."

"So what about their line at Bruno?" Caldwell asked again, looking mystified. "It doesn't fit."

There was a short silence before Packard proceeded. "How's this for a theory? Controlling minorities never have anything to gain from change. That explains their traditional opposition to technology all through history, unless it offered something to advance their interests. That meant it was okay as long as they controlled it. Hence we get the traditional stance of their kind through to the end of the last century. But by that time it was becoming obvious from the way the world was going that if something didn't change soon, somebody was going to start pressing buttons, and then there wouldn't be any kind of pond left to be a fish in. The only choice was nuclear reactors or nuclear bombs. So this revolution they made happen, and they managed to maintain control in the process—which was neat.

"But Thurien and everything it could mean was something else. This group would have been swept away by the time the dust from that kind of revolution finally settled. So they cornered the UN handling of the matter and put up a wall until they got some ideas about where to go next." He threw out his hands and looked around the room to invite comment.

"How did they find out about the relay?" Norman Pacey asked from a corner. "We know from what Gregg and Lyn said that the coded signals had nothing to do with it. And we know Sobroskin wasn't mixed up with it."

"They must have been involved with getting rid of it," Packard replied. "I don't know how, but I can't think of anything else. They could have used some personnel of UNSA who they knew wouldn't talk, or maybe a government or commercial outfit that operates independently to send a bomb or something out there . . . probably as soon as the first signal from Gistar came in months ago. So what they've been doing is stalling things until it got there."

Caldwell nodded. "It makes sense. You've got to hand it to them—they almost had it tied up. If it wasn't for McClusky . . . who knows?"

A solemn silence descended and persisted for a while. Eventually Lyn looked inquiringly from one man to another. "So what happens now?" she asked.

"I'm not sure," Packard replied. "It's a complicated situation all around."

She looked at him uncertainly for a second. "You're not saying they might get away with it?"

"It's a possibility."

Lyn stared as if she couldn't believe her ears. "But that's ridiculous! You're telling us that for . . . I don't know how many years, people like this have been keeping whole nations backward, sabotaging education, and supporting all kinds of idiot cults and propaganda to stay on top of the pile, and there's nothing anybody can do? That's crazy!"

"I didn't put the situation as definitely as that," Packard said. "I said it's complicated. Being pretty sure of something and being able to prove it are two different things. We're going to have to do a lot more work to make a case out of it."

"But, but . . ." Lyn searched for words. "What else do you need? It's all wrapped up. Bombing that relay outside Pluto has to be enough on its own. They weren't acting for the whole planet when they did that, and certainly not in its interests. There has to be enough in that to nail them."

"We don't have any way of *knowing* for sure that they did it," Packard pointed out. "It's pure speculation. Maybe the relay just broke down. Maybe Calazar's organization did it. You couldn't pin anything on Sverenssen that'd stick."

"He knew it was going to happen," Lyn objected. "Of course he was mixed up in it."

"Knew on whose say-so?" Packard countered. "One little girl at Bruno who thinks she might have overheard something that she didn't understand, anyway." He shook his head. "You heard Norman's story. Sverenssen could produce witnesses lined up all down the hall to state that he never had anything to do with her. She became infatuated, then went running to Norman with a silly story to get even when Sverenssen wasn't interested. Such things happen all the time."

"What about the fake signals he got her to send?" Lyn persisted.

"What fake signals?" Packard shrugged. "All part of the same game. She made up that story. They never existed."

"But the Thurien records say they did," Lyn said. "You don't have to tell the whole world about Alaska right now, but when the time's right you can wheel in a whole planet of Ganymeans to back you up."

"True, but all they confirm is that some strange signals came in that weren't sent officially. They don't confirm where they came from or who sent them. The header formats could have been faked to resemble Farside's." Packard shook his head again. "When you think it through, the evidence is not anywhere near conclusive."

Lyn turned an imploring face toward Caldwell. He shook his head regretfully. "He's got some good points. I'd like to see them all go down just as much as you would, but it doesn't look as if the case to do it is there yet."

"The problem is you can never get near them," Benson said, coming back into the conversation. "They don't make many slips, and when they do you're never around. Now and again you get something leaking out like what happened at Bruno, but it's never enough to be a clincher. That's what we need—something to clinch it. We need to put somebody on the inside, close to Sverenssen." He shook his head dubiously. "But something like that needs a lot of research and planning, and it takes a long time to select the right person for the job. We'll start working on it, but don't hold your breath waiting for results."

Lyn, Caldwell, and Pacey were all staying at the Washington Central Hilton. They ate dinner together that evening, and over coffee Pacey talked more about what they had learned in Packard's office.

"You can trace the same basic struggle right down through history," he told them. "Two opposed ideologies—the feudalism of the aristocracies on one side, and the republicanism of the artisans, scientists, and city-builders on the other. You had it with the slave economies of the ancient world, the intellectual oppressions of the Church in Europe in the Middle Ages, the colonialism of the British Empire, and, later on, Eastern Communism and Western consumerism."

"Keep 'em working hard, give 'em a cause to believe in, and don't teach 'em to think too hard, huh?" Caldwell commented.

"Exactly." Pacey nodded. "The last thing you want is an educated, affluent, and emancipated population. Power hinges on the restriction and control of wealth. Science and technology offer unlimited wealth. Therefore science and technology have to be controlled. Knowledge and reason are enemies; myth and unreason are the weapons you fight them with."

Lyn was still thinking about the conversation an hour later when the three of them were sitting around a small table in a quiet alcove that opened off one end of the lobby. They had opted for a last drink before calling it a night, but the bar had seemed too crowded and noisy. It was the same war that Vic, consciously or not, had been fighting all his life, she realized. The Sverenssens who had almost shut down Thurien stood side by side with the Inquisition that had forced Galileo to recant, the bishops who had opposed Darwin, the English nobility who would have ruled the Americas as a captive market for home industry, and the politicians on both sides of the Iron Curtain who had seized the atom to hold a world to ransom with bombs. She wanted to contribute something to his war, even if only a token gesture to show that she was on his side. But what? She had never felt so restless and so helpless at the same time.

Eventually Caldwell remembered an urgent call that he needed to make to Houston. He excused himself and stood up, saying he would be back in a few minutes, then disappeared into the arcade of souvenir and menswear shops that led to the elevators. Pacey lounged back in his seat, put his glass down on the table, and looked across at Lyn. "You're being very quiet," he said. "Eat too much steak?"

She smiled. "Oh . . . just thinking. Don't ask what about. We've talked too much shop today already."

Pacey stretched out an arm to pick up a cracker from the dish in the center of the table and popped it into his mouth. "Do you get up to D.C. much?" he asked.

"Quite a bit. I don't stay here very often, though. I usually put up at the Hyatt or the Constitution."

"Most UNSA people do. I guess this is one of the two or three favorite places for political people. It's almost like an after-hours diplomatic club at times."

"The Hyatt's pretty much like that for UNSA."

"Uh huh." Pause. "You're from the East Coast, aren't you?"

"New York originally—upper East Side. I moved south after college to join UNSA. I thought I was going to be an astronaut, but I ended up flying a desk." She sighed. "Not complaining though. Working with Gregg has its moments."

"He seems quite a guy. I imagine he'd be an easy boss to get along with."

"He does what he says he's going to do, and he doesn't say he's going to do what he can't. Most of the people in Navcomms respect him a lot, even if they don't always agree with him. But it's mutual. You know, one of the things he always—"

A call from the paging system interrupted. "Calling Mr. Norman Pacey. Would Norman Pacey come to the front desk, please. There is an urgent message waiting. Urgent message for Norman Pacey at the front desk. Thank you."

Pacey rose from his chair. "I wonder what the hell that is. Excuse me."

"Sure."

"Want me to order you another drink?"

"I'll do it. You go ahead."

Pacey made his way across the lobby, which was fairly busy with people coming and going and parties assembling for late dinner. One of the clerks at the desk raised his eyebrows inquiringly as he approached. "My name is Pacey.

You paged me just now. There should be a message here somewhere."

"One moment, sir." The clerk turned to check the pigeonholes behind him, and after a few seconds turned back again holding a white envelope. "Mr. Norman Pacey, Room 3527?" Pacey showed the clerk his key. The clerk passed over the envelope.

"Thanks." Pacey moved a short distance away to open the envelope in a corner by the Eastern Airlines booth. Inside was a single sheet of paper on which was handwritten:

Important that I talk to you immediately. Am across lobby. Suggest we use your room for privacy.

Pacey frowned, then looked up and from side to side to scan the lobby. After a few seconds he picked out a tall, swarthy man in a dark suit watching him from the far side. The man was standing near a group of half a dozen noisily chattering men and women, but he appeared to be alone. He gave a slight nod. Pacey hesitated for a moment, then returned it. The man glanced casually at his watch, looked around, and sauntered toward the arcade that led through to the elevators. Pacey watched him disappear, and then walked back to where Lyn was sitting.

"Something just came up," he told her. "Look, I'm sorry about this, but I have to meet somebody right away. Give Gregg my apologies, would you."

"Want me to tell him what it's about?" Lyn asked.

"I don't know myself yet. I'm not sure how long it'll take."

"Okay. I'll be fine just watching the world go by. See you later."

Pacey walked back across the lobby and entered the arcade just in time to miss a tall, lean, silver-haired and immaculately dressed figure turning away from the reception desk after collecting a room key. The man moved unhurriedly to the center of the lobby and stopped to survey the surroundings.

The swarthy man was waiting a short distance from the elevators when Pacey emerged a minute or so later on the thirty-fifth floor. As Pacey approached him, he turned silently and led the way to 3527, then stood aside while Pacey unlocked the door. Pacey allowed him to enter first, then followed and closed the door behind them as the other turned on the light. "Well?" he demanded.

"You may call me Ivan," the swarthy man said. He spoke in a heavy European accent. "I am from the Soviet Embassy here in Washington. I have a message that I have been instructed to deliver to you in person: Mikolai Sobroskin wishes to meet with you urgently concerning matters of some considerable importance which, I understand, you are aware of. He suggests that you meet in London. I have the details. You may convey your response back to him through me." He watched for a few seconds while Pacey stared back uncertainly, not knowing what to make of the message, then reached inside his jacket and drew out what looked like a folded sheet of stiffened paper. "I was told that if I gave you this, you would be satisfied that the message is genuine."

Pacey took the sheet and unfolded it. It was a blank sample of the pink, red-bordered document wallet used by the UN for confidential information. Pacey stared at it for a few seconds, then looked up and nodded. "I can't give you an answer on my own authority right at this moment," he said. "I'll have to get in touch with you again later tonight. Could we do that?"

"I had expected as much," Ivan said. "There is a coffee shop one block from here called the Half Moon. I will wait there."

"I may have to take a trip somewhere," Pacey warned. "It could take awhile."

Ivan nodded. "I will be waiting," he said, and with that, he left.

Pacey closed the door behind him and spent a few minutes walking thoughtfully back and forth across the room. Then he sat down in front of the datagrid terminal, activated it, and called Jerol Packard's private home number.

Downstairs in the alcove to one side of the lobby, Lyn was thinking about Egyptian pyramids, medieval cathedrals, British dreadnoughts, and the late-twentieth-century arms race. Were they all parts of the same pattern too? she wondered. No matter how much more wealth per capita improving technology made possible, always there had been something to soak up the surplus and condemn ordinary people to a lifetime of labor. No matter how much productivity increased, people never seemed to work less, only differently. So if they didn't reap the fruits, who did? She was beginning to see lots of things in ways she hadn't before.

She didn't really notice the man in the seat that Pacey had vacated a few minutes earlier until he started speaking. "May I sit with you? It is so relaxing to do nothing for a few minutes at the end of a hectic day and just watch the human race going about its business. I do hope you don't mind. The world is so full of lonely people who insist on making islands of themselves and a tragedy of life. It always strikes me as such a shame, and so unnecessary."

Lyn's glass nearly dropped from her hand as she found herself looking at a face that she had seen only hours before on one of the charts that Clifford Benson had hung on the wall in Packard's office. It was Niels Sverenssen.

She downed the rest of her drink in one gulp, almost choking herself in the process, and managed, "Yes . . . it is, isn't it."

"Are you staying here, if you don't mind my asking?" Sverenssen inquired. She nodded. Sverenssen smiled. There was something about his aristocratic bearing and calculated aloofness that set him apart from the greater part of the male half of the race in a way that many women find alluring, she admitted to herself. With his elegant crown of silver hair and well-tanned noble features, he was . . . well, not exactly handsome by *Playgirl* standards, but intriguing in some undeniable way. And the distant look in his eyes made them almost hypnotic. "On your own?" he asked.

She nodded again. "Sort of."

Sverenssen raised his eyebrows and motioned his head in the direction of her glass. "I see you are empty. I was on my way to have an unwinder myself in the bar. It seems that, temporarily at least, we are both islands in a world of nine billion people—a most unfortunate situation, and one which I am sure we could do something to correct. Would you consider it an impertinence if I invited you to join me?"

* * *

Pacey stepped into the elevator and found Caldwell there, evidently on his way back down to the lobby.

"It took longer than I thought," Caldwell said. "There's a lot of hassle going on at Houston about budget allocations. I'm going to have to get back there pretty soon. I've been away too long as it is." He looked at Pacey curiously. "Where's Lyn?"

"She's downstairs. I got called away." Pacey stared at the inside of the doors for a second. "Sobroskin's been in touch via the Soviet Embassy here. He wants me to meet him in London to talk about something."

Caldwell raised his eyebrows in surprise. "You're going?"

"I'll know later. I just called Packard, and I'm going to take a cab over to his place right now to tell him about it. I've arranged to meet somebody later tonight to let them know." He shook his head. "And I thought this would be a quiet night."

They came out of the elevator and walked through the arcade to where Pacey had left Lyn. The alcove was empty. They looked around, but she was nowhere in sight.

"Maybe she went to the little girls' room," Caldwell suggested.

"Probably."

They stood for a while talking and waiting, but there was no sign of Lyn. Eventually Pacey said, "Maybe she wanted another drink, couldn't get served out here, and went into the bar. She might still be in there."

"I'll check it out," Caldwell said. He about-faced and stumped away across the lobby.

A minute later he returned, wearing the expression of somebody who had been hit from behind by a tramcar while minding his own business in the middle of the Hilton. "She's in there," he announced in a dull voice, slumping down into one of the empty seats. "She's got company. Go see for yourself, but stay back from the door. Then come back and tell me if it's who I think it is."

A minute later Pacey thudded down into the chair opposite. He looked as if he had been hit by the same tram on its return trip. "It's him," he said numbly. A long time seemed to pass. Then Pacey murmured, "He's got a place up in Connecticut somewhere. He must have stopped off in D.C. for a few days on his way back from Bruno. We should have picked some other place."

"How'd she look?" Caldwell asked.

Pacey shrugged. "Fine. She seemed to be doing most of the talking, and looked quite at home. If I hadn't known any better, I'd have said it was some guy swallowing a line and well on his way to ending up a few hundred poorer. She looks as if she can take care of herself okay."

"But what the hell does she think she's trying to do?"

"You tell me. You're her boss. I hardly know her."

"But Christ, we can't just leave her there."

"What can we do? She walked in there, and she's old enough to drink. Anyhow, I can't go in there because he knows me, and there's no point in making problems. That leaves you. What are you going to do—make like the boss who can't see when he's being a wet blanket, or what?" Caldwell scowled irritably at the table but seemed stuck for a reply. After a short silence Pacey stood up and spread his hands apologetically. "Look, Greg, I know this sounds kind of bad, but I'm going to have to leave you to handle it in whatever way you want. Packard's waiting for me right now, and it's important. I have to go."

"Yeah, okay, okay." Caldwell waved a hand vaguely. "Call me when you get back and let me know what's happening."

Pacey left, using a side entrance to avoid crossing the lobby in front of the bar. Caldwell sat brooding for a while, then shrugged, shook his head perplexedly, and went back up to his room to catch up on some reading while he waited for a call from Pacey.

chapter twenty-two

Danchekker gazed for a long time at the two solid images being displayed side by side in a laboratory in Thurien. They were highly magnified reproductions of a pair of organic cells obtained from a species of bottom-dwelling worm from an ocean on one of the Ganymean worlds, and showed the internal structures color-enhanced for easy identification of the nuclei and other components. Eventually he shook his head and looked up. "I'm afraid I am obliged to concede defeat. They both appear identical to me. And you are saying that one of them does not belong to this species at all?" He sounded incredulous.

Shilohin smiled from a short distance behind him. "The one on the left is a single-cell microorganism that contains enzymes programmed to dismantle the DNA of its own nucleus and reassemble the pieces into a copy of the host organism's DNA," she said. "When that process is complete, the whole structure is rapidly transformed into a duplicate of whatever type of cell the parasite happens to be residing in. From then on the parasite has literally become a part of the host, indistinguishable from the host's own naturally produced cells and therefore immune to its antibodies and rejection mechanisms. It evolved on a planet subject to intense ultraviolet radiation from a fairly hot, blue star, probably from a cell-repair mechanism that stabilized the species against extreme mutation. As far as we know it's a unique adaptation. I thought you'd be interested in seeing it."

"Extraordinary," Danchekker murmured. He walked across to the device of gleaming metal and glass from which the data to generate the image originated, and stooped to peer into the tiny chamber containing the tissue sample. "I would be most interested in conducting some experiments of my own on this organism when I get back. Er . . . do you think the Thuriens might let me take a sample of it?"

Shilohin laughed. "I'm sure you'd be welcome to, Professor, but how do you propose carrying it back to Houston? You're forgetting that you're not really here."

"Tch! Stupid of me." Danchekker shook his head and stepped back to gaze at the apparatus around them, the function of most of which he still failed to comprehend. "So much to learn," he murmured half to himself. "So much to learn . . ." He thought for a while, and his expression changed to a frown. Eventually he turned to face Shilohin again. "There's something about this whole Thurien civilization that has been puzzling me. I wonder if you can help."

"I'll try. What's the problem?"

Danchekker sighed. "Well . . . I don't know . . . after twenty-five *million* years, it should be even *more* advanced than it is, I would have thought. It is far ahead of Earth, to be sure, but I can't see Earth requiring anywhere near that amount of time to reach a level comparable to Thurien's today. It seems . . . strange."

"The same thought occurred to me," Shilohin said. "I talked to Eesyan about it."

"Did he offer a reason?"

"Yes." Shilohin paused for a long time while Danchekker looked at her curiously. Then she said, "The civilization of Thurien came to a halt for a very long time. Paradoxically it was as a result of its advanced sciences."

Danchekker blinked uncertainly through his spectacles. "How could that be?"

"You have studied Ganymean genetic-engineering techniques extensively," Shilohin replied. "After the migration to Thurien, they were taken even further."

"I'm not sure I see the connection."

"The Thuriens perfected a capability that they had been dreaming of for generations—the ability to program their own genes to offset the effects of bodily aging and wasting . . . indefinitely."

A moment or two went by before Danchekker grasped what she was saying. Then he gasped. "Do you mean immortality?"

"Exactly. For a long time it seemed that Utopia had been achieved."

"Seemed?"

"Not all the consequences were foreseen. After a while all their progress, their innovation, and their creativity ceased. The Thuriens became too wise and knew too much. In particular they knew all the reasons why things were impossible and why nothing more could be achieved."

"You mean they ceased to dream." Danchekker shook his head sadly. "How unfortunate. Everything that we take for granted began with somebody dreaming of something that couldn't be done."

Shilohin nodded. "And in the past it had always been the

younger generations, too naive and inexperienced to recognize the impossible when they saw it, who had been foolish enough to make the attempt. It was surprising how often they succeeded. But now, of course, there were no more younger generations."

Danchekker was nodding slowly as he listened. "They turned into a society of mental geriatrics."

"Exactly. And when they realized what was happening, they went back to the old ways. But their civilization had stagnated for a very long time, and as a result most of their spectacular breakthroughs have occurred only comparatively recently. The instant-transfer technology was developed barely in time for them to be able to intervene at the end of the Lunarian war. And things like the h-space power-distribution grid, direct neural coupling into machines, and, eventually, VISAR came much later."

"I can imagine the problem," Danchekker murmured absently. "People complain that life is too short for the things they want to do, but without that restriction perhaps they would never do anything. The pressure of finite time is surely the greatest motivator. I've often suspected that if the dream of immortality were ever realized, the outcome would be something like that."

"Well, if the Thuriens' experience was anything to go by, you were right," Shilohin told him.

They talked about the Thuriens for a while longer, and then Shilohin had to return to the *Shapieron* for a meeting with Garuth and Monchar. Danchekker remained in the laboratory to observe some more examples of Thurien biological science presented by VISAR. After spending some time at this he decided he would like to discuss some of what he had seen with Hunt while the details were fresh in his mind, and asked VISAR if Hunt was currently coupled into the system.

"No, he's not," VISAR informed him. "He boarded a plane that took off from McClusky about fifteen minutes ago. If you want, I could put you through to the control room there."

"Oh, er . . . yes, if you would," Danchekker said.

An image of a communications screen appeared in midair a couple of feet in front of Danchekker's face, framing the features of the duty controller at McClusky. "Hello,

Professor," the controller acknowledged. "What can I do for you?"

"VISAR just told me that Vic has left for somewhere," Danchekker replied. "I wondered what was happening."

"He left a message for you saying he's gone to Houston for the morning. It doesn't go into any details, though."

"Is that Chris Danchekker? Let me talk to him." Karen Heller's voice sounded distantly from somewhere in the background. A few seconds later the controller moved off one side of the screen, and she came into view. "Hello, Professor. Vic got fed up waiting for Lyn to get back from Washington with some news, so he called Houston. Gregg is back there, but Lyn isn't. Vic's gone to find out what's going on. That's really about all I can tell you."

"Oh, I see," Danchekker said. "How strange."

"There was something else that I wanted to talk to you about," Heller went on. "I've been doing a lot of looking into some parts of Lunarian history with Calazar and Showm, and it's becoming rather interesting. We've some questions I'd like your answers to. How soon do you think you'll be back?"

Danchekker muttered under his breath and looked wistfully around the Ganymean laboratory, then realized that he was getting signals through VISAR that his body was getting hungry again. "Actually I'll be coming back now," he replied. "Perhaps I could talk to you in the canteen, ten minutes from now, say?"

"I'll see you there," Heller agreed and disappeared with the image of the screen.

Ten minutes later Danchekker was heartily demolishing a plate of bacon, eggs, sausage, and hash browns at McClusky while Heller talked over a sandwich from the opposite side of the table. Most of the UNSA people were busy refitting one of the other buildings to afford more permanent storage facilities, and apart from some clatterings and bangings from the adjoining kitchen there were no signs of life in their immediate vicinity.

"We've been analyzing the rates of development of the Lunarian civilization and Earth's," she said. "The difference is staggering. They were into steam power and machines in a matter of a few thousand years after starting to use stone tools. We took something like ten times as long. Why do you think that was?"

Danchekker frowned while he finished chewing. "I thought that the factors responsible for the accelerated advancement of the Lunarians were already quite obvious," he replied. "For one thing, they were closer chronologically to the original Ganymean genetic experiments. Therefore they possessed a greater genetic instability, and with it a tendency to a more extreme form of mutation. The sudden emergence of the Lambians is doubtless a case in point."

"I'm not convinced that it explains it," Heller replied slowly. "You've said yourself a few times that tens of thousands of years isn't enough to make a lot of difference. I got VISAR to do some calculations based on human genetic data that ZORAC acquired when the *Shapieron* was on Earth. The results seem to bear it out. And the pattern was already established long before the Lambians appeared. That was only two hundred years before the war."

Danchekker sniffed as he buttered a piece of toast. Politicians had no business playing at being scientists. "The Lunarians would have found a profusion of remnants of the earlier Ganymean civilization on Minerva," he suggested. "The knowledge gained from sources of that nature gave them a flying start over Earth."

"But the Cerians who came to Earth were from a civilization that was already advanced," Heller pointed out. "So that balances. What else made the difference?"

Danchekker wrinkled his nose up and scowled. *Female* politicians playing at being scientists were intolerable. "The Lunarian culture developed during the deteriorating environmental conditions of the approaching Ice Age," he said. "That provided additional pressures."

"The Ice Age was here when the Cerians arrived, and it lasted for a long time afterward," Heller reminded him. "So that balances too. So again—what caused the difference?"

Danchekker stabbed his fork into his meal in a show of exasperation. "If you wish to doubt my word as a biologist and an anthropologist, you have of course every right to do so, madam," he said airily. "For my part, I see no justification whatsoever for elaborating any hypothesis beyond the simple minimum required to account for the facts. And what we already know is perfectly adequate for that purpose."

Heller seemed to have been expecting something like that, and didn't react. "Maybe you're thinking too much like a biologist," she suggested. "Try looking at it from a sociological angle, and asking the question the other way around."

Danchekker's expression said that there couldn't be any other way around. "What do you mean?" he demanded.

"Instead of telling me what speeded the Lunarians up, try asking what slowed Earth down."

Danchekker stared darkly down at his plate for a few seconds, then raised his head and showed his teeth. "The upheavals caused by the Moon's capture," he pronounced.

Heller looked at him in open disbelief. "And regressed them to a point that needed tens of thousands of years to recover from? No way! A few centuries at the most, maybe, but not *that* much. I couldn't buy it. Neither could Showm. Neither could Calazar."

"I see." Danchekker looked a bit taken aback. He attacked his bacon in silence for a while and then said, "And what alternative explanation, if any, are you offering, might I ask?"

"Something you haven't mentioned so far," Heller answered. "The Lunarians developed rational, scientific thinking early on, and relied on it totally from the beginnings of their civilization. By contrast Earth went off into thousands of years of believing that magic, mysticism, Santa Claus, the Easter Bunny, and the Tooth Fairy would solve its problems. It only started to change comparatively recently, and even today there's still a lot of that around. We got VISAR to estimate the effects, and it eclipses all the other factors put together. *That's* what caused the difference!"

Danchekker thought about it for a while, then replied a trifle grudgingly, "Very well." He thrust his chin out defensively. "But I fail to see the need for any melodramatic suggestion that it poses a different question. It's as valid to argue that the early adoption of rational methods accelerated one race as it is to say that its absence retarded the other. What point are you making?"

"I've been thinking a lot about it since I talked to Calazar and Showm, and asking what the reason was. Vic says everything has to have a reason, even if it takes some digging to find it. So what would the reason be for a whole planet clinging obstinately to a lot of nonsense and superstitions for thousands of years when even a little bit of observation and common sense should have shown it doesn't work?"

"I think perhaps you underestimate the complexities of scientific method," Danchekker told her. "It takes centuries . . . scores of generations to evolve the techniques necessary to distinguish reliably between facts and fallacies, and truth and myth. Certainly it couldn't happen overnight. What else did you expect?"

"So why didn't that stop the Lunarians?"

"I have no idea. Have you?"

"That was the question I was leading up to." Heller leaned forward to look at him intently across the table. "What do you think of this for a suggestion: The reason that belief in myths and magic became so deeply rooted in Earth's cultures and persisted for so long could be that, in the earliest stage of our first civilizations, it *did* work?"

Danchekker gagged over the mouthful of food that he had been about to swallow and colored visibly. "*What?* That's preposterous! Are you suggesting that the laws of physics that dictate the running of the Universe could have changed in the last few thousand years?"

"No, I'm not. All I'm—"

"I've never heard such an absurd suggestion. This whole matter is already complicated enough without introducing attempts to explain it by astrology, ESP, or whatever other inanities you have in mind." Danchekker looked about him impatiently and sighed. "Really, it would take far too long to explain why if you are unable to distinguish between science and the banalities dispensed in adolescent magazines. Just take my word that you are wasting your time . . . mine too, I might add."

Heller maintained her calm with some effort. "I am *not* suggesting anything of the kind." An edge of strain had crept into her voice. "Kindly listen for two minutes." Danchekker said nothing and eyed her dubiously across the table as he continued eating. She went on, "Think about this scenario. The Jevlenese have never forgotten that they're

Lambians, and we're Cerians. They still see Earth as a rival and always have. Now put them in the situation where they've been taken to Thurien and are making the most of the opportunity to absorb all that Ganymean technology, and the rivals on Earth have just been sent back to square one by the Moon showing up. They've gained control of the surveillance operation, and probably by this time they can do their own instant moving of ships and whatever around the Galaxy because they've got their own independent computer, JEVEX, on their own independent planet. Also they're *human* in form—physically indistinguishable from their rivals." Heller sat back and looked at Danchekker expectantly, as if waiting for him to fill in the rest himself. He stopped with his fork halfway to his mouth and gaped at her incredulously.

"They could have *made* magic and miracles work," Heller went on after a few seconds. "They could have put their own, shall we say, 'agents' into our culture way back in its ancient history and deliberately instilled systems of beliefs that we still haven't entirely recovered from—beliefs that were guaranteed to make sure that the rival would take a long, long time to rediscover the sciences and develop the technologies that would make it an opponent worth worrying about again. Meanwhile the Jevlenese have bought themselves a lot of time to become established on their own system of worlds, expand JEVEX, milk off more Ganymean know-how, and whatever else they've been up to." She sat back, spread her hands, and looked at Danchekker expectantly. "What do you think?"

Danchekker stared at her for what seemed a long time. "Impossible," he declared at last.

Heller's patience finally snapped. "Why? What's wrong with that theory?" she demanded. "The facts are that something slowed Earth's development down. This accounts for it, and nothing that you came up with does. The Jevlenese had the means and the motive, and the answer fits the evidence. What more do you want? I thought science was supposed to be open-minded at least."

"Too farfetched," Danchekker retorted. He became openly sarcastic. "Another principle of science, which you appear to have overlooked, is that one endeavors to test one's hypotheses by experiment. I have no idea how you intend testing this far-flung notion of yours, but for suggestions I recommend that you might try consulting the illustrators of *Superman* comics or the authors of the articles one finds in those housewives' journals found on sale in supermarkets." With that he returned his attention fully to his meal.

"Well if that's your attitude, enjoy your lunch." Heller rose indignantly to her feet. "I heard that Vic had a hell of a time getting you to accept that the Lunarians existed at all. I can see why!" She turned and marched out of the room.

Karen Heller was still fuming thirty minutes later as she stood by one of the buildings on the edge of the apron watching a UNSA crew installing a more permanent generator facility. Danchekker came out of the door of the mess hall some distance away, saw her, then walked slowly off in the opposite direction, his hands clasped behind his back. He stopped at the perimeter fence and stood for a long time staring out across the marshes, turning his head every now and then to glance back at where Heller was standing. Eventually he turned and paced thoughtfully back to the door of the mess hall. When he was almost there he stopped, looked across at her again, hesitated for a few seconds, then changed direction and came over to her.

"I, er—I apologize," he said. "I think you may have something. Certainly your conclusions warrant further investigation. We should contact the others and tell them about it as soon as possible."

chapter twenty-three

"She what?!"

Hunt caught Caldwell's arm and drew him to a halt halfway along the corridor leading toward Caldwell's office at the top of the Navcomms Headquarters Building.

"He told her to give him a call next time she was in New York to see her mother," Caldwell said. "So I told her to take some vacation and go see her mother." He lifted Hunt's fingers from the sleeve of his jacket and resumed walking.

Hunt stood rooted to the spot for a second, then came to life once more and caught up in a few hurried paces. "What in hell? . . . You can't do that! She happens to be very special to me."

"She also happens to be my assistant."

"But . . . what's she supposed to do when she sees him—read poetry? Gregg, you can't do that. You've got to get her out of it."

"You're sounding like a maiden aunt," Caldwell said. "I didn't do anything. She set it up herself, and I didn't see any reason not to use the chance. It might turn up something useful."

"Her job description never said anything about playing Mata Hari. It's a blatant and inexcusable exploitation of personnel beyond the limits of their contractual obligations to the Division."

"Nonsense. It's a career-development opportunity. Her job description stresses initiative and creativity, and that's what it is."

"What kind of career? That guy's only got one track in his head. Look, it may come as kind of a surprise, but I don't go for the idea of her being another boy-scout badge for him to stitch on his shirt. Maybe I'm being old-fashioned, but I didn't think that that was what working for UNSA was all about."

"Stop overreacting. Nobody said a word about anything like that. It could be a chance to fill in some of the details we're missing. The opportunity came out of the blue, and she grabbed it."

"I've heard enough details already from Karen. Okay, we know the rules, and Lyn knows the rules, but he doesn't know the rules. What do you think he's going to do—sit down and fill out a questionnaire?"

"Lyn can handle it."

"You can't let her do it."

"I can't stop her. She's on vacation, seeing her mother."

"Then I want to take some special leave, starting right

now. I've got personal emergency matters to attend to in New York."

"Denied. You've got too much to do here that's more important."

They fell silent as they passed through the outer office and into Caldwell's inner sanctum. Caldwell's secretary looked up from dictating a memo to an audiotranscriber and nodded a greeting.

"Gregg, this is going too far," Hunt began again when they got inside. "There's—"

"There's more to it than you think," Caldwell told him. "I've heard enough from Norman Pacey and the CIA to know that the opportunity was worth seizing when it presented itself. Lyn knew it too." He draped his jacket on a hanger by the door, walked around the other side of his desk, and dumped the briefcase that he had been carrying down on top of it. "There's a hell of a lot about Sverenssen that we never dreamed of, and a lot more we don't know that we'd like to. So stop being neurotic, sit down and listen for five minutes, and I'll give you a summary."

Hunt emitted a long sigh of capitulation, threw out his hands in resignation, and slumped down into one of the chairs. "We're going to need a lot more than five minutes, Gregg," he said as Caldwell sat down facing him. "You wait till you hear about the things we found out yesterday from the Thuriens."

Four and a half thousand miles from Houston, Norman Pacey was sitting on a bench by the side of the Serpentine lake in London's Hyde Park. Strollers in open-necked shirts and summery dresses making the best of the first warm days of the year added a dash of color to the surrounding greenery topped by distant frontages of dignified and imposing buildings that had not changed appreciably in fifty years. That was all they had ever wanted, he thought to himself as he took in the sights and sounds around him. All that people the world over had ever wanted was to live their lives, pay their way, and be left alone. So how had the few with different aspirations always been able to command the power to impose themselves and their systems? Which was the greater evil—one fanatic with a cause, or a hundred men free enough not to care about causes? But caring about freedom enough to defend it made it a cause and its defenders fanatics. For ten thousand years mankind had wrestled with the problem and not found an answer.

A shadow fell across the ground, and Mikolai Sobroskin sat down on the bench next to him. He was wearing a heavy suit and necktie despite the fine weather, and his head was glistening with beads of perspiration in the sunlight. "A refreshing contrast to Giordano Bruno," he commented. "What an improvement it would be if the *maria* were really seas."

Pacey turned his head from staring across the lake and grinned. "And maybe a few trees, huh? I think UNSA has got its work cut out for a while with the proposals for cooling down Venus and oxygenating Mars. Luna's way down the list. Even if it weren't, I'm not sure that anybody has come up with any good ideas for what they could do about it. But who knows? One day, maybe."

The Russian sighed. "Perhaps we had such knowledge in the palm of our hand. We threw it away. Do you realize that we have witnessed what could be the greatest crime in human history? And perhaps the world will never know."

Pacey nodded, waited for a second to assume a more businesslike manner, and asked, "So? . . . What's the news?"

Sobroskin drew a handkerchief from his breast pocket and dabbed his head. "You were right about the coded signals from Gistar when you suspected that they were in response to an independent transmitting facility established by us," he replied.

Pacey nodded without showing surprise. He knew that already from what Caldwell and Lyn Garland had revealed in Washington, but he couldn't say so. "Have you found out how Verikoff and Sverenssen fit in?" he asked.

"I think so," Sobroskin said. "They seem to be part of a global operation of some sort that was committed to shutting down communications of any kind between this planet and Thurien. They used the same methods. Verikoff is a member of a powerful faction that strongly opposed the Soviet attempt to open another channel. Their reasons were the same as the UN's. As it turned out, they were taken by surprise before they could organize an effective block, and some transmissions were sent. Like Sverenssen, Verikoff was instrumental in causing additional messages to be sent secretly, designed to frustrate the exercise. At least we think so. . . . We can't prove it."

Pacey nodded again. He knew that too. "Do you know what they said?" he inquired out of curiosity, although he had read Caldwell's transcripts from Thurien. ´

"No, but I can guess. These people knew in advance that the relay to Gistar would deactivate. That says to me that they must have been responsible. Presumably they arranged it months ago with an independent launching organization, or maybe a part of UNSA that they knew they could trust . . . I don't know. But my guess is that their strategy was to delay the proceedings via both channels until the relay was put out of action permanently."

Pacey stared across the lake to an enclosed area of water on the far side in which crowds of children were swimming and playing in the sun. The sounds of shouting and laughter drifted across intermittently on the breeze. Apart from the confirmation of Verikoff's involvement, he hadn't learned anything new so far. "What do you make of it?" he asked without turning his head.

After a long, heavy silence, Sobroskin replied, "Russia had a tradition of tyranny through to the early years of this century. Ever since it threw off the yoke of Mongol subjugation in the fifteenth century, it was obsessed with preserving its security to the point that the security of other nations became a threat that could not be tolerated. It expanded its borders by conquest and held on to its acquired territories by oppression, intimidation, and terror. But the new lands in turn had borders, and there was no end to the process. Communism changed nothing. It was merely a banner of convenience for rallying gullible idealists and rationalizing sacrifice. Apart from a few brief months in 1917, Russia was no more Communist than the Church of the Middle Ages was Christian."

He paused to fold his handkerchief and return it to his pocket. Pacey waited without speaking for him to continue. "We thought that all that began to change in the early decades of this century with the end of the threat of thermonuclear war and a more enlightened view of internationalism. And superficially it did. Many like myself dedicated themselves to creating a new climate of understanding and common progress with the West as it emerged from its own style of tyranny." Sobroskin sighed and shook his head sadly. "But the Thurien affair has revealed that the forces that plunged Russia into its own Dark Age did not go away, and their purpose has not changed." He looked at Pacey sharply. "And the forces that brought religious terror and economic exploitation to the West have not gone away, either. On both sides they have merely modified their stance to avert what would have guaranteed their destruction along with everything else. There is a web across this whole planet that connects many Sverenssens with many Verikoffs. They pose behind banners and slogans that call for liberation, but the liberation they seek is their own, not that of the people who follow them."

"Yes, I know," Pacey said. "We've uncovered some of it too. What's the answer?"

Sobroskin raised an arm and gestured at the far side of the lake. "For all we know, those children might have grown up to see other worlds under other suns. But the price of that would have been knowledge, and knowledge is the enemy of tyranny in any disguise. It has freed more people from poverty and oppression than all of the ideologies and creeds in history put together. Every form of serfdom follows from serfdom of the mind."

"I'm not sure what you're saying," Pacey said. "Are you saying you want to come over to us or something?"

The Russian shook his head. "The war that matters has nothing to do with flags. It is between those who would set the minds of children free, and those who would deny them Thurien. The latest battle has been lost, but the war will continue. Perhaps one day we will talk to Thurien again. But in the meantime another battle is looming in Moscow for control of the Kremlin, and that is where I must be." He reached behind him for a package that he had placed on the bench behind him and passed it to Pacey. "We have a tradition of ruthlessness in handling our internal affairs that you do not share. It is possible that many people will not survive the next few months, and I could be one of them. If so, I would like to think that my work has not been for nothing." He released the package and withdrew his arm. "That contains a complete record of all that I know. It would not be safe with my colleagues in

Moscow since their future, like my own, is full of uncertainties. But I know that you will use the information wisely, for you understand as well as I do that in the war that really matters we are on the same side." With that he stood up. "I am glad that we met, Norman Pacey. It is reassuring to see that on both sides, bonds exist that are deeper than the colors on maps. I hope that we meet again, but in case that is not to be . . ." He let the words hang and extended a hand.

Pacey stood up and grasped it firmly. "We will. And things will be better," he said.

"I hope so." Sobroskin released his grip, turned, and began walking away along the side of the lake.

Pacey's fingers tightened around the package as he stood watching the short, stocky figure marching jerkily off to keep its appointment with fate, possibly to die so that children might laugh. He couldn't let him, he realized. He couldn't let him walk away without knowing. "Mikolai!" he called.

Sobroskin stopped and looked back. Pacey waited. The Russian retraced his steps.

"The battle was not lost," Pacey said. "There's another channel to Thurien operating right now . . . in the United States. It doesn't need the relay. We've been talking to Thurien for weeks. That was why Karen Heller returned to Earth. It's okay. All the Sverenssens in the world can't stop it now."

Sobroskin stared at him for a long time before the words seemed to register. At last he moved his head in a slow, barely perceptible nod, his eyes expressionless and distant, and murmured quietly, "Thank you." Then he turned away and began walking again, this time slowly, as if in a trance. When he had covered twenty yards or so he stopped, stared back again, and raised his arm in a silent salutation. Then he turned away and began walking once more, and after a few steps his pace lightened and quickened.

Even at that distance Pacey had seen the exultation in his expression. Pacey watched until Sobroskin had vanished among the people walking by the boathouses farther along the shoreline, then turned away and walked in the opposite direction, toward the Serpentine bridge.

chapter twenty-four

Niels Sverenssen's million-dollar home was situated in Connecticut, forty miles from New York City, on the shore side of a two-hundred-acre estate of parkland and trees that overlooked Long Island Sound. The house framed two sides of a large, clover-leaf pool set among terraced banks of shrubs. A tennis court on one side and outbuildings on the other completed the pool's encirclement. The house was fashionably contemporary, spacious, light, and airy, with sections of roof sweeping in clean, unbroken planes from crest almost to ground level in some places to give the complete structure the lines and composition of an abstract sculpture, and drawing back in others to reveal vertical faces and slanted panels of polished brownstone, tiled mosaic, or glass. The imposing central structure rose two levels and contained the larger rooms and Sverenssen's private quarters. One wing fell to single level and comprised six extra bedrooms and additional living space to accommodate the guests of his frequent weekend parties and other functions. The other was two-storied, though not as high as the central portion; it contained offices for Sverenssen and a secretary, a library, and other rooms dedicated to his work.

There was something odd about the history of Sverenssen's house.

Lyn had flown up to New York accompanied by one of Clifford Benson's agents, who had introduced her to a local office of the CIA to examine their records for additional information on Sverenssen. It turned out that his house had been built for him ten years previously by the construction division of Weismand Industries, Inc., a large, diversified corporation. The company was a builder of industrial premises, not private dwellings, which was no doubt why they had called in several outside architects and designers

as consultants. What made the project even stranger was
that Weismand was based in California; why would Sverenssen have used them when any number of qualified
firms existed in the area?

Further checks revealed that Weismand Industries stock
was held mainly by a Canadian insurance consortium that
was closely linked to the same British banking fraternity
that, along with its French and Swiss connections, had
launched Sverenssen's spectacular career upon his sudden
return from obscurity. Had Sverenssen simply been repay-
ing a favor, or were there other reasons why he felt it necessary to build his house using a company with which he
had close, and presumably confidential, connections?

Lyn asked herself the question again as she reclined in a
bikini on a chaise by the pool and studied the house
through the intervening flower beds and shrubs. Sverenssen, wearing sunglasses and clad in a pair of scarlet bathing trunks, was sitting a few feet away at an umbrellaed
table drinking iced lemonade and talking with a man he
had introduced as Larry. A blonde named Cheryl was bask-
ing face-down and naked on another chaise a short distance
away, while two other girls, Sandy and Carol, were laughing and shouting in the pool with a Mediterranean-looking
character by the name of Enrico. Sandy was topless, and
the object of the mêlée in progress was evidently to render
her bottomless as well. Another couple had been around
earlier, but had been gone for the last hour or so. It was
Friday afternoon, and more people were expected to arrive
as the evening wore on, plus a few the next morning. Sverenssen had described the occasion as "a pleasant get-
together of some interesting friends" when Lyn called him
on Thursday morning.

The only thing that seemed even slightly unusual about
the house was the office wing, she decided as she looked at
it. Sverenssen had stressed that it was not open to visitors
when he showed her around earlier. That seemed reasonable enough, but something *was* different about it, she realized. This part of the building wasn't built to the same airy
and open design as the rest of the place, with yards of
plate-glass windows and sliding glass doors that led through
to the inside. Instead it was solid, with small windows set
high off the ground. They looked thick and seemed more

suited to keeping sunlight out, along with everything else. As she looked closer, she was sure that what had seemed at first to be ornamental trim across the windows was in fact carefully disguised bars guaranteed to exclude any possibility of entry—not just by burglars, but by a tank. There were no doors to the outside at all; the only access to the wing was from inside the house. If she hadn't been looking specifically, she would never have noticed it, but the office wing, beneath its veneer of tiled designs and paintwork to match the rest of the house, was virtually a fortress.

The noise from the pool rose to a crescendo that culminated in a shriek as Enrico emerged from a flurry of water and bodies waving the lower half of Sandy's swimsuit triumphantly over his head. "One down, one to go," he yelled.

"Not fair!" Sandy screamed. "I was drowning. That's an unfair advantage."

"Carol's turn," Enrico shouted.

"Like hell," Carol laughed. "That's inequality. Sandy, give me a hand and let's get the bastard." The commotion started all over again.

"It sounds as if they could use some help," Sverenssen said, turning his head to look across at Lyn. "Go ahead and join in. There aren't any restrictions on how you enjoy yourself here, you know."

She let her head fall back on the raised end of the chaise and forced a smile. "Oh, sometimes spectator sports are just as much fun. Anyway, they seem to be managing okay. I'll be the reserve division."

"She's being smart and saving her energy," Larry said, speaking to Sverenssen and sending Lyn a broad wink. She did a good job of pretending not to notice.

"Very wise," Sverenssen said.

"The real fun starts later," Larry explained, grinning. Lyn managed a half-smile, at the same time wondering how she was going to handle that. "We'll find you lots of new friends. They're great people here."

"I can't wait," Lyn said drily.

"Isn't she charming," Sverenssen said, glancing at Larry and looking approvingly back at Lyn. "I met her in Washington, you know—a most fortunate encounter. She has people that she visits here in New York." It made her feel like a piece of merchandise, which was probably a pretty close assessment of her situation. She wasn't especially surprised; if she hadn't been prepared to play along for appearance's sake, she wouldn't have come in the first place.

"I get to Washington a lot," Larry said. "You work there or something?"

Lyn shook her head. "Uh uh. I'm with the Space Arm in Houston—computers, lasers, and people who talk numbers all day . . . but it's a living."

"Ah, but we're going to change that, aren't we, Lyn," Sverenssen said. He looked at Larry. "As a matter of fact I was thinking of something in Washington that would suit her perfectly, and prove far more interesting, I'm sure. Do you remember Phil Grazenby? I had lunch with him one day while I was there recently, and he wants somebody bright and attractive to manage the new agency he's opening. And he is talking about really worthwhile money."

"We'll have to get together there if you make it," Larry said to Lyn. He made a face. "Aw, but that's business, and it's a long time away. Why wait until Washington? We can get to know each other right here. Are you here alone?"

"Yes, she's free," Sverenssen murmured.

"That's great!" Larry exclaimed. "Me too, and I'm the perfect guy for introducing new faces around here. Believe me, honey, you've made the right choice. You must have good taste. Tell you what—you can partner me in one of the games later. So we've got a deal, right?"

"I live for the present," Lyn said. "Suppose we let later take care of itself later, okay?" She stretched to squint up at the sun, then looked at Sverenssen. "Right now all I'm going to be good for is a case of radiation sickness if I don't cover up. I'm going to go inside in the shade and put on something else until it cools down a bit. I'll see you later?"

"By all means, my dear," Sverenssen said. "The last thing we want is for you to end up on the casualty list." Lyn unfolded herself from the chaise and walked toward the house. "I think you may have a little game of playing hard to get to win before—" she heard Sverenssen murmur. The rest was drowned out by another burst of screaming from the pool.

Cheryl raised her head and watched as Lyn disappeared between the shrubs. "You've got nothing to offer, Larry," she said. "Now *I* could show her a good time that's really different."

"So what's wrong with both of us?" Larry asked.

Lyn's room contained twin king-size beds and was as luxuriously furnished and fitted as every other part of the house. She was supposed to be sharing it with somebody called Donna, who hadn't arrived yet. Inside, she took off her bikini and put on a shirt and shorts. Then she stood by the window thinking for a while.

There was a datagrid screen in the room, but she didn't want to make any calls since there was a good chance it was bugged. Anyway she didn't need to if she wanted to get out because Clifford Benson's people had already anticipated that. Inside her shoulder bag in the closet was a microelectronic transmitter that looked like a powder compact but would send out a signal when she unlocked a safety catch and pressed a disguised button. If she pressed it once, a CIA agent would call the house within seconds, posing as a brother with news of a family emergency and stating that a cab was on its way to collect her. If she pressed it three times, the two agents in the airmobile parked a mile down the road from the front gate would arrive in under half a minute, but that option was for use only if she got into real trouble. But she didn't want to get out just yet. The house was empty and quieter than it would be at any time for the rest of the weekend. There would never be another chance like this for a look around the place with little risk of being disturbed. She sure-as-hell wasn't going to chicken out after a couple of hours with nothing to report, she told herself.

She took a deep breath, bit her lip nervously, walked over to the door, inched it open, and listened. Everything seemed still. As she let herself out into the passage a half-stifled giggle came from behind the door opposite. She stopped for a second; there was no other sound, and she moved quietly on toward the central part of the house.

The passage led through a small den into a large, central, open room that rose the full height of the building, one side a sloping wall of glass panels facing the rear of the house. The room was elbow-shaped, thickly carpeted, and had a sunken floor in front of a large fireplace of brickwork, with areas of raised floors around it angling away to openings and stairways which gave access to other parts of the house.

Muffled voices and kitchen noises were coming from one of the corridors, but she didn't detect any sign of Sverenssen's domestic staff in her immediate vicinity. She slowly examined the furnishings, ornaments, the pictures on the walls, and the fittings overhead, but found nothing that looked out of place. After pausing to replay her mental model of the layout, she picked out a narrow corridor that seemed to lead toward the office wing and followed it.

Eventually, after exploring the system of rooms that the corridor brought her to, most of which she had already seen in the course of the quick tour that Sverenssen had given her, she came back to what seemed to be the only door anywhere that opened through into the office wing. She tried the handle gently, but it was locked, as she had expected. When she tapped it with a knuckle, the sound it produced was flat and solid, even from the parts that looked like ordinary wood panels. They might have been wood on the surface, but there was a lot of something else underneath; that door had been put there to keep out a lot more than just drafts. Without a rock drill or an army demolition squad, she wasn't going to get any farther in that direction, so she turned to go back to the center part of the house. As she began moving, she recalled one of the sculptures that she had seen in the central room. It hadn't really struck her at the time, but now as she thought about it again, she realized that there had been something vaguely familiar about it. Surely not, she thought as she tried to visualize it again in her mind. There was no way it could be possible. She frowned, and her pace quickened a fraction.

The piece was standing in an illuminated recess on one side of the brick fireplace—an abstract form rendered in some kind of silver and gold translucent crystal, about eight inches high and mounted on a solid black base. At least, when she glanced over it casually a few minutes earlier she had thought it to be abstract. But now as she picked it up and turned it slowly over in her hands, she became more convinced than ever that its form couldn't be simply a coincidence.

Its lowermost part was a composition of surfaces and shapes that could have meant anything, but projecting up from the center to form the main body of the design was a tapering column of finely carved terraces, levels, and intervening buttresses flowing upward in distinctive curves. Could it represent a tower? she wondered. A tower that she had seen not long ago. Three slim spires continued upward from the top of the main column—three spires supporting a circular disk just below their apexes. A platform? The disk had more finely cut details on its surface. She turned the sculpture over . . . and gasped. There were more details, defining a readily discernible pattern of concentric rings—on the *underside* of the platform! She was looking at a representation of the central tower of the city of Vranix. It couldn't possibly be. But it couldn't be anything else.

Her hand was shaking as she carefully replaced the sculpture in its recess. What the hell had she gotten herself into? she asked herself. Her first urge was to go back to her room, collect her things, and get out fast; but as she forced herself to calm down and her mind to think more clearly, she fought back the feeling. The opportunity to learn more was unique, and it would never present itself again. If there were more, nobody might ever know unless she found it now. She closed her eyes for a second and took a deep breath to summon up her reserves of nervous energy to see it through.

She had to find out more about the office wing, but there seemed no way to get inside. Maybe she could get nearer in some other way . . . under it, perhaps? A house like this would surely have cellars. There would probably be stairs somewhere in the direction of the kitchen. She moved across to the end of the corridor leading that way; voices were still audible, but they sounded closed off. Two doors proved to be closets. The third that she tried revealed a flight of wooden stairs going down. She entered, eased the door shut behind her, and descended.

The cellar that she found herself in looked ordinary, with a bench and some tool racks, a storage space, and lots of pipes and conduits. Machinery of some kind, probably a central air conditioner, was humming behind a louvered door to one side. Two other cellars opened off from this one, one in each direction of the two arms of the house; she moved on into the one leading toward the office wing. It was another storage area, full of boxes and leftover decorating materials. A partition wall with a gap in its center screened off the far end. Lyn crossed the area and peered through the gap. The cellar did not continue on beneath the office wing, but ended at a bare wall on the far side of the small space behind the partition. As Lyn looked around and studied the surroundings, she realized that the part of the cellars she had entered was strangely different from the rest structurally, particularly the blank wall facing her.

The line where the wall and ceiling met was formed by a steel girder that must have measured fifteen inches across the flange at least, and it was supported by two more, equally massive members running down the corners and terminating in what looked like solid concrete foundations partly visible along the lower part of the walls and going down into the floor. The ceiling, too, was reinforced with girders and cross-ties gusseted at the angles. All was painted white to blend in with the general background of the other cellar rooms, and the casual visitor would probably never have noticed; but to somebody who was looking for the unusual and who had a special interest in that end of the house, the heavy structures stood out unmistakably.

So the office wing itself was not over any part of the cellars but was built on solid ground, and she was looking at one side of its foundation and underpinning. It was built from materials and in a fashion that would have supported a battleship. What could there be upstairs that would have crushed the foundations of an ordinary house and had made all this necessary? she wondered.

And then she remembered the holes she had seen punched through the concrete at McClusky.

A Thurien interstellar communications system contained a microscopic, artificially generated, black-hole toroid when it was switched on and operating.

But that idea was even more insane. The house had been built ten years before. Nobody had heard of the Ganymeans, let alone Thurien, in 2021.

She backed slowly away from the partition and turned dazedly back toward the stairs.

At the top of the stairs she stopped for a while to give the thumping in her chest time to slow down and to bring her reeling mind under some kind of control. Then she opened the door a fraction and brought her eye close to it just in time to catch a glimpse of Sverenssen moving out of sight behind an angle in the wall back near the corner room. He had been turning his head from side to side as he moved, as if he were looking for something . . . or somebody. Lyn immediately erupted into a new spasm of shaking and shivering. Suddenly Navcomms and Houston seemed very far away. If she ever got out of this, she'd never want to leave the coziness of her own office again.

If Sverenssen was looking for her, he would already have tried knocking on the door of her room. The part of her that felt guilty told her that she needed a reason for not being there. She thought for a few seconds, then let herself out into the corridor and went the other way, into the kitchen. A minute later she reemerged holding a cup of coffee and began making her way back to the guest section of the house.

"Oh, *there* you are." Sverenssen's voice sounded from behind her when she was halfway across one of the raised floors around the periphery of the corner room. She froze; had she done anything else, the coffee and the cup would have been all over the carpet. Sverenssen came out of one of the side rooms as she turned to face him. He was still wearing his bathing trunks, but had put sandals on his feet and thrown a shirt loosely over his shoulder. He was eying her uncertainly, as if he were mildly suspicious about something but not sufficiently sure of himself to be direct.

"I went to get some coffee," she said, as if it weren't obvious. Immediately she felt like the classical dumb broad; but at least she managed to stop herself from following up her statement with an inane laugh. She was certain that Sverenssen was looking past her shoulder at the sculpture in its recess. She could picture it in her mind's eye with a neon sign in six-inch letters above shouting, "I HAVE BEEN MOVED." Somehow she resisted the compulsion to turn her head.

"I wouldn't have thought that somebody from Houston would be bothered by the sun," he remarked. "Especially somebody with a tan like yours." His voice was superficially casual, but had an undertone that invited an explanation.

For a second or two she felt trapped. Then she said, "I just wanted to get away for a while. Your friend . . . Larry, was starting to come on a bit strong. I guess I need time to get used to this."

Sverenssen looked at her dubiously, as if she had just confirmed his fears about something. "Well, I do hope you manage to loosen up a little before too much longer," he said. "I mean, the whole idea of being here is to enjoy oneself. It would be such a shame if one person allowed her inhibitions to ruin the atmosphere for everyone else, wouldn't it."

Despite her confusion, Lyn couldn't keep a sharp edge out of her voice. "Look . . . I didn't exactly come here expecting this," she told him. "You never said anything about playing musical people."

A pained expression came over Sverenssen's face. "Oh dear, I do hope you're not going to start preaching any middle-class morals. What did you expect? I said I would be entertaining some friends, and I expect them to be entertained and made to feel welcome in a manner appropriate to their tastes."

"*Their* tastes? That's very nice of you. They must love you for it. What about my tastes?"

"Are you suggesting that *my* acquaintances fail to come up to *your* standards? How amusing. You've already made your tastes quite plain—you aspire to luxury and the company that goes with it. Well, you have them. Surely you don't expect anything in this life to come free."

"I didn't expect to be treated like a piece of candy to be dangled in front of those overgrown kids out there."

"You're talking like an adolescent. Do I not have a right to expect you, as my guest, to behave sociably in return for my hospitality? Or did you imagine that I was some kind of a philanthropist who opens his home to the world for reasons of pure charity? I can assure you that I am nothing of the kind, and neither is anybody else who has the intelligence to understand the realities of life."

"Who said anything about charity? Doesn't respect for people come into it anywhere?"

Sverenssen sneered. Evidently it didn't. "Another middle-class opiate. All I can say to you is that whatever fantasies you have been harboring appear to have been sadly unfounded." He sighed and shrugged, apparently having already dismissed the matter as a lost cause. "The opportunity is yours to enjoy a life quite free from worries financial or otherwise, but seizing it requires that you throw off a lot of silly protective notions left over from childhood and make a pragmatic assessment of your situation."

Lyn's eyes blazed, but she managed to keep her voice under control. "I think I just made it." Her tone said the rest.

Sverenssen appeared indifferent. "In that case I suggest that you call yourself a cab without further delay and return to your world of misplaced romanticism and unfulfillable dreams," he said. "It really makes no difference to me. I can get somebody else here within the hour. The choice is entirely yours."

Lyn stood absolutely still until she had fought down the urge to hurl her coffee in his face. Then she turned away and, mustering the effort to maintain her calm, walked off in the direction of her room. Sverenssen followed her coldly with his eyes for a few seconds, then shrugged contemptuously and hurried out through a side door to rejoin the others at the pool.

Two hours later Lyn was sitting in a Washington-bound plane beside the CIA agent who had accompanied her to New York. Around them sat families, couples, people alone, and people together; some were dressed in business suits, some in jackets, and others in casual shirts, sweaters, and jeans. They were talking, laughing, reading, and sleeping—just ordinary, sane, civilized people, minding their own business. She wanted to hug every one of them.

chapter twenty-five

In the illusory world of VISAR's creations, Karen Heller was half a billion miles tall and floating in space. A loosely coupled binary system of Ping-Pong-ball-sized stars, one yellow and one white, was revolving slowly in front of her while a myriad more glowed as pinpoints of light in the infinite blackness stretching away on every side. The center of mass of the two stars was located at one of the foci of a highly elongated ellipse, superposed on the view by VISAR, tracing the orbit of the planet Surio.

Hanging in space beside Heller and looking like some cosmic god contemplating the material universe as if it were a plaything, Danchekker extended an arm to point at the planet sliding along its trajectory in VISAR's speeded-up simulation. "The conditions that Surio encounters at opposite ends of the ellipse are completely different," he said. "At one end it's in close proximity to both its suns and therefore very hot; at the other it's remote from them and therefore quite cool. Its year alternates between a long oceanic phase during the cool period, and an equally long hot phase during which Surio possesses practically no hydrosphere at all. Eesyan tells me it's unique among the worlds that the Thuriens have discovered so far."

"It's fascinating," Heller said, enthralled. "And you're saying that life has emerged there despite those conditions. It sounds impossible."

"I thought so too," Danchekker told her. "Eesyan had to show me this before I'd believe otherwise. That was what I wanted to show you. Let's go down and take a closer look at the planet itself."

They seemed to be rushing toward Surio as VISAR responded to the verbal cue. The stars vanished away behind them, and the planet grew rapidly and swelled into a sphere that flattened out beneath them as they descended from the sky. It was in a cool, oceanic phase, and as they plunged downward they shrank in size so that the sea stretching from horizon to horizon looked normal. Then they were underwater, with strange alien life forms swimming and twisting in the ocean around them.

A black, fishlike creature, vaguely reminiscent of some shark species, seemed to single itself out, their viewpoint moving progressively as they followed it. Then, as VISAR altered the content of the information being injected into their visual systems, the body and soft tissues of the creature became a translucent haze to reveal clearly the structure of its skeleton. The light filtering through the water from above went out suddenly, then came on again, then continued to flicker steadily like a slow-motion stroboscope. The image of the fish remained motionless in front of them. "Day and night cycles," Danchekker explained in answer to Heller's questioning look. "VISAR is speeding them up and freezing this image artificially so that we can observe it. Have you noticed yet that the intensity of the daylight periods is increasing?"

Heller had. She also noticed that the creature's skeleton was beginning to change subtly. Its spine was shortening and getting thicker, and the bones inside its fins were elongating and differentiating into clearly discernible jointed segments. Also, the fins were slowly migrating toward the creature's underside. "What's happening there?" she asked, pointing.

"It's an adaptation that I thought you might be interested in seeing," Danchekker replied. "The year is growing warmer, and the oceans around us have begun evaporating rapidly." VISAR obligingly raised them high above the surface again to confirm the statement. The face of the planet had already changed beyond recognition since their arrival. The oceans had retreated to a series of steep-sided basins, uncovering broad shelves that now connected into vast land masses what had previously been scattered islands and minor continents. Carpets of vegetation were creeping outward behind the receding shorelines and upward into what had been barren mountainous regions. A dense cloud blanket had formed, from which continuous rains were drenching the highlands.

They watched the surface transformation continue for a

while, and then descended once more to follow local events in a shallow estuary formed where a river draining water from the rainy areas inland had carved a trench across the exposed continental shelf to one of the diminishing ocean basins. The creature that they had studied previously was now an amphibian living on the mud flats, with rudimentary legs already functioning and a fully differentiated, mobile head. "It dissolves its bones by means of specially secreted fluids triggered by environmental cues, and grows a new skeleton more suited to an existence in its changed environment," Danchekker commented. "Quite remarkable."

To Heller this seemed an overly drastic solution. "Couldn't it stay a fish and simply move out into the oceans?" she asked.

"Very soon there won't be any oceans," Danchekker told her. "Wait and see."

The oceans shrank into isolated pools surrounded by mud, and then dried up completely. As the climate grew hotter the rivers from the highlands became trickles as they flowed downhill, finally evaporating away before reaching the basins, and what had been the seabeds turned into deserts. The vegetation receded across the shelves until it had been reduced to scattered oases of life clinging doggedly to the highest plateaus and mountain peaks. The creature had migrated upward and was now a fully adapted land dweller with a scaly skin and prehensile forelimbs, not unlike some of the earliest terrestial reptiles. "Now it's in its fully transformed state," Danchekker said. "As Surio goes through a year, the animal cycles are repeated from one extreme of morphology to the other. An amazing example of how tenacious life can be under adverse conditions, wouldn't you agree."

The day lengthened as light periods from the two suns overlapped, and then shortened again as Surio came around the tip of its orbit and began its long swing outward into another cold phase. The vegetation began advancing down the mountainsides, the creature's limbs commenced reducing, and the whole sequence went slowly into reverse. "Do you think intelligence could ever emerge in a place like this?" Heller asked curiously.

"Who can say?" Danchekker replied. "A few days ago I

would have said that what we have just witnessed was unthinkable."

"It's fantastic," Heller murmured in awe.

"No, it's reality," Danchekker said. "Reality is far more fantastic than anything that unaided human imagination could ever devise. The mind could not, for example, visualize a new color, such as infrared or ultraviolet. It can only manipulate combinations of elements that it has already experienced. Everything that is truly new can only come from the Universe outside. And uncovering the truth that lies out there is, of course, the function of science."

Heller looked at him suspiciously. "If I didn't know you better, I'd think you were trying to start an argument," she teased. "Let's get back before this conversation goes any further and see if Vic's called in yet."

"I agree," Danchekker said at once. "VISAR, back to McClusky, please."

He got up from the recliner, moved out into the corridor of the perceptron, and waited for a moment until Heller emerged from one of the other cubicles. They exited through the antechamber, were conveyed down to ground level, and a few seconds later were walking along the side of the apron toward the mess hall.

"I'm not going to let you get away with that," Heller began after a short silence. "I started out in law, which has a lot to do with uncovering the truth too, you know. And its methods are just as scientific. Just because you scientists need computers to do your work for you, that doesn't give you a monopoly on logic."

Danchekker thought for a moment. "Mmm . . . very well. If one is hampered by mathematical illiteracy, law does provide something of an alternative, I suppose," he conceded loftily.

"Oh really? I would say it demands far more ingenuity. What's more, it taxes the intellect in ways that scientists never have to bother about."

"What an extraordinary statement! And how would that be, might I ask?"

"Nature is often complex, but never dishonest, Professor. How often have you had to contend with deliberate falsification of the evidence, or an opponent with as much vested interest in obscuring the truth as you have in revealing it?"

"Hmph! And when was the last time that you had to subject your hypotheses to the test of rigorous proof by experiment, eh? Answer me that," Danchekker challenged.

"We do not enjoy the luxury of repeatable experiments," Heller responded. "Not many criminals will oblige by recommitting their crimes under controlled laboratory conditions. So, you see, we have to keep our wits sharp enough to be right the first time."

"Hmm, hmm, hmm . . ."

They had timed their return to McClusky well. Hunt called just as they entered the control room. "How quickly can you get back here?" Danchekker asked him. "Karen has had some remarkable thoughts which after some reflection I find myself forced to agree with. We need to discuss them at the earliest opportunity."

"Gregg and I are leaving right away," Hunt told him. "We've just heard about John's visit to the city. It puts a whole new light on everything. We need to talk to the board ASAP. Can you fix it?" It meant that Packard's report of Pacey's meeting with Sobroskin had arrived in Houston, and a meeting with Calazar and the Thuriens was urgently called for.

"I'll see to it immediately," Danchekker promised.

An hour later, while Hunt and Caldwell were still on their way and after Danchekker had made arrangements with Calazar, Jerol Packard called from Washington. "Hold everything," he instructed. "Mary's back. We're putting her on a plane up to you right now. Whatever you think you already know, I guarantee it's not half of it. She just blew our minds here. Don't do anything until she's talked to you."

"I'll see to it immediately," Danchekker sighed.

chapter twenty-six

For Imares Broghuilio, Premier of the Federation of Jevlenese Worlds and head of the Thurien civilization's Jevlenese component, the past few months had been beset with unexpected crises that had threatened to disrupt the carefully laid plans of generations.

First there had been the sudden and completely unpredictable reappearance of the *Shapieron* on Earth. The Thuriens had known nothing about that until the signal sent out by the Terrans at the time of the ship's departure was somehow relayed directly to VISAR without going through JEVEX. How that had happened had been, and still was, a mystery. Broghuilio had been left with no choice but to preempt awkward questions by going to Calazar first with the Jevlenese account of what had transpired, namely that the Jevlenese had felt apprehensive at the thought of inviting Thurien intervention in a situation already made precarious by the belligerence and instability of the Terrans and therefore, rightly or wrongly, had decided to postpone announcing any news until the ship was safely clear of Earth. The explanation had by necessity been hastily contrived, but at the time Calazar had seemed to accept it. The device that had relayed the signal was not something that the Thuriens had placed near the solar system, Calazar had insisted in response to Broghuilio's accusation; the Thuriens had not broken their agreement to leave Earth surveillance to the Jevlenese. Privately, however, Broghuilio's experts had been able to suggest no other explanation for the relay. It seemed possible, therefore, that the Thuriens were, after all, more prudent than he had given them credit for.

This suspicion had been reinforced some months later when the Thuriens secretly reopened their dialogue with Earth for the unprecedented purpose of double-checking information supplied by JEVEX. Broghuilio had been unable to challenge this development openly since doing so would have revealed the existence of information sources on Earth that the Thuriens could not be allowed to discover, but with some fast footwork he had neutralized the attempt, at least for the time being, by securing control of the Earth end of the link. His bid to counter the surprise Soviet move of opening a second channel had not proved as successful, and he had been forced to resort to more desperate measures by having the link put out of action—something which he had avoided until that point because of the risk of the Thuriens electing to continue the dialogue by more direct means. He had calculated that they would hesitate for a long time before breaking their agreement in so open a fashion.

The Thuriens had not chosen to divulge their contact with Earth by mentioning the incident. Broghuilio's advisors had interpreted this as confirmation that the measures taken to persuade the Thuriens that Earth was responsible for the destruction of the relay had succeeded. A further implication was that the image that had been created of a hostile and aggressive Earth had survived intact, which, it was felt, would suffice to dissuade the Thuriens from taking things further by contemplating a landing.

After some anxious moments, therefore, the gamble appeared to have paid off. The only remaining problem was the *Shapieron*, outward bound from the solar system and already beyond the point where an interception could be staged with only a moderate risk of disturbing planetary orbits. Broghuilio had guessed that the Thuriens, being the cautious breed that they were, would play safe and allow an ample safety margin. Accordingly he had put the relay first in order of priority, using it as a test of how easily the Thuriens would accept a suggestion of an overtly hostile act on the part of the Terrans. If they did accept it, then the odds would be acceptable they would hold Earth responsible for the destruction of the *Shapieron* as well. The Thuriens had passed the test, and now only a matter of minutes stood between Imares Broghuilio and the elimination of the last element of a problem that had been plaguing him for too long.

He felt a deep sense of satisfaction at a difficult challenge met as he stood at one end of the War Room, deep below a mountain range on Jevlen, surrounded by his entourage of advisors and military strategists, following the reports coming in through JEVEX from the instruments tracking the *Shapieron* many light-years away. As he looked slowly around at the ranks of generals in the all-black uniforms of the Jevlenese military and at the arrays of equipment bringing information from and carrying his directions to every corner of his empire, he felt a deep and stirring anticipation of fulfillment at the approaching appointment that destiny had set for him. It was a manifestation of the Jevlenese superiority and iron willpower of which he was both the last in a long succession of architects and the ultimate personification, and which would soon assert itself across the Galaxy.

The uniforms were not yet worn openly, and this place was not known to the Ganymeans who visited Jevlen and on occasion remained for protracted periods for various reasons. Organization, planning, and training operations were still conducted in secret, but already an embryonic officer corps was ready to emerge with an established command chain to a nucleus of trained active units upon which a carefully worked-out recruitment program could begin building at short notice. The factories hidden deep beneath the surface of Uttan, one of the remote worlds controlled by Jevlen, had been steadily accumulating weapons and munitions for several years, and the plans to switch the whole Jevlenese industrial and economic machine fully to a war footing were in an advanced stage.

But the time was not yet quite right. On one or two occasions the events of the past few months had almost prompted him into being swayed by the overreactions and panickings of his lesser aides and acting prematurely. But by thinking clearly and with courage and sheer willpower he had steered them through the obstacles and annihilated the problems one by one until finally only the matter of the *Shapieron* remained. And that would be disposed of very soon now. He had been tested and found not to be lacking, as the Cerians would discover for themselves as soon as the inhibiting yoke of Thurien had been cast off. But not yet . . . not quite yet.

"Target closed to within one scan period," JEVEX announced. The atmosphere in the room was tensely expectant. The *Shapieron* was approaching the device that had been transferred into its path via a toroid projected several days earlier in order for the gravitational disturbance to be outside the range of any Thurien tracking instruments following the ship at the time. The device itself, packing a nucleonic punch of several gigatons and programmed to detonate automatically on proximity, was gravitationally passive and would not register on the Thurien tracking system, which operated by computing the spatial location of the stress field produced by the ship's drive. JEVEX's statement meant that the bomb would go off before the tracking system delivered its next update.

Garwain Estordu, one of Broghuilio's scientific advisors, seemed nervous. "I don't like it," he muttered. "I still say we should have diverted the ship and interned it at Uttan or somewhere. This . . ." He shook his head. "It's too extreme. If the Thuriens find out, we'll have no defense."

"This is a unique opportunity. The Ganymeans are psychologically ready to blame Earth," Broghuilio declared. "Such an opportunity will not come again. Such moments are to be seized and exploited, not wasted by timidity and indecision." He looked at the scientist disdainfully. "That is why I command and you follow. Genius is knowing the difference between acceptable risk and rashness, and then being willing to play for high stakes. Great things were never achieved by half-measures." He snorted. "Besides, what could the Thuriens do? They cannot match strength with strength. Their heritage has left them sadly ill-equipped to deal with the realities of the Universe on the terms that the Universe dictates."

"They have survived for a long time, nevertheless," Estordu observed.

"Artificially, because they have never faced the test of opposition," General Wylott declared, taking up the party line from one side of Broghuilio. "But trial by strength is the Universe's natural law. When the more natural course of events unfolds, they will not prevail. They are not tempered to spearhead the advance into the unknowns of the Galaxy."

"There speaks a soldier," Broghuilio said, scowling balefully at Estordu and the rest of the scientists. "You bleat like Ganymean sheep while you are in the safety of the fold, but who will protect you when you go out onto the mountain to face the lions?".

At that moment JEVEX spoke again: "Latest update now analyzed." A hush fell at once across the Jevlenese War Room. "Target no longer registering in scan data. All traces have vanished. Destruction effected with one-hundred-percent success. Mission accomplished."

The tension lifted abruptly, and a flurry of relieved murmurings broke out on all sides. Broghuilio permitted a grim smile of satisfaction as he drew himself up to his full height to acknowledge the congratulations being directed toward him from around the floor. His chest swelled with the feeling of power and authority that his uniform symbolized. Wylott turned and threw his arm out in a crisp Jevlenese salute acknowledging the leader. The rest of the military followed suit.

Broghuilio made a perfunctory return, waited a few moments for the excitement to subside, then raised an arm. "This is but a small foretaste of what is to come," he told them, his voice booming to carry to the far corners of the room. "Nothing will stand in our path when Jevlen marches forward to its destiny. The Thuriens will be wisps of straw lost in the hurricane that will sweep across first the solar system, and then the Galaxy. DO YOU DARE TO FOLLOW ME?"

"WE DARE!" came the response.

Broghuilio smiled again. "You will not be disappointed," he promised. He waited for the room to quiet and then said in a milder tone, "But in the meantime we have our good *duty* to perform for our Ganymean masters." His mouth writhed in sarcasm as he wrung out the final word, causing grins to appear on the faces of some of his followers. He raised his head a fraction. "JEVEX, contact Calazar through VISAR and request that Estordu, Wylott, and I see him at once on a matter of gravest urgency."

"Yes, Excellency," JEVEX acknowledged. A short delay followed. Then JEVEX reported, "VISAR informs me that Calazar is currently in conference and asks if the matter can wait."

"I have just received news of the most serious nature," Broghuilio said. "It cannot wait. Convey my apologies to Calazar and inform VISAR that I must insist on going to

Thurien immediately. Tell VISAR we have reason to believe that the *Shapieron* has met with a catastrophe."

A minute or two went by. Then JEVEX announced, "Calazar will receive you immediately."

chapter twenty-seven

At Houston, Caldwell had described to Hunt the network of real power that had lain hidden across the world possibly for centuries, operating to preserve privilege and promote self-interest by opposing and controlling scientific progress. The attempt first to frustrate and then to shut down communications with Thurien had seemed consistent with such a power structure and policy.

Then Danchekker had called in a visibly excited state from McClusky with the news that Karen Heller had opened up a completely new dimension to the whole situation. On arriving in Alaska hours later, Hunt and Caldwell learned of the evidence for supposing that the Jevlenese had been interfering with Earth's technological development since the dawn of its history while they grew in numbers, reorganized, and profited from their access to Ganymean knowledge. This notion had proved so astonishing that nobody made the connection between the two sets of information until Lyn arrived from Washington with the staggering announcement that not only was Sverenssen in communication with the Jevlenese, as he apparently had been for many years, but that, from the evidence of the sculpture, the Jevlenese were still staging physical visits to Earth, at least intermittently. In other words the Jevlenese had not been interfering merely way back in early times; what Pacey and Sobroskin had started to uncover parts of right now was a Jevlenese-controlled operation.

This news immediately threw up a host of whole new questions. Was Sverenssen simply a native Terran working as a collaborator, or was he actually a Jevlenese agent injected into Earth's society and using the identity of a Swede killed in Africa years before? Whatever the answer, how many more like him were there and who were they? Why had the Jevlenese been distorting their reports to make Earth appear warlike? Could the reason be that they wanted a pretext to justify to the Ganymeans their maintaining a military strength of their own as an "insurance" against the possibility of future terrestrial aggression beyond the solar system? If so, who had the Jevlenese been intending to direct the military strength against—the Thuriens, to end what was seen as an era of Ganymean domination; or Earth, to settle an account that went back fifty thousand years? If Earth, had the activities of Sverenssen's network to promote strategic disarmanent and peaceful coexistence during recent decades been a deliberate ploy calculated to render Earth defenseless and set it up to be taken over as a going industrial and economic concern instead of the ball of smoking rubble that would have been left had it been able to offer resistance? And if this were true, how had the Jevlenese then intended to deal with the Thuriens, who would hardly have just sat and done nothing while it all happened?

There had been more than enough reasons to talk straight away to the Ganymeans, so Calazar had called everybody together at Thurios—including Garuth, Shilohin, and Monchar from the *Shapieron*. After the ensuing debate had droned on for over two hours, VISAR interrupted to announce that something had just destroyed the object substituted for the *Shapieron*. Minutes later Imares Broghuilio, Premier of the Jevlenese group of worlds, contacted Calazar to request an immediate appointment.

Sitting off to one side of a room in the Government Center at Thurios with the others from McClusky, Hunt waited tensely for the confrontation with the first Jevlenese they would meet face to face, who were due to appear at any second. Garuth and his two companions from the *Shapieron* formed another small group on the far side; and Calazar, Eesyan, Showm, and a few more Thuriens were clustered at one end. The Ganymeans were still somewhat shaken by what they had learned of deception and subterfuge that went beyond their wildest imaginings. Even Frenua Showm had conceded that without the apparently uniquely human ability to penetrate such deviousness, it was doubtful that the Ganymeans would ever have reached the bottom of it. It seemed that being suspicious of another's motives was something that came with the conditioning of predatorial thinking, and Ganymeans simply were not predators. "On Earth they say you must set a thief to catch a thief," Garuth had remarked. "It appears just as true that to catch a human you must set a human."

"They might be great scientists, but they'd make lousy lawyers," Karen Heller murmured in Danchekker's ear. Danchekker snorted and said nothing.

Calazar was curious to see how far the Jevlenese would go in their fabrications if fed sufficient rope; also, there was more that he hoped to learn from them before exposing just how much he knew. For these reasons he did not want to confront them immediately with the presence of the Terrans and the *Shapieron* Ganymeans. He therefore instructed VISAR to edit out of the datastream sent to JEVEX, and hence to the participants on Jevlen, all information pertaining to those two groups. It meant that Hunt, Garuth, and their companions would, after a fashion, be there, but remain completely invisible to the Jevlenese. Such a tactic was a flagrant violation of good manners and Thurien law, and unprecedented throughout the many centuries for which VISAR had been in use. Nonetheless Calazar decreed that by their own actions the Jevlenese had warranted making this occasion an exception. Hunt was looking forward to the consequences.

"Premier Broghuilio, Secretary Wylott, and Scientific Advisor Estordu," VISAR announced. Hunt stiffened. Three figures materialized at the end of the room opposite Calazar and the Thuriens. The one in the center had to be Broghuilio, Hunt decided at once. He stood six-foot-three at least, and had dark eyes that blazed fiercely from a face made all the more intimidating by a mane of thick, black hair and a pugnacious mouth surrounded by a short, cropped beard. His body was clad in a short coat of gold sheen worn over a mauve tunic covering a barrel-like chest and powerful torso.

"What of the *Shapieron*?" Calazar demanded in an unusually clipped voice. Hunt would have expected that for one of Broghuilio's rank some form of opening formality

would have been appropriate. The flicker of surprise that
he caught on the faces of the other two Jevlenese seemed to
say so too. One of them looked directly at where Hunt was
sitting and stared straight through. It was a strange feeling.

"I regret the intrusion," Broghuilio began. His voice was
deep and harsh, and he spoke stiffly, in the manner of
somebody performing a duty that demanded a greater show
of feeling than he could muster readily. "We have just received news of the most serious nature: all traces of the
ship have disappeared from our tracking data. We can only
conclude that it has been destroyed." He paused and cast
his eyes around the room for effect. "The possibility that
this could be the result of a deliberate act cannot be dismissed."

The Thuriens stared back in silence for what seemed a
long time. They did not attempt playacting any show of
concern or dismay . . . or even surprise. The first glimmer of uncertainty crept into Broghuilio's eyes as he
searched the Ganymean faces for a reaction. Evidently this
was not going as he had anticipated.

One of the other two, also tall, dressed somberly in dark
blue and black, with icy blue eyes, slicked-back silver hair,
and a florid face that tended toward puffiness, seemed not
to have read the signs. "We tried to warn you," he said,
spreading his hands imploringly in a good imitation
of sharing the anguish that the Thuriens were presumably
supposed to be feeling at that moment. "We urged you to
intercept the ship before now." That was hardly true;
possibly he placed a lot of faith in his powers of suggestion.
"We told you that Earth would never allow the *Shapieron*
to reach Thurien."

Across the room Garuth's eyes turned steely, and his ex-
pression was about as close to malevolence as that of a
Ganymean could get. "Patience, Garuth," Hunt called out.
"You'll get your shots in before long."

"Luckily Ganymeans possess plenty of that," Garuth replied. The Jevlenese didn't hear a thing. It was uncanny.

"Really?" Calazar responded after a pause. He sounded
neither convinced nor impressed. "Your concern is most
touching, Secretary Wylott. You almost sound as if you believe your own lies."

Wylott froze with his mouth hanging half open, obviously taken completely aback. The third Jevlenese, who had to be Estordu, was a lean, thin-faced man with a hooked nose, wearing an elaborate two-piece garment of light green embroidered with gold over a yellow shirt. He threw up his hands in shock. "Lies? I don't understand. Why do you say that? You have been tracking the ship yourselves. Hasn't VISAR confirmed the data?"

Broghuilio's expression darkened. "You have insulted us," he rumbled ominously. "Are you telling us that VISAR does not corroborate what we have said?"

"I'm not disputing the data," Calazar told him. "But I would advise you to think again about your explanation for it."

Broghuilio drew himself up to his full height to face the Thuriens squarely. Evidently he was going to brazen it out. "Explain yourself, Calazar," he growled.

"But we are waiting for *you* to explain *your*self," Showm said from one side of Calazar. Her voice was low, little more than a whisper, but it held the tension of a tightly wound spring. Broghuilio jerked his face around to look at her, his eyes darting suspiciously from side to side as a sixth sense told him he had walked into a trap. "Let's forget the *Shapieron* for a moment," Showm went on. "How long has JEVEX been falsifying its reports of Earth?"

"What?" Broghuilio's eyes bulged. "I don't understand. What is the—"

"How long?" Showm asked again, her voice rising suddenly to cut the air sharply. Her tone and the expressions of the other Thuriens spelled out clearly that any attempt at a denial would have been futile. The hue of Broghuilio's face deepened to purple, but he seemed too stunned to form a reply.

"What grounds do you have for such an accusation?" Wylott demanded. "The department that conducts the surveillance is responsible to me. I consider this a personal attack."

"Evidence?" Showm uttered the word offhandedly, as if the demand were too absurd to take seriously. "Earth disarmed strategically in the second decade of its current century and has pursued peaceful coexistence ever since, but JEVEX has never mentioned it. Instead JEVEX has reported nucleonic weapons deployed in orbit, radiation projectors sited on Luna, military installations across the solar system, and a whole concoction of fictions that have never existed. Do you deny it?"

Estordu was thinking frantically as he listened. "Corrections," he blurted suddenly. "Those were corrections, not falsifications. Our sources led us to believe that Earth's governments had discovered the surveillance, and they had conspired to conceal their warlike intentions. We instructed JEVEX to apply a correction factor by extrapolating the developments that would have taken place if the surveillance had not been discovered, and we presented these as facts in order to insure that our protective measures would not be relaxed." The stares coming from the Thuriens were openly contemptuous, and he finished lamely, "Of course, it is possible that the corrections were . . . somewhat exaggerated unintentionally."

"So I ask you again, how long?" Showm said. "How long has this been practiced?"

"Ten, maybe twenty years . . . I can't remember."

"You don't know?" She looked at Wylott. "It's your department. Have you no records?"

"JEVEX keeps the records," Wylott replied woodenly.

"VISAR," Calazar said. "Obtain the records from JEVEX for us."

"This is outrageous!" Broghuilio shouted, his face turning black with anger. "The surveillance program is entrusted to us by long-standing agreement. You have no right to make such a demand. It has been negotiated."

Calazar ignored him. A few seconds later VISAR informed them, "I can't make any sense of the response. Either the records are corrupted, or JEVEX is under a directive not to release them."

Showm did not seem surprised. "Never mind," she said, and looked back at Estordu. "Let's give you the benefit of the doubt and say twenty years. Therefore anything reported by JEVEX before that time will not have been altered. Is that correct?"

"It might have been more," Estordu said hastily. "Twenty-five . . . thirty, perhaps."

"Then let's go back further than that. The Second World War on Earth ended eighty-six years ago. I have examined some of the accounts of events during that period as reported by JEVEX at the time. Let me give you some examples. According to JEVEX, the cities of Hamburg, Dresden, and Berlin were devastated not by conventional saturation bombing but by nuclear weapons. According to JEVEX, the Korean conflict in the 1950s escalated into a major clash of Soviet and American forces; in fact, nothing of the kind took place. Neither were tactical nuclear devices used in the Middle East wars of the '60s and '70s, nor was there an outbreak of Sino-Soviet hostilities in the 1990s." Showm's voice became icy as she concluded, "And neither was the *Shapieron* taken into captivity by a United States military garrison on Ganymede. The United States has never had a military garrison on Ganymede."

Estordu had no answer. Wylott remained immobile, staring straight in front of himself. Broghuilio seemed to swell with indignation. "We asked for *evidence!*" he thundered. "That is not evidence. Those are allegations. Where is your proof? Where are your witnesses? Where is your justification for this intolerable behavior?"

"I'll take it," Heller said, rising to her feet beside Caldwell. There was no way she was going to let him beat her to it this time. From where Hunt was sitting nothing appeared to change, but the way the three Jevlenese heads snapped around to gape at her left no doubt that VISAR had suddenly put her on stage.

Before any of them could say anything, Calazar spoke. "Allow me to introduce somebody who might satisfy your requirement—Karen Heller, Special Envoy to Thurien from the State Department of the United States."

Estordu's face had turned white, and Wylott's mouth was opening and closing ineffectively without producing any sound. Broghuilio was standing with his fists clenched and paroxysms of rage sweeping in visible tremors through the length of his body. "We have many witnesses," Calazar said. "Nine billion of them, in fact. But for now, a few representatives will suffice." The Jevlenese's eyes opened wider as the remainder of the Terran delegation became visible. None of them glanced in the opposite direction, indicating that Calazar had not yet instructed VISAR to reveal Garuth and the others from the *Shapieron.*

Karen Heller had compiled a long list of suspicions concerning Jevlenese manipulations of events on Earth, none of which she could prove. The opportunity for bluffing the confirmation from the Jevlenese would never again be quite what it was at that moment, and she plunged ahead without giving them a second's respite. "Ever since the Lambians were taken from Luna to Thurien after the Minervan war, they have never forgotten their rivalry with the Cerians. They have always seen Earth as a potential threat that would one day have to be eliminated. In anticipation of that day, they took advantage of their access to Ganymean sciences and devised an elaborate scheme to insure that their rival would be held in a state of backwardness and prevented from reemerging to challenge them until they had absorbed the last ounce of the knowledge and technologies that they thought would make them invincible." She was unconsciously addressing her words to Calazar and the Thuriens as if they were judge and jury, and the proceedings were a trial. They remained silent and waiting as she paused for a moment to shift to a different key.

"What is knowledge?" she asked them. "*True* knowledge, of reality as it is, as opposed to how it might appear to be or how one might wish it to be? What is the only system of thought that has been developed that is effective in distinguishing fact from fallacy, truth from myth, and reality from delusion?" She paused again for a second and then exclaimed, "*Science!* All the truths that we *know*, as opposed to beliefs which some choose blindly to adopt as if the strength of their convictions could affect facts, have been revealed by the rational processes of applied *scientific method*. Science alone yields a basis for the formulation of beliefs whose validity can be *proved* because they predict *results* that can be *tested*. And yet . . ." Her voice fell, and she turned her head to include the Terrans sitting around her. "And yet, for thousands of years the races of Earth clung persistently to their cults, superstitions, irrational dogmas, and impotent idols. They refused to accept what their eyes alone should have told them—that the magical and mystical forces in which they trusted and which they aspired to command were fictions, barren in their yield of results, powerless in prediction, and devoid of useful application. In a word, they were *worthless*, which of course made any consequences *harmless*. And this, from the Lambian, or Jevlenese, viewpoint, constituted a re-markably convenient situation. It was too convenient to be just a coincidence." Heller turned her head to look coldly at the Jevlenese. "But we know that it was not merely a coincidence. Far from it."

Danchekker turned an astonished face to Hunt, leaned closer, and whispered, "How extraordinary! I'd never have believed I'd hear *her* make a speech like that."

"I'd never have believed it, either," Hunt muttered. "What have you been doing to her?"

Still looking at the Jevlenese, Heller went on, "We know that the early beliefs in the supernatural were established by miracle workers whom *you* recruited and trained, and injected as agents to found and popularize mass movements and countercultures based on myth, and to undermine and discredit any tendencies toward the emergence of the rational systems of thought that could lead to advanced technology, mastery over the environment, and a challenge to your position. Can you deny it?" She could read on their faces that her bluff had succeeded. They were standing rigid and unmoving, too numbed with shock to respond. Feeling more confident, Heller looked over at the Thuriens and resumed, "The superstitions and religions of Earth's early cultures were carefully contrived and implanted. The beliefs of the Babylonians, the Mayas, the ancient Egyptians, and the early Chinese, for example, were based on notions of the supernatural, magic, legend, and folklore, to sap them of any potential for developing logical methods of thought. The civilizations that grew upon those foundations built cities, developed arts and agriculture, and constructed ships and simple machines, but they never evolved the sciences that could have unlocked true power on any significant scale. They were harmless."

Low mutterings and murmurs were rippling among the Thuriens as some of them only began to realize for the first time the full extent of what the Terrans had uncovered. "And what of Earth's later history?" Calazar asked, mainly for the benefit of those Thuriens who had not been as involved in everything as he.

"The same pattern traces through to modern times," Heller replied. "The saints and apparitions who created legends by conveying messages and performing miracles were agents sent from Jevlen to reinforce and reassure. The cults and movements that perpetuated beliefs in spiritualism and the occult, in paranormal sciences and other such nonsenses that were in vogue in Europe and North America in the nineteenth century, were manufactured in an attempt to dilute the progress of true science and reason. And even in the twentieth century, the so-called popular reactions against science, technology, positive economic growth, nuclear energy, and the like were in fact carefully orchestrated."

"Your answer?" Calazar demanded curtly, staring at Broghuilio.

Broghuilio folded his arms, drew a long breath, and turned slowly to face directly toward where Heller was standing. He seemed to have recomposed himself and was apparently far from conceding defeat yet. He glared defiantly at the Terrans for a few seconds and then turned his head toward Calazar. "Yes, it was so. The facts are as stated. The motive, however, was not as described. Only a *Terran* mind could conceive of such motives. They are projecting into us their own evils." He threw out an arm to point at the Terrans accusingly. "You know the history of their planet, Calazar. All the violence and bloodthirstiness that destroyed Minerva is preserved today on Earth. I do not have to repeat to you their unending history of quarrels, wars, revolutions, and killing. And that, mark you, was *despite* our efforts to contain them! Yes, we planted agents to steer them away from the sciences and from reason. Do you blame us? Can you imagine the holocaust that would be sweeping across the Galaxy today if they had been allowed to return into space tens of thousands of years ago? Can you imagine the threat that it would have posed to you as well as to us?" He looked again at where the Terrans were sitting, and scowled distastefully. "They are primitives. Insane! They always will be. We kept their planet backward for the same reason that we would not give fire to children—to protect them as well as ourselves, and you too. We would do the same again. I have no apologies to offer."

"Your actions betray your words," Frenua Showm retorted. "If you believed that you had pacified a warlike planet, you would have been proud of the achievement.

You would not have concealed the fact. But you did the opposite. You presented a falsified picture of Earth that showed, it as warlike when in fact it was moving in exactly the direction that you should have considered desirable. You successfully delayed its advancement until its Minervan inheritance had been diluted sufficiently for it to advance wisely. But not only did you conceal that fact, you distorted it. How do you explain that?"

"A temporary aberration," Broghuilio replied. "Underneath nothing has changed. We altered the more recent developments so that you would not be misled. A final solution to the problem was still called for."

Heller was thinking rapidly as she listened. The "final solution" had to mean that the Jevlenese had used Earth's belligerence as an excuse to maintain their own military forces as she had suspected. It seemed to support another line of thought that her researches had caused her to wonder about, and here was an opportunity to test it. But to do so she would have to resort to bluff again. "I challenge that explanation," she said. "What I have described so far is only part of what the Jevlenese have been doing." All the heads in the room turned toward her. "By the time of the nineteenth century, it was obvious that Western civilization was rapidly spreading science and industrial technology across the globe in spite of all their efforts. At that point the Jevlenese changed their tactics. They actually began to stimulate and accelerate scientific discovery by leaking information in various quarters that precipitated major breakthroughs." She turned her head a fraction. "Dr. Hunt. Would you like to comment, please?"

Hunt had been expecting the question. He stood up and said, "The sharp discontinuities and nonlinearities that attended the major breakthroughs in physics and mathematics in the late nineteenth and early twentieth centuries have been a mystery for a long time. In my opinion, such conceptual revolutions could not have happened in the time they did without some external influence."

"Thank you," Heller said. Hunt sat down. She looked back at the Thuriens, more than a few of whom appeared puzzled. "Why would the Jevlenese do such a thing when their policy up until then had been to retard their rival? Because they were forced to accept the fact that they would not be able to keep Earth back any longer. Therefore, if Earth was about to become a high-technology planet anyway, the Jevlenese decided to use their already established infrastructure of influence to steer that advancement in such a direction that their rival would eliminate itself. In other words they set out to engineer events in such a way that the sciences which they themselves had helped develop would be used not to eradicate the scourges that had plagued mankind throughout history, but to wage war on a global scale and with unprecedented ferocity." She watched Broghuilio carefully as she spoke, and saw that she had hit the mark. Now was the moment to go for the kill.

"Deny that it was Jevlenese agents who infiltrated the European nobility at the end of the nineteenth century and created the rash of internecine jealousies that culminated in the horrors of the First World War," she challenged in a suddenly loud and cutting voice. "Deny that it was a Jevlenese-controlled organization that seized control of Russia after the 1917 revolution and developed the prototype for the totalitarian police state. And deny that you set up a Jevlenese group in the wreckage of postwar Germany to resurrect the hatreds that the League of Nations was formed to resolve by peaceful means. They were led by some very carefully selected and trained individuals, weren't they? What happened to the real Adolf Hitler? Or perhaps you operated from behind the throne—Alfred Rosenberg, perhaps?" The three Jevlenese did not have to say anything. Their frozen postures and stunned expressions provided all the confirmation needed. Heller turned her head toward the Thuriens and explained, "World War II was supposed to be nuclear. The necessary scientific, political, social, and economic prerequisites had all been taken care of. It didn't quite work as planned, but it came frighteningly close."

A new wave of mutterings broke out among the Thuriens. Heller waited for it to subside and then concluded in a quieter voice, "The tensions continued for over half a century, but despite the continuing Jevlenese efforts, the global catastrophe that they sought never quite took place." The next part was pure guesswork, but she continued without any change of tone. "They concluded that one day they would have to confront their rival themselves, and so embarked on a program of exaggerating Earth's wars and armament developments to justify to the Thuriens their creation of a 'protective' strength of their own. At the same time they reversed their policy on Earth and used their network to defuse tensions, promote disarmament, and permit its people to develop their talents and resources creatively in the ways they had always wanted to. The object of this, of course, was to turn Earth into a defenseless target. To maintain the justification for increasing their own armed forces, they supplied the Thuriens with what gradually became a total fantasy manufactured inside JEVEX."

Heller paused again, but this time there was no sound. She wheeled around to point at the Jevlenese, and her voice rose to an accusing shout. "*They* accuse *us* of killing each other, when all the time they know full well that *their agents* have orchestrated the worst episodes of havoc and bloodshed in Earth's history. *They* have murdered more people than all the leaders of planet Earth put together." Her voice fell to an ominous whisper. "But the unexpected arrival of the *Shapieron* threw all those plans into confusion. Here was a group of Ganymeans who would expose the lie if they were allowed to make contact with Thurien. Now we see the *real* reason why its existence was never disclosed." The color was draining from Broghuilio's face. Wylott had turned scarlet and seemed to be having difficulty breathing, while on Broghuilio's other side Estordu was dripping with perspiration and shaking visibly. Across the room Garuth, Shilohin, and Monchar were sitting forward tensely as they sensed the moment approaching for them to reveal themselves.

"And now we come to the question of the *Shapieron*," Heller said. Her tone was almost soft, but menace was glittering in her eyes as she fixed them upon the Jevlenese. "We heard earlier a suggestion that Earth had sabotaged it. The suggestion is based on what we have seen to be lies. The *Shapieron* was never in any jeopardy at any time during the six months it was on Earth. On the contrary, our relationship with the Ganymeans was very friendly. We have ample records to prove that." She paused for a second. "But we do not have to rely on those records to prove that Earth did nothing to harm that ship or its occupants. We have far more convincing evidence than that." Across the room Garuth and his companions stiffened. Calazar was about to give the instruction to VISAR.

And the Jevlenese vanished.

The floor where they had been standing was suddenly empty. Surprised murmurs broke out on all sides. After a few seconds VISAR announced, "JEVEX is cutting all its links. I have no access to it at all. It is ignoring requests to reconnect."

"What do you mean?" Calazar asked. "You have no communications to Jevlen at all?"

"The whole planet is isolating itself," VISAR replied. "All the Jevlenese worlds are disconnecting. JEVEX has detached and become an independent system. No further communications or visits within its operating zone are possible."

The consternation breaking out among the Thuriens meant that something very unusual was happening. Hunt turned to meet an inquiring look from Danchekker and shrugged. "It looks as if JEVEX has broken off diplomatic relations," he said.

"What do you suppose it means?" Danchekker asked.

"Who knows? It sounds like a siege. They're inside their own zone controlled by JEVEX, and JEVEX isn't talking to anyone. So I guess that short of sending ships in there's no way anyone can get at them now."

"It might not be that easy," Lyn said from Hunt's other side. "If they've been setting themselves up as a Galactic police force, there could be a problem there."

A strange silence fell over the Thuriens. Calazar and Showm looked uneasily at each other; Eesyan looked down and fiddled awkwardly with his knuckles. The Terrans and the *Shapieron* Ganymeans looked at them curiously. Eventually Calazar looked up with a sigh. "Your demonstration of how to get truth from the Jevlenese was remarkable. You were wrong on one of your assumptions, however. We have never agreed to any proposal by the Jevlenese that they maintain a military force either to counter possible aggressive expansionism by Earth or for any other reason."

Heller didn't seem too reassured by the statement as she

sat down. "You know now what they're like," she said. "How can you be certain that they haven't been secretly arming themselves."

"We can't," Calazar admitted. "If they have, the implications of the situation that would confront both of our civilizations are serious."

Caldwell was puzzled. He frowned for a moment as if to check over what was going through his mind, stared at Heller for a second, then looked across at Calazar. "But we assumed that was why they invented the phony stories," he said. "If that wasn't the reason, then what was?"

The Thuriens looked even more uncomfortable. Showm turned to Calazar and spread her hands as if conceding there was something that couldn't be concealed any longer. Calazar hesitated, then nodded. "It is clear to us now why the Jevlenese falsified their reports," Showm said, turning her head to address the whole room. An expectant hush fell as she paused. She took a long breath and resumed, "There is more to this, which up until now we have felt it wiser not to talk about . . ." She turned her head momentarily sideways to glance at Garuth and his colleagues, ". . . to any of you." They waited. She went on, "For a long time the Ganymeans have been haunted by the specter of Minerva repeating itself, and this time possibly spilling out into the Galaxy. Just under a century ago, the Jevlenese persuaded our predecessors that Earth was on the verge of doing just that, and urged a solution to contain Earth's expansion permanently. The Thuriens commenced working on a contingency plan accordingly. Because of the false picture that we were given by the Jevlenese, we have continued with the preparations to implement that plan. If we had known the true situation on Earth, we would have abandoned the idea. Clearly the Jevlenese were misleading us in order to harness our technology to contain their rival permanently and eliminate it from competing with them across the Galaxy in times to come. That was what Broghuilio meant when he referred to the final solution."

The Terrans needed a few seconds to digest what Showm was saying. "I'm not sure I follow what you mean," Danchekker said at last. "Contained Earth's expansion by what means? You don't mean by force, surely."

Calazar shook his head slowly. "That would not be the

Ganymean way. We said contain, not oppose. The choice of word was deliberate."

Hunt frowned as he tried to fathom what Calazar was driving at. Contain Earth? It was too late for that; mankind's civilization had already spread a long way beyond Earth. Then it could only mean . . . His eyes widened suddenly in disbelief. Surely not even Thurien minds could think on a scale as vast as that. "Not the solar system!" he gasped, staring at Calazar in awe. "You're not telling us you were going to shut in the whole solar system."

Calazar nodded gravely. "We devised a scheme for using our gravitic science to create a shell of steepened gravitational gradient that nothing—not Earthmen, nor Earthmen's aggression, nor even light itself, would escape from. Inside the shell conditions would be normal, and Earth would be free to pursue whatever way of life it chose. And beyond the shell, so would we." Calazar looked around and took in the appalled stares coming back at him. "That was to have been our final solution," he told them.

chapter twenty-eight

And so for the first time in the long history of their race the Ganymeans found themselves at war, or at least in a situation so akin to war that the differences were academic. Their response to the Jevlenese was swift and devastating. Calazar ordered VISAR to withdraw all its services from the Jevlenese who were physically present on Thurien and the other Ganymean-controlled worlds. A whole population who throughout their lives had taken for granted the ability to communicate or travel instantly anywhere at any time, to have information of every description available on request, and who had relied completely on machines for every facet of their existence, found themselves suddenly cut off from the only form of society that they knew how to function in. They were isolated, powerless, and panic-stricken. Within hours they had been reduced to helplessness and were speedily rounded up and detained, as much for their own safety and sanity as to keep them out of any unlikely mischief, until the Ganymeans decided what to do with them. The whole Jevlenese contingent scattered across all the Ganymean worlds had thus been eliminated in a single lightning blow that left no survivors.

That left the enemy headquarters planet of Jevlen together with its system of allied worlds, which were serviced by JEVEX and not by VISAR. This, it turned out, was going to be a far harder nut to crack since it was unassailable by simply sending in ships as Hunt had thought of doing earlier.

The problem was that Jevlen was light-years away from Gistar, and the only way of getting ships there was through black-hole toroids projected by VISAR. But when VISAR attempted to project a few test beams into JEVEX's operating zone, it found that JEVEX was able to disrupt the beams easily; evidently the Jevlenese had been planning to break from Thurien for some time. Neither was it feasible for VISAR to transfer ships through toroids projected to just beyond the fringe of JEVEX's effective jamming radius to make their own way to Jevlen from there. The problem in this case was that all the Thurien vessels relied on power, as well as navigational and control signals, beamed through the Thurien h-grid from centralized generating and supervisory centers, and JEVEX could disrupt those beams just as easily. In other words, nothing could get into the Jevlenese system as long as JEVEX was operating, and the only way to stop it from operating was to send something in. It was a deadlock.

More serious was the possibility that the Jevlenese might have been amassing weapons secretly for a long time, and, in anticipation of exactly the kind of situation that now existed, building vessels to transport them that operated with self-contained propulsion and control capability. If so, they would be in a position to move their forces with impunity into VISAR-controlled regions and proceed unopposed with whatever threats or actions they had been planning. Time was crucial. The events at Thurios had clearly forced the Jevlenese to make their break sooner than they had intended, and the more swiftly the Thuriens reacted, the better the chances would be of catching the Jevlenese at a disadvantage with their preparations incomplete. But what kind of reaction was possible from a race that had no experience of resisting an armed opponent, possessed no weaponry to react with even if they had, and couldn't get near their opponent anyway? Nobody had any solution to offer until a day after the confrontation in Thurios, when Garuth, Shilohin, and Eesyan requested a private audience with Calazar.

"No disrespect, but your experts are missing the obvious," Garuth said. "They've taken advanced Thurien technology for granted for so long that they can't think in any other terms."

Calazar raised his hands protectively. "Calm down, stop waving your arms about, and tell me what you're trying to say," he suggested.

"The way to get in at Jevlen is in orbit over Thurien right now," Shilohin said. "The *Shapieron*. It might be obsolete by your standards, but it's got its own on-board power, and ZORAC flies it perfectly well without any need for anybody's h-grid."

For a few seconds Calazar stared mutely back at them in astonishment. What they had said was true—none of the scientists who had been debating the problem without a break since JEVEX had severed its connections had even considered the *Shapieron*. It seemed so obvious that Calazar was convinced there had to be a flaw. He looked questioningly at Eesyan.

"I can't see why not," Eesyan said. "As Shilohin says, there's no way JEVEX could stop it."

There was something deeper behind this proposal, Calazar sensed as he searched Garuth's face. What was equally obvious, and had not been said, was that even if JEVEX could not prevent the *Shapieron* from physically entering its operating zone, it might well have plenty of other means at its disposal for stopping the ship once it got in there. Garuth had been itching to confront the Jevlenese yesterday, and had been frustrated at the last moment. Was he now ready to risk himself, his crew, and his ship in recklessly settling something that he saw as a personal vendetta against Broghuilio? Calazar could not permit that. "The

Shapieron would still be detected," he pointed out. "The Jevlenese will have sensors and scanners all over their star system. You could be walking into anything. A ship on its own, isolated from any communications with Thurien, with no defensive equipment of any kind? . . ." He let the sentence hang and allowed his expression to say the rest.

"We think we have an answer to that," Shilohin said. "We could fit the ship's probes with low-power h-link communicators that wouldn't register on JEVEX's detectors and deploy them as a covering screen twenty miles or so out from the *Shapieron*. That would give them, effectively, faster-than-light communications back to the ship's computers. ZORAC would be able to generate cancellation functions that the probes would relay outward as out-of-phase signals added to the optical and radar wavelengths reflected from the ship so that the net readings registered at a distance in any direction would be zero. In other words it would be electromagnetically invisible."

"It would still show up on h-scan," Calazar objected. "JEVEX could detect its main-drive stress field."

"We don't have to use main drive at all," Shilohin countered. "VISAR could accelerate the ship in h-space and eject it from the exit port with sufficient momentum to reach Jevlen passively in a day. When it got near, it could retard and maneuver on its auxiliaries, which radiate below detection threshold."

"But you'd still have to project an exit port outside the star system," Calazar said. "You couldn't hide that scale of disturbance from JEVEX. It would know that something was going on."

"So we send another ship or two as decoys . . . unmanned ships," Shilohin replied. "Let JEVEX jam those and think that's all there is to it. In fact that would be a good way of diverting its attention from the *Shapieron*."

Calazar still didn't like the proposal. He turned away, clasped his hands behind his back, and paced slowly across the room to stare at the wall while he thought it over. He was not a technical expert, but from what he knew, the scheme was workable theoretically. Thurien ships carried on-board compensators that interacted with a projected toroid, compacting it and minimizing the gravitational disturbance created around it. That was why Thurien ships could travel out of a planetary system and transfer into h-space after only a day of conventional cruising. The *Shapieron* had not been built with such compensators, of course, which was why months had been necessary for it to clear the solar system. But even as the thought struck him, Calazar realized there was a simple answer to that too: the *Shapieron* could be equipped with a Thurien compensator system in a matter of days. Anyway, if there were serious technical difficulties, Eesyan would already have found them.

Calazar did not have to ask what the purpose of the exercise would be. JEVEX consisted of a huge network similar to VISAR, and in addition to its grid of h-communications facilities possessed a dense mesh of conventional electromagnetic signal beams that it employed for local communications over moderate distances around Jevlen. If the Thuriens could intercept one, or preferably several, of those beams, simulating regular traffic in order to be inconspicuous, there was a chance that they might be able to gain access to the operating nucleus of JEVEX and crash the system from the inside. If they succeeded, the whole Jevlenese operation would come down with it, and the same thing would happen to the whole empire that had happened on a smaller scale to the Thurien Jevlenese a day earlier. But the problem was how to get the necessary hardware physically into a position to intercept the beams. Eesyan's scientists had been debating it for over a day and so far had produced no usable suggestions.

At last Calazar wheeled around to face the others again. "Very well, you seem to have that side of it all figured out," he conceded. "But tell me if I'm missing something. There's something else that you haven't mentioned: the kind of computing power you'd need to bring down a system like JEVEX would be phenomenal. ZORAC could never do it. The only system in existence that would stand a chance is VISAR, but you couldn't couple VISAR into ZORAC because that would require an h-link, and you couldn't close an h-link while JEVEX is running."

"That's a gamble," Eesyan admitted. "But ZORAC wouldn't have to crash the whole JEVEX system. All it would have to do is open up a channel to let VISAR in. Our idea is to equip the *Shapieron* and a set of its daughter probes with h-link equipment that VISAR can couple in through, and disperse them to intercept a number of channels into JEVEX. Then if ZORAC can just get far enough into JEVEX to block its jamming capability, we can throw the whole weight of VISAR in behind ZORAC and hit JEVEX from all directions at once. VISAR would do the rest."

There was a chance, Calazar admitted to himself. He didn't know what the plan's odds of success were, but it was a chance; and Garuth's idea was more than anybody else had been able to come up with. But the vision in his mind's eye of the *Shapieron* venturing alone into a hostile region of space, unarmed and defenseless, and the tiny ZORAC pitting itself against the might of JEVEX, was chilling. He walked slowly back to the center of the room while the other three Ganymeans watched him intently. It was clear from their expressions what they wanted him to say. "You realize, of course, that this could mean subjecting your ship to what could be a considerable risk," he said gravely, looking at Garuth. "We have no idea what the Jevlenese have waiting there. Once you are in, there will be no way for us to get to you if you encounter difficulties. You would not even be able to contact us without revealing your presence, and even then the channel would immediately be jammed. You would be entirely on your own."

"I know that," Garuth answered. His expression had hardened, and his voice was uncharacteristically tense. "*I* would go. I would not ask any of my people to follow. It would be for them to decide individually."

"I have already decided," Shilohin said. "A full crew would not be necessary. More would come forward than would be needed."

Inside, Calazar was beginning to yield to the irrefutable logic of their argument. Time was precious, and the effectiveness of anything that could be done to thwart the Jevlenese ambitions would be amplified by an enormous factor with every day saved. But Calazar knew, too, that Garuth's scientists and ZORAC would not possess the knowledge of Thurien computing techniques viably to wage a war of wits with JEVEX; the expedition would have to include some expertise from Thurien as well.

Eesyan seemed to read his mind. "I will go too," he said quietly. "And there will also be more volunteers among my experts than we will require. You can count on it."

After a long, heavy silence, Shilohin said, "Gregg Caldwell has a method that he uses sometimes when he has to make a difficult decision quickly: forget the issue itself and consider the alternatives; if none of them is acceptable, the decision is made. It fits this situation well."

Calazar drew a long breath. She was right. There were risks, but doing nothing and having to face at some later date what the Jevlenese had been preparing anyway, with their plans correspondingly more advanced, might be taking a greater risk in the long run. "Your opinion, VISAR?" he said.

"Agreed on all points, especially the last," VISAR replied simply.

"You're confident about taking on JEVEX?"

"Just let me at it."

"You could operate effectively with access only through ZORAC? You could neutralize JEVEX on that basis?"

"Neutralize it? I'll tear it apart!"

Calazar's eyebrows lifted in surprise. It sounded as if VISAR had been talking with Terrans too much. His expression grew serious again as he thought for a few seconds longer, then nodded once. The decision was made. At once his manner became more businesslike. "The most important thing now is time," he told them. "How much thought have you given to that? Do you have a schedule worked out yet?"

"A day to select and brief ten of my scientists, five days to equip the *Shapieron* with entry compensators for it to clear Gistar in minimum time, and five days to fit the ship and probes with h-link and screening hardware," Eesyan replied at once. "But we can stage those jobs in parallel and conduct testing during the voyage. We'll need a day to clear Gistar and another to make Jevlen from the exit port, plus an extra day to allow for Vic Hunt's Murphy Factor. That means we could be leaving Thurien in six days."

"Very well," Calazar said, nodding. "If we are agreed that time is vital, we must not waste any. Let us begin immediately."

"There is one more thing," Garuth said, then hesitated.

Calazar waited for a few seconds. "Yes, Commander?"

Garuth spread his hands, then dropped them to his sides again. "The Terrans. They will want to come too. I know them. They will want to use the perceptron to come physically to Thurien to join us." He looked appealingly at Shilohin and Eesyan as if for support. "But this . . . war will be fought purely with advanced Ganymean technologies and techniques. The Terrans would be able to contribute nothing. There is no reason why they should be allowed to place themselves at risk. On top of that, we have been helped enormously so far by information from Earth, and we might well be again. In other words we cannot afford to be without the communications channel to McClusky at a time like this. They have a more valuable function to perform there. Therefore I would rather we deny any such request . . . for their own good as much as anything else."

Calazar looked into Garuth's eyes and saw again the hardness that he had glimpsed at the moment when Broghuilio had announced the *Shapieron*'s destruction. It was as Calazar had suspected—a personal score to be settled with Broghuilio. Garuth wanted no outsiders, not even Hunt and his colleagues. It was a strange reaction to find in a Ganymean. He looked at Shilohin and Eesyan and could see that they had read it too. But they would not offend Garuth's pride and dignity by saying so. And neither would Calazar.

"Very well," he agreed, nodding. "It will be as you request."

chapter twenty-nine

Night surrounded the Soviet military jet skimming northward over the ice between Franz Josef Land and the Pole. The clash that had occurred inside the Kremlin and throughout the ruling hierarchy of the Soviet Union was still far from resolved, and the loyalties of the nation's forces were divided; the flight was therefore being made secretly to minimize risks. While Verikoff sat rigidly between two armed guards at the back of the darkened cabin and the half-dozen other officers dozed or talked in lowered voices in the seats around him, Mikolai Sobroskin stared out at the blackness through the window beside him and thought about the astounding events of the past forty-eight hours.

The aliens didn't stand up very well under interrogation, he had discovered. At least, the alien Verikoff hadn't. For that was what Verikoff was—a member of a network of agents from the fully human contingent of Thurien that ran the surveillance operation, and who had been infiltrating Earth's society all through history. Niels Sverenssen was another. The demilitarization of Earth had been engineered in preparation for their emergence as a ruling elite to be established by the Jevlenese, with Sverenssen as planetary overlord. Earth would eventually be deindustrialized to provide a playground for the aristocracy of Jevlen and extensive rural estates as rewards for its more faithful servants. How a planet reduced to this condition would support the portion of its population not required for labor and services had not been explained.

Once this much had been established, the value of Verikoff's skin had fallen markedly. To save it he had offered to cooperate, and to prove his credibility he had divulged details of the communications link between Jevlen and its operation on Earth, located at Sverenssen's home in Connecticut and installed by Jevlenese technicians employed by a U.S. construction company set up as a front for some of the Jevlenese's other activities. Through this link Sverenssen had been able to report details of the Thurien attempt to talk to Earth secretly via Farside and had received his instructions for controlling the Earth end of the dialogue. Sobroskin had detected no hint that Verikoff knew anything about the U.S. channel that Norman Pacey had mentioned. Despite the elaborate Jevlenese information-gathering system, therefore, Sobroskin had concluded that at least that secret had been kept safe.

Sobroskin had decided that the first step toward breaking up the network would have to be the severing of the link through Connecticut while its discovery was still unknown, and the Jevlenese were therefore off guard and vulnerable. Obviously that could only be accomplished with the help of somebody in Washington, and since nobody, not even Verikoff, knew the full extent of the network or who might be among its members, that had meant Norman Pacey. Sobroskin had called "Ivan" at the Soviet embassy and, using a prearranged system of innocuous-sounding phrases, conveyed a message for relaying to Pacey. A call from the U.S. State Department to an office in Moscow eight hours later, stating that hotel reservations had been made for a group of visiting Russian diplomats, confirmed that the message had been received and understood.

"Five minutes to touchdown," the pilot's voice sounded from an intercom in the darkness overhead. A low light came on in the cabin, and Sobroskin and the other officers began collecting the cigarette packages, papers, and other items strewn around them, then put on heavy arctic coats in preparation for the cold outside.

Minutes later the plane descended slowly out of the night and settled in the center of a dim pool of light that marked the landing area of an American scientific research base and arctic weather station. A U.S. Air Force transport stood in the shadows to one side with its engines running and a small group of heavily muffled figures huddled in front of it. The door forward of the cabin swung open, and a set of steps telescoped downward. Sobroskin and his party descended and walked quickly across the ice with Verikoff and the two officers escorting him making up the middle of the group. They halted briefly in front of the waiting Americans.

"You see, it wasn't such a long time, after all," Norman Pacey said to Sobroskin as they shook hands through the thick gloves they were wearing.

"We have much to talk about," Sobroskin said. "This whole thing goes further than your wildest imaginings."

"We'll see," Pacey replied, grinning. "We haven't exactly been standing still, either. You may have some surprises coming too."

The group began boarding while behind them the engine note of the Soviet jet rose, and the plane disappeared back into the night. Thirty seconds later the American transport lifted off, its nose swinging northward onto the course that would take it over the Pole and down across eastern Canada to Washington, D.C.

* * *

It was late evening at McClusky. The base was quiet. A short distance from the line of parked aircraft brooding silently in the subdued orange glow cast by lamps spaced at intervals along the perimeter fence, Hunt, Lyn, and Danchekker were staring in the direction of the constellation Taurus.

They had argued, inveigled, and protested that the business was as much Earth's as anybody's, and that if Garuth and Eesyan were risking themselves, honor and justice demanded that Earthpeople should also be there to share whatever consequences were in store, but to no avail; Calazar had been adamant that the perceptron could not be moved. They had not dared call in higher authority in the form of the UN or the U.S. Government to back their case because there was no way of knowing who might be working for the Jevlenese. Therefore they could do nothing but resign themselves to hoping and waiting.

"It's crazy," Lyn said after a while. "They've never fought a war in their history, and now they're going in on a commando raid to try and take out a whole planet. I never knew Ganymeans were like that. Do you think Garuth has flipped out or something?"

"He just wants to fly his ship one more time," Hunt murmured and snorted humorlessly. "You'd think that after twenty-five million years of it he'd have had enough." The thought had also crossed Hunt's mind that perhaps Garuth had decided to go down with it like the proverbial captain. He didn't say so.

"A noble gesture, nevertheless," Danchekker said. He shook his head with a sigh. "But I feel uneasy. I don't see why the perceptron had to remain here. That sounded like an excuse. Even if we could not have contributed anything technically, we could still contribute something else which I fear Garuth and his friends might well find themselves in need of if they encounter difficulties."

"How do you mean?" Lyn asked.

"I'd have thought it was obvious," Danchekker answered. "We have seen already how differently Ganymean and human minds function. The Jevlenese may possess some talent for intrigue and deception, but they are not the masters of the art that they appear to imagine. It requires a human insight, however, to recognize and exploit their blunders."

"They've only had Ganymeans to deal with," Hunt said. "We've had a few thousand years of practice handling one another."

"My point entirely."

A short period of silence elapsed, then Lyn said absently, "You know what I'd like to see? If those Jevlenese guys think they're so smart, I'd like to see them come up against some real professionals and find out what deception is all about. And with VISAR on our side, we ought to have the right equipment to do it with, too."

Hunt looked at her and frowned. "What are you talking about?"

"I'm not sure really." She thought for a moment and shrugged. "I was just thinking that with JEVEX faking all that information for years and feeding it to the Thuriens, it would be kind of nice if we did something like that to them . . . just for the hell of it."

"Did something such as what?" Hunt asked, still puzzled.

Lyn looked back up at the night sky with a distant expression. "Well, imagine this as a for-instance. JEVEX must have all those stories about weapons and bombs and things that it's been inventing stored away someplace in its records, right? And someplace else in its records, it must have all the genuine information about Earth that it's collected through its surveillance system—in other words, all the stuff about Earth that it knows is true. But how does it know which is which? How does it know which records are real and which are phony?"

"I don't know." Hunt shrugged and reflected for a second. "I suppose it'd have to tag them with some kind of header-label system."

"That's what I thought," Lyn said, nodding. "Now suppose VISAR did manage to get inside JEVEX, and it scrambled those labels around so that JEVEX couldn't tell the difference anymore. It could make JEVEX really believe all those stories were true. Imagine what would happen if it started saying things like that. Broghuilio and his bunch would go bananas. See what I mean—it'd be nice to watch."

"What a delightful thought," Danchekker murmured, intrigued. An evil smile crept across his face as he pictured it. "How unfortunate that we never mentioned it to Calazar. War or not, the Ganymeans would have been unable to resist it."

Hunt was smiling distantly too as he thought about it. The idea could be taken a lot further than Lyn had suggested. If VISAR got into JEVEX's memory system sufficiently to change the labels, it would only be a short step from there for it to add in some extra fiction of its own devising. For example, if it could gain access to the part of JEVEX that handled the incoming surveillance data from Earth, VISAR could probably make JEVEX think anything it wanted about what was happening on Earth—such as a whole armada being readied to blow Jevlen out of the Galaxy. As Danchekker had said, a delightful thought.

"You could fake an agreement with Thurien to use their toroids to transport a strike force to Jevlen," Hunt said. "That way you could have JEVEX saying it would arrive in days. And if you'd already scrambled its records from way back, that would be fully consistent with what it would think it had been reporting for years. The Jevlenese would know it hadn't . . . but then if they've never questioned it all their lives, maybe they wouldn't know what to think. What do you think Broghuilio would make of that?"

"He'd have a heart attack," Lyn said. "What do you think, Chris?"

Danchekker turned serious all of a sudden. "I have no idea," he replied. "But this is an example of precisely the kind of thing I was referring to. The idea of finding ways to bewilder a foe is something that comes naturally to humans but not to Ganymeans. They are going to attempt the straightforward approach of simply crashing JEVEX—direct, logical, and without any thought of deviousness. But suppose that the Jevlenese have prepared themselves by providing backup systems capable of operating autonomously even without JEVEX. If so, the *Shapieron* could still find itself exposed to considerable dangers when it reveals itself by bringing down JEVEX, assuming it succeeds. I trust you see my point." Danchekker directed a solemn stare at the other two, then continued: "But on the other hand, if their plan had been to *control* JEVEX rather than disable it, and to disorient the Jevlenese by subterfuge of the kind you have been describing, then perhaps all manner of opportunities to exploit and exacerbate the resulting situation further might have presented themselves, which as things stand will never be created." He looked up at the sky again and shook his head sadly. "I can't for a moment imagine our Ganymean friends adopting such a tactic, I'm afraid."

The amusement of a few minutes earlier had drained from Hunt's face as he listened. He had tried, Caldwell had tried, and Heller had tried, but still he couldn't escape the lingering discomfort that perhaps they could have tried harder still. Now that Danchekker had voiced them, he recognized the same thoughts that he had been suppressing. "We should have gone with them," he said in a heavy voice. "We should have made Gregg bully them into it."

"I doubt that it would have made any difference," Danchekker said. "Couldn't you see that Garuth had a personal score to settle with Broghuilio? He didn't want anybody else involved as a matter of principle. Calazar knew it too. Nothing we could have said would have made any difference."

"I guess you're right." Hunt sighed. He looked toward Taurus again, stared at it for a while, then suddenly snapped out of his reverie and looked from side to side at the others. "It's getting cold," he said. "Let's go inside and get some coffee."

They turned and began walking slowly back across the apron toward the mess hall.

Many light-years away, the *Shapieron* slipped quietly out of orbit above Thurien. For a little over a day VISAR tracked it to beyond the Gistar system and monitored its transfer through h-space to a point just outside JEVEX's zone of control on the fringe of the Jevlenese star system. The power and control beams to the two unmanned decoy ships sent with it were promptly jammed, and while they drifted helplessly on the edge of JEVEX-space, the *Shapieron* continued moving inward and vanished from the view of VISAR's instruments into the cloak of impenetrability that surrounded the enemy star.

chapter thirty

The construction floating in space was in the form of a hollow square. It measured over five hundred miles along a side. From each of its corners a bar, twenty miles thick, extended diagonally inward to support the two-hundred-mile-diameter sphere held in the center. The surfaces of the outer square bristled with angular protuberances, sections of ribbing, and domed superstructures, all etched harshly in black and shades of metallic gray, and immense windings girded parts of the central sphere and its supporting members. Receding away into space behind it, a line of identical objects spaced at two-thousand-mile intervals diminished in size with distance until they were lost in the background of stars.

Imares Broghuilio, formerly Premier of the Jevlenese faction of Thurien and now Overlord of the recently proclaimed Independent Protectorate of Jevlenese Worlds, stood in his black Supreme Military Commander's uniform, his arms folded across his chest, and scowled out at the scene from inside a blisterdome on the hull of a spacecraft riding several thousand miles off. Low to one side, the dark, rugged sphere of the planet Uttan hung as a crescent against the blackness, appearing the size of a tennis ball held at arm's length. Wylott and a number of generals from various commands of the Jevlenese military were standing behind him with Estordu and a handful of civilian advisors. To one side, not looking very happy, were Niels Sverenssen and Feylon Turl, technical coordinator of the quadriflexor construction program.

Broghuilio waved an arm at the scene outside. "*We* have been forced to revise *our* timetables just as drastically and in just as little time," he said curtly, glaring at Turl. "I expect you to do at least as well."

"But engineering on this scale can't be accelerated by

that kind of factor simply by ordering it to be," Turl protested. "We are still short by fifty units. It will take two years at least, even with round-the-clock shifts in all critical—"

"Two years is unacceptable," Broghuilio said flatly. "I've given you our requirement, and I want your confirmation, today, that it will be met as stipulated. Tell me what *can* be done for a change. The Protectorate is now operating on a war economy, and whatever resources are needed will be made available."

"It isn't simply a question of production resources," Turl insisted. "The power to transfer that number of quadriflexors to the target won't be available for two years. Crallort's latest estimates show that—"

"Crallort has been removed," Broghuilio informed him. "That office is now under military control. The generator battery will be expanded under an emergency program that is already in effect, and the power requirement will be met as stipulated."

"I—" Turl began, but Broghuilio cut him off with an impatient motion of his hand.

"You have until twenty-four hours from now to discuss the revisions with your staff. I shall expect you at the Directorate of Strategic Planning on Jevlen at that time to report. I will *not* expect to hear lame excuses. Do I make myself understood?"

"Yes, Excellency," Turl mumbled.

Subvocally Broghuilio instructed JEVEX to remind him later in the day to review possible candidates for Turl's replacement at Uttan, then turned his eyes contemptuously toward Sverenssen. "And it appears that my 'able lieutenant' who was supposed to have had the situation on Earth 'well under control' is equally incompetent," he sneered. "Well, what have you been able to find out? How did the Thuriens manage to communicate with Terrans right under your noses? Where is their facility located? What is your plan to eliminate it? How did they penetrate your operation? Who has been betraying it? I hope you have good answers, Sverenssen."

"I must protest," Sverenssen said in a shocked voice. "Yes, I admit that the Thuriens did establish a link somehow. But the accusation that we have allowed our operation to be penetrated is without foundation. There is no evidence to—"

"Then you are either blind or stupid!" Broghuilio spat. "I was there, in Thurios. You were not. I tell you they knew everything. The Terrans must have turned half the imbeciles in your organization and had them working against us for years. How long have they had a link on Earth direct into VISAR?"

"We . . . have not been able to ascertain that yet, Excellency," Sverenssen admitted.

"Obviously since long before they started anything on Farside," Broghuilio said. "The whole Bruno operation was a façade to fool you and keep you occupied, and you swallowed every inch of it." He screwed up his face and mimicked a fawning tone. " 'We have gained complete control, Excellency,' I was told. Pah!" Broghuilio slammed a fist into his other palm. "Control! They were manipulating you like a puppet. They probably have been for years. Overlord of Earth? You'd be a laughingstock trying to govern a kindergarten." Sverenssen paled, and his jaw strained, but he said nothing.

Broghuilio raised his arms in front of the rest of the company as if inviting them to witness his predicament. "You see what I have to contend with—imbecile engineers and imbecile agents. And what of you? Clearly the enemy will not sit idly by and do nothing while we complete our preparations. But we are told that it will take two years. Thus we have a problem situation that demands some form of action now, while we retain the initiative. What are your plans?"

Some of the generals looked uncertainly at one another. Eventually Wylott replied hesitantly, "We are still analyzing the latest developments. The situation calls for a complete revision of every—"

"Never mind your academic analyses and evaluations. Do you have firm *plans* drawn up for offensive *action*, *now*, to secure our position while the quadriflexor program is being completed?"

"No, but we've never—"

"The general does not have a plan," Broghuilio told the rest of them. "You see—on all sides I have to deal with imbeciles. But fortunately for all of us, I do have a plan.

Our weapons production program here at Uttan has begun showing results, has it not? We have ships, armaments, and sufficient generating capacity to transfer them to Gistar at once, while the Thuriens have nothing. It is a time for boldness."

Wylott seemed worried. "That is not the way we have always intended," he said. "Our plans have never included launching an unprovoked assault on Thurien. The weapons were to be used against the Cerians. We would find it hard to justify such an action to the people. It would not be popular."

"Did I say anything about attacking Thurien?" Broghuilio asked. "Can you conceive of no methods other than brute force and clumsiness? Have you no sense of subtlety?" He turned his head to address all present. "War is as much a matter of psychology as it is of weapons, and in particular of understanding the psychology of one's enemy. Study the history of Earth, or even of Minerva. Many great victories have been won by seizing an opportune psychological moment. And such a moment presents itself to us now."

"What are you proposing?" Estordu asked uneasily. "That we might intimidate Thurien into submission?"

Broghuilio looked at him in surprise and with unconcealed approval. "For a scientist you are thinking quickly for once," he said. He raised his voice. "You hear? The scientist is thinking more like a general than any of you. The Thuriens have no taste for war, nor even any concept of it. At this moment they believe that we have retreated into a shell and will not trouble them for a long time to come. They feel secure for the time being, and that is why they are vulnerable."

He strode slowly to one side of the dome and stared out at the distant ball of Uttan for a few seconds. Then he came back to the center and resumed, "I will tell you what the Thuriens are thinking at this moment. They realize that we present a threat which they do not have the stomach to face, but which the Terrans do. On the other hand they possess the technology necessary to counter that threat, whereas the Terrans do not. So what will be their obvious strategy?"

Wylott was beginning to nod slowly. "To arm and equip

the Terrans as proxy troops," he said. "Thurien will enlist Earth to fight on its behalf."

"Exactly!" Broghuilio exclaimed. "But Earth is demilitarized and not competent to match us technically anyway, and at this moment the Thuriens have nothing to arm them with." He looked around with a triumphant glint in his eyes. "In other words their solution will require *time*. But we do not need time because right now we have something, and they have nothing. Our forces might be small compared to what they will be in times to come, but that situation gives us a ratio of something to zero, which equates to infinite superiority. That advantage will not exist indefinitely, and it will never again be in our favor to the extent that it is now. And *that* is why the time to act is *now*, and not later."

Wylott's eyes gleamed as he began to see what Broghuilio was driving at. "With self-powered ships we can send a task force in and issue an ultimatum to the Thuriens to place VISAR under our control," he said. "Being Ganymeans, they will have no choice. Then they'd be helpless, and we would assume full control of the combined empires of JEVEX and VISAR."

"And the Terrans will be deprived of their armorers," Broghuilio completed. "In two years they could never hope to match us without the Thuriens. Thus we will have bought the time we need to complete our preparations for dealing with Earth, and for neutralizing Thurien permanently." He turned to confront Wylott squarely, folded his arms across his chest, and stuck out his chin. "That, General, is the plan—*my* plan."

"A stroke of genius," Wylott declared. A chorus of murmurs from the ranks behind endorsed the statement. "We will commence detailed preparations at once."

"See to it," Broghuilio ordered. He turned and glowered at Sverenssen. "And you, if you think you have the ability to redeem yourself, go back to Earth. I want every one of the traitors in your organization uncovered, tracked down, and dealt with. All except Rank B2 and above. *Those* are to be held while we arrange a landing to bring them back to Jevlen. I will deal with *them* personally." His voice fell to an ominous growl, and his eyes smoldered. "And if you fail in this, Sverenssen, *you* will certainly be brought back, even if I have to come physically to Earth myself to do it."

chapter thirty-one

Several days went by without news from the *Shapieron*. VISAR analyzed all the available data on the design of JEVEX and gave ZORAC a five-percent chance of electronically lock-picking its way through the layers of security checks and access restrictions protecting the enemy system. The problem was that JEVEX's Ganymean-designed molecular circuits worked at subnanosecond speeds, enabling an enormous amount of self-checking to be interleaved with its regular operations. The odds were overwhelming that any chink in JEVEX's armor that ZORAC managed to slip a wedge into would be detected and closed before VISAR could be brought in to drive the wedge home. In other words JEVEX could scan its own internal processes too rapidly, or as Hunt put it to Caldwell, "It's got too much instant-to-instant awareness of what's going on inside itself. If we could distract its attention somehow, even for a few seconds at the speeds those machines work at, ZORAC might be able to neutralize the jamming system and let VISAR in." But how could they distract JEVEX when the only channel they had to it was through ZORAC, and ZORAC couldn't get in until JEVEX had been distracted?

And then VISAR reported a series of gravitational disturbances outside Gistar's planetary system, followed by a steady accumulation of objects that seemed to be ships of some kind being transferred through from somewhere. Shortly afterward, the objects began moving toward Thurien. VISAR could detect no h-grid power or control beams and was unable to check their progress. They were self-powered, heavily armed Jevlenese war vessels, and there were fifty of them. As they fanned out to maneuver into positions around Thurien, JEVEX reopened contact briefly with VISAR to deliver the Jevlenese ultimatum: the Thuriens had forty-eight hours to place their entire world-system under Jevlenese control. If at the end of that period they had not agreed, obliteration of Thurien cities one at a time would commence, starting with Vranix. Those were the terms. There was nothing to discuss.

The atmosphere inside the Government Center at Thurios was strained and tense. All of the Terran group from McClusky were present with Calazar, Showm, and a selection of engineering and technical experts that included Eesyan's deputy, Morizal. They were already six hours into the ultimatum period.

"But there must be something you can do," Caldwell protested, stamping backward and forward across the center of the room in frustration. "Couldn't you try using remote-controlled ships to ram them? Couldn't VISAR make a few black holes to suck them into or something? There has to be a way."

"I agree," Showm said, looking at Calazar. "We should try. I know it's distasteful, but the Jevlenese have made the rules. Have you considered the alternatives?"

"They could pick off ramships long before they even got near," Morizal said. "And they could detect a black hole forming and evade it long before it could trap them. And even then you could only hope to get a few at the most. The rest would incinerate Thurien then and there without waiting for the deadline."

"And besides, that's not the way," Calazar said at last, throwing up his hands. "Ganymeans have never sought solutions by war or violence. I couldn't condone anything like that. We will not descend to the level of Jevlenese barbarism."

"You've never faced this kind of threat before," Karen Heller pointed out. "What other way is there to meet it?"

"She's right," Showm said. "The Jevlenese force is not large. There's a good chance that it's all they possess right now. Six months from now that could change. Earth's logic is harsh, but nevertheless realistic in this kind of situation: losing some people now could buy the time to save many more later. It's a lesson they have learned, and we may have to as well."

"It's not the way," Calazar said again. "You've seen Earth's history. That kind of logic always leads to escalation without limits. It's insane. I won't allow us to start down that road."

"Broghuilio is insane," Showm insisted. "There's no other way."

"There must be. We need time to consider."

"We don't have any time."

A heavy silence descended. On one side of the room, Hunt caught Lyn's eye and shrugged hopelessly. She raised her eyebrows and sighed. There was nothing to say. The situation didn't look good. A short distance away Danchekker was becoming restless. He removed his spectacles, squinted through them while he twisted them first this way and then that in front of his face, then replaced them and began pinching his nose with his thumb and forefinger. Something was going through his mind. Hunt watched him curiously and waited.

"Suppose . . ." Danchekker began, thought for a second longer, then swung his head toward Calazar and Morizal. "Suppose we could induce the Jevlenese to postpone their offensive intentions and switch their force to the defensive . . . in other words take it back to Jevlen," he said. "That would gain us some time."

Calazar looked at him, puzzled. "Why should they do that? To defend against what? We have nothing to threaten any attack against them with, and neither have you."

"Agreed," Danchekker said. "But perhaps there is a way in which we could persuade them that we do." The Ganymeans stared back at him nonplussed. He explained, "Lyn and Vic were talking recently about an idea to *simulate* an all-out assault on Jevlen inside VISAR and inject it into JEVEX, assuming ZORAC gains access of course. And by suitably manipulating JEVEX's internal records, VISAR could, perhaps, then instill in JEVEX the conviction that the existence of such forces was consistent with what it has been observing for years. You see my point? Such a ruse might create enough confusion inside the Jevlenese camp for them to withdraw their forces. And given a sufficient level of uncertainty, they would probably not risk firing upon Thurien until they had determined the true situation. What we would do then I have no idea, but it would at least gain us some respite from the current predicament."

Showm was listening with a strange look on her face.

"That would be almost identical to what they did to us," she murmured. "We'd be turning their own tactic right back at them."

"Yes, it does have a certain appeal of that nature about it," Danchekker agreed.

In response to some questions from Morizal, Danchekker went on to describe the idea in greater detail. When he had finished, the Ganymeans looked at one another dubiously, but none of them could pick out a fatal flaw in the argument. "What do you say, VISAR?" Calazar asked after they had talked for some time.

"It might work, but it still rests on a five-percent probability at best," VISAR replied. "It's still the same problem: the only way I could get into JEVEX is if ZORAC can switch off its jamming system, and so far ZORAC doesn't seem to be having much luck. I still haven't heard a thing from it."

"What else can you suggest?" Calazar asked.

A few seconds went by. "Nothing," VISAR admitted. "I could get to work and manufacture the information with some help from the Terrans and have it ready to beam through on the off-chance ZORAC does get me in, but it's still five percent. In other words don't bank on it."

A faraway look had been coming into Hunt's eyes while the discussion was going on. One by one the heads in the room turned toward him curiously as they noticed. "It's this problem about distracting JEVEX's attention again," he said, "isn't it? If we could just freeze its self-checking functions for the couple of seconds ZORAC would need to switch off the jamming routines and open an h-link, VISAR would be able to hold that link open permanently and do the rest."

"True, but what's the point?" VISAR said. "We've already been through all this. We can't do anything like that because the only way in is through ZORAC in the first place."

"I think maybe we can," Hunt said in a distant voice. The room became very still. His eyes cleared suddenly as he gazed around at the others. They waited. "We can't create a diversion through ZORAC because ZORAC is outside the system trying to get in," he said. "But we've got another channel that goes straight through to the *inside*—direct into the core of JEVEX."

Caldwell shook his head and looked puzzled. "What are you talking about? What channel? Where?"

"In Connecticut," Hunt told them. He glanced at Lyn for a second and then looked back at the others. "I'm betting that what's inside Sverenssen's house is a complete communications facility into JEVEX—probably one with its own neural coupler. What else could it be? We could get at it through that."

A few seconds elapsed before what he had said registered fully. Morizal seemed mystified. "Get at it and do what?" he asked. "How would you use it?"

Hunt shrugged. "I haven't really thought about it yet, but there has to be something. Maybe we could use it to tell JEVEX all the things that VISAR's inventions will corroborate—Earth is fully armed and has been for years; an attack is on its way to wipe Jevlen out now . . . supporting evidence, that kind of thing. That ought to shake it up for a second or two."

"That's the craziest thing I ever heard." Caldwell shook his head helplessly. "Why would it believe you? It wouldn't even know who you were. And anyhow, would you sit down in that thing and let JEVEX inside your head?"

"No, I wouldn't," Hunt said. "But JEVEX knows Sverenssen. And it would believe what he told it. That would really shake it up."

"Why would Sverenssen ever do something like that?" Heller asked. "What makes you think he'd want to cooperate?"

Hunt shrugged. "We put a gun to the bastard's head and make him," he replied simply.

Silence fell once again. The suggestion was so outrageous that nobody had a ready comment to offer. The Ganymeans were looking at each other in amazement, all except Frenua Showm, who seemed ready to go along with the scheme without further ado. "How would you get in?" Caldwell asked dubiously at last. "Lyn said it'd take an army."

"So use the Army," Hunt said. "Jerol Packard and Norman Pacey must know some people who could pull it off."

The idea was taking root as they thought about it. "But how do you know you could force him to do something like that without JEVEX knowing you were there doing it?"

Heller asked. "I mean, VISAR can see somebody in the perceptron at McClusky even before they sit down in a recliner. How do you know Sverenssen's place isn't the same?"

"I don't," Hunt conceded. He spread his hands appealingly. "It's a risk. But it's a hell of a lot less of a risk than the one you were asking Calazar to take. And besides, the Ganymeans have taken enough of the risks already."

Caldwell nodded curtly as soon as Hunt said this. "I agree. Let's do it."

"VISAR?" Calazar inquired, still somewhat dazed by the sudden turn of events.

"I've never heard of anything like it," VISAR declared. "But if it increases the odds above five percent, it's worth a try. How soon can I start working on the movies?"

"Right away," Caldwell said. He moved to the center of the group and suddenly felt the old, familiar feeling of being in command once again. "Karen and I will stay here to help out with that side of it. You'd better stay too, Chris, to explain the whole idea again. Vic needs to go to Washington to tell Packard what we want, and Lyn had better go with him because she knows the layout of the house."

"It sounds as if we should consider you in charge of this operation," Calazar said.

"Thanks." Caldwell nodded and looked around the room. "Okay," he said. "Let's go through the whole thing in detail from the beginning and work out as much as we can to synchronize the two ends of it."

Hunt and Lyn arrived in Washington late that afternoon. Caldwell had already called Packard from Alaska, so they were expecting to find Packard, Pacey, and Clifford Benson of the CIA waiting for them. What they were not expecting to find was a contingent of Soviet military officers there too, headed by Mikolai Sobroskin. To their further and total amazement they learned that a Jevlenese defector in the form of the scientist Verikoff was also present in another part of the building.

Most of the Russians were too stunned by what they heard from Hunt and Lyn to be capable of contributing very much to the proceedings. Sobroskin, however, digested their story quickly and confirmed from what Verikoff had already told him—that the office wing of Sverenssen's house

did indeed contain a full communications system into
JEVEX, including a neural coupler. In fact Verikoff himself had used it on numerous occasions to make quick visits
to Jevlen. This led Sobroskin to propose a means of simpli-
fying considerably the plan that Hunt and Lyn had described. "As you say, the big risk in forcing Sverenssen to
do it is that JEVEX might be able to observe what is happening," he said. "But perhaps there is no need for that at
all. If we could just gain access to the device, Verikoff
might be persuaded to do what is required voluntarily.
JEVEX already knows Verikoff. It would have no reason to
see anything amiss."

Ten minutes later they all left the room and descended
one story of the building to enter a door that had two
armed guards stationed outside it. Verikoff was inside with
two more of Sobroskin's officers. At Sobroskin's request,
Verikoff sketched a plan of Sverenssen's house on a mural
display, indicating the location of the communications
room and the access door into the wing in which it was
located, as well as describing the building's protective features. "What's your verdict?" Pacey asked, looking at Lyn,
when Verikoff had finished.

She nodded. "One-hundred-percent accurate. That's it,
just the way it is."

"He seems to be telling the truth," Packard said, sounding satisfied. "And everything else he told Sobroskin
checks with what Vic Hunt has told us. I think we can
trust him."

Verikoff's eyes widened in surprise. He waved a hand at
the sketch he had drawn, and then at Lyn. "She knows this
already? How could that be? How could she know about
the coupler?"

"It would take too long to explain," Sobroskin said. "Tell
us what kind of visual sensors JEVEX has around the
house. Are there some in all rooms, outside, inside the
communications room, or what?"

"Only inside the communications room itself," Verikoff
answered. He was looking from side to side uncomprehend-
ingly.

"So JEVEX would not know about anything that was
happening in the rest of the house outside that room," Sobroskin said.

Verikoff shook his head. "No."

"How about conventional intruder alarms around the grounds?" Pacey inquired. "Is the place equipped with anything like that? Would it be possible to get in over the walls and fences without being detected?"

"It's extensively wired," Verikoff replied. His expression became alarmed as he realized the implication of the questions. "Detection would be certain."

"Is the place watched from orbit by Jevlenese surveillance?" Hunt asked. "Could it be assaulted without it being reported?"

"As far as I know it is checked periodically, but not continuously."

"How frequently?"

"I don't know."

"How about Sverenssen's domestic staff?" Lyn asked. "Are they Jevlenese too, or just help that he hires locally? How much do they know?"

"Specially picked Jevlenese guards—all of them."

"How many?" Sobroskin demanded. "Are they armed? What armaments do they have?"

"Ten of them. There are always at least six in the house. They are armed at all times. Conventional Terran firearms."

Packard looked over at the others. One by one they returned slow nods. "It looks as if we could be in with a chance," he said. "It's time to bring in the professionals and see what they think."

Verikoff suddenly seemed apprehensive. "What is this talk of an assault?" he asked. "You are going in there?"

"*We* are going in there," Sobroskin told him.

Verikoff started to protest but stopped when he saw the menace in Sobroskin's eyes. He licked his lips and nodded. "What do you want me to do?" he asked.

An hour later a VTOL personnel carrier flew the whole party across the Potomac to the army base at Fort Myer. They were met by a Colonel Shearer, who commanded a Special Forces antiterrorist unit that had already been called to alert and was standing by. The planning and briefing session that followed went on until the early hours of the morning. The first gray light of dawn was showing in the east as an Air Force transport took off from Fort Myer and followed the coast toward New England. It landed with a whisper less than thirty minutes later at an out-of-the-way military supply depot situated among wooded hills twenty miles or so outside Stamford, Connecticut.

chapter thirty-two

The Jevlenese were still tapping into Earth's communications net. Earth knew they were, and the Jevlenese knew that Earth knew. Therefore, Caldwell reasoned, the Jevlenese would expect any high-level communications between Earth's governments, especially anything to do with an impending attack on Jevlen, to be encoded by methods that were generally thought to be unbreakable; anything else would not look authentic. But if the codes were indeed unbreakable, little purpose would be served by planting authentically encoded information in JEVEX since JEVEX wouldn't be able to unravel what it said.

At Caldwell's request the scientists at McClusky beamed details of the coding algorithms currently used for high-security terrestrial communications through to the perceptron. VISAR studied them and announced that JEVEX would have no problem. The scientists were skeptical. As a test VISAR invited them to compose an encoded message and send it over the beam, which they did. VISAR returned the plaintext translation less than a minute later. The stunned scientists decided that they still had a lot to learn about algorithms. But the implication was satisfactory: JEVEX could be led plausibly to believe that it was eavesdropping on Earth's highest-level secure communications.

Since then VISAR had been busy manufacturing a revised history of the last few decades on Earth in which the superpowers had not disarmed but gone on to escalate their strategic forces to insane levels of overkill capability, concluding with an account of Earth's leaders meeting secretly and agreeing to a hasty alliance to hurl their combined strength at Jevlen with the Thuriens transporting the force to within striking distance. Its latest creation, being previewed in the Government Center in Thurios, showed a conference hookup in which some of the senior officers engaged in the joint planning of the operation were delivering a preliminary briefing to their staffs. A General Gearvey, whom VISAR had already appointed as the American Supreme Commander, began speaking.

"We are about to engage an enemy who possesses a technology incalculably ahead of our own, and of unknown strength and retaliatory capability. But against that we have two factors in our favor that could redress the balance—*time* and *preparedness*. We are in a position to move now, while all our intelligence from the Thuriens leads us to believe that the enemy is not. Our strategy is therefore based on exploiting these factors to the fullest. We will forego detailed planning and rely heavily on the initiative of local commanders in order to move fast and aim at total devastation of the enemy in a single, surprise, all-out, lightning strike with no compromises. This is not a time to ponder about morality. We might not have a second chance."

A Russian general leaned forward and took it from there. "The opening phase of the assault is designated OX-BOW. Fifteen long-range radiation projectors will commence area-obliteration of selected targets on Jevlen, firing from one million miles standoff behind screens of destroyers and close-support tactical units. Five more will be held in reserve at ten million miles. The bombardment is intended to draw and engage the defensive forces while the spearheads move in to commence operations around the planet itself."

A European Air Force chief continued, "Phase BANSHEE will begin with a high-level sweep of Jevlenese near-space to clear it of all enemy hardware. This will be followed immediately by rapid deployment of a mixed-strike orbital system to neutralize major military installations and observed ground concentrations. A secondary force will concentrate on population centers and administrative focal points to dislocate the defenses by creating panic and disrupting communications. Simultaneously, lower-altitude intercept units and killsats will contest Jevlenese air space, with carrier-based tactical groups operating in selective ground-strike and counterfire roles. Our objective here is to gain complete control above the surface within twelve hours of the spearheads going in. The codeword CLAY-MORE will be issued upon the successful completion of this phase."

A Chinese general summed up the last part. "When CLAYMORE is declared, conditions will have been established to permit the seizure of bridgeheads on the surface. This phase is designated DRAGON. The first descents will be made by remote-controlled decoy landers to enable surviving defensive installations to be identified and destroyed by a portion of the orbital bombardment groups held in reserve for that purpose. The remaining orbiting groups will redeploy to provide close-support fire for the landings, and the carrier groups assigned to ground suppression will commence launching aircraft. When descent corridors have been cleared, the ground forces will be landed initially at twelve strategic points. Details of those operations are currently being finalized with the respective bridgehead commanders. Strategic bombardment from high level will continue throughout to prevent the defenses from concentrating on the landing areas."

"That concludes the overview," Gearvey said. "Individual unit assignments, timetabling, and call signs will follow immediately. Remain on standby."

"What do you think?" Caldwell asked as the image cut out.

"I'm impressed," Heller said. "It'd sure scare the hell out of me."

"Horrifying," Calazar pronounced numbly. "It is just as well that you did not go with the *Shapieron*. We would never have conceived anything like that."

Danchekker did not seem completely happy. "It still doesn't contain the sense of urgency that we have to convey," he said. "It doesn't mention any specific dates."

"I did that on purpose," Caldwell told him. "If we're going to be credible, we'd have to allow Earth ships months to get out of the solar system. The best thing seemed to be to leave it uncertain. What other way is there?"

"I don't know, but I still don't like it," Danchekker said.

Nobody spoke for a few seconds, then Morizal said, "Well, we've already got the Thuriens providing the transfer ports outside the solar system. We could take it a step further and have the Terran vessels fitted with Thurien-supplied h-grid boosters. That way we could get them out of the solar system in a day."

"A whole fleet?" Heller said dubiously. "Could a whole fleet be fitted out that quickly?"

"Conceivably yes," Morizal replied. "It's quite a simple job. With unlimited assistance from Ganymean engineers, it would be feasible."

"How does that sound?" Caldwell asked, looking at Danchekker.

"It sounds more like what we want," Danchekker agreed, nodding.

"Suppose I change the last part to this," VISAR offered. The image reappeared and showed General Gearvey again, just about to sum up.

"That concludes the overview," he said. "There are no major revisions to the schedule to report. The h-beam boosters are currently being fitted by the Thuriens, and the first assault elements should commence moving out from Earth, on time, at eighteen hundred hours today. Current indications are that the full force will complete its assembly outside the enemy star system three days from now as planned. The force will then reenter h-space and be accelerated to reexit into normal space at a velocity that will move it to Jevlen in twenty-two hours. Therefore we should be going into action four days from now. Good luck to you all. Individual unit assignments, timetabling, and call signs will follow immediately. Remain on standby." The image vanished.

"Excellent," Danchekker murmured.

"The next thing I need to start working on is some surveillance data from Earth to back it all up," VISAR said. "But first I need some reference information on contemporary Terran military hardware and installations. Can you get it beamed in through McClusky?"

"Give me a line," Caldwell said. "I'll get something moving right away." He turned his head away and stared grimly for a few seconds at another view, constructed from VISAR's locally collected data, of the pattern of Jevlenese warships positioned around Thurien. "Any news about the *Shapieron* yet?" he asked.

"Nothing," VISAR told him. Its tone was neutral.

An image in the form of a frame enclosing the features of the controller at McClusky appeared in the air a few feet in front of Caldwell's face. Caldwell turned his head away from the view of the Jevlenese threat and returned his attention to the matter to hand.

chapter thirty-three

"Damn! Damn! Damn!" Niels Sverenssen hammered savagely at the touchboard of the datagrid terminal, then brought his fist down heavily on top of the unit as the screen remained dead. He turned away and marched furiously toward the L-shaped central room. "Vickers!" he shouted. "Where are you, for God's sake? I thought those confounded dataphone people were supposed to be here by now."

Vickers, the heavily built and swarthy chief of Sverenssen's domestic staff, appeared from one of the passages. "I only returned ten minutes ago. They said they'd be right over."

"Well, why aren't they?" Sverenssen demanded irritably. "I have calls waiting that must be made immediately. The service *must* be restored at once."

Vickers shrugged. "I already told 'em that. What else was I supposed to do?"

Sverenssen began massaging a fist with his other hand and pacing to and fro, cursing beneath his breath. "Why do such things always have to happen at a time like this? What kinds of buffoon are unable to maintain a simple communications service competently? Oh, the whole thing is intolerable!"

The first faint hum of an approaching aircar drifted in from the direction of the window. Vickers cocked his head to listen for a second, then walked over to peer out through one of the sliding glass panels that formed part of a wall. "It's a cab," he said over his shoulder, "coming down over the roof." They heard the cab land on the other side of the house, in the front driveway. The door chime sounded shortly afterward, followed by the footsteps of one of the maids as she hurried to the front hallway. He heard a muted exchange of female voices, and a few moments later the maid ushered in a smiling Lyn Garland. Sverenssen's mouth dropped open in a mixture of surprise and dismay.

"Niels!" she exclaimed. "I tried to call you, but you seem to be having problems with the line. I thought you wouldn't mind me showing up, anyway. I've been thinking about what you said. You know, maybe you were right. I thought maybe we could patch things up a little." Her hand was resting casually on the top of her shoulder bag as she spoke. Sverenssen was not inside the communications room, which was the one thing Colonel Shearer had insisted on before he could move in. Inside the top of the bag, Lyn's finger found the button on the microtransmitter and pressed it three times.

"Oh, not now!" Sverenssen groaned. "You should know better than to barge in like this. I am an extremely busy man, and I have things to attend to. Anyway, I thought I made myself perfectly clear on the not-so-memorable occasion of our last meeting. Good day. Vickers, kindly show Miss Garland back to her cab."

"This way," Vickers said, taking a step forward and nodding his head toward where the maid was still hovering.

"Oh, but you did," Lyn said, looking at Sverenssen and ignoring Vickers. "You made it very clear. And I was being so silly, wasn't I, just like you said. But now I've had a chance to think about it, it sounds so—"

"Get her out of here," Sverenssen muttered, turning away. "I don't have time to waste listening to any inane female prattling today." Vickers gripped Lyn's upper arm and steered her firmly back along the corridor to the front hall while the maid ran on ahead to hold the door open. The cab was still there. Just as they reached the door, a Southern New England Dataphones repair truck rounded the bend in the driveway and drew up in front of the house, halting so close to the cab that the ladders slung on its side overhung and blocked its ascent path.

The cabbie wound down his window and leaned out to yell in the direction of the front end of the truck. "Hey, asshole! Who taught ya ta drive dat thing? How the hell am I supposed ta get outa here?" Two repairmen had jumped out of the passenger-side door of the truck, and another was emerging from the rear. The truck's engine came to life again in a series of laboring electric whines, then shuddered and died.

"I've got problems," a voice shouted through the open driver's window of the truck. "The same thing happened just now when we left the office."

"Well, do something with the goddam thing, willya. I've got a living ta make."

Vickers had released Lyn's arm and was growling profanities beneath his breath. With what was going on in the driveway, neither he nor the maid noticed her backing quietly away across the hall.

"Back up for Chrissakes. What's the matter? Don't you know how to reverse a cab?"

"How can I back up? Don't those look like flowers behind me to you? You need lenses or sump'n?"

Another technician was coming out of the back of the truck. There were already more of them than would have been sent on a simple domestic repair job, but Vickers and the maid were too preoccupied with the argument to register the fact for a few vital seconds. Also they failed to notice the sound of air engines growing steadily louder from beyond the treetops flanking the driveway.

When Lyn reappeared in the corner room Sverenssen was on the far side at one of the windows, peering out and upward as sound deluged the house suddenly, seemingly from all directions. All in the same moment, two Army assault landers dropped into sight from above and came down on the terrace by the pool with khaki-clad figures already bursting from their doors, explosions and the sounds of shattering glass came from the upper part of the house, and there was a brief glimpse of Vickers and the maid being bowled over by more figures pouring into the front hall before additional concussions followed by clouds of smoke blotted out the view along the corridor.

. Lyn snatched the respirator from her bag, clamped it over her face and eyes, and snapped its retaining band into position behind her head just as the barrage of stun grenades and gas bombs crashed in through the ground-floor windows of the house. Detonations and smoke were everywhere, punctuated by shouting, splintering glass, the thuds of doors being smashed down, and a few scattered shots. One of the domestics appeared in the archway that led through to the main stairs, gesticulating frantically upward and behind him. "They're on the roof! There's soldiers coming in off the roof! They're—" The rest was drowned by more explosions, and he was engulfed by a cloud of smoke and gas erupting behind him.

Sverenssen had recoiled from the window, and Lyn could see him clawing at his eyes in the middle of the room as he tried to get his bearings. Whatever happened, he couldn't be allowed to get to the communications room now. She began picking her way cautiously around the wall to get between him and the passageway leading to the office wing. He saw the movement through the smoke and came nearer. "*You!*" His face twisted into a mask of fury as he recognized her, made even more grotesque by the watery streaks cutting through the smoke grime on his cheeks. Lyn's heart did a backflip in her chest. She backed away, but kept moving toward the passageway. Sverenssen's shape came looming through the smoke, straight at her.

Then barked military commands sounded inside the house, seemingly from not far away in the direction of the guest annex. Sverenssen threw a glance back over his shoulder and hesitated. Shadowy figures were struggling in the corridor outside the kitchen, and there was more movement on the side of the house facing the pool. He changed direction and made a bolt toward the office wing. Without realizing what she was doing, Lyn scooped up a wicker chair and hurled it across the floor at his legs. Sverenssen went down heavily and struck his head on the wall as he sprawled full-length on the floor.

But through the smoke Lyn could see he was still moving. She looked around desperately, picked up a large vase from a side table, swallowed hard and tried to stop her hands from shaking, and forced herself to move nearer.

Sverenssen was half sitting up, one hand clutching at his head, a small trickle of blood oozing through his fingers. He braced a foot beneath himself, stretched out an arm to steady himself against the wall, and started to haul himself up. Lyn raised the vase high with both hands. But Sverenssen's legs had turned to jelly. He swayed for a second, groaned aloud, and then collapsed back against the baseboard. Lyn was still standing paralyzed in the same position when the first figures wearing respirators and Army combat uniforms and carrying assault rifles materialized out of the fumes around her. One of them took the vase lightly from her hands. "We'll take care of him," a gruff voice told her. "Are you okay?" She nodded mutely while in front of her two Special Forces troopers lifted Sverenssen roughly to his feet.

"Bloody good show that," an English voice commented from somewhere behind her. "You know, if you worked at it, you might even get a job with the S.A.S." She turned and found Hunt looking at her approvingly. Shearer stood next to him. Hunt moved beside her, slipped an arm around her waist, and squeezed reassuringly. She pressed the side of her head against his shoulder and clung tightly as the tension released itself in a spasm of trembling. Talking could wait until later.

Around them the noise had subsided, and the smoke was clearing to reveal Sverenssen's domestic staff being brought into the corner room to be searched and relieved of their weapons before they were herded away into the guest annex. As the assault troops and the others already inside the house removed their respirators, a knot of American and Soviet officers came in through the wreckage. They were accompanied by men wearing civilian clothes beneath combat jackets. Sverenssen's eyes bulged in disbelief as they refocused. "Hi," Norman Pacey said, with a trace of deep satisfaction. "Remember us?"

"For you the war is over, my friend," Sobroskin informed him. "In fact, everything is over. It's a shame that you did not find Bruno up to your standards. It's quite luxurious compared to where you will be going." Sverenssen's face writhed with anger, but he still seemed too dazed to make any reply.

A sergeant crossed the room, saluted, and reported to

Shearer. "No casualties, sir. Just some cuts and bruises, mainly on the other side. None of them got away. The whole house is secured."

Shearer nodded. "Start getting them out right away. Let's get those landers away before they're spotted by the surveillance. Where are Verikoff and the CIA people?" Even as he spoke, another group of figures pushed into the room. Sverenssen's head jerked around, and his jaw dropped as he heard the name. Verikoff halted a few feet away from him and stood eying him defiantly.

"So, it's you . . ." Sverenssen hissed. "You . . . *traitor!*" He lunged forward instinctively and was promptly doubled over by a sharp blow delivered to the solar plexus by a rifle butt. As he sagged two of the troopers caught him and held him.

"He carries the key to the facility on him at all times," Verikoff said. "It should be on a chain around his neck." Shearer ripped open the front of Sverenssen's shirt, found the key, removed it, and passed it to Verikoff.

"You'll pay for these atrocities, Colonel," Sverenssen wheezed weakly. "Mark my words. I've ruined bigger men than you."

"Atrocities?" Shearer turned his head aside quizzically. "Do you know what he's talking about, Sergeant?"

"I've no idea, sir."

"Did you see anything?"

"Didn't see a thing, sir."

"Why do you think this man is holding his stomach?"

"Probably indigestion, sir."

As Sverenssen was hustled away to join his staff, Shearer turned to Clifford Benson. "I'm pulling my men out right away, apart from ten that I'll leave as guards for the house. I guess it's ready for you to take over."

"You did a fine job, Colonel," Benson acknowledged. He turned to the others. "Well, time's precious. Let's get on with it."

They stood aside while Verikoff led the way into the passage toward the office wing, and followed a few paces behind. At the end of the passage he came to a large, solid-looking, wooden door. "I am not sure how far JEVEX's visual field extends," he called to them. "It would be better if you kept well back." The others fell back into a small dense huddle with Hunt, Sobroskin, Lyn, Benson, and Pacey together at the front. "I need a minute to compose myself," Verikoff told them. They waited while he brushed a few specks of soot from his clothes, smoothed his hair, and wiped his face with a handkerchief. "Do I look as if all is normal?" he asked them.

"Fine," Hunt called back.

Verikoff nodded, turned to face the door, and unlocked it. Then he drew a deep breath, grasped the handle, and pushed the door open. The others caught a glimpse of elaborate instrumentation panels and banks of gleaming equipment, and then Verikoff stepped inside.

chapter thirty-four

The strain on the Command Deck of the *Shapieron* had been hovering around breaking point for days. Eesyan was standing in the center of the floor gazing up at the main display screen, where an enormous web of interconnected shapes and boxes annotated with symbols showed the road map into JEVEX that ZORAC had laboriously pieced together from statistical analyses and pattern correlations of the responses it had obtained to its probe signals. But ZORAC was not getting through to the nucleus of the system, which it would have to penetrate if it was going to disrupt JEVEX's h-jamming capability. Its attempts had been repeatedly detected by JEVEX's constantly running self-checking routines and thwarted by automatically initiated correction procedures. The big problem now was trying to decide how much longer they could allow ZORAC to try before the tables of fault-diagnostic data accumulating inside JEVEX alerted its supervisory functions that something very abnormal was happening. Opinions were more or less evenly divided between Eesyan's scientists from Thurien, who already wanted to call the whole thing off, and Garuth and his crew, who seemed willing to risk almost anything to pursue what was beginning to look, the more Eesyan saw of it, like some kind of death wish.

"Probe Three's function directive has been queried for the third time," one of the scientists announced from a nearby station. "Header response analysis indicates we've triggered a veto override again." He looked across at Eesyan and shook his head. "It's too dangerous. We'll have to suspend probing on this channel and resume regular traffic only."

"Activity pattern correlates with a new set of executive diagnostic indexes," another scientist called. "We've initiated a high-level malfunction check."

"We have to shut down on Three," another, standing by Eesyan, pleaded. "We're too exposed as it is."

Eesyan stared grimly up at the main screen as a set of mnemonics unrolled down one side to confirm the warning.

"What's your verdict, ZORAC?" he asked.

"I've reduced interrogation priority, but the fault flags are still set. It's tight, but it's the nearest we've come so far. I can try it one more time and risk it, or back off and let the chance go. It's up to you."

Eesyan glanced across to where Garuth was watching tensely with Monchar and Shilohin. Garuth clamped his mouth tight and gave an almost imperceptible nod. Eesyan drew a long breath. "Give it a try, ZORAC," he instructed. A hush fell across the Command Deck, and all eyes turned upward toward the large screen.

In the next second or two a billion bits of information flew back and forth between ZORAC and a Jevlenese communications relay hanging distantly in space. Then, suddenly, a new set of boxes appeared in the array. The symbols inside them were etched against bright red backgrounds that flashed rapidly. One of the scientists groaned in dismay.

"*Alarm condition,*" ZORAC reported. "General supervisor alert triggered. I think we just blew it." It meant that JEVEX knew they were there.

Eesyan looked down at the floor. There was nothing to say. Garuth was shaking his head dazedly in mute protest as if refusing to accept that this could be happening. Shilohin moved a step nearer and rested a hand on his shoulder. "You tried," she said quietly. "You had to try. It was the only chance."

Garuth was staring around him as if he had just awakened from a dream. "What was I thinking?" he whispered. "I had no right to do this."

"It had to be done," Shilohin told him firmly.

"Two objects a hundred thousand miles out, coming this way fast," ZORAC reported. "Probably defensive weapons coming to check out this area." It was serious. The screen hiding the *Shapieron* would never stand up to probing at close range.

"How long before we register on their instruments?" Eesyan asked hoarsely.

"A couple of minutes at most," ZORAC replied.

In the Jevlenese War Room, Imares Broghuilio stood gazing at a display showing the deployment of his task force in the vicinity of Thurien. Although the ships were in VISAR-controlled space, VISAR had not jammed their communications beams to Jevlen. No doubt the Thuriens had guessed that the force had standing orders to commence offensive action automatically if it was interfered with in any way. At least, they hadn't risked it, which was precisely the kind of reaction he had expected from a timid and overcautious race like the Ganymeans. Again his instincts had proved infallible. Exposed at last for what they were, the Thuriens had shown again that they had nothing with which to oppose the combination of nerve, strength, and willpower that he had forged. A deep sense of satisfaction and fulfillment swept through him with the realization that the issue was already as good as decided.

If a response had not been received by a certain time, the plan called for some selected uninhabited areas of Thurien's surface to be devastated as a demonstration that the ultimatum was serious. That time had now arrived, and Broghuilio's aides were waiting with a tense expectancy. "Report the current status of the fleet," he instructed curtly.

"No change," JEVEX replied. "Bombardment squadron standing by and awaiting order. Secondary beams unlocked and primed for area saturation. Coordinates programmed for targets as selected."

Broghuilio gazed around his circle of generals to savor the moment for a while longer, then opened his mouth to issue the command. At that instant JEVEX spoke again. "I have to interrupt, Excellency. A channel has just opened from Earth, top priority. Your response is requested at once."

The smirk vanished from Broghuilio's face. "I have nothing to talk to Sverenssen about. He has his instructions. What does he want?"

"It isn't Sverenssen, Excellency. It's Verikoff."

Broghuilio's expression changed to an angry frown. "Verikoff? What business does he have there at this time? He should be handling the situation in Russia. What does he mean by ignoring protocols in this fashion?"

JEVEX seemed to hesitate for a moment. "He . . . says he has an ultimatum to deliver to you personally, Excellency."

Broghuilio looked as if he had suddenly been punched in the face. He stood absolutely motionless for a few seconds while an ominous tide of deep purple crept slowly upward behind his beard, starting at his collar and eventually finding its way to his scalp. The generals around him were exchanging shocked, uncomprehending looks. Broghuilio licked his lips, and his fists opened and closed by his sides. "Get him here," he growled. "And JEVEX, do *not* disconnect him until *I* say so."

"I regret that is impossible, Excellency," JEVEX replied. "Verikoff is not coupled neurally into the system. I have audio and visual contact only." A screen on one wall of the room came to life to show Verikoff standing in the center of Sverenssen's communications room, · evidently having thought better of committing himself to the recliner that was partly visible behind him. Something had happened to him since he had entered the room. He was staring out from the screen with his arms folded solidly across his chest, and he looked calm and assured.

"Behold, the textbook warlord." Verikoff allowed his lip to curl into a contemptuous sneer. "You should not have sent us to Earth, Broghuilio. It has been an honor and an education to meet *real* warriors. Believe my words—you would be even more of a fool than the fool you are to pit your rabble of amateurs against the Terrans. If you do, they will destroy you. That is my message."

Broghuilio's eyes widened. The veins at the sides of his

neck began pulsating. "*You* are the traitor!" he spat. "Now we see the vermin exposing himself at last. What is this talk of an ultimatum?"

"Traitor? No." Verikoff remained unperturbed. "Merely a question of calculating the winning odds, which after all is your own dictum. You have set us up well to assume control of Earth very soon, and we thank you for it, but unfortunately for you that puts us on the winning side. Which do you think we'd rather be—caretakers of an outpost of your empire, or rulers of our own? The answer should not be difficult."

"What do you mean by *we*?" Broghuilio demanded. "How many of you are behind this?"

"All of us, of course. We manipulate all of Earth's major national governments and therefore have control over its strategic forces. And we have enjoyed the cooperation of the Thuriens for a very long time now. How else do you think they've been able to talk to the Terrans without your knowing anything about it? They know that you, not the Terrans, are the real threat to the Galaxy, and we have persuaded them to allow us a free hand to deal with it. So we command a fully armed planet, backed by Thurien technology. It's all over, Broghuilio. All you have left to save now is your skin."

A short distance back from the open door through which Verikoff was speaking, Hunt turned an astounded face toward Lyn and leaned close to whisper in her ear. "I didn't think he had it in him. The guy deserves an Oscar." Beside them, Sobroskin, looking as if he didn't really believe it either, had lowered the automatic with which he had been covering Verikoff from the passageway.

Broghuilio was looking bewildered. "Strategic forces? What strategic forces? Earth doesn't have any strategic forces."

Then JEVEX interrupted again. "We have an alarm condition in Sector Five. Something unidentified is attempting to penetrate the net. Two destroyers have been detached from station and sent to investigate."

"Don't bother me with such things now," Broghuilio raged, waving his arms impatiently. "Delegate to Sector Control and report later." He looked back at Verikoff again. "Earth demilitarized years ago."

"Is that what you believe?" Verikoff leered openly. "You poor simpleton. You don't really imagine we'd allow Earth to disarm when we knew this day was coming, do you? That story was purely for your consumption. Ironically you almost changed it back into the truth. It has given the Thuriens a lot of amusement."

Broghuilio still couldn't make any sense out of it. "Earth has disarmed," he insisted. "Our surveillance . . . JEVEX has shown us—"

"JEVEX!" Verikoff scoffed. "VISAR has been pumping fairy tales into JEVEX for years." His expression became hard and threatening. "Listen to me, Broghuilio, for I am in no mood to repeat myself. This demonstration at Thurien has taken things too far. The Ganymeans have seen now what you represent, and they are not of a mind to hold us back by scruples. So this is our ultimatum to you: either you withdraw from Thurien now, and agree to place your entire military command under our jurisdiction unconditionally, or the Thuriens will transfer through to Jevlen a combined Terran force that will blow you to stardust—you, your whole planet, and that laughable aggregation of scrap that you call a computer network."

Somewhere deep inside JEVEX something hiccuped. A million tasks that had been running inside the system froze in the confusion as directives coming down from the highest operating levels of the nucleus redefined the whole structure of priority assignments to force an emergency analysis of the new data. And in the middle of it all, the routines that had been scanning for inquisitive probes through h-space faltered. It was only for a few seconds, but . . .

On Thurien, VISAR spoke suddenly to end a long vigil that had been dragging silently by for hours. "Something's happened! I've got a link to ZORAC!" Even as Caldwell was jumping to his feet, and Heller and Danchekker were looking up with startled faces on the other side of the room, streams of binary were pouring across the gulf to the *Shapieron,* light-years away, and VISAR had begun analyzing the patterns assembled by ZORAC.

"What's the situation?" Calazar asked tensely. "Is the ship all right? How far into JEVEX have they penetrated?"

"They've got problems," VISAR said after a short delay.

"Give me a few more seconds. This is going to need some fast footwork."

On the Command Deck of the *Shapieron,* a familiar voice that had not been heard for several days spoke suddenly to break the silence that had fallen with despair. "Say, you're in a bit of a mess here. Sit tight. I'll handle this."

Eesyan's jaw dropped in disbelief. Garuth looked up speechlessly from where he had sunk down into a chair at one of the empty crew stations. Around them a score of other dazed Ganymeans had heard it too, but didn't believe it, either. "VISAR?" Eesyan whispered, as if half fearing an aural hallucination. "ZORAC, was that VISAR?"

"It's busy," ZORAC's voice answered. "Don't ask me what's happened, but yes it was. Something deactivated the self-checking functions, and I've switched off the jamming routine. We're through to Thurien."

While ZORAC was speaking, VISAR decoded the access passwords into JEVEX's diagnostic subsystem, erased a set of data that it found there, substituted new data of its own, and reset the alarm indicators. Inside the Jevlenese Defense Sector Five control center, a display screen changed to announce a false alarm caused by a malfunctioning remote communications relay. Far off in space, the two destroyers turned away to return to their stations and resume routine patrolling. Already VISAR was pouring volumes of information into JEVEX that it had no time to explain, not even to ZORAC. At the same time it broke its way into JEVEX's communications subsystem and gained control of the open channel to Earth.

A voice that Verikoff recognized as VISAR's spoke suddenly in the communications room in Sverenssen's house. "Okay, we've done it. If Vic Hunt and the others are there somewhere, you can bring them in to watch what happens next. I can edit them out of the datastream to Jevlen on a one-way basis. Get off the line now as quick as you can."

Somehow Verikoff kept his astonishment from showing. Behind him Hunt and the others had heard and were slowly moving in through the door, too astounded to say anything. Broghuilio, obviously unaware of them, was still staring dumbstruck from one of the screens. Verikoff pulled himself together and reacted swiftly. "You have one hour to give your reply, Broghuilio," he said. "And hear this—if one of those ships at Thurien makes so much as anything that even looks like a hostile move, we will attack under an order that will be irrevocable once issued. You have one hour."

Nothing changed on the screen, but VISAR announced, "Okay, you're off the air." At once a bewildered Verikoff was assailed by congratulations and back-slapping from all sides. Pacey and Benson were watching incredulously from the doorway, while just inside the room Sobroskin slipped his automatic surreptitiously back inside his jacket.

Another screen came to life to show the Command Deck of the *Shapieron* as VISAR continued to integrate the communications functions of JEVEX that it was taking over into its own network. A few seconds later another screen brought the view from the Government Center in Thurios. It had to be the most bizarre computer hookup ever, Hunt thought as his eyes jumped from side to side to take it all in. Caldwell, Heller, and Danchekker were physically in Alaska, yet he was seeing them through a link that extended from Connecticut to a Jevlenese star light-years away, back to the *Shapieron* and from there to a second star, and from Gistar back to the perceptron at McClusky.

"You . . . apparently believe in cutting things close," Eesyan said from the *Shapieron*, still looking distinctly shaken.

"You worry too much," Caldwell told him, addressing a point offscreen. "We know how to manage a business." He shifted his gaze to look straight out of the screen in Connecticut. "How'd it go? Is everybody okay? Where's Sverenssen?"

"We had a change of plans," Hunt replied. "I'll tell you about it later. Everybody's fine here."

On the screen that showed the Jevlenese War Room, Broghuilio had demanded a report from JEVEX on its current surveillance intercepts from Earth. JEVEX responded by producing accounts of Earth's leaders meeting secretly to agree on details of a combined attack on Jevlen. That was already historical, JEVEX declared in answer to questions from a completely stunned Broghuilio. Currently the plans for the assault were complete, and preparations were well advanced. JEVEX's latest intercept was a briefing from the senior officers of the joint Terran command staff, which it proceeded to replay. Broghuilio grew more perplexed and more flustered as he listened.

"Explain this, JEVEX," he demanded in a strangled voice. "What forces were those primitives talking about? What were those weapons?"

"My respects, Excellency, but it would appear to be self-explanatory," JEVEX answered. "The strategic forces that Earth has been building for some time. The weapons referred to are typical of those deployed by the various nations of Earth at the present time."

Broghuilio's brow knotted, and his beard quivered. He scowled at the nervous faces around him as if seized by the sudden suspicion that only he among all of them might be sane. "Typical of what weapons deployed by Earth at the present time? You have never informed us of such weapons."

Invisible fingers raced through JEVEX's memory, interchanging hundreds of thousands of record descriptors in a fraction of a second. "I regret that I must dispute the statement, Excellency. I have reported the details consistently."

The color of Broghuilio's face darkened even further. "What are you talking about? Reported details of what?"

"The sophisticated interplanetary offensive and defensive capabilities that Earth has been developing for several decades," JEVEX informed him.

"JEVEX, WHAT ARE YOU TALKING ABOUT?" Broghuilio exploded. "Earth disarmed years ago. You have reported *that* consistently. Explain this."

"There is nothing to explain. I have always reported what I have just said."

Broghuilio brought his hands up to massage his eyes, then wheeled around suddenly to throw out his hands in an imploring gesture to those around him. "Am I going mad, or is that idiot machine having some kind of a fit?" he demanded. "Will somebody tell me that I have been seeing and hearing what I think I have been seeing and hearing for all these years. Have I been imagining things? Were we told that Earth had disarmed, or were we not? Do those weapons that we just heard about exist, or do they not? Am I the only sane person in this room, or am I not? Somebody tell me what's happening."

"JEVEX reports the facts," Estordu said lamely, as if that explained everything.

"HOW CAN IT BE REPORTING FACTS?" Broghuilio shouted. "It's contradicting itself. Facts are facts. They can't contradict."

"I have contradicted nothing," JEVEX objected. "My records all indicated that—"

"Shut up! Speak when you are spoken to."

"My apologies, Excellency."

"What Verikoff said about VISAR must be true," Estordu muttered in a worried voice. "VISAR could have been manipulating JEVEX when they were coupled together, before JEVEX disconnected—for years, maybe. Now that JEVEX is isolated, possibly we're receiving the truth for the first time." A ripple of alarmed voices ran around the War Room.

Broghuilio licked his lips and looked suddenly less sure of himself. "JEVEX," he commanded.

"Excellency?"

"Those reports—they were received direct from the surveillance system?"

"Of course, Excellency."

"Those weapons exist? They are being mobilized now?"

"Yes, Excellency."

Wylott was looking uncertain. "How can we be sure?" he objected. "JEVEX says first one thing and then another. How do we know what is true?"

"So, do we do nothing?" Broghuilio asked him. "Would you just sit there and hope that the Terran assault force doesn't exist? What would it take to convince you—a hundred thousand of them coming for your throat? And what would you do then? Imbecile!" Wylott fell silent. The others around the War Room looked at one another with apprehension.

Broghuilio clasped his hands behind his back and began pacing slowly. "We still have a card up our sleeve," he said after a few seconds. "We have decoded their top-level secure communications, and we know their plans. We may have fewer weapons, but we are immeasurably ahead of Earth technically. We command a vastly superior firepower." He looked up, and his eyes began to gleam. "You heard those primitives—the main advantage they were counting on was surprise. Well, they no longer have that advantage. So, Verikoff calls us a rabble, does he? Let him send in his horde of Terran primitives. We will be waiting for them. He will find out who are the rabble when they come up against *Jevlenese* weapons."

Broghuilio turned back to face Wylott. "The operation at Thurien must be suspended for the time being," he declared. "Recall our forces at once and redeploy them for defense of Jevlen. This is not a time to be concerned about upsetting orbits at Gistar. Project the transfer ports in to where the ships are now, and get them back here as soon as possible. I want them in position by this time tomorrow."

New orders went out to the commanders of the task force at Thurien, who prepared their vessels for immediate transfer back. But they were in VISAR-controlled space, and JEVEX reported that its attempts to project entry ports into that region were being jammed; the ships could not be brought back without getting clear of Gistar first. Broghuilio had no choice but to extend his deadline by an extra day and order his force to get away under its own power. An hour later it was streaming in full flight back toward the edge of the Thurien planetary system.

"Phase One completed successfully," Caldwell announced with satisfaction from Thurios as he watched the data displays being presented inside the Government Center. "We've got the bastards on the run. Now let's make sure we keep things going that way."

chapter thirty-five

The transfer ports were ready and waiting outside the system of Gistar as arranged, and the Jevlenese warships peeled out of formation to enter them in relays with crisp, disciplined, military precision. What they didn't know was that by then VISAR was controlling the transfer system, not JEVEX, and such were VISAR's manipulations of JEVEX's internal functions that JEVEX didn't know it, either. Upon exiting back into normal space, one squadron found itself at Sirius, another at Aldebaran, and another near Canopus, while the rest reappeared strewn in ones and twos across Arcturus, Procyon, Castor, Polaris, Rigel, and assorted other stars in between. Thus they were out of harm's way for the time being and could be rounded up later. That completed Caldwell's Phase Two.

With a cigarette in one hand and a cup of black coffee in the other, Hunt stood on the patio outside Sverenssen's house, watching a protesting group of people in brightly colored garb being herded into an Air Force personnel carrier by the pool while a vigilant semicircle of Special Forces troopers looked on from a short distance back. The most recent captives had arrived at Sverenssen's expecting a party, but had found the CIA waiting instead. With VISAR controlling the surveillance there was no longer any need to conceal the activity around the house from orbital observation, but Clifford Benson had decided to maintain a low profile all the same, mainly to take advantage of just this kind of opportunity to extend further his suspect list of Sverenssen's acquaintances. But that was really just a precaution to identify any collaborators that might have been recruited locally. VISAR had found included among JEVEX's records a complete organizational chart of the Jevlenese operation on Earth, and with that information now in Benson's and Sobroskin's hands, the rest of the network would soon be mopped up.

A concentration of Ganymean spacecraft had been building up on the periphery of the Jevlenese planetary system, and at that point it would have been possible for VISAR to shut off all of JEVEX's services from the Jevlenese in the same way that it had done with the Jevlenese element across the Thurien-administered worlds. The problem, however, was that the Jevlenese had clearly been preparing for a war situation for some time, and there was no way of telling what other stand-alone and backup systems they might possess that were capable of operating without JEVEX. Hunt and Caldwell therefore decided that simply pulling the plug, sending in the Ganymeans, and hoping for the best was not the way to go. Instead they opted to continue applying pressure until either they obtained the unconditional surrender that Verikoff had demanded, or the Jevlenese operation somehow fell apart from the inside. Also they hoped that the reactions they observed inside the Jevlenese War Room would reveal whether or not, and if so to what degree, the Jevlenese could in fact carry on without JEVEX.

Behind Hunt, a flap opened in the plastic sheeting with which the back of the house had been temporarily repaired, and Lyn stepped out through what had been a glass-panel wall of the corner room. She moved over to where he was standing and slipped an arm lightly through his. "I guess this place is off the list for the party rounds from now on," she said, looking across at the VTOL down by the pool.

"Just my luck," Hunt murmured. "As soon as some of the girls I've been hearing about show up, they take 'em away again. Who ever deserved a life like this?"

"Is that all you were worried about?" she asked. Her eyes were twinkling, and there was an elusive, playfully challenging note in her voice.

"And to see pal Sverenssen off on his way, of course. What else?"

"Oh, really," Lyn said softly and mockingly. "That wasn't exactly the way I heard it from Gregg."

"Oh." Hunt frowned for a moment. "He, er . . . he told you about that, huh?"

"Gregg and I work pretty well together. You should know that." She wriggled her arm more tightly inside his. "It sounded to me like somebody was pretty upset."

"Principles," Hunt said stiffly after a pause. "Fancy me being stuck up in a place like McClusky while somebody else was down here in the sun, getting all that action. It was the principle of it. I have very strong principles."

"Oh, you idiot," Lyn said with a sigh.

They walked back into the house. Sobroskin was standing nearby with a couple of his officers, and Verikoff was sitting on a couch on the far side of the room, talking with Benson and a mix of CIA officials and more Soviets. Norman Pacey was nowhere in sight; probably he was still in the communications room where Hunt had left him a while earlier. Hunt caught Sobroskin's eye and inclined his head slightly in Verikoff's direction. "That guy's done a good job, and he's trying hard," he muttered in a low voice. "I hope he gets a big remission."

"We'll see what we can do," Sobroskin said. His tone was noncommittal, but there was something deep down in it that Hunt found reassuring.

"WHAT?" A voice that sounded like Broghuilio's shrieked distantly from the direction of the passageway that led through to the communications room. "YOU'VE MANAGED TO LOCATE THEM WHERE?"

"Oh-oh. I think somebody's just found his fleet," Hunt said, grinning. "Come on. Let's go and watch the fun." They moved across toward the passageway, and all around the room figures began standing up and converging behind them. Nobody, it seemed, wanted to miss the excitement.

"There must have been a malfunction in JEVEX," the Supreme Commander of the Thurien task force pleaded, cringing as Broghuilio advanced menacingly toward him. "Everything has been premature. There was no time to test the transfer system thoroughly."

"It's true," a white-faced Wylott said from behind. "There wasn't enough time. An interplanetary operation could not be organized on such a schedule. It was impossible."

Broghuilio whirled around and pointed a finger at a screen showing the latest details of the Terran order of battle. "WELL THEY'VE DONE IT!" he raged. "Every bicycle and bedpan factory on the planet is making weapons." He turned to appeal to the whole room. "And what do my *experts* tell me? Two years to complete the quadriflexor program! Twelve months to bring the extra generators on line! 'But we have the overwhelming technical superiority, Excellency,' I'm told." He turned purple and raised his clenched fists over his head. "WELL WHERE IS IT? Do I have all the imbeciles in the Galaxy on my side? Give me a dozen of those Earthmen and I'd conquer the Universe." He wheeled upon Estordu. "Get them back here. Even if you have to exit them here in the middle of the planetary system, get them back here today."

"It . . . seems that it isn't quite that simple," Estordu mumbled bleakly. "JEVEX is reporting difficulties in controlling the transfer system."

"JEVEX, what is this oaf babbling about?" Broghuilio snapped.

"The central beam synchronization system is not responding, Excellency," JEVEX answered. "I am confused. I have not been able to interpret the diagnostic reports."

Broghuilio closed his eyes for a moment and fought to keep control of himself. "Then do it without JEVEX," he said to Estordu. "Use the standby transfer facility at Uttan."

Estordu swallowed. "The Uttan system is not general purpose," he pointed out. "It was only set up to handle supply transfers to Jevlen. The fleet is scattered across fifteen different stars. Uttan would have to recalibrate for every one. It would take weeks."

Broghuilio turned away in exasperation and began pacing furiously back and forth across the floor. He halted suddenly in front of the commanding general of the local defense system. "They've got their attack planned all the way down to who will dig the latrines after they've wiped out the last imbecile in your army. You have a direct line into their communications network, and you can decode their signals. You know their intentions. Where is your defense plan?"

"What? I . . ." the general faltered helplessly. "How do you—"

"YOUR PLAN OF DEFENSE. WHERE IS IT?"

"But . . . we have no weapons."

"You have no reserves? What kind of a general are you?"

"A few robot destroyers only, all controlled by JEVEX. Can they be relied upon? The reserves were sent to Thurien." That had been at Broghuilio's insistence, but nobody chose to remind him of the fact.

A deathly silence enveloped the Jevlenese War Room. At last Wylott said firmly. "A truce. There is no alternative. We must sue for a truce."

"What?" Broghuilio looked toward him. "The Protectorate has barely been declared, and already you are saying we should crawl to primitives? What kind of talk is this?"

"For time," Wylott urged. "Until Uttan is in full production and the stockpiles are built up. Give the army time to be brought up to strength and trained. Earth has been geared to war for centuries. We have not, and there is the difference. The break from Thurien was forced too soon."

"It looks as if it may be the only chance we have, Excellency," Estordu said.

"JEVEX has reopened a channel," VISAR announced. "Broghuilio wishes a private audience with Calazar." Calazar had been expecting the call and was sitting alone on one side of the room in the Government Center waiting for it, while Caldwell, Danchekker, Heller, and the Thuriens watched from the far side.

A head-and-shoulders image of Broghuilio appeared in a frame before Calazar. Broghuilio looked surprised and uncertain. "Why are we talking like this? I asked to come to Thurien."

"I do not feel that the intimacy of proximity would be appropriate," Calazar replied. "What did you wish to discuss?"

Broghuilio swallowed and forced his words with a visible effort. "I have had an opportunity to consider the recent . . . developments. On reflection, it seems that perhaps we were disoriented by the arrogance of the Terrans. Our reactions were, perhaps, a little . . . hasty. I would like to propose a debate to reconsider the relationship between our races."

"That is no longer an affair that concerns me," Calazar told him. "I have agreed with the Terrans to leave the matter to be settled between yourselves. They have given you their terms. Do you accept them?"

"Their terms are outrageous," Broghuilio protested. "We have to negotiate."

"Negotiate with the Terrans."

Alarm showed on Broghuilio's face. "But they are barbarians . . . savages. Have you forgotten what leaving them to settle things their way will mean?"

"I choose not to. Have you forgotten the *Shapieron*?"

Broghuilio paled. "That was an inexcusable error. Those responsible will be punished. But this . . . this is different. You are Ganymeans. We stood beside you for millennia. You can't stand aside and abandon us now."

"You deceived us for millennia," Calazar replied coldly. "We wanted to keep Lunarian violence from spreading into the Galaxy, but it is loose in the Galaxy already. Our attempts to change you have failed. If the only solution left lies with the Terrans, then so be it. The Ganymeans can do no more."

"We must discuss this, Calazar. You can't allow this."

"Will you accept the Terran terms?"

"They cannot be serious. There must be room for negotiation."

"Then negotiate with the Terrans. I have nothing more to say. Excuse me now, please." The image of Broghuilio vanished.

Calazar turned to confront the approving faces across the room. "How did I do?" he asked.

"Terrific," Karen Heller told him. "You should apply for a seat in the UN."

"How does it feel to be hard-nosed, Terran-style," Showm asked curiously.

Calazar stood up, drew himself up to his full height, and filled his lungs with air while he considered the question. "Do you know, I find it rather . . . invigorating," he confessed.

Caldwell turned his head toward an image showing the observers on Earth. "It's not looking so bad," he said. "They can't get their ships back, and they don't seem to have a lot else. We could pull the rug out now. What do you think?"

Hunt was looking dubious. "Broghuilio's shaky, but he hasn't cracked yet," he replied. "He might have enough there to turn nasty with, especially if only unarmed Thurien ships show up. I'd like to see him a bit more unhinged first."

"So would we," Garuth said from the *Shapieron*. His tone left no room for doubt about the matter.

Caldwell thought for a second, then nodded. "I'll go along with that." He stroked his chin and cocked an eye at Hunt. "And VISAR has done a helluva job preparing all this material. It'd be a shame to waste it, wouldn't it."

"A terrible shame," Hunt agreed solemnly.

chapter thirty-six

The scene being presented inside the Jevlenese War Room was a view of the combined Terran battle fleet forming up as it moved from Earth. In the foreground a formation of destroyers, sleek, gray, and menacing, was moving into position to become part of an unfolding armada that extended away as far as the eye could see. As the first shrank into the distance to merge into the array, more formations slid majestically inward from the sides of the view and were absorbed in turn into the growing panorama. The first groups carried the Red Star of the Soviet Union, the next ones the Stars and Stripes of the U.S.A., and after those came the emblems of U.S. Europe, Canada, Australia, and the Republic of China. Farther away, moving slowly behind the vessels maneuvering and turning in the foreground, were lines of immense warships, their stark, solid contours broken by sinister weapon housings and ominous clusters of externally mounted missile pods. And behind them were the task groups and supply convoys—carriers, bombardment platforms, battle cruisers, interceptor mother ships, ground-suppression orbiters, shuttle launchers, troop and armor carriers, transports, all attended by swarms of support and escort craft—diminishing away to become pinpoints that seemed to be hardly moving at all against the stars. But appearances were deceiving. The whole awesome constellation was speeding silently and relentlessly away from Earth—toward the Ganymean transfer ports.

JEVEX's comments came through on audio. "The first wave, moving out from its forming-up area near Luna. Measured acceleration is consistent with the arrival time that the Terrans have indicated."

Broghuilio turned a shade paler. "First wave?" he gasped. "There's more?"

In response the scene changed to show a view looking

277

down on what appeared to be a huge base of some kind, enclosed by a perimeter fence and surrounded by desolate, sandy terrain. Lines of dots along one side expanded rapidly as the view enlarged, and resolved themselves into rows of surface shuttles in the process of being loaded. The area in front of them was packed with lines of tanks, artillery, personnel carriers, and thousands of troops waiting in neat, geometric groupings. "Chinese regular divisions embarking to be ferried up for the second wave now assembling in orbit," JEVEX announced.

The view changed again to show a similar scene, but this time set among thickly forested hills. "Conventional low-level supersonic bombers and high-altitude interceptors being loaded in Siberia."

And another view. "Missile batteries and antitank laser units embarking in the western U.S.A. There're more coming in from all over. Contingency plans are being drawn up for a third wave."

Perspiration was showing on Broghuilio's face. He closed his eyes, and his lips moved soundlessly as he struggled to remain calm. "Might I suggest, Excellency, that—" Wylott began, but Broghuilio cut him off with a sharp wave of his hand.

"Quiet. I need time to think." Broghuilio brought his hand up to his chin and began tugging at his beard nervously. He clenched his other fist behind his back and paced to the far end of the War Room. Then he turned to face back again. "JEVEX."

"Excellency?"

"VISAR must have a link into the Terran communications net through the Thurien facility there. Get me a channel into it through VISAR. I want to talk to the President of the United States of America, the Soviet Premier, or anybody else in high authority that VISAR can get hold of. Do it immediately."

"How do you want me to play it?" VISAR asked in the Government Center at Thurios.

"We can't let the plan bog down," Caldwell said. "Unconditional surrender has to be his only way out. Fix it so that he thinks he's cut off from everybody except Verikoff."

Anxious and impatient, Broghuilio had started pacing

again. Then JEVEX announced, "VISAR is denying the request. It has been directed to conform to Thurien policy, which is to dissociate itself from Terran-Jevlenese affairs."

Broghuilio's legs almost buckled beneath him. "The Thuriens are transferring those warships here to wipe us out!" he shouted. "What kind of dissociation policy is that? Tell VISAR I insist."

"VISAR has instructed me to advise you, with respect, Excellency, to go to hell."

Broghuilio was too numbed with shock to react violently. "Then tell VISAR to connect me to Calazar again," he choked.

"VISAR refuses."

"Then connect VISAR through to me."

"VISAR has severed all connections. I am unable to obtain further responses."

Broghuilio had begun trembling with a mixture of rage and fear. He spun his head wildly from side to side, his eyes white and staring. "Verikoff is your only choice," Wylott said. "You have to accept the ultimatum."

"*Never!*" Broghuilio shouted. "I'll never surrender my force intact. We still have two days. We can evacuate the entire officer corps, our scientists, our best engineers, and consolidate at Uttan. We will make our stand there. Uttan has permanent defenses that the Terrans will find themselves hard put to match. They will still have some surprises in store for them if they try to follow us there." He looked at Wylott. "Work out a schedule with JEVEX to evacuate the maximum of value from Jevlen in two days. Begin at once. Ignore all other tasks."

"I think we ought to try the switch," Hunt said, watching. "They're just about ready."

"Are you really going to try that?" Shilohin asked from the *Shapieron*. She sounded skeptical. "It's too illogical, surely."

"What do you think, Chris?" Caldwell asked, glancing over his shoulder.

"They have been conditioned to accept contradictions now," Danchekker said. "At this moment there is a good chance that they will be incapable of thinking sufficiently clearly to question it."

"And they are close to panic," Sobroskin observed from beside Hunt. "Panic and logic are impossible companions."

"I'm still not sure I understand this phenomenon you call panic," Eesyan said from the *Shapieron*.

"Let's see if we can show you," Caldwell said, and gave an instruction to VISAR.

"Pardon, Excellency," JEVEX queried. "But your figure of two days appears irrelevant."

"What?" Broghuilio stopped dead in his tracks. "What do you mean, irrelevant?"

"I don't understand why you have specified two days," JEVEX answered.

Broghuilio shook his head, nonplussed. "It's obvious, isn't it? The Terran attack will begin two days from now, will it not?"

"I don't follow, Excellency."

Broghuilio sent a puzzled frown around the room. His aides stared back at him equally bemused. "The attack is due in two days, is it not?" he said again.

"There has been no postponement, Excellency. The attack is still expected today, twelve hours from now."

Nothing happened for a few seconds.

Then Broghuilio brought his hand up to his face and beat it slowly and deliberately several times against his brow. "JEVEX," he said. His voice was quiet as his effort to control himself overcompensated. "You have just told us that the first wave is only now in the process of leaving Earth."

"Pardon, Excellency, but I have no record of saying any such thing."

It was too much. Broghuilio's voice began to rise and shake uncontrollably. "How can the Terrans be less than a day away?" he demanded. "Are they or are they not departing from Earth now?"

"They began departing from Earth two days ago," JEVEX replied. "They have entered Jevlenese planetary space and will commence their attack in twelve hours' time."

Broghuilio's color was deepening rapidly. "Those surveillance reports that you just presented. Were they or were they not live from Earth as of this moment, as you stated?"

"They were records obtained two days ago, as I stated."

"YOU DID NOT SAY THAT!" Broghuilio screamed.

"I did. My records confirm it. Shall I replay them?"

Broghuilio turned to appeal to the rest of the room. "You all heard it. What did that idiot machine say? Were those views live or were they not?" Nobody was listening. One of the aides was rushing back and forth and jabbering incoherently, another was clutching at his face and moaning, while among the rest consternation was breaking out on every side.

"They couldn't be from two days ago."

"How do you know? How do you know what's happening and what isn't? How do you know anything?"

"JEVEX said so."

"It said the opposite too."

"Maybe JEVEX is mad."

"But JEVEX said—"

"JEVEX doesn't know what it's saying. We can't trust anything."

"The Terrans are coming! They're only hours away!"

On one side of the room the scientist, Estordu, quietly vanished. In the confusion, nobody noticed.

Broghuilio was waving his arms and shouting above the clamor. "Twelve hours! *Twelve hours!* And you tell me you have no weapons! They'll be coming straight in for the kill because they don't know what opposition to expect. . . . AND WE HAVE NO OPPOSITION TO OFFER! A shipful of children could walk in and take us over, and the Terrans don't even know it. And what do I have to stop them? Imbecile generals, imbecile scientists, and an imbecile computer!"

Wylott shouldered his way through to where Broghuilio was standing. "There is no choice," he insisted. "You have to accept Verikoff's terms. At least that way there will come another day." Broghuilio turned his head and glowered, but the inevitability of what Wylott had said was written in his eyes. But still he could not bring himself to give the order. Wylott waited for a few seconds, then raised his head to call above the commotion still going on around them. "JEVEX. Call Earth via your own channel to Sverenssen. Get Verikoff on the line."

"At once, General," JEVEX acknowledged.

In the communications room in Connecticut, Hunt

turned his head toward Verikoff, who was watching from the doorway. "You'd better come on in. It looks as if you'll be on again in a few seconds to accept the surrender. It's just about all over." Verikoff moved to the center of the room while the others fell back to clear a small circle around him. On the screen showing the Jevlenese War Room, Wylott and Broghuilio had turned to look directly out at the room and were waiting expectantly for JEVEX to make the connection. Verikoff folded his arms and assumed a domineering posture in readiness.

And suddenly the screen went blank.

Puzzled looks appeared all around the room. "VISAR?" Hunt said after a few seconds. "VISAR, what's happened?" There was no reply. The screens that had been connecting them to Thurien and the *Shapieron* had gone blank as well.

Verikoff moved quickly over to a bank of equipment on one side of the room and ran rapidly through a sequence of tests. "It's dead," he announced, looking up at the others. "The whole system is dead. We don't have any channels to anywhere, and I can't open any. Something has cut us off from JEVEX completely."

In the Government Center at Thurios, Caldwell was equally bewildered. "VISAR, what's happened?" he demanded. "Where did the views from Earth and Jevlen go? Have you lost them or something?"

A few seconds went by, then VISAR answered. "It's worse than that. I haven't only lost Connecticut and the War Room, I've lost everything from JEVEX. I don't have anything into it at all. The whole system has switched off."

"Don't you know anything that's happening at Jevlen at all?" Morizal asked, aghast.

"Nothing," VISAR said. "The only channel I've got to anywhere in the whole of the JEVEX-controlled world-system is the one through to the *Shapieron*. JEVEX seems to be dead. The whole system has just gone down."

Broghuilio found himself reclining in his private quarters deep underground in the complex that housed the Directorate of Strategic Planning. He sat up sharply, unsure of what had happened. A moment before he had been in the War Room with Wylott, waiting for a connection to

Verikoff. Even as he remembered, he saw again in his mind's eye the armada from Earth, at that moment sweeping inward toward Jevlen. He looked around wildly. "JEVEX?"

No response.

"JEVEX, answer me."

Nothing.

Something cold and heavy turned over deep in his stomach. He leaped to his feet, fumbled his way into a robe to cover his shorts and undershirt, and hurried into the next room to check the status indicators of the suite's monitor panel. Lighting, air conditioning, communications, services . . . everything had reverted to emergency backup mode. JEVEX was not operating. He tried activating the communications console, but the only thing he could raise on the screen was a message stating that all channels were saturated. It meant that the condition was general and not due simply to some local failure; the complex was in panic. He rushed through into his bedroom and began frantically tearing clothes out of a closet.

He was still buttoning his tunic when a tone sounded from the outside door in the hallway. Broghuilio hastened out and pressed his thumb against a printlock plate to dematerialize the door. Estordu was there with two other aides. The sounds of shouting and commotion came in from behind them.

"What's happened?" Broghuilio demanded. "The whole system is dead."

"I deactivated it," Estordu told him. "I threw the manual override breakers in the master nucleus control room. I've shut JEVEX down totally."

Broghuilio's beard quivered, and his eyes widened. "You *what*—" he began, but Estordu waved a hand impatiently to silence him. The gesture was so out of character that Broghuilio just stared.

"Can't you see what's happened?" Estordu said, speaking rapidly and urgently. "JEVEX was not functioning coherently. Something was affecting it from the *inside*. It could only have been VISAR. Somehow VISAR gained access to it. That meant that the Thuriens could have been watching every move we made. We still have twelve hours, and if we move quickly we can still get away. We still have emergency communications channels to Uttan, and the standby transfer system can project an entry port to Jevlen. With JEVEX inoperative and VISAR therefore blind, we can make our arrangements without risking interference from the Thuriens or the Terrans. The nearest Terran ships are still twelve hours away. By the time they get here we can be gone, and they'll have no way of knowing where to. By the time they think of looking for us at Uttan, we will be well prepared. Don't you see? It was the only way. With JEVEX running we couldn't have planned a move without them knowing."

Broghuilio thought rapidly as he listened. There was no time for arguing, and anyway, Estordu was right. He nodded. "Everyone with their wits about them will go physically to the War Room," he said. He looked at Estordu. "Find Lantyar and tell him I want five reliable crews mustered and brought to Geerbaine by eighteen hundred hours today. You . . ." He directed his gaze at one of the two aides standing behind Estordu. "Contact the operations commander at Geerbaine and tell him I want five E-class transports ready for launch not one minute later than then, and power standing by on-line at Uttan to project ports as soon as the transports clear Jevlen." He gestured to the other aide. "And you, find General Wylott and tell him to mobilize four companies of guards and organize air transportation from here to Geerbaine, ready to leave by seventeen thirty hours. I'll need capacity for two thousand persons. Commandeer it from wherever you need to, and don't hesitate to use force. Do you understand?" Broghuilio straightened his collar and went back through to the bedroom to buckle on his belt and sidearm. "I am going to the War Room now," he called out to them. "The three of you will report to me there not later than one hour from now. Do as I say, and this time tomorrow we will all be on Uttan."

chapter thirty-seven

The *Shapieron* had moved closer to Jevlen to await the arrival of the Ganymean ships from Thurien, which had begun moving inward from the edge of the planetary system but were still many hours away. The main screen on the Command Deck was showing views of Jevlen's surface being sent back from probes at lower altitudes. The planet seemed to be in chaos. Nothing was flying anywhere, but in many places people had begun leaving the cities on foot and in disorderly streams of ground vehicles that had soon jammed solid on highway systems never intended for more than minor local or recreational traffic. Disturbances and rioting had broken out in a few places, but in most the populations were merely assembling in the open spaces, leaderless and bewildered. Communications traffic from the surface was garbled and revealed no organization for maintaining order or vital services. In short, the Ganymeans were going to have a big job on their hands putting the pieces of the mess together again.

Garuth was tense and apprehensive as he stood in the center of the Command Deck taking in the reports. VISAR had not crashed JEVEX, so the culprit had to have been the Jevlenese themselves. Somehow they had discovered they were the unwitting objects of surveillance through JEVEX, and had shut down the system to blind VISAR to what they were doing. In other words they were up to something, and there was no way of knowing what. Garuth didn't like it.

The other thing that was bothering him at a deeper level was the feeling that he had failed. Despite the reassurances of Eesyan, Shilohin, Monchar, and the others that his bringing the *Shapieron* to Jevlen had saved Thurien, Garuth was acutely conscious of how near to disaster he had brought them, and that only the fast action of Hunt and the others on Earth had saved things. He had risked his crew and Eesyan's scientists irresponsibly, and others had bailed him out. Yes, the threat to Thurien had been removed; but Garuth didn't feel he deserved very much credit for that. He would have liked to have contributed more and the congratulations that had poured through from Thurien had only added to his discomfort.

On a smaller screen to one side, Hunt was talking over his shoulder to the others who were crowded into the room in the Connecticut house that had been the headquarters of the Jevlenese operation to infiltrate Earth. "Can you imagine the problems we might have created for lots of people on this planet in years to come?"

"What do you mean?" the voice of Norman Pacey, the American government representative, asked from somewhere in the background.

Hunt half turned to wave at the screen in front of him. "One day people might be sending their kids to college on Thurien. Suppose the kids figure out this stunt for themselves and start calling home collect."

After JEVEX had gone off the air and shut down the communications facility, the group in Connecticut had reestablished contact by the simple expedient of telephoning the control room at McClusky and linking back into VISAR via the databeam to the perceptron. They had called on two lines from the datagrid terminals in Sverenssen's office, next door to the communications room, and had one screen to the *Shapieron* and another to the Government Center at Thurios.

"I still don't believe it," the CIA official, Benson, said from a chair by a window, partly visible over Hunt's shoulder. "When I see somebody picking up the phone and calling talking computers in an alien spaceship out at some other star, I don't believe it." Benson turned his head to address somebody offscreen. "*Jeez!* The CIA should have had something like this years ago. We could even have tuned into what you guys were talking about in the men's room inside the Kremlin."

"I think the days of that kind of thing will very soon be over, my friend," a voice replied from somewhere in an accent that Garuth assumed was Russian.

It would have made no difference if they were physically present in the *Shapieron*, he thought to himself. They would banter and laugh in the same way whatever the risks and whatever the unknowns. They could try, fail, forget, laugh, and try again—and probably succeed. The thought that they had been within a hair's breadth of disaster didn't trouble them. They had won the round, now it was dismissed and in the past, and their only thoughts now were for the next. Sometimes Garuth envied Earthmen.

ZORAC spoke suddenly. Its tone was urgent. "Attention please. There is a new development. Probe Four has detected ships rising fast from the surface on the far side of Jevlen—five of them in tight formation." At the same instant the view on the main screen changed to show the curving, cloud-blotched surface of the planet with five dots creeping across the mottled background.

On the auxiliary screen Hunt was leaning forward while others crowded behind him. They had stopped talking. An adjacent screen showed Calazar and the observers at Thurios, all equally tense.

"It has to be Broghuilio and his staff," Calazar said after a few seconds. "They must be making a break for Uttan. Estordu said they've got a standby transfer system that operates between Jevlen and Uttan. That's what they've been planning! We should have thought of it."

Eesyan had joined Garuth in the center of the Command Deck. Shilohin, Monchar, and some of the scientists were gathering around from the sides of the room. "They have to be stopped," Eesyan said, sounding worried. "They could have Uttan prepared and defended as a fallback base. If they reach it and regroup, they could decide to fight it out. It would only be a matter of time before they realized that we don't have anything to challenge them with. With Uttan in their hands, we'd be in real trouble."

"What is Uttan?" Hunt asked from the screen.

Eesyan turned away from Garuth and answered in a faraway voice as he tried to think. "An airless, waterless ball of rock on the fringe of Jevlenese space, but very rich in metals. The Jevlenese were granted it long ago as a source of raw materials to build up their industries. It's obviously where their weapons came from. But if what we suspect is right, they've turned the whole planet into a fortified armaments factory. We've got to prevent Broghuilio's getting there."

While Eesyan was speaking to Hunt, Garuth quickly reviewed what he could recollect of the Thurien h-transfer system. VISAR or JEVEX could jam h-beams projected into their respective regions of space by virtue of the dense networks of sensors they possessed, which enabled them to monitor the field parameters of a transfer toroid just beginning to form, and disrupt the energy flow through from h-space. Without the sensors, jamming wouldn't work. But the only sensors that existed in the vicinity of Jevlen were JEVEX's and VISAR would not be able to use them since it could only do so through JEVEX, and JEVEX was dead. Hence a beam from Uttan couldn't be disrupted by VISAR. So *that* was why the Jevlenese had shut down the system.

"There's nothing we can do," Calazar was saying from the other screen. "We haven't got anything near there. Our ships are still eight hours away at least."

An agonized silence fell on the Command Deck. Calazar was looking helplessly from one side to another about him, while to one side of him Hunt and the Terrans on Earth had frozen into immobility. On the main screen the five Jevlenese vessels had cleared the edge of the planet's disk.

A feeling of composure and confidence that he had not known for a long time flowed slowly into Garuth's veins as the situation unfolded in sudden crystal clarity. There was no doubt about what he had to do. He was himself again, in control of himself and in command of his ship. "We are right here."

Eesyan stared for a second, then turned his head to gaze uncertainly at the five dots on the main screen, now diminishing rapidly into the starry background of space. "Could we catch them?" he asked dubiously.

Garuth smiled grimly. "Those are just Jevlenese planetary transports," he said. "Have you forgotten? The *Shapieron* was built as a starship." Without waiting for a response from Calazar, he raised his head and called in a louder voice, "ZORAC, dispatch Probe Four in pursuit immediately, recover deployed probes, lift the ship into high orbit, charge all on-board probes for maximum range, and bring the main drives up to full-power readiness. We're going after them."

"And what will you do then?" Calazar asked.

"Worry about that later," Garuth replied. "The first thing is not to lose them."

"Tally ho!" ZORAC cried, mimicking a flawless English accent.

Hunt sat up and blinked in astonishment on one of the screens. "Where the hell did it pick that up?" he asked.

"Documentaries of World War II British fighter pilots," ZORAC announced. "That was for your benefit, Vic. I thought you'd appreciate it."

chapter thirty-eight

Broghuilio stood on the bridge of the Jevlenese flagship and scowled while the technicians and scientists clustered around a battery of datascreens in front of him took in the details of the report coming through from the long-range scanning computers. Gasps of disbelief sounded among the rising murmur of voices. "Well?" he demanded as his patience finally exhausted itself.

Estordu turned from the group. His eyes were wide with shock. "It can't be possible," he whispered. He made a vague gesture behind him. "But it's true . . . there's no doubt about it."

"What is it?" Broghuilio fumed.

Estordu swallowed. "It's . . . the *Shapieron*. It's pulling away from Jevlen and turning this way."

Broghuilio stared at him as if he had just gone insane, then snorted and pulled two of the technicians out of the way to see the screens for himself. For a second his mouth clamped tight, and his beard quivered as his mind refused to accept what his eyes were seeing. Then another screen came to life to show a magnified view from the long-range optical imagers that left no room for dissent. Broghuilio spun around to glare at Wylott, who was watching numbly from a few feet back. "*HOW DO YOU EXPLAIN THIS?*" he shouted.

Wylott shook his head in protest. "It can't be. It was destroyed. I *know* it was destroyed."

"*THEN WHAT IS THAT COMING AT US RIGHT NOW?*" Broghuilio whirled to the scientists. "How long has it been at Jevlen? What is it doing here? Why didn't any of you know about it?"

The captain's voice came from the raised section of the bridge above them. "I've never seen acceleration like it! It's vectoring straight after us. We'll never outrun it."

"They can't do anything," Wylott said in a choking voice. "It's not armed."

"Fool!" Broghuilio snapped. "If it wasn't destroyed, it must have been transferred to Thurien. And Terrans could have been transferred to Thurien. So it could have Terrans on board it with Terran weapons. They could blow us apart, and after your bungling, the *Shapieron*'s crew won't lift a finger to stop them." Wylott licked his lips and said nothing.

"Stress field around the *Shapieron* building up rapidly," the long-range surveillance operator called from one of the stations above. "We're losing radar and optical contact. H-scan shows it's maintaining course and acceleration."

Estordu was thinking furiously. "We may have a chance, Excellency," he said suddenly. Broghuilio jerked his head around and thrust his chin out demandingly. Estordu went on, "The Ganymean ships from that period did not possess stress-field transmission correction, and h-scan equipment was unknown. In other words they have no means of tracking us while they're under main drive. They'll have to aim blind to intercept our predicted course and slow down at intervals to correct. We might be able to lose them by changing course during their blind periods."

At that instant another operator called out, "Gravitational anomaly building up astern and starboard, range nine eighty miles, strength seven, increasing. Readings indicate a Class Five exit port. H-scan shows conformal entry-port mapping to vicinity of *Shapieron*." The tension on the bridge rocketed. It meant that VISAR was projecting two beams to create a linked pair of transfer ports—a "tunnel" through h-space from the *Shapieron* to the Jevlenese vessels. A Class Five port would admit something relatively small. The operator's voice came again, rising with alarm. "An object has emerged at this end. It's coming this way, fast!"

"A bomb!" somebody screamed. *"They've exited a bomb!"* Consternation broke out around the bridge. Broghuilio was wide-eyed and sweating profusely. Wylott had collapsed onto a chair.

The operator's voice came again. "Object identified. It's one of the *Shapieron*'s robot probes . . . matching us in course and speed. The exit port has dissolved."

And the long-range surveillance operator: *"Shapieron* closing and still accelerating. Range two-twenty thousand miles."

"Get rid of it," Broghuilio barked up at the level above. "Captain, shake that thing off."

The captain gave a set of course-correction instructions, which the computers acknowledged and executed.

"Probe matching," came the report. "Evasion ineffective. *Shapieron* has corrected to a new vector and is still closing."

Broghuilio turned a furious face toward Estordu. "You said they'd be blind! They're not even slowing down." Estordu spread his hands and shook his head helplessly. Broghuilio looked at the rest of the group of scientists. "Well, how are they doing it? Can't any of you work it out?" He waited for a few seconds, then pointed a finger angrily at the screens showing the tracking data of the *Shapieron.* "Some genius on *that* ship has thought of something. Everywhere I am surrounded by imbeciles." He began pacing back and forth across the bridge. "How does this happen? They have all the geniuses, and I have all the imbeciles. Give me—"

"The probe!" Estordu groaned suddenly. "They must have fitted the probe and the *Shapieron* with h-links. The probe will be able to monitor every move we make and update the *Shapieron*'s flight-control system through VISAR. We'll never lose it now."

Broghuilio glared at him for a second, then looked across at the communications officer. "We have to make the jump to Uttan now," he declared. "What's the status there?"

"The generators are up to power and standing by," the officer told him. "Their director is locked onto our beacon, and they can throw a port here immediately."

"But what if that probe transfers through with us?" Estordu said. "VISAR would locate it when it reenters at Uttan. It would reveal our destination."

"Those geniuses will have guessed our destination already," Broghuilio retorted. "So what could they do? We can blow anything that comes near Uttan to atoms."

"But we're still too close to Jevlen," Estordu objected, looking alarmed. "It would disrupt the whole planet . . . chaos everywhere."

"So would you rather stay here?" Broghuilio sneered. "Hasn't it occurred to you yet that the probe was just a warning? The next thing they tunnel through at us *will* be a bomb." He sent a stare around the bridge that defied anybody to argue with him. Nobody did. He raised his head. "Captain. Transfer now, to Uttan."

The command was relayed to Uttan, and within seconds huge generators were pouring energy into a tiny volume of space ahead of the five Jevlenese ships. The fabric of spacetime wrinkled, then buckled, heaved, and fell in upon itself to plummet out of the Universe. A spinning vortex began growing to open up the gateway to another realm, first as a faint circle of curdled starlight against the void, then getting stronger, thicker, and sharper, and expanding slowly to reveal a core of featureless, infinite blackness.

And then a counterspinning pattern of refractions materialized inside the first. The resultant composite of vortices shimmered and pulsated as filaments of space and time writhed in a tangle of knotted geodesics. Something was wrong. The port was going unstable. "What's happening?" Broghuilio demanded.

Estordu was turning his head frantically from side to side to take in the displays and data reports. "Something is deforming the configuration . . . breaking up the field manifolds. I've never seen anything like this. It can only be VISAR."

"That's impossible," one of the other scientists shouted. "VISAR can't jam. It has no sensors. JEVEX is shut down."

"That's not jamming," Estordu muttered. "The port began to form. It's doing something else. . . ." His eye caught the view of the *Shapieron* again. "The probe! VISAR is using the probe to monitor the entry-port configuration. It couldn't jam the beam, so it's trying to project a complementary pattern from Gistar to cancel out the toroid from Uttan. It's trying to neutralize it."

"It couldn't," the other scientist protested. "It couldn't get enough resolution through a single probe. It would be aiming virtually blind from Gistar."

"The Gistar and Uttan beams would interact constructively in the same volume," another pointed out. "If an unstable resonance developed, anything could happen."

"That *is* an unstable resonance," Estordu shouted, pointing at the display. "I tell you, that's what VISAR'S doing."

"VISAR would never risk it."

Ahead of the ships, a maelstrom of twisting, convulsing, multiply-connected relativity was boiling under the clash of titanic bolts of energy materializing and superposing from two points, each light-years away. The core shrank, grew again, fragmented, then reassembled itself. And still they were heading directly for its center.

Broghuilio had listened enough. He turned his head up to where the captain was watching him, waiting. Then at the last second, something about Estordu pulled his attention away.

Estordu was standing absolutely still with a strange look on his face as he stared at the view of the *Shapieron*. He was mumbling to himself, and seemed to have forgotten everything going on around him. "H-links through the probes," he whispered. "That was how VISAR got into JEVEX." His eyes opened wider, and his face became ashen as the full realization hit him. "That was how . . . *everything* got into JEVEX! It never existed, any of it. They were doing it through the *Shapieron* all the time. . . . We're running away from a single unarmed ship."

"What is it?" Broghuilio snapped. "Why are you looking like that?"

Estordu looked at him with a bleak stare. "It doesn't exist. . . . The Terran strike force doesn't exist. It never did. VISAR wrote it into JEVEX through the *Shapieron*. The whole thing was a fabrication. There was nothing there but the *Shapieron* all the time."

The captain leaned over from above. "Excellency, we have to . . ." He stopped as he saw that Broghuilio was not listening, hesitated for a second, then turned away to call to somewhere behind him. "Disengage forward compensators. Cut in emergency boost and reverse at full power. Compute evasion function and execute immediately."

"*What? —What did you say?*" Broghuilio turned to face the semicircle of cowering figures behind him. "Are you telling me the Terrans have been making fools out of all of you?"

From above the synthetic voice of a computer came tonelessly: "Negative function. Negative function. All measures ineffective. Ship accelerating on irreversible gradient. Corrective action now impossible. Repeat: Corrective action now impossible."

But Broghuilio didn't hear, even as the craft plunged into the knot of insanely tangled spacetime looming around them. "You imbeciles!" he breathed. His voice rose and began shaking uncontrollably as he lifted his fists high above his head. "*Imbeciles!* IMBECILES! You *IM-BE-CILES!!*"

"My God, they're going straight into it!" Hunt gasped from a screen on the Command Deck of the *Shapieron*. The view on the main screen was being sent back from the probe two hundred thousand miles away, still clinging doggedly to the heels of the Jevlenese ships. A horrified silence had fallen all around.

"What's happening?" Eesyan whispered from the center of the floor.

"An oscillating instability is coupling positively to an h-frequency alias caused by discrepancies in the beam spectra," VISAR answered. "The properties of the region created are beyond analysis."

On another screen Calazar, openmouthed with shock, was shaking his head in protest. "I never intended this," he said in a strangled voice. "Why didn't they turn away? I just wanted to deny them the port."

"ZORAC, cut the main drives and decelerate," Garuth instructed in a voice that was clipped and expressionless.

"Present an optical scan of the area as soon as we reintegrate."

A background of turbulent light and blackness now filled the entire main screen. The five dots grew smaller in front of it . . . and were suddenly swallowed up in the chaos. The turmoil seemed to rush out as the probe followed in after them, and then the view changed abruptly as the *Shapieron*'s stress field dispersed and ZORAC switched through the long-range image from the ship's own scanners. "The instability is breaking down," VISAR reported. "The resonances are degenerating into tubulence eddies. If there was a tunnel there, it's caving in." On the screen the patterns broke up into swirling fragments of light that spiraled rapidly inward, at the same time growing smaller, dimmer, and redder. They faded, and then died. The region of the starfield that was left shimmered for a few seconds to mark where the upheaval had been, and then all was normal just as if nothing had happened.

For a long time an absolute silence gripped the Command Deck, and nobody moved. The faces on the screens showing Earth and Thurien were grim.

And then VISAR spoke again. There was a distinct note of disbelief in its voice. "I have a further report. Don't ask me how right now, but it looks as if they got through. The probe was still transmitting when the tunnel closed in behind it, and its last signal indicates that it reentered normal space." While surprise was still evident all over the Command Deck, the view on the main screen changed to show the last image transmitted by the probe. The five Jevlenese ships were hanging in ragged formation in what looked like ordinary space sure enough, studded with what looked like ordinary stars. And up near one corner was a larger speck that could have been a planet. The image froze at that point. "The transmission ceased there," VISAR said.

"They survived that?" Eesyan stammered. "Where is it? Where in space did they emerge?"

"I don't know," VISAR answered. "They must have been trying for Uttan, but anything could have happened. I'm trying to match the starfield background with projections from Uttan now, but it could take awhile."

"We can't risk waiting," Calazar said. "Even though Uttan might be defended, I'll have to send in the reserve ships from Gistar to try and cut Broghuilio off before he reaches that planet." He waited for a few seconds, but nobody could disagree. His voice became heavier. "VISAR, connect me to the reserve-squadron commander," he said.

"There is nothing more for us to do here," Garuth said in a voice that had become very quiet and very calm. "ZO-RAC, return the ship to Jevlen. We will await the arrival of the Thuriens there."

While the *Shapieron* was turning to head back, a set of toroids opened up briefly some distance outside the planetary system of Gistar, and the squadron of Thurien vessels that had been held in reserve there transferred into h-space, then reemerged outside the system of Uttan. The Jevlenese long-range surveillance instruments detected them as a series of objects hurtling inward at a speed not much below that of light. The commander at Uttan decided that a portion of the Terran strike force had been diverted, and within minutes every emergency signal band was carrying frantic offers of unconditional surrender. The Thuriens arrived at Uttan some hours later and took over without opposition.

That result had been unexpected. The reason for it was even more unexpected: Broghuilio's ships had not, after all, appeared at Uttan, or anywhere near it. Uttan control had lost contact when they vanished from the vicinity of Jevlen, and had been unable to relocate them. Without their leaders, the defenders at Uttan opted to capitulate without a fight.

So where had the five Jevlenese ships gone? VISAR reported that they had not rematerialized anywhere inside the regions of space that it controlled, and when it projected small transfer ports to the scores of worlds previously run by JEVEX and sent search probes bristling with sensors and instruments, the ships were not to be found at any of those places, either. They seemed to have vanished entirely from the explored portion of the Galaxy.

The Thuriens did find something else at Uttan, however—something that left them shaken and mystified. Hanging in space, all at various stages of construction, they found lines of immense engineering structures. Each was in the form of a hollow square that measured five hundred miles along a side, and carried at its center a two-hundred-mile-diameter sphere supported by bars extending diagonally inward from the corners.

chapter thirty-nine

"I don't understand this," Calazar said as he stared out from one of the Thurien vessels floating near Uttan. "Those are full-scale quadriflexors, exactly as we designed them. The Jevlenese have been building hundreds of them."

"I don't know," Showm replied, shaking her head beside him. "It makes no sense."

Heller, Caldwell, and Danchekker looked at each other. "What's a quadriflexor?" Caldwell asked.

Calazar sighed. There was no point in being evasive. "They are the devices with which we were going to enclose the solar system," he said. "They were to be positioned at a considerable distance outside Pluto at points defining a quasi-spherical surface around the system. Every quadriflexor would couple through h-fields to the four adjacent to it in the grid, and collectively they would create a cumulative deformation of spacetime at that boundary which would equate to an escape-proof gravitic gradient.

"We performed preproduction testing on some scaled-down prototypes, and we did in fact begin building some of the full-size versions, but we are still a long way from being in a position to implement the final plan." Calazar waved at the view outside the ship. "But the Jevlenese have obviously been copying our designs in secret, and their program was far more advanced. I can't understand why."

Danchekker was blinking behind his spectacles and frowning to himself while he wrestled with the riddle. Somehow he had the feeling that the last layer of the enigmatic onion that seemed to surround everything connected with the Jevlenese was about to be peeled away. By at first exaggerating Earth's aggressiveness and later manufacturing false evidence, the Jevlenese had persuaded the Ganymeans that Terran expansion had to be checked, and nothing short of physical containment would check it. The Ganymeans had, until very recently, been convinced, and had set the necessary preparations in motion accordingly. But the Jevlenese had embarked on an identical venture and concealed the fact from the Ganymeans. Why? What did it mean?

Danchekker looked over at the images that VISAR was presenting of the Command Deck of the *Shapieron* and Sverenssen's office in Connecticut, but there were no suggestions forthcoming from those directions. The Ganymeans in the *Shapieron* were preoccupied with something that was happening on the main screen inside the ship, while in the other view he could see only the backs of Hunt and the others as they crowded around the terminal on the other side of the room, which connected them to the *Shapieron*. A lot of excited talking was going on in both places, but what it was about was obscure.

"Could they have been planning to do the same thing themselves?" Karen Heller said at last.

"For what reason?" Calazar asked. "We were already working on it. What could they have stood to gain?"

"Time?" Caldwell offered.

Calazar shook his head. "If time was so critical to them, they could have persuaded us to accelerate our own program with a fraction of the effort that they must have put into this. Certainly we have the resources to have been able to beat any schedule they could have been aiming at."

Frenua Showm was looking thoughtful. "And yet it's strange," she mused. "On several occasions when we wanted to speed up our program, the Jevlenese actually seemed to play down the risks of Terran expansion. It was as if they were trying to keep our research moving, but weren't in a hurry to see us move into production."

"They were milking off the know-how," Caldwell grunted. "Making sure that their program stayed well ahead of yours." He paused for a few seconds, then asked,

"Could those things be used for shutting in anything else apart from a star system?"

"Hardly," Calazar replied, then added, "Well, I suppose they could be used to close in anything of comparable size . . . or something smaller, come to that."

"Mmm . . ." Caldwell lapsed back into thought.

Heller shrugged and turned up her hands. "If they weren't going to enclose the solar system, they must have been planning to enclose some other . . ." Her voice trailed away as the answer suddenly became plain, to her and to everybody else at the same time.

Calazar and Showm stared speechlessly at each other for a few seconds. "*Us?*" Calazar managed at last in a strained voice. "*The Thuriens?* They were going to shut in Gistar?" Showm brought her hand up to her brow and shook her head as she struggled to take in the implication of it. Caldwell and Heller were standing dumbstruck.

The whole thing slowly became clear in Danchekker's mind. "*Yes!*" he exclaimed. He moved forward to the center of the group and stood for a moment checking his thoughts, then began nodding his head vigorously. "Yes!" he said again. "Surely it's the only acceptable explanation." He looked excitedly from one to another of the others as if he expected them to agree with something there and then. They stared back at him blankly. Nobody knew what he was talking about. He waited for a moment and then elaborated. "I have never been able to accept fully that the obsessive Lambian-Cerian rivalry could have persisted in the minds of the Jevlenese for all that time, especially with their exposure to Ganymean influence. Did it never strike you as strange? Didn't any of you ever feel that there had to be something more behind it than just that?" He looked at the others questioningly again.

After a few seconds Caldwell said, "I guess not, Chris. Why? What are you getting at?"

Danchekker moistened his lips. "It's an interesting thought, wouldn't you agree, that there was one entity that was always there at the back of things, permanent and unchanging while generations of Jevlenese came and went."

There was a moment of silence. Then Heller stared at him and gasped. "JEVEX? Are you saying the computer was behind the whole thing?"

Danchekker nodded rapidly. "JEVEX was established a long time ago. Is it completely inconceivable that its basic design and programming couldn't somehow have embodied as some kind of innate driving instinct the ruthlessness and ambitions of its creators—the descendants of the original Lambians? And to realize those ambitions, could it not have harnessed the Jevlenese elite as its instruments? But if that were so, it would have found itself confronted by a serious obstacle in the form of the restraints imposed on it by the Thuriens."

Caldwell was beginning to nod. "It would have had to get the Thuriens out of the way somehow," he agreed.

"Precisely," Danchekker said. "But not too quickly. There was a lot that it wanted to learn from them first. And the really cunning part was that at the end of it all, the Thuriens' own ingenuity and technology would provide the means whereby the Jevlenese would get rid of them. Then, armed with stolen Ganymean science and with JEVEX as their leader, the Jevlenese would have had the Galaxy at their mercy. Think of all those developing worlds . . . and a technology that could cross light-years in moments. They would become the masters of every part of explored space, poised to expand their empire without limit, and the only potential opposition would be safely locked up inside a gravitic shell that nothing could get out of." Danchekker gripped his lapels and turned from side to side to take in the astounded expressions around him. "So now at last we see what was behind it all—the ultimate design that they had been working on, probably ever since Minerva. And how near they came to succeeding!"

"So the weapons at Uttan . . ." Calazar said falteringly, still struggling to grasp the enormity of it all. "They were never intended to be used against Thurien at all?"

"I doubt it," Danchekker said. "I suspect that they were for afterward, to add teeth to their expansion when the time came."

"Yes, and guess who'd have been first on the list," Heller said. "They were Lambians, and we were Cerians."

"Of course!" Showm whispered. "Earth would have been defenseless. *That* was why they concealed your demilitarization from us." She nodded slowly in grudging admiration. "It was neatly worked out. First they work to retard

Earth's advancement while they grow strong and learn. Then they accelerate Earth's rate of discovery suddenly, engineer the results into a threat which they enlist Ganymean aid to eliminate. And finally they remove the threat to themselves but conceal the fact from the Ganymeans, and use the very technique that they have induced the Ganymeans to develop as the means of eliminating the Ganymeans instead. That would have left them in a position to settle the old score with the Cerians without interference, and with the odds overwhelmingly in their favor."

"We wouldn't have stood a chance," Caldwell breathed, for once genuinely staggered.

"And the Jevlenese would have repossessed the solar system, which I suspect has always been their first goal," Danchekker said. "I would imagine they have always considered it rightly theirs. And they would no longer have had to play second fiddle to the Ganymeans, a position they clearly have never been able to come to terms with gracefully."

"It all makes sense," Calazar said in a resigned voice. "Why they were so insistent about administering their own, autonomous group of worlds . . . why they needed a system independent of VISAR, controlling its own volume of space." He looked at Showm and nodded. "A lot of things are beginning to make sense now."

He fell silent for a few seconds. When he spoke again his voice was lighter. "If all this is true, then our problem of what to do next could be eased considerably. If the roots of it all lay not so much in the Jevlenese people but in JEVEX, then maybe there is hope for them after all. Distasteful punitive measures may not be necessary."

A distant look came into Showm's eyes. "Ye-es," she said slowly, and began nodding. "Perhaps, given the right help, they might rebuild their civilization upon a new model and emerge from it all as a mature and benign race. All may not be lost yet."

"It does give us a positive goal to aim at and a task to accomplish," Calazar said, sounding more enthusiastic. "Despite all the setbacks, things might work out to a successful conclusion. As you say, all is not lost."

"Er, at present this is merely a hypothesis, you understand," Danchekker said hastily. "But there might be a way to test it. If the whole thing did in fact begin with JEVEX, it might be possible to trace the origins of some of the things we've been talking about back to conceptual sub-nets of some form buried in JEVEX's older archives." He looked at Calazar. "I assume that once your people are fully in control of Jevlen, it would be possible to reactivate parts of JEVEX in a controlled fashion and allow VISAR to examine its records thoroughly."

Calazar was already nodding. "I would have thought so. Eesyan is really the person we should talk to about that." He looked across at the view coming from the Command Deck of the *Shapieron*. "Isn't he free yet? What's happening there?"

Consternation was breaking out among the Ganymeans crowded below the main screen in the image. At the same time a chorus of shouts erupted from the other image, showing the view from Earth, in which Hunt and the others were bumping into each other in their haste to get back across the room to the terminal that connected them to the Thurien ship at Uttan. Danchekker, Calazar, and the others with them forgot their conversation of a few moments earlier and stared in astonishment. Hunt was almost incoherent with excitement as he got to the screen. "We've found them! ZORAC reprocessed the planet. We know where they went. It's impossible!"

Danchekker blinked at him. "Vic, what are you babbling about? Kindly calm down, and simply say whatever it is that you're trying to say."

Hunt recomposed himself with some effort. "The five Jevlenese ships. We know what happened to them." He paused for a second to get his breath back, then turned his head away to call over the people behind him to the terminal connecting them to the *Shapieron*. "ZORAC, pass that shot over to VISAR, would you. Tell VISAR to display it at Uttan." In the ship where Danchekker was, an image appeared of the final shot of the Jevlenese vessels sent back by the *Shapieron*'s probe just before the tunnel caved in. "Have you got it?" Hunt asked.

Danchekker nodded. "Yes. What about it?"

"The spot in the upper right-hand corner is a planet," Hunt said. "We asked ZORAC if there was any way it could reprocess that part of the image and enhance it to give us a better look at it. It did. We know what planet it is."

"Well?" Danchekker asked, puzzled, after a second or two. "Where is it?"

"A better question would be *when*?" Hunt told him.

Danchekker frowned and looked around him only to be met by expressions as confused as his own. "Vic, what are you talking about?" he asked.

"VISAR, show them," Hunt said in reply.

The speck enlarged in an instant to become a full disk occupying the whole frame. It was a world shining brightly against the stars with cloud formations and oceans. The resolution was not good, but there were continental outlines discernible on its surface. Calazar and Showm froze. A split second later, Danchekker realized why.

What he was looking at was not unfamiliar. Like Hunt, he had studied every island, isthmus, estuary, and coastline sandwiched between the two enormous ice caps of that planet many times—at Houston, in the course of the Lunarian investigations over two years earlier. He looked away. Calazar and Showm were still staring in silent awe, and now Caldwell too was wide-eyed with disbelief. Danchekker slowly turned his head to follow their gaze once again. It was still there. He hadn't imagined it.

The planet was Minerva.

chapter forty

Nobody could say for certain exactly how it had come about in those final few seconds as VISAR and the projector at Uttan fought for control of the same speck of spacetime light-years away, and many believed that nobody ever would. But Hunt was forced at last to accept the truth of the claim that Paul Shelling had made at Houston on the day that Karen Heller and Norman Pacey had come to talk to Caldwell: the Ganymean physical equations that described the possibility of point-to-point transfers through space had solutions that admitted transfers through time too. Or both. For somehow the five Jevlenese ships had been hurled across light-years of space and backward through tens of thousands of years of time to emerge in the solar system when Minerva was still in existence. In fact, by careful measurement of the positions of background stars, the Ganymean scientists determined to a high degree of accuracy when; it came out to be about two hundred years before the final Lunarian war.

And that, of course, explained where the superbreed of Lambians, who had emerged seemingly overnight with a technology far in advance of anything else anywhere on the planet, had come from. And it explained why a planet that had, by and large, mended its warlike ways and commenced working constructively and cooperatively toward an eventual migration to Earth became divided into the two rival factions that in the end had destroyed each other. The Cerians were native, having evolved from the terrestrial primates transported to Minerva twenty-five million years earlier by the Ganymeans, while the Lambians were from Jevlen and fifty thousand years in the future. The Lambians never emerged at all; they *arrived*.

There were more than enough riddles in this for the scientists to argue over for many years to come. How, for example, could the Lambians have been the descendants of their own descendants? Their greed and power lust were seen at last as characteristic of them as a group rather than of the human race as a whole, but that being so, where had those characteristics originated? The Jevlenese had inherited them from the Lambians, who had inherited them from the Jevlenese that had landed on Minerva. So where and when had it started? Danchekker speculated that their passage through the zone of dislocated spacetime might have induced some form of psychological aberration that had started the whole thing off, but the suggestion was not very satisfying since the meaning of the word "started" in this context was obscure to say the least.

Another enigma arose from the knowledge of subsequent events that the Jevlenese would presumably have taken back to Minerva with them. If they knew about the next two hundred years, the war, the millennia after that with the Thuriens, and their own eventual defeat at the hands of VISAR, why would they have allowed those very things to happen? Had they been powerless to change the sequence? Surely not. Had a whole new history somehow been written into the timeloop to erase and replace something else that had existed there "before," whatever that meant? Or had they perhaps taken few hard records with them in their haste and suffered some kind of stress-induced amnesia such that they arrived not knowing who they were or where they had come from, thus dooming themselves to launch again into an endless, unaltering cycle?

The Thuriens didn't know the answers to these questions either, which raised issues that were on the fringes of their own theoretical researches. Possibly, one day, future generations of Ganymean and Terran mathematicians and physicists would deduce the strange logic within which such things could happen. Then again, possibly no one would ever know.

But one mystery was solved that had been perplexing the Terrans, the Ganymeans, and the Jevlenese alike—the mystery of the device out beyond Pluto that had responded to that first message beamed from Farside in ancient Ganymean code, and relayed it directly to VISAR. The Thuriens had assumed it was something that the Jevlenese had positioned, the Jevlenese had assumed it was something that the Thuriens had emplaced, and because of the circumstances neither side had ever been able to challenge the other. And now that it had been destroyed, there was no way of investigating it. So what had it been, and how had it gotten there?

The answer could only be the probe that had gone through the tunnel on the heels of the Jevlenese ships. Naturally it had been programmed to respond to the communications protocols used by its own mother ship, and it had been fitted with an h-link to Thurien. By analyzing the log of messages exchanged during those last few seconds, Shilohin's scientists established that, just before the tunnel closed behind it, the probe had been in a passive mode awaiting its next command from the *Shapieron*. Apparently it had waited for a long time. After exiting near Minerva under the impetus that VISAR had imparted in accelerating it in pursuit of the Jevlenese ships, it climbed away from the Sun and eventually stabilized in a distant orbit out beyond Pluto. And it waited. And eventually it heard a command that it understood, and relayed it to VISAR because that was what its instructions told it to do. It didn't know that fifty thousand years had gone by in the meantime.

And so the full circle that linked Minerva and the early Ganymeans, the Lunarians both Lambian and Cerian, Charlie and Koriel, Earth and *Homo sapiens*, and the Giants' Star, was complete. It had begun with its own ending, and in the process JEVEX, Broghuilio, and the Lambians had become locked in an unbreakable loop that was firmly and permanently embedded in the past. Ironically their prison was even more escape-proof than the one that they themselves had devised.

Deprived of their corrupt element, the people of Jevlen turned out to be not so unlike human beings anywhere else after all, and set themselves to the task of rebuilding their society with a new mood of cooperation and optimism. This would require a great deal of physical hard work as well as social and political reforms because of the widespread damage, mainly from flooding, that had been caused by the gravitational upheaval of Broghuilio's spectacular departure, so Calazar installed Garuth as temporary planetary governor to supervise and coordinate the operation. Jevlen would be on probation for a while to come, and for some time there would be no planet-wide system after the pattern of JEVEX; planning and other functions would require extensive information-processing capacity nevertheless, and fortunately a machine of just the right size presented itself in the form of ZORAC. The *Shapieron* was permanently based at Jevlen, and ZORAC became the nucleus of a new pilot network that one day would assume interplanetary dimensions and be merged into VISAR.

Furthermore the temporarily decomputerized world of Jevlen would provide an ideal environment for Garuth's people from the *Shapieron*, displaced twenty-five million years from their own civilization, to recuperate and readjust to the ways of the Thuriens. At the same time they would be able to play a key role in helping Garuth rebuild the planet and inaugurate a new system of Jevlenese government. So Garuth, his people, and ZORAC had a worthwhile job to do, a challenging future ahead, and a home of their own once again.

On Earth, Mikolai Sobroskin became the Soviet Foreign Minister under the new order that emerged from the wreckage of the previous regime. Through some machinations inside the Kremlin that would never be fully disclosed, Verikoff ended up as an advisor on extraterrestrial sciences, having made history as the first alien ever to apply for and be granted Terran citizenship.

In the U.S. State Department, Karen Heller and Norman Pacey headed a team assigned by Packard to draft a policy aimed at breaking down the barriers of East-West suspicions that had festered for over a century, and forging an era of universal prosperity from the combined economic and industrial might of the U.S. and Soviet giants, and the material and human resources of the emerging Third World. Already the international web that had precipitated World War I, financed both the Bolshevik Revolution and the rise of Hitler, manufactured the Middle East and Southeast Asian crises of later years, contrived for a whole world to fund its own blackmail through the nuclear arms race, and been behind a long list of other interesting things found recorded in great detail inside JEVEX, was well on its way to being broken up for good.

The UN, purged of the influences that would have manipulated it into a focal point of global power to be delivered wholesale into the hands of the Jevlenese, would be remolded into the instrument through which Earth would take its place in the interstellar community. And it would have an important role to play in that community—a role in which people like Clifford Benson, Colonel Shearer, and Sobroskin's generals would still have a place. For despite their sciences and their technology, the Ganymeans had learned the wisdom of preserving a strong right arm; there was no telling how many more Broghuilios might be waiting in the unexplored reaches of the Galaxy.

Such days would come, but they were still far in the future. In the meantime there were preparations to be made—a whole planet to reeducate, and a whole system of natural sciences to be revised and brought up to date. UNSA drew up tentative plans for merging Navcomms into a new superdivision under Caldwell, who would move to Washington to begin the mammoth task of rewriting the long-range plans for the space program in the light of Ganymean technology and initiate studies for integrating selected parts of Earth's communications net into VISAR. Hunt would become Deputy Director of the new organization, and Danchekker, fired by the vision of unlimited access to scores of alien worlds each with its own alien biology and alien evolution, accepted an offer to go too as Director of Alien Life Sciences. At least, that was why Danchekker said he wanted to move to Washington. Caldwell reserved a box in the organization chart for Lyn too, of course.

But the real hero of the war, for which neither anybody nor anything else in existence anywhere could conceivably have substituted, was VISAR. Calazar agreed that VISAR would take over Uttan and run the planet exclusively, to enjoy its own measure of independence, and in the process be free to evolve further its own brand of intelligence in its own way and to its own design. But VISAR's ties to its creators would not be broken, and in the years and centuries ahead, the expansion into the Galaxy would manifest the same alliance of human and Ganymean, organic and inorganic instincts and abilities that had already proved to be a formidable combination.

epilogue

The procession of black limousines drew slowly to a halt
before the military guard of honor and lines of foreign am-
bassadors standing by the side of the field of Andrews Air
Force Base, Maryland, a few miles from Washington, D.C.
The day was sunny and clear, and the thousands filling the
area outside the boundary fence all around were strangely
quiet.

Feeling somewhat odd and formal in his black pinstripe
three-piece suit, stiffened cuffs and collar, and tightly
knotted necktie, Hunt stepped out of the second car back
from the one flying the presidential pennant on its hood,
and helped Lyn out after him while the chauffeur held the
door. Danchekker, similarly attired though nothing seemed
to fit exactly as it was supposed to, came next, followed by
Caldwell and a group of senior UNSA executives.

Hunt looked around and picked out the perceptron
among a line of aircraft parked some distance away in the
background. "It's not really like home, is it," he commented. "There aren't any windows boarded up, and it
needs some snow and a few mountains around."

"I never thought you were sentimental," Lyn said. She
looked up. "Blue sky, and lots of green. I'll stick with this."

"Not a romantic who hankers for old times, I perceive,"
Danchekker said.

Lyn shook her head. "After the amount of flying that I
did back and forth to that place, I don't care if I never see
McClusky again."

"We might be sending you a lot farther than that before
very much longer," Caldwell grunted.

The Soviet Premier and his delegation had not yet
emerged from the car immediately in front of them, but
ahead of that the U.S. President and his entourage were
assembling. Karen Heller and Norman Pacey detached

themselves from the group and walked back. "Well, get used to it," Pacey said, making a sweeping gesture with his arm. "It's going to be your new home for a while. I've got a feeling this place will get to feel like your own private airport. You people are going to be pretty busy."

"We were just talking about it," Lyn said. "Vic seems to prefer McClusky."

"When will you be moving up to D.C.?" Heller inquired.

"It'll be a few months yet at least," Caldwell said.

She looked at Danchekker. "The first thing we'll have to do is have dinner somewhere, Chris. It'll make up for all those canteen meals in Alaska."

"An admirable suggestion," Danchekker replied. "And one with which I concur fully." Lyn nudged Hunt in the ribs. Hunt looked away and grinned.

Pacey glanced at his watch and looked over his shoulder. Sobroskin was leading the Soviet party from the car ahead. "It's almost time," he said. "We'd better move on up." They walked forward to join the Soviet contingent, all of whom they had already met individually in the Executive Lounge earlier, and the whole group moved on to join the President and his party at the front of the cavalcade of limousines. Sobroskin moved closer to Pacey as they came to a halt. "The day has arrived, my friend," he said. "The children will see other worlds under other stars."

"And I told you you'd see it happen," Pacey said.

Packard was looking at Pacey curiously. "What did that mean?" he asked.

Pacey smiled. "It's a long story. I'll have to tell you about it sometime."

Packard turned his head toward Caldwell. "Well, at least I know what to expect this time, Gregg. You know, I don't think I'll ever live that down."

"Don't worry about it," Caldwell told him. "The rest of us were only a few seconds behind you."

They moved toward the open area of the base and came to a halt again, arranged in orderly rectangular groups with the McClusky team, including Jerol Packard, at the front, the U.S. and Soviet leaders alongside each other behind them with Pacey and Sobroskin standing ahead of their respective national delegations, and the UNSA and other groups from the remaining cars arrayed at the back. Every head was turned upward, waiting. And suddenly, sensed rather than heard, a wave of excitement rippled across the entire base and through the crowds packed outside.

The ship was already visible as a faint dot enlarging in the flawless blue above. As it grew larger, it took on a brilliant silvery sheen that glinted with reflected highlights in the sun, and resolved into a slender wedge with gracefully curved leading edges flaring to merge into two needle-pointed nacelles at the tips. And still it was getting larger.

Hunt's mouth dropped open as the raised bulges along its hull, ancillary housings swelling from its underside, fairings, pods, blisterdomes, and turrets gradually revealed themselves in a steadily unfolding hierarchy of detail to give the first real hint of the craft's awesome size. Gasps of wonder were coming from either side of him and behind, and the crowd outside seemed paralyzed. It must have been miles in length . . . tens of miles; there was no way of telling. It expanded above their heads to fill half the sky like some huge, mythical bird that seemed to be hanging over the entire state of Maryland. And still it might have been in the stratosphere, or even beyond that.

He had seen the Thurien power generators and been told they were thousands of miles across, but that had been out in empty space where there were no references. His senses had been spared the impact of direct confrontation, leaving only his imagination to grapple with what the numbers had meant. This was different. He was standing on Earth, surrounded by trees, buildings, and everything else that made up the world of the familiar and the unquestioned, in which intrusions like this were forbidden. Even the distance from one horizon to another, which he sensed unconsciously although it was not visible directly, set a perspective that defined the permissible, imposed rules, and forced limits. The Thurien spaceship had no place in that scheme. It belonged to a different order of magnitude, breaking every known rule and making nonsense of the usual limits. He felt like an insect that had just grasped the meaning of the toenail in front of it, or a microbe that had glimpsed an ocean. His mind had no model to accommodate it. His senses rebelled from taking in the totality of what he was seeing. His brain fought to reconcile it with something that was manageable within a lifetime's stored experiences, couldn't, and gave up.

At last a light moving across his field of view against the underside of the ship broke the hypnotic trance that had taken hold of him. The figures that had been frozen into immobility around him began stirring as they saw it too. Something was coming down, and was already much nearer than the ship; it had to have been descending for some time, and had only just become visible. It moved swiftly and silently on a direct line toward the center of the base and turned into a flattened, highly elongated ellipsoid of pure gold, completely smooth except for two low, sharply swept fins projecting from its upper surface. It landed without a sound a short distance away, its nose pointing to where Hunt and the others were standing. For perhaps ten seconds not a sound or a movement disturbed the total stillness that had enveloped the base.

And then the forward section of the underside hinged slowly downward to form a broad, shallow ramp leading down to the ground. The point where the ramp entered the body was lost in a glow of brilliant yellow light. Lyn's fingers found Hunt's and squeezed as the first eight-foot-tall shapes appeared a dozen or so abreast out of the light and began moving down the ramp. At the bottom of the ramp, they halted to survey the waiting lines of Terrans.

In the center was Calazar, easily recognizable even without his familiar short silver cape and green tunic, and on one side of him were Frenua Showm, Porthik Eesyan, and Eesyan's deputy, Morizal. Garuth was at Calazar's other side, with Shilohin, Monchar, and other Ganymeans from the *Shapieron* whose light gray skins set them apart as a group from the darker, less heavily built Thuriens. The team that had gone to McClusky had been waiting a long time for this moment. For the first time since the perceptron's landing and their first hesitant entry into it, they were not seeing the Thuriens via neural stimulations transmitted from light-years away. This time the Thuriens were real.

Massed bands had begun playing in the background. The crowd, still overwhelmed by the spectacle filling the sky above their heads, was quiet. Then with orderly, unhurried dignity the Ganymeans started moving again, and Caldwell stepped forward to lead the McClusky team to meet them at the halfway point.

"It was a bit scary at times, but I think Earth has made it," Lyn whispered as they began moving.

"You're making it sound as if it's all over," Hunt murmured beside her. "This is just the start of it."

And it was. For the Ganymeans, it was the end of a task they had been working on for millennia; for the inhabitants of Jevlen, it was a change of heart and direction; and for VISAR, it was a new phase of existence.

But for *Homo sapiens*, it was a whole new beginning.

The heirs to the stars were about to claim their inheritance.

appendix

Answers to Crossword

ACROSS

1 SHANNON—Irish river. (flow-er, not flower).

5 DECODE—find the meaning of. "Ode" (poem) added *to* "DEC."

9 INNOCENT—opposite of "guilty." "O" (zero) "cent" (money) *after* "inn" (pub).

10 BEACON—guiding light. Literally *in* "could (*be a con*)fused."

12 DEEP END—profound conclusion. "Pen" (writer) jumping into (hint) "deed" (action).

13 EXTREME—ultimate. Literally *in* "t"(*ext reme*)dies.

14 EULER—Swiss mathematician. "E" (east, i.e. oriental) plus *changed* (anagram of) "rule."

16 INTRO—colloquial *short* form of "introduction," i.e. preamble. *Wild* (anagram of) "riot" *about* (around) "N" (compass point).

17 EXTRA—something more. "Ex" ("expert" less four letters of six) plus "tra," i.e. "art" *back*(ward).

18 APART—separated. A-part (piece).

20 AFRICAN—continental. *Maybe* (anagram of) "i" (one) "fan car."

21 ANNULAR—ring-shaped, around. Annul (abolish) a "r" (right).

23 RETAIN—keep. "E" and "T" (head and tail of "elephant") *in*(side) "rain."

24 DISTRESS—heartache. Di's (Dianna's) tress (lock of hair).

25 YEMENI—type of Arab. "Men" and "I" *after* "ye" (half of "year," i.e six months).

314

26 ENCASES—surrounds. "Ease" *surrounding* (double use) "NC" added *to* "S" (compass point).

DOWN

1 SWINDLE—something not fair. "Win" *in*(side) *perhaps* (anagram of) "sled."

2 ANNIE—noted (musical) lady. Advised to get a gun (arms).

3 NUCLEAR REACTION—*power*ful reaction (response) from nucleus (heart). Extra hint: "r" (right) taken *from* "heart" gives "heat."

4 NON-ADDICTING—not habit-forming. *Possibly* (anagram of) "did on gin can't."

6 ELECTROMAGNETIC—a (kind of) wave. Generated *from* charges of the kind (brigade) that produce light (i.e., accelerating electric ones).

7 ORCHESTRA—something that makes harmony. "H" (chemical symbol for hydrogen) *in*(side) *turbulent* (anagram of) "star core."

8 ERNIE—man's name. "N" (head of "Norman") *in*-(side) "Erie" (lake).

11 TEST DATA FILE—experimental results. *Reorganized* (anagram of) "let's fit a date."

15 LOGARITHM—type of number. Phonetically similar to "logger" (lumberjack) "rhythm" (music).

19 THRUSTS—urges progress (mechanically, not politically). "H" (*initial* of "Hoover") *in*(side) "trust," *over* (literally) "S" (South).

20 ARRAY—matrix. "Ar" (chemical symbol for argon) plus "ray" (beam).

22 LOESS—geological deposit. "O" (nothing) *in*(side) "less" (smaller amount).

ABOUT THE AUTHOR

JAMES HOGAN was born in London in 1941 and educated at the Cardinal Vaughan Grammar School, Kensington. He studied general engineering at the Royal Aircraft Establishment, Farnborough, subsequently specializing in electronics and digital systems.

After spending a few years as a systems design engineer, he transferred into selling and later joined the computer industry as a salesman, working with ITT, Honeywell, and Digital Equipment Corporation. He also worked as a life insurance salesman for two years ". . . to have a break from the world of machines and to learn something more about people."

In mid-1977 he moved from England to the United States to become a Senior Sales Training Consultant, concentrating on the applications of minicomputers in science and research for DEC.

At the end of 1979, Hogan opted to write full-time. He is now living in northern California.